Mirrors of the Unseen
An Unexpected Light

THE NETWORK

JASON ELLIOT

BLOOMSBURY

LONDON · BERLIN · NEW YORK

First published in Great Britain 2010

Bloomsbury Publishing Plc
36 Soho Square
London W1D 3QY

www.bloomsbury.com

Bloomsbury Publishing, London, New York and Berlin
A CIP catalogue record for this book is available from the British Library

ISBN 978 1 4088 0347 9

10 9 8 7 6 5 4 3 2 1

Typeset by Hewer Text UK Ltd, Edinburgh
Printed in Great Britain by Clays Limited, St Ives plc

Mixed Sources
Product group from well-managed
forests and other controlled sources
www.fsc.org Cert no. SGS-COC-2061
© 1996 Forest Stewardship Council
FSC

'Look at the inmost causes of things, stripped of their husks; note the intentions that underlie actions; study the essences of pain, pleasure, death, glory; observe how man's disquiet is all of his own making, and how troubles come never from another's hand, but like all else are creatures of our own opinion.'

Marcus Aurelius, *Meditations*

PART ONE

April 2001
Herefordshire, England

Five months before 9/11

I

For a few moments the illusion is complete, as if my work is done and I am finally at rest after every threat and uncertainty has passed. My eyes are open but I am not awake, and my senses are suspended in a dream that ignores the ordinary rules of time and space. I feel neither cold nor pain. Above me stretches an expanse of sky, as featureless as you would expect for an April morning in England, onto which my eyes have opened. At the centre of this hypnotic whiteness a solitary hawk is hovering.

I see nothing else but his lonely silhouette, and my mind goes through none of its normal efforts to assign any scale or context to this vision. He hovers directly above me, like a captive of my own gaze, and seems to defy both gravity and the laws of motion. Even though his body is in constant motion, his head is as still as a sniper's, held in a perfect equilibrium against the invisible stream in which he swims. As the wind flows over his wings, the trailing feathers tremble and flutter, and his wedge-shaped tail treads the air with incalculable speed and precision. The leading edges of his wings sweep back like those of a fighter plane, his head is streamlined like the point of a lance, and his beak resembles a scimitar poised high above its victim. Every line and movement of his body expresses the beauty and lethal prowess of the raptor. For a strange few moments it seems as though I enter into the spirit of the bird and feel what it feels. But all this takes shape in a different language, free of thinking itself, because I'm spellbound by the silhouette overhead, and my mind has yet to intervene.

Then, too fast for the eye to follow, he swerves downwards a few feet, brakes to a sudden stop, beats his wings to compensate for the loss in speed, and hovers again. He repeats the movement in an upward direction, to get a better view of his prey on the floor of the forest. I watch this faultless airborne ballet, mesmerised all the while, until a cry comes from his mate, its sound carried unevenly on the wind. The shrill call repeats, then falls in pitch and fades to silence. It is this sound that breaks the spell.

I hear a sudden breath, which is my own, entering my body like the gasp of an infant at birth and bearing with it all the burden of the senses. I struggle up in a spasm of fear, and the world and its nightmare tumbles in. My hands are swollen from scratches and thorns and I feel the toxin of fatigue that makes every muscle ache. I get to my feet and throw off the bracken that I have used for my improvised bed, which is a muddy crater left by the torn-up roots of a giant beech, and I curse out loud. I have already broken the only rule: *never stop*.

I wonder how long I've slept. Not long, going by the feeling of exhaustion. Under a half-moon I have run, walked, staggered, waded and crawled through the night. I am filthy and freezing but am grateful for the jacket that fends off the bite of the wind, which is more dangerous than the cold. Running my hands over my pockets I'm reminded they've been emptied, so there is no point returning to my car, even if I did know how to find my way back to it. The sudden recollection of my capture sends a shiver through my body. It's only yesterday but, separated by the long and hateful night, now seems like years ago.

I'm returning home after a weekend session with H, most of it spent learning about improvised explosive devices and how to set them off. Useful skills, he tells me, even if we never have to call on them, though he says this about all our sessions together. He shows me how to make an anti-disturbance device from two U-shaped nails, how to use a clothes peg for a tripwire-activated circuit, and how to make a pressure pad, suitable for detonating

4

the explosive of one's choice, from two bits of old drawer and a thin copper strip from a household draught excluder. He also demonstrates the more modern technique of using a mobile phone to fire one or multiple ignition circuits, an operation which can be accomplished with disturbing ease from anywhere in the world with a single phone call. Useful skills, as he says.

When I stop for petrol on the outskirts of Hereford, where H, between frequent trips to seldom-heard-of African republics, teaches these and related skills to his Regimental apprentices, I suspect nothing. I'm tired after having spent the night on a freezing hillside in the Black Mountains, and not feeling at my sharpest. Even after all our sessions devoted to security, which is H's business, it hasn't occurred to me to check whether I'm being followed, which explains my surprise and anger when a black Range Rover parks neatly in front of my car just as I'm getting out.

The driver stays in the vehicle but from the rear doors emerge two short-haired and mustachioed men in casual clothes, one of whom addresses me in a neutral accent by my own name and requests that I accompany him. They're not hostile but speak with the muted ambition of people whose agenda is fairly clear to themselves.

'Are you arresting me?' I ask.

'Nothing like that, sir.'

'So it's social, is it? You're not behaving very socially.'

'If you'd just like to come with us please, sir.' They look fit and have the poised restraint of men who turn readily to physical exertion. I have no wish to tangle with them. They don't behave like men from the Regiment, who tend to have a better sense of humour. I wonder what the worst thing is that can happen. This is England. I cannot be held against my will. Perhaps Seethrough, with all his love of cloak-and-dagger, has arranged to have me escorted to a classified location. I wonder if it's Pontrilas or some subterranean comms facility nearby.

To buy time, I protest indignantly that I can't leave my car on a garage forecourt, thinking that from the safety of the car I'll call Seethrough before going anywhere with these purposeful-looking strangers.

'We'll take care of that, sir,' says one of them. I am not sure if the 'sir' is an expression of genuine or artificial deference until my head is pushed down in the manner of a prisoner as we enter the Range Rover, and the two of them squeeze in on either side of me and request that I empty my pockets. It definitely doesn't feel very social, but perhaps it's a security requirement like having to surrender your mobile phone inside the Firm's headquarters at Vauxhall Cross. As I'm complying the driver gets out, reverses my car, parks it at the edge of the forecourt and returns. My possessions, including my watch, are put in a ziplock freezer bag, to which my car keys are now added, and stowed in a seat pouch. There's a squawk of static from a discreet two-way radio on the driver's belt, which he adjusts without looking down. We pull out from the garage.

'If you wouldn't mind leaning forward, sir,' says one of the men next to me. I'm forced to fold my arms over my knees and can't keep my head up to keep track of the route. We drive for sixteen minutes, during which nobody speaks, and I count the minutes on my fingers, folding them into my palm in turn. Judging from the frequency of turns and stops, we're sticking to country roads. Then a mobile phone rings from inside the bag in the seat pouch. It's mine, and they've forgotten to turn it off. After a moment's thought, the man to my left extracts it and looks at the screen.

'Lili Marlene. Who's Lili Marlene?' I feel his body turn slightly towards the other man, as if he's consulting him.

'It's my girlfriend,' I say, which is a calculated risk. 'She's wondering why I haven't called her back.' I can't see his face, but I can sense that he's deciding whether he should pass me the phone or not. 'I'm supposed to be meeting her later,' I add.

'You'd better cancel, then.' He hands me the phone without looking at me, but pushes me firmly forward again so that I can't see where we are. 'Make it quick.'

Lili Marlene is the alias I've assigned to the number that's calling, but the voice at the other end belongs to H, a lifetime soldier and twenty-two-year veteran of the Special Air Service, better known to its members as the Regiment. I've never been quite so glad to hear it.

'Listen,' he says in a tone that sounds concerned but not worried. It reassures me, but not much. 'I just heard you've been picked up. Sounds like you're in a vehicle. Just give me yes or no answers.' He lowers his voice. 'Can anyone hear what I'm saying?'

'I don't think so.'

'Do you know where you are?'

'No.'

'Have they told you where they're taking you?'

'No. Very sorry.'

'Sounds like there's been a bit of a balls-up. I can't explain it all now, but you need to get out of that vehicle.'

'Yes,' I say, after a pause.

'Whatever it takes. Just get away. It doesn't matter where to. Never stop, remember? Don't give them anything till you see me again.' A grittiness has entered his voice. 'Not a word, just the big four. Have you got me?'

'Alright,' I say.

'I'll catch up with you as soon as I can. Now get out of that vehicle and get moving.'

I hand back the telephone to the sullen man at my side, who looks straight ahead as he returns it to the seat pouch.

'She sends her love,' I tell him. 'You should try a bit of romance yourself sometime.' There is no visible reaction.

The truth is I'm not ready for this and feel a kind of dread rising from my abdomen. I need a plan to focus on and to control what H calls the fear factor. It is nearly dusk. Within half an hour I will have darkness on my side. So fifteen minutes later I decide it's time to act and start making the appropriate gestures.

'I'm going to be sick,' I say.

There is no immediate answer. I imagine the two of them exchanging a questioning glance behind me.

'I'm going to be sick all over you if I don't get some fresh air.'

'Pull over, Snapper,' says the one who does the talking. 'Passenger needs to make a pit stop.'

'Quickly, please,' I say, with my hand over my mouth.

The nearside door opens and I feel a hand on my right arm.

'Watch him,' growls the one who stays behind.

The hand stays on my arm as I walk diagonally to the rear of the vehicle, where I'm hoping the driver won't be able to see us in his mirrors. There's a fence by the side of the road, and woods beyond the adjacent fields which will give me the cover I need.

I kneel compliantly by the verge on all fours, and for a minute imitate the violent spasms that accompany the worst kind of hangover, throwing in some profane muttering for extra effect. My adopted minder stands mutely behind me.

As I stand up, I turn but not all the way, and raise my right hand in a gesture of exasperation, complaining that no one carries a handkerchief these days. I repeat the gesture, which will have the effect, I'm hoping, of distracting any attention away from my left hand, which is about to connect with the bridge of my victim's nose. A second later the two meet in a crunching embrace, and a jolt of pain travels up my arm as my victim topples backwards. While he's struggling to figure out what's happened, I hit him again.

I am over the fence and a good few seconds into my sprint across the field when the first shout goes up. When I risk a backward glance half a minute later, I see the car skidding and lurching, lights blazing, across the field towards me. There's no time for hesitation when I reach the chalky escarpment at the far side, which cuts steeply downwards to what looks like a broad river beyond the trees. I'm under the barbed wire and slithering down before I hear more shouts as the three men above me spread along the lip of the escarpment. I catch a glimpse of their silhouettes and the drawn weapons at their sides. Their hesitation gives me precious extra seconds. By the time they plunge down the slope after me, I've already sprinted to the far side of the trees, and the current of freezing water which has taken my breath away has already carried me more than fifty yards downstream. Providing I don't drown, I rate my chances of a successful escape as being fairly even.

Now I have lost time to make up, even if I do lack a destination. H's house seems like the best haven to aim for, if I can only find out where I am. I'm guessing it's within twenty miles. I must find a map in a bus shelter or an unlocked car. After the cold and bewilderment of the darkness, the daylight seems like a luxury. I rub some mud on my face and move to the edge of the trees that have sheltered me, keeping below the ridge that runs above so that I'm not silhouetted and won't become instantly visible from a distance.

The landscape below and beyond is a picture postcard of the English countryside. The hills are low and rounded, and their slopes a patchwork of different shades of green separated by dark lines of hedgerows. Bands of well-maintained forest reach across their contours and resemble the angular shapes of a children's puzzle. There's no movement except that of the clouds, which are steaming in a swift mottled convoy of greys from one side of the world to the other. No part of the sky is brighter than any other, so I cannot even judge the position of the sun. I wonder again how far I've come during the night, and how well my pursuers have organised themselves in the meantime.

If I stick to the patches of forest I will be harder to spot, and I begin to plot the best route across them. There are some scattered houses and I wonder if anyone in them will be on the lookout for a fugitive on foot. It depends, I reason, on the resources that the hunters have brought to the capture of their game. This thought has just taken hold when I hear a sound that ignites a sudden feeling of dread: dogs. A pack of them, by the sound of it, coming from some buildings that look like a farm, about a mile away and several hundred feet below. A dark-coloured Land Rover is moving towards the farm on a sliver of road, but I can't afford the time to watch its progress. With dogs after me I have no time to rest and must find a way to break free of the net before it closes on me. My whole body is shivering violently and I must run to keep warm. I will think on the move.

A rough formula is trying to take shape in my head, although pushing my fear aside is like leaning on a heavy door that refuses to close. I want to keep moving downwind from the dogs, which I'm hoping will make things harder for them, but I don't know how much harder. If I find an empty plastic bag or sack I'll tie it around my shoes to weaken my scent, but in the meantime the only hope of evading them is to find a wide enough river and cross it far enough downstream to break the trace of my own scent. It means losing my precious height and descending into the valley on the far side of the hill. I run to the ridge, break out of the trees and find myself on a single-track road between two enclosing walls of tall pines. To judge from the worn surface it's not a public road but belongs to the Forestry Commission. There will be no traffic on it. I can make better speed on a hard road than cross-country, and I run along it for about half a mile until the land opens up again. I'm grateful for the running I've been doing every day under H's supervision, which allows me a steady pace even if my lungs are putting up their usual complaint.

I reach a second track, which descends to the bottom of the hill in a straight line along the edge of the forest. I take it without stopping. Several times what sounds like the hiss of tyres against the wet surface of the track makes me leap into the undergrowth, but it's the sound of wind in the tops of the pines, not a vehicle. A jay cries from somewhere in the woods, and ahead of me a pheasant runs a few panicky yards and disappears into the undergrowth. I stop twice just to listen. There is nothing but the wind and the sound of raindrops hitting the leaves around me. No barking, which is a mercy. I put my lips to a tiny rivulet of flowing water at the road's edge to soften a horrible thirst. I cannot allow my pace to slow.

Downhill I make better speed, but my lungs are still protesting. I reach the bottom of the track, where it turns sharply to the left. Here the unexpected sight of a man less than ten yards ahead brings me to a lurching halt. I leap sideways in a reflex of shock and slip on the wet ground, realising in the half-second it takes for me to break my fall that the man isn't after me. He's standing perfectly still beside an open gate, wearing a tweed cap and jacket, farmer's boots and carrying in the crook of his arm a twelve-bore shotgun with polished side-by-side barrels. A leash in his left hand restrains a muddy spaniel, which cowers in surprise as I lurch into view.

'You're out early. Gave me a hell of a fright,' I say as nonchalantly as is possible under the circumstances. I attempt a reassuring wave and brush myself off as I recover, taking a few steps towards him. He is about fifty, stocky, with a thick black beard, and his eyes don't move from me. I've probably given him just as much of a fright as he's given me, and if I can win his confidence and get him to help me, this is good news. But it has to happen quickly.

'I didn't expect to see anyone—' I begin, taking another step towards him, but his words bring me to a stop.

'That's close enough, I reckon.' His voice is deep and steady, and his accent, whatever it is, is thick. Herefordshire? Shropshire? It isn't Welsh. Six or seven paces will close the distance between us, so I take another.

'Captain Taverner, SAS,' I say, extending my arm. 'Is this your land?' He's not reciprocating the gesture, so I point over my shoulder. 'There's some people on the other side of that hill trying to catch up with me. Trouble is I'm not supposed to let them. I don't suppose you can help me by giving me a lift somewhere?' I'm hoping that this unlikely suggestion will lighten his look of suspicion, but it doesn't. The barrels snap shut with a jerk of his left hand and the butt moves under his armpit.

'That'll do,' he says, more sternly now.

'There's no need for that,' I say, putting my hands protectively in front of me. 'I'm an army officer and I can prove it. Lower your weapon please.'

The reply stuns me.

'I know who you are, you murdering bastard.' The evenness of his voice, and its conviction, stop me from going any closer. 'Don't waste your breath on me.'

Anything, H has told me in our sessions together, can be used to counter an attacker: soil in a sock, swung fast enough, that can knock a man unconscious; a rolled-up newspaper jabbed into the throat; even the unfolded foil of a tube of toothpaste that can sever a jugular vein. But I have nothing. My close-quarter train-ing with H is for disarming an Afghan carjacker with an AK-47, not an English farmer with a shotgun.

'I haven't murdered anyone,' I tell him as calmly as I can muster. 'I'm an army officer on an escape and evasion training exercise. I can prove it,' I tell him again, realising as I utter the words that I can do no such thing. In my mind's eye I see a pack of dogs swerv-ing over my tracks as they climb the hillside.

'Army officer don't make you less of a murderer. Save it for the police.' A jerk of the barrels indicates his intention. 'Both hands on the gate.'

I comply, moving to the edge of the track and wondering how they have managed to get to him. The top bar of the metal gate is cold.

'You're making a mistake,' I say.

'See about that,' he growls.

At a safe distance and to my side, and without taking his eyes off me, he transfers the leash from the hand that grips the stock to the hand that grips the butt. Then with his free hand he takes a mobile phone from his jacket pocket and his thumb works the keypad. As he listens to the ringing tone he glances downwards to his dog, who is looking expectantly at its master.

'Steady, girl,' he says. At the other end, someone answers. 'Tom here. Make it quick. I got the slippery-tongued fucker right in front of me.' A macabre chuckles escapes his throat. 'Right. I'll take him to the entrance gate and wait for you there.'

The best moment for escape, H has also told me, is as soon after the moment of capture as possible. The longer the enemy has to consolidate his control, the slimmer one's chances of getting away and the greater the likelihood of recapture. To fail to make the utmost effort to escape from the enemy is – as any soldier, former or otherwise, knows – classified as misconduct in action. And anyone who points a weapon at me, I affirm to myself, is an enemy.

Another jerk of the barrels indicates his intended route, which lies beyond the gate in the direction of what looks like a barn and some other buildings a few hundred yards away. I do not want to go there. I keep up a steady patter of protest in the hope that, eventually, Farmer Tom will be distracted enough to bring his shotgun close enough for me to knock it, and its owner, to the ground. I tell him I will give him a number to call to confirm my identity. I tell him he can speak to my commanding officer. I tell him the SAS don't take kindly to civilian interference. It's all fiction, but he's not to know.

'Hands where I can see them,' he says in the same steady tone, listening to nothing I have said. He keeps his distance cautiously as I move beyond the gate and onto a watery footpath, and follows me into the field. Then, being a conscientious farmer, he gives a sharp push to the gate, which swings closed into its latch and the whole gate reverberates with a *clang*. The result is one of those events that restores one's faith in the idea of providence. A female pheasant, which has been hiding in the undergrowth at our feet, flies upwards in surprise at the noise, and the dog leaps after it, pulling at the leash, which is still attached to Farmer Tom's right wrist. He keeps hold of the gun, but it's pulled out from under his arm, and in the effort to restrain his dog he turns his back on me.

'*Down*, damn you,' yells Tom. Into this slender moment is compressed my chance. I take it.

I dive to one side and roll through the line of trees that separates the track from the field beyond, cursing as I hit the ground more heavily than usual because I'm so tired. Without looking back, I am sprinting along the edge of the field as I hear the first shot. The pellets tear into the leaves behind me but Tom is out of luck and I am untouched. His second shot comes a few seconds later and also misses. I reach a hedge, turn sharp left across the field and keep up the sprint. At the far side I cross a farm track, slither into the grassy ditch on the far side, try to get my breath back for a few seconds, and try to think.

What H has called a 'balls-up' has nearly killed me, and now I wonder if my new status as a murderer is a calculated lie, a coincidence or an accident. Whichever the case, whoever is pursuing me has influence. The drone of an airborne motor seems to confirm this unpleasant thought, and I look up to see a light aircraft bearing directly towards me at about 200 feet. How they can possibly have found me so quickly is another mystery I'll dwell on later.

I curl into the soaking grass, praying I can't be seen if I keep still, not daring to look up in case the whiteness of my face betrays me. The aircraft flies overhead without deviating from its course and after it has passed I notice that its drop in altitude has the characteristic gradient of a final approach. I watch it bank into a gentle turn and sink below the line of trees towards the floor of the valley less than half a mile away. It does not emerge from the treeline on the far side, and this convinces me of two things:

firstly, that the light aircraft flying overhead is indeed a coincidence and not a cause for panic. Secondly, that there must be an airfield nearby, which for the purposes of my new plan is more important. I'm not thinking much of the consequences. It's the only plan I have.

I run in as much of a straight line as possible in the direction of the last point I saw the aircraft, across two open fields alongside another hedge. I cross a small country road and pass near the long windowless shape of a battery chicken farm and a cluster of buildings alongside it. My lungs are splitting again as I reach a second, broader road. The hedge on its far side is impenetrable and I must risk running along it. It is free of traffic for the moment. Reminded suddenly of the presence of other human beings, I try my best to wipe the mud from my face in the hope that I won't alert any onlooker to my status as a fugitive, but it's probably too late for that.

A municipal sign announces the identity of the village I am entering: SHOBDON. I've never heard of it. A few hundred yards beyond, to avoid the buildings that are beginning to cluster ahead, I turn left on a small road which winds almost imperceptibly downhill. Then I break off in the direction of where I saw the plane disappear and keep running on unsurfaced tracks between fields, finding nothing for a further desperate mile. Then, just as I begin to doubt whether this is even the same valley where the plane landed, I glimpse the roof line of some prefabricated buildings and head towards them. A fluttering orange windsock confirms I am in the right place. I creep along the base of the hedge that encloses the airfield and come to a line of white trailers which, judging from their length and strange shape, must contain gliders.

I lie down on my back under one of them and wait for the heaving of my chest to subside. Then I turn in the direction of the airfield buildings to look for any sign of life. There is none. Nothing stirs by the big hangar a hundred yards away. The control tower, which looks more like a shed perched on a twelve-foot-high platform, is empty. In my imagination I see Tom explaining his encounter to the dog handlers, who are probably in the process of making a succession of phone calls. My close observation lasts only ten minutes but I can't wait any longer.

There are about a dozen single-engined aircraft parked on the grass alongside the runway, pointing down it. The majority have blue winter covers draped over their canopies like horse blankets, but several are uncovered. Concrete weights or ten-gallon plastic drums are tied to the undersides of the wings as anchors. I can still hear nothing but my own breathing. It's now or never. I walk with as much confidence as possible from my hiding place and try the doors of the uncovered aircraft in turn. The Piper and the Cessna 172 are locked. The third, a 152 and the aircraft I first learned to fly, is open. Nothing moves by the buildings, and the possibility of success is now making my hands tremble.

I check the fuel in the nearest wing: enough for my purposes. I won't fly much more than fifty miles. I'll stay in class G airspace, keep the transponder off, hope there aren't too many low-flying military fighters on exercise, and head west until I hit the coast and put down in a remote field. Then I'll find a way to call H, who will get me out of the shit I'm in. A moment later I'm in the cockpit. The ignition switch lacks a key but after some groping under the cowling I have worked free the P-wires to the two magnetos, and bypassed the ignition circuit. I turn the fuel to rich and the carburettor heat to cold. I prime. I open the throttle half an inch. The master switch is on, the brakes off. I need only prop the aircraft manually and remove the tie-downs.

I have to prop the aircraft by hand because I have effectively removed the ignition. It's the wrong order in which to do things, but I want more than anything to get the engine going first. There is no time for the usual checks. I get out and heave down on the propeller with all my effort: there is a thud and a hiss from the engine.

'Bitch,' I hear myself shout.

I heave again. Another thud. And another. On my fifth try there's a miraculous succession of thuds and muted explosions and the engine bursts into glorious life. The airframe begins to strain forward like a dog at its leash. All that remains is the tie-downs. With a sharp knife I might have cut them off within seconds and been airborne within a minute. There are no tie-downs in films about aircraft theft, much less tie-downs with stiff ropes tied too tightly to undo with cold and trembling hands.

I try my best, but the ropes won't budge. The forward motion of the aircraft is putting tension on them and making the task even harder. I am contemplating shutting down the engine when through the perspex of the cockpit doors I see the vehicles hurtling through the gate beyond the hangar. Two Range Rovers with lots of bodies inside. I will not give up. One skids to a halt in front, and the other behind the aircraft. Reason suggests that at this point I concede defeat because I cannot possibly take off, but I'm reluctant to part from my closeness to success and climb back into the cockpit. H has said I must *never* give up. I pull the throttle to its maximum extent and let the handbrake off. The plane is creeping forward and vibrating like a spin drier and men in jackets and fleeces are tumbling out of the vehicles. A musta-chioed face appears at the door to my left and tries the handle. I kick it open towards him and the face disappears but the other door is open now and hands are tearing at my arm. A fist reaches my head. Two bodies now occupy the left door frame and are grabbing at my flailing legs. They do not shout, which impresses me. Now I am being prised from the cockpit like a worm from its hole and someone is pounding on my arms to make me let go of the seat. As I fall to the ground a knee connects with my left eye, and little flashes of light tumble across my vision against a dark background. This is not supposed to happen.

The engine revs subside and I realise someone has found the throttle and pushed it in. I hear the air go out of my lungs with another blow, and a cracking sound spreads from my ribs. I wonder how much force it really takes to break a rib. I feel no pain. Someone is jamming my face into the ground, and I smell the grass and the mud. There are two sets of knees on my back and another two on my legs. A plastic tie tightens over my wrists.

As I am dragged to one of the cars I notice that at the far end of the runway the sun has broken through the clouds, and a vast and slanting beam of golden sunshine is spreading downwards in a mockery of benediction.

2

I am not sure how much time passes, whether I've lost consciousness, or whether I've been drugged. My right eye, because my
left has swollen shut by now, opens as if into a tunnel running
beneath a long row of lights with metal shades, some of which
are unlit. The floor on which I'm lying on my side is concrete
and the walls are wooden. I have the impression it's dark outside
but I can't say why. Remembering the long structures I passed
earlier, I eliminate tunnel and barn and decide on chicken farm,
disused. A rank smell supports my guess. Turning my head
slowly, because it hurts too much when I try to move my eyes, I
now see the man whose face appeared at the door of the aircraft
during my ill-fated attempt at flight, which has imprinted itself
on my memory with extra clarity. He's squatting beside me in
scuffed Timberlands, black denim jeans and a brown leather
jacket with a belt which he's had the presence of mind to keep
off the floor.

'Wakey wakey,' says the Face in a tone of perverse intimacy.
South London accent, I'm guessing. He's watching me closely
for any reaction, which is perhaps his training and suggests the
shrewd observational skills of the streetwise. 'Looks like our
stunt pilot here is in need of a bit of refreshment,' he says. Then,
more loudly, and without taking his eyes from mine, 'Billy, get
the man some refreshment.' There is a scraping noise behind me
from a second face which I've not yet seen. 'Do you fancy that,
Mr Stunt Pilot? A nice bit of tucker to warm you up after all your
recreational activities?'

Food would be good, but I say nothing. This is a dance in which I and my captors will make our chosen moves. The sing-song in the Face's voice is calculated to provoke.

'Cat's got his tongue,' says the Face. 'Shame about your flight plan being denied. Who's that actor who's a pilot? You look a bit like him. Is it John Travolta? Billy,' he calls to whoever is behind me, 'who's that actor who's always flying around in his own private jet? Isn't it John Travolta?' He stands and takes a few steps backwards.

'Fuck knows,' mutters Billy, who at the moment of replying is preparing to throw a bucket of cold water over me, which he now does. His heavy northern accent registers simultaneously with the shock of the water.

'Sorry about that,' says the Face, squatting down again. 'Ran out of hot.'

My hands are tied behind my back and I cannot wipe the water from my eyes. I want to tell him this. I'm just able to tilt my head to allow a few drops to fall from my eyebrows onto my tongue, which is enough to moisten the inside of my mouth, but not more. He sees me shivering.

'Chilly, isn't it? Catch your death lying on a cold floor like that. Shall we get you up? Stretch your legs a bit?' He studies my face with an exaggerated look of enquiry. 'You can even have a go at me and Billy if you want. Get your blood going a bit. Fancy your chances?'

He raises his fists in a pantomime boxer's stance.

'Because we're going to get you up now, and if you do fancy your chances,' he says, opening the left side of his jacket to show me the paddle holster on his belt with the SIG Sauer pistol in it, 'if you really do, we'll shoot you. You alright with that?'

He looks up and nods towards Billy, who is behind me cutting through the plastic cable tie on my wrists. The relief is indescribable. I bring one arm over my body and the other from under me and squeeze my hands together to ease the pain in them.

'Get up, cunt,' says Billy in a matter-of-fact tone. I feel two strong hands pulling me up. The Face stands and steps back while Billy, who's the larger of them, does the lifting. As I come to my feet, I lean on him more than I need to, partly to get the measure of his strength and partly to appear weaker than I am. The Face spots this ploy in an instant, and circles round me like a hyena whose prey isn't quite dead yet.

'Oh look, he's feeling faint. Shall we put him back on the floor and tie him up again? Maybe something in his mouth this time? Billy? See if you can find a dead rat, can you?' A sudden lethality enters his voice. 'Don't fuck around with us, soldier boy.'

So he knows I was in the army, I register, which means that my identity is known. It's a mistake on his part, I can't help thinking, and this error, however small, gives me a feeling akin to hope. It means these people are fallible, human. Billy is manhandling me meanwhile, spreading my arms against the wall and kicking my ankles away from it, so that I'm leaning forward like a man about to be frisked.

'Now give the man his nice hat,' says the Face.

Billy obliges by putting a white pillowcase over my head. I am thus deprived of any chance to observe my surroundings, but the warmth of my own breath on my face is a comfort which they can't guess at. I'm also able to move my face without being observed. To flex my eyebrows, gauging thereby the extent of the wound to my eye, brings a feeling of secret victory. It doesn't last. The stress position is an innocent-looking technique designed to reduce to nothing what little reserves are left to an exhausted man. After lying on the cold ground with my hands tied, the first few minutes are a relief. But soon I feel the strain on my wrists and ankles, especially where they've been kicked, and the pain begins to spread.

The urge to move my limbs becomes irresistible. I want first to let my head drop and relax my neck. Billy has evidently been left in the room to make sure I don't do this. Whenever my head begins to fall, I hear his northern charm from behind me.

'Fucking head up, cunt.'

I comply, not from fear of him but so as not to give any impression of defiance. If I show no reaction, I am winning, because I am overcoming my wishes, which requires a measure of control. I cannot change the world, but I have a tiny degree of control over my reactions, which, however infinitesimally, does have an influence on events. I must guard this control. I have been taught that in small choices great consequences are often hidden.

My second wish is to bring my legs closer together to reduce the feeling that I'm sinking into the ground, like a sagging beam which is beginning to split under its own weight. Billy is trained to notice this too.

'Fucking legs apart,' is his way of putting it. The third time I shift my legs he comes over and kicks my ankles to increase the distance between them, and then slaps the back of my head down for good measure.

'Fucking head up, I said. You fucking deaf, or what?'

And before too long, after what is commonly called an eternity, not only am I unable to keep my head up for more than a few seconds at a time, but my legs are beginning to tremble with fatigue. Only slightly at first, but visibly later on. Twice my legs simply buckle under me as I fall asleep before righting myself by reflex, and it is perhaps this indication I won't last much longer that prompts the arrival of a third and unfamiliar voice to enter my deprived world. I cannot hear it distinctly, but I think the words are 'Take that off, for God's sake,' and the tone is more smoothly modulated and unexpectedly deep.

I hear the calculated cheeriness of the Face near my ear.

'You still in there, Captain?' The pillowcase is pulled off my head. 'Nice bit of fresh air for you. All the comforts of home. Don't say we don't look after you. Have a seat, there's a good fellow, and say hello to the CO.'

The Face leads me by the arm towards a folding chair with a torn plastic seat placed several feet from a table where a man in uniform is sitting. He does not look up as I am steadied into the chair but with my good eye I can make out his jumper, the three pips on each shoulder that identify him as a captain, and the rose and laurel cap badge on his distinctively coloured beret that identifies the regiment to which he belongs.

'Get this over with quickly and you can have that eye seen to,' he says in a quiet but firm tone. I cannot help but feel, after my treatment by the Face and his friend Billy from up north, a kind of kinship with this fellow officer, but dare not let my hopes rise. I must bring myself to a state of indifference, of greyness, as H would call it. Each breath brings a sharp pain into my side and I am at the edge of total exhaustion. My head falls forward.

'Head UP,' screams Billy from behind me at the top of his voice. My head jerks up in reflex, and this is when I notice that the three pips on the officer's rank slides are not identical. One is a crown. He is not a captain but a full colonel. My mind is struggling to understand the significance of this. Military protocol dictates that only an officer of equal or senior rank may interrogate another officer, but the sight of such a senior officer is disturbing me.

He unscrews the cup of a Thermos, fills the cup, drinks from it and puts it down beside a trio of files. I can smell the coffee. Perhaps the visual metaphor is a deliberate one, calculated to weaken me.

'Can you confirm that you are Captain Anthony Hugh Taverner, 1st Battalion, Scots Guards, latterly SO3/E2 in Kuwait City serving under the Joint Services Interrogation Wing?'

The big four to which H referred are name, rank, serial number and date of birth. But since they seem to know this and more, I see no reason to speak. Even were I to confirm my identity, I don't know how it would help him, since I haven't been in the army for nine years and service law is inapplicable to me as a civilian.

'Ah,' he exclaims, as if my silence itself has given him the answer he requires. '*Nemo me impune lacessit*. Good show at Tumbledown, but I suppose that's before your time.'

The colonel knows my regimental motto and its battle honours, which suggests a level of personal knowledge, or research, which makes me uncomfortable. One of the files is a familiar red colour, and I wonder if it's my 108, record of service from my stint with the Green Team. I dread to think. He's probably got eyewitness statements from the Thursday nights in Abbots and a menu from the Roast Seagull Chinese restaurant in Ashford.

He purses his lips pensively.

'Are you going to co-operate, Taverner? We won't need long if you are. I expect you'd like to get home, as would I. What's your answer?'

His apparent sincerity is like a lifeline towards which I'm tempted to reach. I must assume it is all part of his plan, although what the overall purpose is I can't yet guess. I'm almost disappointed at the ridiculousness of the charade – the semblance of a military interrogation, as if the trappings and manners of an authority to which I once bowed will intimidate me into compliance. I am wondering who has concocted this infantile scheme when the colonel speaks again.

'In case you think you're not in the army any more, you *are*.' He looks directly at me, without expression, then down again. 'I have here your additional duties commitment document, dated 17 March. That is your signature, isn't it?' He holds up a piece of paper that appears to confirm this. But I haven't signed any such document and my mind is starting to turn in tighter circles now. The only document I put my signature to a month ago is the paperwork handed to me by Seethrough at Vauxhall Cross, which I took to be the Official Secrets Act. But now I begin to wonder if I've been deceived, which is, I remind myself, the prerogative of the service to which Seethrough so proudly belongs. I must escape from this anxiety or at least find a way to regulate it. It is time to give voice to my chosen mantra, as recommended by H.

'I can't answer that question. Sir.' To speak brings relief.

'Ah. So you *do* talk.'

And now I recall Seethrough's joke at the moment I was about to look over the pages. More draconian than before, he'd said, or something like it. I'd thought it strange at the time: you only sign Section 5 of the OSA once, because it's for life. Was his joke to distract me from looking too closely at the pages? Is it possible that I've been tricked into signing a document that makes me accountable under military law? Is it possible that everything that has preceded this moment has been a set-up? That the op in Afghanistan is no more than a ploy? Or have I been tricked into thinking that I've been tricked? Doubt is stalking me now. But perhaps that is the colonel's job: to feed my doubt.

'Always read the small print, isn't that what they say?' He says this almost to himself.

I tilt my head back to get a better look at him from under the swelling ridge of my eyebrow. Would he bother, I'm wondering now, with such a throwaway line if he didn't mean it?

He drives home his attack. 'In that case, I must caution you under Section 52 of the Armed Forces Act, "whereby a charge may be heard summarily if the accused is an officer below the rank of lieutenant colonel, and if the accused is subject to service law". Which you *are*, Taverner. Offences that may be dealt with at a summary hearing include any offence under Section 13, Contravention to Standing Orders, Section 30, Allowing Unlawful Release of Prisoners, and Section 42, Criminal Conduct. I remind you also that a court martial has jurisdiction to try any service offence under Section 328, Giving False Answer During Enlistment in a Regular Force. And in case you want to drag things out in the hope that someone's going to swoop from the heavens to rescue you, I remind you also that any review of custody may be postponed if the person in service custody is being questioned and the commanding officer is satisfied that an interruption of the question would prejudice the investigation. In your case, the first review of your custody here will be in ninety-six hours. Are you with me, Taverner? Ninety-six hours can be a long time.'

Now, for the first time, I am beginning to feel uncertain as to the true purpose of our encounter. It is paradoxical that this unextraordinary-looking man with his precise gestures and his even tones evokes more distress in me than any of the threats of violence from his more theatrical subordinates. But that is the interrogator's art. I have seen a few of them. The best never have to lay a finger on their charges to bring about a state of total compliance, a fact of which I am now reminded.

The colonel looks down at the file again, as if disappointed. His lips are pursed and he's nodding to himself. I wonder how much of the material is genuine, or whether the pages really belong to someone else's file. I recognise the interrogator's 'file and dossier approach', used to convince a prisoner that everything about him is known and recorded.

'Allow me to take you back nine years to Kuwait.' He has my attention, such as I can summon. 'You were detailed with confinement of Cat 1 PW number,' he looks down, 'LBN428571, better known as Elias Rashid Gemayel, were you not? I know, you can't answer the question. So let me answer it for you. You're E2 ops officer with the Joint Forward Interrogation Team tasked with assessing said internee's IP and drafting relevant TIRs. Coming back to you?'

'I can't answer that question.'

'Can't answer it, *sir*.'

I have forgotten the army's obsession with acronyms and abbreviations. It's another language. E2 is my function as an extra-regimentally employed officer with the JFIT, IP is the prisoner's intelligence potential, and a tactical interrogation report is what an ops officer, on occasion, is tasked to write up after an interrogation has taken place.

'Would you like to describe for me your relationship with Gemayel? You gave him a high co-operation level, low potential intelligence rating. Which is strange, don't you think? Did you imagine all the effort that went into finding him was just for fun?' He allows himself a pause, during which he takes a sip of coffee. 'You liked him, didn't you? *Your* words, not mine,' he remonstrates, as if I've challenged him on the point.

There had been no reason to dislike him. He had been scooped up in Kuwait City by 14 Int after a tip-off. It was near the end of hostilities, and he'd been brought to the EPW facility for priority processing. We'd rained so much high explosive onto the length and breadth of Iraq that the war was about to end with spectacular speed, and technically Gemayel hadn't been an enemy prisoner of war at all. He was later classed as a civilian internee and given private but secure quarters. Despite the circumstances, our sessions were friendly. Gemayel was a Lebanese Arab, whose mother had been Christian before her marriage. He was pushing fifty, an educated and cultured man with a sense of humour. He claimed to have been visiting relatives in the city when the war had started, and I had no reason to doubt his story. In the course of our interviews we'd talked about Lebanese food and wine, and the literary outputs of Gibran and Naimy. But a week after his arrival his interviews were taken over by a team from a newly formed unit I'd never even heard of. They wore civilian clothes and concealed sidearms, and their treatment of him grew too harsh for my liking. As E2 and translator I was obliged to be present, and after several days of seeing him manhandled and deprived of food I protested that under the definitions of the Geneva Convention his treatment was inhumane. I'd brought him cigarettes in his room and urged him to tell his interrogators what they needed to know. He'd always dismissed my suggestions with a mirthless laugh, claiming they would never give up. They will come for me, he said. I never understood what he'd meant. But this should all be ancient history, I'm thinking. This was all cleared up years ago.

'Let's go on, then,' says the colonel. 'On the morning of 9 February the facility is breached by persons unknown whose intention, you purport, is to kidnap Gemayel.'

Purport? My left eye protests as the muscles try to open in surprise. 'Persons unknown' is a commando team with explosives and automatic weapons, the ammunition for which is later shown to be Israeli. They didn't come for a tea party, I want to say. Unless they were planning to have one in a corridor of a prison facility filled with smoke from the plastic explosive they'd used to blow Gemayel's door off its hinges while their screaming victim was being dragged out by his hair. Purport?

'Let me ask: at the time when the facility was breached, what were your actions on in the event of a security failure? After the cessation of hostilities on 7 February were they not to issue a verbal challenge to any intruder? And *did* you issue a verbal challenge to the intruder?'

'I can't answer that question, sir.' Because it's the stupidest question I've ever heard.

'You did not.'

Of course I fucking did not. When a man points an automatic weapon at you, you don't engage him in conversation.

'You shot and killed him instead. You fired eight rounds from your weapon into him.' The colonel takes a sip of coffee. 'There are some people – I'm not saying I'm one of them – who are still unhappy about that. There's a family in Tel Aviv without a father, and there are people who want to know more about your motives that morning.'

Motives? He's pushing all my buttons now. My motives were to save my own life and prevent my prisoner from being kidnapped. There has never been any doubt about this – until now. I've relived the scene often enough. Relived the trauma, relived the debriefs, relived the guilt, relived the questions that cannot be answered.

The assault team hadn't expected to be challenged. They had planned for the guards at the entrance to the facility, who were disarmed and held at gunpoint at the outset of the raid, but not for two extra armed officers inside, who should have been quartered on the other side of the compound. I had slept in my office in my clothes after a late night of writing up reports, and across the corridor my best friend and fellow E2 had done the same. The first we knew of the raid was when the door to Gemayel's cell was blown open with charges to the hinges and locks. I tripped the emergency lighting and ran with my weapon to the prisoners' rooms, where the air was thick with shouts and smoke.

It didn't look like a tea party. I raised my Browning towards the figure in black who was dragging Gemayel out of his room. His weapon came up as he saw me, but for reasons I will never know he hesitated, allowing me in his second of doubt to fire. I kept firing until he went down. His partner returned a long burst from an automatic weapon from beyond him and I was forced back into cover. My friend and 2i/c had come out of his room before me and received a rifle butt in his face before he could reach his weapon. He was taken with Gemayel, and had never been found. At our debrief all the facility personnel signed extra secrecy clauses and the event was sealed up tighter than radioactive waste.

End of story, Colonel, I want to say. Don't drag me back there now. Because this wasn't the kind of conflict I signed up for in any case. Not for the frenzied slaughter by American jets of the retreating Iraqis at the Mutla Gap, not for the fuel-air bombs that sucked the lungs and eyes out of their victims, or the conscripts bulldozed alive into their trenches, or the depleted uranium that's poisoned the desert for a thousand years, and not for the disappearance of my best friend. Don't drag me back to that.

'I have to tell you,' the colonel continues, 'there are those who think you might have got just a bit too friendly with your prisoner. They think you might have struck a deal with him. Did you strike a deal with him, Taverner?'

It's an abhorrent suggestion, but it's getting me where it hurts. It is so perversely twisted a suggestion that I'm wondering if an equally twisted deal has been struck in which I'm the scapegoat, and am filled with misery at this possibility. I can't think about it now. But the colonel isn't letting up.

'What did you agree? Agree to defend him? Fight off his kidnappers? Kill a Jew or two? Or were you just going to ask them to go away back to Israel? Because if it's found to be that, you're looking at an increase in sentence for Racial Aggravation, Section 240. That is unless you're charged with Unlawful Killing, Section 42, which carries up to a life sentence. Do you want to talk about it now, sort it out? Or do you want to play the hero and go to prison? You *will* go to prison. Do you want to go to prison?'

'I can't ...' *Just breathe.* 'I can't answer ...' *Breathe.* 'That question. Sir.'

My eyes are closed now. From another room comes the scraping sound of someone getting up from his chair. It's the Face and he's back to escort me to my place against the wall.

'Nice chat with the colonel?' I hear him ask. 'Oh dear, was he a bit hard on you? Speaking strictly personally, it sounds to me like you're *fucked*. Right, hats on, everybody.'

And I'm back against the wall with the pillowcase over my head now, wondering if there really is an Israeli unit claiming its pound of flesh for the accidental death of one of its commandos. The colonel's report will set the tone for everything that follows, and I'm not co-operating. But it's too much effort now to think this through. My mind is grinding to a halt like a film that's being slowed down, and it's frame by frame now.

'Shall we try a bit of white noise on him, Billy?'

I shudder in anticipation, and not being able to see amplifies my fear.

'Put it right by his ear and turn it on.'

I hear their bodies drawing near and wonder how I'll cope. Then I hear a strange sonorous whine by my ear and realise after a few seconds that it's Billy, whistling a tuneless rendition of 'Rule Britannia'.

'That's *torture*, that is,' says the Face, and they both burst into heartless guffawing.

I am falling asleep. My legs buckle several times, but Billy is always there to offer his own special encouragement. Twice I collapse, but he's there to pick me up and remind me, in his own way, that I'm messing him around and he's not fucking having any more of this shit from me. The pillowcase comes off again and I look up at him out of one eye. He towers over me and seems monstrously large. I doubt if I will take much more. My body does not co-operate any longer. Billy hauls me into the chair, and the colonel is waiting patiently for me. I no longer care whether he is really a colonel or not. Something has gone badly wrong but I don't know what. They can't treat me like this.

'Let's talk about Afghanistan,' he says, turning a few pages in the file. Someone has given him a brief and accurate history of my two years with the Trust in Kabul, and I wonder who. I make a note that I must find out how, then wonder if I really care. He asks me who I met there, and he lists names I have never heard, over and over again. Some of them are Arab names, some Afghan. He asks in turn whether I met them, and whether, to use his stupid expression, I 'went native' in the course of my time in Afghanistan. Whether I met Abdullah Salafi in Kabul. Ahmad Popalzai in Kandahar. Khalil Razzaq in Herat. Someone else in Jalalabad. He describes their crimes, of which I lose track because I'm not hearing much of what he's saying any more.

And I'm not hearing him because I've found what I wanted now. I'm walking across the most beautiful landscape I have ever seen, in the region of the Shibar Pass, on the high slopes above Bamiyan, where the light dispels all the ugliness of the world and cuts into the soul with a clarity I've never seen anywhere else. We're walking because our vehicle has finally given up and there's no radio contact with Kabul because of the mountains. We can't walk out through Bamiyan because there's fighting there and Salahuddin my driver is a Hazara and the Taliban will kill him. We head for Hajigak to the south instead and hope for the best, living off a few strips of Afghan bread for three days. Then, on the fourth day, Salahuddin quietly produces something from his bag which surprises all three of us because we thought there was no more food. He unwraps a roast chicken from what looks like a bundle of rags.

Billy props me up against the wall because it's obvious I can't stand any more, and takes off the pillowcase.

In size it's more like a pigeon than a chicken, and it's obviously led a hard but honourable life, like most Afghans, and there's barely more than a mouthful for each of us. Salahuddin divides it up reverently after uttering a *Bismillah* over the miserable carcass, and we eat it together, listening to the distant gunfire and explosions coming from the valleys where the Taliban are killing Salahuddin's Hazara relatives, making us wonder whether we'll get out of the mountains alive. The flesh has a smoky flavour that comes from the wood it's been cooked over, and it's the most delicious meal I've ever had. I'm savouring it now for the second time, picking the flesh from the bones and sucking on them until they're smooth, and the satisfaction is indescribable. And I realise that my satisfaction has been transmitted to my face, because Billy is looking into it with a puzzled expression, asking me what the fuck is so funny. He cannot know that I am eating a chicken and, despite everything, taking more pleasure in it than he can possibly imagine.

And now all I know is that I have been alone for a long while in my ill-lit tunnel, and Billy and the Face are striding towards me with a new look of determination on their faces. Whatever is coming next, I have had enough. *Nemo me impune lacessit.* Or to put it more colloquially, nobody fucks with me and gets away with it. I will put my elbow into Billy's groin, headbutt the Face and sink my teeth into whatever part of him I can. Then I will take his pistol and get away, because I have no reason to believe, Section 29, 'that this custody is lawful'.

I'm being lifted up on both sides, but not roughly this time.

'Come on, Captain,' says the Face in a tone I haven't heard before. 'Let's get you in your carriage before it turns into a pumpkin.' The hostile banter has dropped clean out of his voice, and the effect on my plan is disarming. His voice is real. My feet are dragging under me. I pass through another smaller room and then outside into darkness and feel the cold air on my face. Hands manoeuvre me into the back of a car, where I lie on my side and the pain in my rib flares up and leaves me gasping. The engine is running.

'Jesus, what have they done to you?' Through the drunkenness of exhaustion, I recognise the voice.

'I cannot answer that question,' I mumble.

'Turn that heater up *now*,' says the voice I recognise. It dawns on me it's H, who gets into the back of the car, props me up and brings a small hip flask to my lips filled with his blessed Glenlivet. 'Easy does it,' he says, 'end-ex, mate. You've done it, you bastard.' He's taking off his coat and sliding it behind my back and over my shoulders. 'What d'you say we get you home?'

I can't stop shivering, but there's an electric warmth spreading across my chest, and I'm so relieved I can't speak, and upset that I can't speak. I try to wink at H, but my eye's already closed, and the effort makes me wince instead. I see the Face come to the rear door, and H lets down the window. The Face rests his arms on the door frame and sighs.

'All yours, skipper,' he says. 'Not a word. Top notch. If he ever gets bored send him over to us, why don't you?' Then Billy appears beside him and passes the ziplock bag with my possessions through the window.

'Give him a fucking fag, then,' says Billy with a look of outrage. The Face hands Billy a cigarette, who lights it and reaches inside the window to put it in my mouth. The smoke goes straight to my head and makes me dizzy.

'You can't whistle for shit, Billy,' I tell him.

'And you're a stubborn cunt, and all,' he replies. And Billy is grinning from one side of his face to the other, like a boy who's made a new friend.

I sleep a whole day and a night, and wake up in the unreal luxury of a clean and warm bed. H has brought the local doctor to me, who doesn't normally make house calls, but the two of them go back a while by the look of it. It's not the first time he's been to the house to look at a minor injury that's never been properly explained by its owner.

'You *have* been in the wars,' says the doctor as he looks me over.

'Only two, actually,' I say.

He tells me there's not much to do for a cracked rib except patience and painkillers, which will also bring down the swelling in my eye and left hand. My eye gets a butterfly suture and a wry suggestion to stay away from doors.

Hot water feels like a miracle, and the breakfast that H cooks is worth any lottery win. After we eat, H asks if I'm ready for a debrief. He gets out one of his laminated maps and points out the crossroads where I stopped to get petrol, and the place where I began my night-time escape. We find the ridge where I woke up, and we find the village of Shobdon and the airfield where my travels came to an end.

'What I don't understand is how you knew I was at the airfield,' I say.

'Clever that,' he says with a knowing smile. 'Where'd I put your jacket?' He retrieves it and goes to work on the stitches of the collar with his penknife, extracting a thin piece of black plastic the size of a large stamp with a six-inch-long tail of fine wire. It dawns on me that I never really had a chance to escape my pursuers after all.

'Tracker,' he says, tossing it in his palm. 'A bit sneaky beaky. Used to use these all the time Over The Water. We were going to let you go a lot longer, but we couldn't have you nick a plane. Nice idea, though.' He grins. The airfield is where the Regiment has been known to practise what he calls hot exfils, which is Regiment-speak for getting people like H in or out of countries where there isn't much time to socialise, and involves driving a Range Rover at high speed on or off the ramp of a moving Hercules aircraft, which H calls a Fat Albert. He doesn't know why Hercs are called Fat Alberts, he says; they just are.

The place I had my tête-à-tête with the colonel is, as I've guessed, an abandoned chicken farm on the periphery of the airfield, and the colonel, he says, really is a colonel with the Green Slime.

'Arrogant bastard, but a good soldier,' he concedes. Billy, he tells me, is just a big softie, and the Face, who's actually called Nick, was the youngest member of Pagoda Troop at the Prince's Gate hostage rescue.

'He said he was going to shoot me,' I tell him.

'Don't be daft,' says H. 'We're not allowed to carry weapons. Probably just a water pistol.' A wink suggests this isn't the whole story, but I let that go.

'What about that fucking farmer who tried to kill me?'

'Old Tom? We knew where you were, so we put him at the bottom of the woods. Wouldn't hurt a fly. Known him for years. Some of the lads practise their OP skills on his farm.'

'What happened to the dogs?' I ask, because this has been puzzling me.

'Dogs?' he asks. 'We didn't have any dogs. Must have been a hunt. Happened to me on my E & E once,' he says, going back to his own selection days. 'Whole pack of them came swarming over us. I was sure I was going to be Platform 4'd. Scared the life out of me, but a minute later they were all gone.' He folds up the map. 'Sorry about all the psycho games. They get quite into it sometimes. Must have liked you.'

'They don't know what I'm used to from my ex,' I say, and the effort to laugh hurts my eye again.

I retrieve the Firm's magic mobile and bring it to life. There's a text message waiting which reads INT LOCSTAT, which is Seethrough's way of asking where I am and what I'm doing. I call London, activate the encryption and listen to the watery-sounding ringing tone until it stops.

'This is Plato for Macavity,' I say.

'Macavity here. I'm told congratulations are in order. Good show.'

Crisp, to the point and ridiculous as ever.

'You've got some travelling coming up. Be here on Saturday, can you? We'll send some transport.'

I have no idea what day it is, but agree.

'Did you really try to steal an aircraft?' he asks.

'Yes.'

'Well, don't make a habit of it. And don't let this go to your head.'

'Roger that,' I say.

But it won't be easy.

PART TWO

3

This is not how it all begins. It begins a month earlier with a minor and, to my mind, forgivable act of theft committed on a grey March morning with Gerhardt, my partner in crime. We have been stealing firewood from a patch of forest not far from home, thanks to an undefended muddy track which Gerhardt has managed with ease, despite the full load of logs carried by his rear axle. It's true that, at sixteen, he's showing his age now and is far from perfect, but he still belongs to the fraternity of the most handsome and instantly recognisable four-wheel-drive vehicles in the world, the Mercedes G-Wagen, built to be indestructible and to go wherever their drivers take them.

I've rescued Gerhardt from a cruel and uncaring owner who kept him locked in a cold garage, understanding nothing of his potential. It's true I keep a hammer in the glove compartment for when the fuel pump misbehaves, and for when the solenoid jams in wet weather. A few blows in the right spot usually do the trick. I also keep handy a spare bottle of transmission fluid, which tends to leak from the torque converter housing, and I try not to think about why the water pump makes a sort of puffing sound like Chitty Chitty Bang Bang. But apart from these foibles, Gerhardt is my pride and joy. Off-road, he comes into his own. He also weighs over two tons, which makes me remember what happens next all the more vividly.

I'm nearly home and travelling at speed along a narrow country lane. Turning a corner I find the road unexpectedly blocked by a tractor towing an evil-looking piece of farm machinery which takes up the entire width of the road. It's a giant tiller with rows of curved shining blades, and as I hit the brakes hard a loud tearing sound comes from underneath me as the nearside wheels lock on the loose wet gravel. Logs come spilling into the front seats and I have a vision of Gerhardt being sliced into wafers at the moment of impact. We come juddering to a very timely halt, six feet short of the gleaming blades.

The driver of the tractor can't hear me swearing. He hasn't even seen me, and creeps forward at a snail's pace. I try to squeeze past, but the road's too narrow, so I follow for a while as my relief turns to frustration. My only chance to get ahead is to divert along a track through long grass and mud. I've driven it once before. It will add half a mile to the journey home but it's a good excuse to put Gerhardt through his paces off-road.

When I reach the sign marked BRIDLEWAY, I turn onto the track with a final curse at the tractor and slip the gearbox into four-wheel drive. The steering stiffens as the differentials lock and the power spreads to all four wheels. Lurching through the deep muddy ruts, Gerhardt is as happy as a horse released into the wild. Further on the track narrows and is choked with undergrowth, which flattens out submissively at our advance. Ten minutes later we rejoin the surfaced road. I push back the differential locks, return to two-wheel drive and head for home, listening to the tyres throwing off mud like a dog shaking water from its fur after a satisfying walk.

I'm a few minutes from home after this little detour when an unfamiliar sight catches my eye. A bright-red late-model Alfa Romeo is parked on the grassy verge with its hazard lights flashing. It's an odd place to leave a car. There's nothing to stop for nearby except empty fields. I slow up alongside and can see that the front wheels have spun themselves into the soft ground. I can see heat rising off the bonnet. Someone has got stuck and needs to be towed out.

I drive on and a hundred yards later see a figure up ahead. It must be the driver: a dark-haired woman, walking on the verge with her back to me. As I draw closer I can't help noticing how well proportioned she is. She's wearing a short wine-coloured jacket embroidered with what look like flowers and beads, dark close-fitting trousers and knee-high boots in cream and brown leather. They're expensive, city clothes and look out of place on a country lane in Wiltshire. She turns her head as she hears Gerhardt's engine and turns back again without changing pace, and I catch a glimpse of a shapely, Far Eastern-looking face.

She makes no effort to stop me as I pass, so I pull over just ahead of her. Leaning over to lower the passenger window I see the striking features of a thirty-year-old woman with long jet-black hair and high cheekbones. Her eyes are dark, narrow and intense, and their opposing curves resemble a pair of leaping dolphins. She brushes a strand of hair from her forehead, and comes to the window with an anxious smile. She looks Japanese, and is very beautiful.

'Nice parking,' I say. A soft leather handbag is slung over her left shoulder. In her right hand is a mobile phone, which she waves in a gesture of embarrassment.

'Can you help me?' she asks. 'No signal!' She sounds Russian, which is unexpected. 'I have to make a phone call. Do you know where there's a telephone?'

'There's no reception here,' I say. 'I have the same problem.' I'm feeling in my pocket for my phone, then realise I've left it at home. 'Maybe I can help,' I suggest, because it's not every day you get to come to the aid of an Oriental damsel in distress. 'I have a rope,' I tell her, wondering how I'll extricate it from under half a ton of logs. 'We can drive back to your car and try to pull it out.'

I open the passenger door for her, and apologise for the logs that have fallen into the front of the car. She looks hesitantly for a moment at the debris of bark on the seat.

'You are *farmer*?'

I can't explain I've been stealing wood, so the simplest thing is to agree.

'I live here,' I say, brushing off the seat and throwing a few logs into the back. Her accent is definitely Russian, though by her looks she's from central Asia. She smiles, gives a girlish shrug of assent, and climbs aboard.

'My name is Anthony,' I say, feeling unexpectedly nervous to have such a beautiful stranger by my side. I turn the car around.

'Anthony,' she repeats. 'I can call you Tony?'

'Absolutely not. My friends call me Ant. Like the animal.' I make a crawling motion on the dashboard. She laughs, and the slender gold circles of her earrings dangle with the motion of her head.

'My name is Ziyba,' she says.

'The word for beautiful.'

'My God!' she squeals. 'You speak Uzbek! How is it possible?'

'A farmer knows many things,' I say. I don't actually speak a word of Uzbek, but the word has the same meaning in Persian, which I know well enough.

'I am lucky to find such a farmer,' she says with irony. But I'm the one who can't believe my luck. Her jacket has fallen open and my eye has been caught by the contours of her sweater and the medallion-like buckle of her belt, which is made from concentric circles of pink coral beads. I've almost driven past her stranded car when I hear her point it out, and pull over. I retrieve the tow rope from under the seat, and make a show of effort hooking up the U-bolts to the towing brackets of both cars.

'Start the engine and drive forward gently, and let's see what happens.'

I drive ahead of her, take up the slack very slowly and in the mirror watch as the Alfa rolls onto the road. Then we both get out to admire our success.

'It worked!' She's beaming. 'Thank you,' she says. There's an awkward pause. I live half a mile away and haven't the courage to ask her back for a coffee. I roll up the tow rope and throw it back into the car, but I can't bear to see her go. She's like a bird of paradise that's landed in my lap, and I'm racking my brains for an idea that will stop her from disappearing.

'If you need to make a phone call, you can follow me to a pub. It's just two minutes away.'

She shrugs again after a moment's thought, and agrees to drive behind me.

It's my local, but I'm not there very often. A couple of scruffy-looking local cars are parked outside, as well as a powerful grey BMW, looking very out of place. We walk in together through the back door, where I point out the payphone in the corridor. I check if she has change for the phone, and ask if I can buy her a drink.

'Just a mineral water,' she says, smiling.

I push open the door to the bar and smell the smoke and beer. A few locals are sitting at tables with their drinks. Standing at the bar itself is a solitary man with his back to me, wearing a Barbour that has lost its shine. I order a mineral water and a pint of local beer, and glance at the man a few feet from me, who's peering thoughtfully into his glass. The drinks appear. I take a few sips of beer as I wait and glance back at the door, but as the minutes pass I lose patience and walk back to see if I can help Ziyba. The corridor's empty.

Outside, Gerhardt is where I've left him, but the Alfa has gone. I feel a pang of disappointment, and walk back to the bar, feeling desolate and stupid. Then, as I raise my glass to my lips, I hear a distinctly upper-class English voice say, 'You look like someone who's just been stood up.'

I turn my head in surprise and look at the face of the man who's been standing near me, which is now fixed on me in a broad and knowing grin.

'Hello, Ant,' he says quietly. 'Fancy meeting you here.'

It's an extraordinary coincidence. I haven't seen the face for six or seven years. It's broad and squarish, with a large and prominent brow framed with neat sandy-coloured hair. It has the same thin lips and prominent chin as I remember, the same mischievous eyes, and bears an uncanny resemblance to Frans Hals' Laughing Cavalier. My most vivid memory of it is from ten years earlier, hanging upside down from the seat belt of an army Land Rover which the two of us have managed to roll over on Salisbury Plain. But it's lost much of its boyish charm since then.

'Captain Seethrough, I presume,' I say with genuine astonishment. 'What the hell are you doing here?' Pronouncing his name out loud makes me want to laugh. His real name is Carlton-Cooper, or something very like it, which in an environment such as the army is as problematic as being called Hyper-Ventilate or Slashed-Peak. When he first made captain, and became Captain Carlton-Cooper, someone had the idea of calling him C3. Not long afterwards a fellow officer in a waggish mood tweaked the name to Seethrough, and for its ragging value and suggestion of lewdness, it stuck firmly. He never liked it much.

'Well may you ask, Ant, well may you ask,' he says, rather as if he knows something I don't. He has the same manner of talking through his teeth in clipped tones that lends a quality of determination to everything he says, and the same playful habit of flexing his eyebrows as if a conspiracy were afoot. 'I'd say the question is what are *you* doing here?' He smiles charmingly. It's a strange way to greet an old friend after such a long time, and I wonder for a moment whether there isn't an hereditary streak of madness in his very distinguished family.

'I'm here,' I explain tolerantly, 'because a tractor was blocking the road on my way home.' I can't decide whether to tell him about my unexpected encounter with the Uzbek girl, so I add, 'I was just dropping a friend off.'

He looks at me with a smile that borders on smugness.

'Naughty boy,' he says as if to admonish a child. 'Telling porkies again.' His tone of voice suggests I'm a complete fool. I feel a mixture of resentment and curiosity towards him, which grows as he says, 'Nice girl, though. Can't blame you for liking her. Knew you would.' He takes a sip from his glass and sighs with exaggerated relish. 'God, you've really got proper beer in the country, haven't you? Here.' He passes me the untouched glass of mineral water. 'Shall we sit?'

We move to a table in a corner of the room, facing the front door. I'm too baffled to speak.

'Father was actually a KGB colonel, would you believe it?' he goes on. 'Unthinkable a few years ago. Now she works for us. Didn't even have to twist her arm.'

'Do you mind if I ask what you're on about?' I interrupt him. 'I met that woman ten minutes ago by chance.'

'Powerful illusion, isn't it, chance?' He takes a slow sip from his glass. 'You met her because you stopped for her. You stopped for her because she was beautiful and driving a sports car. You saw her sports car because you took the long way home. You took the long way home because the road you were on was blocked by a tractor.'

'And I suppose you're going to tell me you put the tractor there.' It's too far-fetched. He's bluffing wildly, but my mind's racing through the possibilities. I can't figure out how he knows I turned off the road, because I haven't told him.

'Actually, yes, we did. A little cash for an obliging farmer.'

'What if I hadn't turned off where I did?'

'I admit we had to choose the right spot in advance. But you don't like to be thwarted, and you do like going off-road. We knew you'd take the dirt track.'

'I didn't have to bring her here,' I counter, wondering who 'we' are.

'She needed to make a phone call. This is the nearest place where there's a phone.'

'I could have let her call from my mobile.'

'You haven't got your mobile with you, Ant. We know you left it at home from the last time it talked to the network. It's called a handshake, and the transmitter density gives us a pretty good idea of the location it came from. Pretty soon all mobiles will be

GPS-enabled and we'll be able to know which pocket they're in.'
He grins smugly and takes another sip of beer.

'I could have taken her home,' I say.

'Oh, come on,' he scoffs dismissively. 'You're much too old-fashioned for that.'

'I might not have come to the bar. I could have left her in the car park.'

'You like a drink, Ant. We both know that.'

He's got me there. I feel strangely violated. He's predicted my every step.

'Why go to all the fuss?' I asked. 'If you wanted to meet why couldn't you just call me like a normal person?'

He takes another sip of beer and his eyes scan the room from left to right as the glass is raised. His voice grows a little quieter.

'This isn't just a joke, Ant. People watch. This way, there's nothing to show we didn't meet by accident. No record, no phone calls, no prior meeting.'

'Please. Who cares?'

'The people you once nearly worked for care,' he says, and turns to me in the manner of a parent admonishing a guilty child.

I feel the hair go up at the back of my neck. No one knows that. I've never told anyone. From wondering whether my old friend has lost his mind, I now have to ask myself how, unless he's seen my personnel file at the Firm, he can possibly know about this secret chapter of my life which I buried a long time ago. My mind is scanning over the little history I really know about Seethrough.

We meet for the first time at Sandhurst, where he's lecturing in Faraday Hall while I'm a still an officer cadet, and once again on exercise near Warminster, where we manage to topple the Land Rover. As a young lieutenant in a Guards regiment he's rebadged during the Gulf War to operate with a branch of the SAS called the Force Projection Cell, based in Riyadh, where we meet again by chance at the end of hostilities. We see each other a few times in London after the Gulf but eventually lose touch. He's always travelling, and the few times we speak by telephone, when I ask him what he's doing he says he can't talk about it. I regret the loss of contact. He's a brave and principled soldier, gifted with charm, energy and a wide circle of distinguished friends, but I move, by choice and temperament, in less exalted circles. It occurs to me now that I've envied his enormous self-confidence, his freedom from introspection and his use of old-fashioned expressions that remind me of my father. But it makes sense now. My old friend Captain Seethrough has become a spy.

'Why the approach?' I ask casually, hoping to disguise my astonishment. 'Am I a target? There's not very much that's secret about the landscaping business. I know some frogs and newts you could recruit.'

'Don't be facetious, Ant,' he says, taking another sip from his glass. 'We thought you might want to go back to Afghanistan. Courtesy of the Firm this time.' He studies my reaction. I try not to have one. 'There's an op there if you want it. The Chief's been looking for someone and I've managed to convince him that this one's got your name on it. Think you might want to give it a try? Nobody's poked around the place as much as you have, or speaks the languages.' He pauses while the proposition sinks in. 'You failed the first time and I'm giving you a second chance.'

'I didn't fail,' I say, 'I opted out.'

'That's not quite what your file says, Ant,' he says with a scepti-cal tilt of his head. So he's seen my PF after all. Then his manner changes completely and he looks around the room as if he's just arrived.

'Do they do food here?' he asks loudly.

'I haven't got much of an appetite,' I say.

Seethrough goes to the bar and orders two more beers, and I watch as he engages the barman in conversation, laughing with him as though the two of them are old friends. He has the gift of immense and apparently spontaneous charm. He can convince a complete stranger of nearly anything with what looks like untainted sincerity, and adapt his conversation to whatever subject comes up, even if he knows nothing about it. I can see he's deliberately misleading the barman with an invented story about his reasons for being in the area, something about buying a yurt for his kids to play in. At the end of this contrived encounter, he reaches into his wallet for a note and hands it over with a theatrical flourish.

As I watch him, my thoughts are shunting back to the chapter I've allowed myself to forget. I didn't fail. I wanted to join the Firm because I'd seen the effects of war first hand and believed that the weaknesses in intelligence that led to conflict could only be shored up by the more diligent use of human assets. I'd gone through the conventional channels, cleared the vetting and selection hurdles, signed Section 5 over tea in a room overlooking the Mall, and sat my qualifying tests in a gloomy office near Admiralty Arch. But the events of my personal life sent me spinning in a different direction. I was in the midst of my divorce at the time and my wife had told me I'd never see my children again if I was posted overseas. I had two young daughters and the prospect of not seeing them was too much. Then my wife had moved back to America with the girls, and my life felt as though it had been cut into small pieces.

When the trap came, I decided to walk into it rather than admit to the ongoing humiliations of my private life. A month after my QTs, while I was still under review, an old friend had contacted me out of the blue. He worked in the City and enjoyed the lifestyle that went with it. He'd introduced me to a new and distracting world, given me flying lessons in his private plane, lent me money and generally raised my spirits. Then came the offer of dinner with a married couple who liked, as he'd put it, to swing.

I'd known it was a set-up, and was deeply disappointed that my prospective employers had managed to persuade a friend to deceive me. The woman propositioned me the same evening, and

I'd taken her up on the offer knowing that it would destroy my chances of a career in the Service. She looked a bit like Madonna, I now remember. But an aspiring Intelligence Branch officer can't afford to be susceptible to sexual entrapment. He might one day be drugged while his computer is searched, or seduced into giving away secrets. The risk is too high. Shortly afterwards a curt letter had informed me that I had no future in the Service. As I'd expected.

'Sorry,' says Seethrough, after I briefly explain my motives for sabotaging my own career. 'I don't buy it. They assessed you in the old-fashioned way, and you fell for it. Don't tell me you saw it coming. Nobody outwits the Firm.'

'I don't know about that,' I say. 'People have been known to run imaginary sources and been paid handsomely for it.'

'Only if it suits us, Ant. Look. Someone wants you on board and I'm willing to approve it. If you don't want the op you can forget we ever met and go back to building ponds.'

'Landscaping,' I correct him. 'Ponds are only a part of what I do, but they're arguably the most fascinating aspect.'

'Don't fuck about, Ant. This affects you.'

I enjoy our sparring, but he sounds serious.

'So where do we go from here?' I ask.

'Talk about it outside,' he says. As he glances at his watch he sees that his shirt cuff is wet with beer, and curses quietly.

'There's a sale on at Turnbull and Asser,' I tell him.

'Ended last week,' he corrects me. 'How would you know, anyway? Can you *afford* to buy shirts in Jermyn Street? Building homes for newts?'

'Actually I have them made by my tailor in Rome.' It isn't entirely true. I only had the one shirt made because it cost so much.

'You haven't changed, Ant,' he says thoughtfully as we stand up, and for a moment the mask drops and I'm reminded of the young soldier I had so much fun with. 'But it's nice to see you.'

We walk through the corridor to the car park, where I unlock Gerhardt. Seethrough climbs into the passenger seat and looks disapprovingly over the dashboard, then tugs absent-mindedly on one of the differential lock levers.

'What's wrong with an English car?' he asks. 'Why can't you just have a Land Rover like a normal person?'

I ignore the question, although it's true I occasionally long for a different car. A later-model version of Gerhardt, with full-time four-wheel drive and electronic centre-diff control.

'Are you going to tell me about the op or not?' I ask.

He sighs to himself, as if making way again for the serious side of his personality. He looks at me, and then out of the windscreen towards some far-off place.

'Not right now. You're going to go home and carry on as normal, building ponds or doing whatever it is you do. You don't call anyone, you don't tell anyone, you don't write anything down. A week today, you come to Legoland at midday.'

'Is that what they call it? Legoland?' A picture of the Secret Intelligence Service headquarters, perched on the lip of the Thames beneath the southern end of Vauxhall Bridge, flashes into my head. It does look a bit like a giant Lego construction.

'You go to the main entrance,' says Seethrough, ignoring my interruption, 'and ask for Macavity at reception. Introduce yourself as Plato, and someone will come for you.'

'Macavity? Plato? They're T. S. Eliot's cats, aren't they? That's very original.'

'Quite,' he replies, ruffled.

He opens the door and turns to me just before stepping out.

'And for God's sake, Ant, just don't blab about it in the meantime. Otherwise,' he adds with a schoolteacherish look, 'Macavity won't be there.'

He's alluding to the poem, a fragment of which now returns to me.

You may meet him in a by-street, you may see him in a square
But when a crime's discovered, Macavity's not there!

The door bangs shut, and his manner changes again as he gives an uncharacteristically cheerful wave as if seeing off an old friend. For the benefit, I suppose, of whoever he thinks might be watching. Perhaps it's his habitual tradecraft kicking in. The grey BMW slides quietly and swiftly away like a shark into deep water, and I'm alone again.

It's only lunchtime, but already the day seems long. I head home, briefly entertaining the fantasy that as I turn into my drive I'll see a red Alfa Romeo parked there, and the beautiful Ziyba will be waiting for me nearby.

I don't, and she isn't.

4

In the course of the following week I make two journeys. The first needs an accomplice. An old friend in London is happy to oblige. We've long ago agreed on an innocuous code word signifying alarm that can be slipped into a telephone conversation, so his suggestion that we have dinner together in London that evening sounds spontaneous enough to anyone who might be listening. It also allows me to name the restaurant, the location of which means I can walk credibly past a certain street corner in Maida Vale and, in the act of posting a letter, leave a chalk mark for an elderly lady to see on her daily walk the following morning. It's old-fashioned, but it works, and allows me to avoid making a phone call which Seethrough's minions are no doubt already authorised to intercept.

Halfway along Pall Mall, and sandwiched between what its occupants consider to be lesser places, stands a stone building said to be inspired by Michelangelo's Palazzo Farnese in Rome. Nine steps lead up to dark heavy doors. It's late morning. I check the time and walk up into the imposing entrance, where the porter, as porters are wont to do in such establishments, looks me up and down with a dour expression of enquiry.

'Baroness K—— is expecting me in the library,' I say.

He glances down at the papers on the kiosk counter and looks up again with a marginally more friendly expression.

'Very good, sir.'

I walk up the second set of steps into the flamboyant atrium. Glancing overhead I can see the graceful arcs of lead-crystal lozenges in the roof and the dark and slender Ionic columns of the upper gallery. I turn left towards the stairs, passing beneath the grand oil paintings on the walls and the marble facings in deep red and green, until I reach the cavernous opulence of the library. After the rush of traffic on the street below, the long room seems magically quiet. A few members glance discreetly up through the ritual dimness at the entry of a stranger, then return to their subdued conversations.

At the eastern end of the room stands the woman I've come to see, studying the spines of a row of leather-bound volumes beside the bay of a tall window. She turns and peers over her glasses just as I enter, and steps forward to meet me.

'My dear boy,' she says as we embrace. 'You look more like your father every time I see you.' And you, I think to myself, look older. It's only been a month since our last meeting, but the radiotherapy has taken its toll on her body. She's grown noticeably thinner, and there's a visible space between the collar of her black cashmere sweater and the sinews of her neck. There's a growing stoop to her bird-like frame, the bones of which seem too narrow and fragile to contain the sum of her life's experience. Yet her movements are nimble and precise, and her voice is still charged with the quiet authority and confidence of an adviser to ministers and confidante to heads of state, and of her lifetime calling of scholar and spy. She ushers me to a marble fireplace and her voice lowers as we settle into a pair of red leather armchairs beneath a worn and austere-looking marble bust of Milton.

'Your signal was awfully faint; I wasn't sure if it was you. Or perhaps it's my glasses. I lose them so often nowadays.'

'They don't make chalk like they used to,' I suggest.

She presses a discreet button by the fireplace. A waiter appears a few moments later and she orders her usual, a whisky and soda with no ice. I ask for the same.

'You're well,' I say.

'Eighty-seven isn't a bad innings, if you think about it. I do have trouble with opening things, which is the worst aspect of getting old, but other than that everything seems to be working.' A gentle smile comes over her gaunt features. 'You must enjoy your youth while you have it. Did I tell you the president of Naronda offered me a state funeral? I don't suppose one can take him up on it. He was a child when we all had to leave but it seems he never forgot the constitution I drafted rather in his favour.'

'I trust you'll keep him waiting,' I said.

We chat for a while and, postponing the inevitable, catch up on personal news. Then she puts her glass gently onto the small table between us. Her cheeks and the skin beneath her eyes droop noticeably downwards and give her a bloodhound's perpetually sad look of enquiry. But the clear grey steely quality of her gaze remains unchanged, and now her eyes fall undistractedly on me.

'But we have more important things to talk about. Tell me.'

I tell every detail of my encounter with Seethrough, the operation he's proposed and the decision I'll soon be forced to make. The Baroness listens intently, and when I've told her everything, she nods gravely and gazes towards the window, reciting in a quiet voice,

'Macavity, Macavity, there's no one like Macavity,
There never was a Cat of such deceitfulness and suavity.'

'Your memory always astonishes me,' I say.

'In our day your father and I had to memorise everything before a mission. He had the advantage of perfect French – not like me. I shall never forget the occasion when he asked a German soldier for directions. We were somewhere in the Vosges. The soldier was perfectly civil, but of course he didn't know our guns were pointed at him in our pockets. If he'd spoken to me, we would've had it. I came from Section D and I don't suppose my Arabic would have got us very far.'

'Section D?'

'Did I say that? It's such a long time ago now. I don't suppose St Ermin's even exists any longer. But your father was a brave man. And a patriot, though he would never admit it. After the Blitz his attitude towards the Germans changed. I don't suppose he ever forgave them, but he never let revenge get in the way. You must above all do the same.'

'I haven't given it much thought,' I say, which is untrue.

'But you must be prepared. Perhaps you know the story of Ali and the knight? Rumi tells it in the *Mathnawi*.'

I haven't heard it, though I know of the reverence in which the famous poet is held in the Persian-speaking world. It's an odd moment to be recounting an eastern fable, but the Baroness always has her reasons.

'I'll tell you, but then we must have some lunch.' She studies the backs of her hands thoughtfully for a moment, then clasps them neatly together and lets them come to rest on her lap.

'You know that the fourth caliph, Ali, was said to have been a courageous fighter as well as a political leader – not like today's, I need hardly say,' she snorts. 'Well. Ali is on the battlefield and engages a Christian knight. They fight, and the Christian falls to the ground. Ali is about to kill him when the knight, in a final act of defiance, spits in his face. But instead of lopping off his head, Ali sheathes his sword, and lets the knight go free. Now, the knight is a bit surprised by this and asks why on earth he didn't kill him when he had the chance. "Because if I'd killed you at that moment," says the great warrior, "it would have been from anger, and against the principles of war." The knight is so impressed he converts to Islam. It's a good story, and of course the Shi'a love it.' The Baroness sighs. 'The man who strives for freedom doesn't allow himself to be provoked, even in the heat of battle. At least that's how I understand it. Freedom. You must strive for the same thing.' She pauses. 'Things will happen quickly now that they've found a role for you. It suits our purpose, and you must play the part.'

'You said you'd arrange a context for me. I won't ask how you managed it.'

She doesn't rise to this but smiles benignly. This frail old woman has succeeded in having me recruited to the Secret Intelligence Service for a purpose unknown even to the Service itself.

'You will jump aboard and must be prepared for the journey. When you know more, contact me in the usual way. In the meantime I shall watch, and pray.'

She says nothing more, but with a simple gesture indicates it's time to move to the coffee room, as the dining room is misleadingly called. We walk down the carpeted stairs in silence, and a jacketed member of staff greets us with a deferential bow and shows us to a table. Two menus are produced, though no prices appear on the one I'm given.

I look out of the window. From it I can just see the Duke of York's Monument and coated figures scurrying past the shrapnel-scarred statues in Waterloo Place. I wonder how many of them have undertaken work about which they can speak to no one, how they have managed the burden of secrecy, and how they have mastered the division in one's life that comes with a double task.

As if from afar I hear the voice of my hostess. I'm reminded that her presence is a comfort, even though we hardly talk. A wine list is in her hand and she's peering at me over her glasses.

'Can we manage a bottle? There's a Montrachet that'll go very well with the sole.'

I nod enthusiastically, but my thoughts are somewhere else. I'm remembering how the plastic sheeting on the windows of the house in Kabul used to balloon inwards whenever there was a detonation in the city, and how the whole house used to shake when a Taliban rocket landed nearby, and how rich I felt just to be alive afterwards.

I'm haunted by the prospect of returning to Afghanistan, a country that has left its mark on me like no other. There's a discovery waiting for me there, and the answer to a secret that I can mention to no one except the Baroness. I'm not sure I'm ready for it. The Baroness long ago taught us the power of a single thought: that in the Network we are never alone. There are always others among its members in similar or more difficult situations, suffering or struggling with the same situations, unable to reveal their true purpose to the world, and this knowledge has often come to my aid, as it does now.

'My dear boy,' I hear her say, 'you're miles away.'

I make the second journey after the agreed interval of a week, the following Sunday. Two hours after leaving home with Gerhardt I'm crossing the Thames at Vauxhall Bridge, trying to decide whether the building looming ahead of me on the left is ugly or not. It still looks brand new, though I wonder how its clean and angular lines will eventually age.

I park in Kennington Lane. Now that Gerhardt is at rest, I can smell the transmission fluid burning off the hot manifold. With a few minutes to spare, I take the opportunity to check the fluid level, to see how much poor Gerhardt has leaked on the way. It isn't good. It's dropped considerably, and the dark liquid streaks all the way from the torque converter to the rear silencer. I feel a pang of regret that I can't afford a new transmission, then remember how old Gerhardt is. Replacing his transmission is akin to giving a heart transplant to an elderly man. Much in life, I reflect gloomily, simply isn't solvable.

At midday I walk through the doors of Number 85 Albert Embankment, and enter the lobby. The place has a stripped-down and anonymous look with the smooth flat colours of a modern hotel, and there is everywhere a slightly greenish hue, cast by the triple-glazed glass of the windows. I announce myself at the reception area, which is overseen by an unexpectedly cheerful pair of young women.

'Plato to see Macavity,' I say.

One of the women picks up a handset, passes on the names and motions me, as might a hotel receptionist, to a black sofa opposite, where I wait next to an imitation *Monstera deliciosa*. Seethrough appears a few minutes later from behind the futuristic door system that stretches across the far side of the entrance lobby, and comes up to me. He's dressed in a charcoal mohair suit, one of his Savile Row shirts with a swept-back collar and antique garnet cufflinks, and a grey silk tie. An identity card hangs from his neck, bearing his photograph but no name. Beside his image is what looks like a globe surrounded by yellow lightning bolts. He sees me looking at it.

'Now, now,' he says, tucking the card into his breast pocket. We shake hands and he looks me up and down approvingly.

'You clean up quite well,' he says.

'Thank you. New shirt?'

'Yes. Had it made in Italy. Little place off Piazza Navona,' he replies with a knowing grin, correctly locating my tailor in Rome. I'm not sure if I'm reassured by this detail. He must have had someone search my credit card records since our meeting a week earlier. At least it means he listens to everything I say.

'Shall we? I need your phone first.' No one, he explains, is allowed a mobile phone inside the main building.

He hands it to the security guard, who gives me a receipt like a raffle ticket.

'Right. Follow me and don't even think of wandering off,' he says. 'And by the way, you never run in this place. Whatever happens, you never run.' We walk to the doors, where he passes his card through a reader and enters a number on a keypad. A door slides open, he goes through, it closes again, and he repeats the process from behind a second door on the far side, allowing me to enter. I'm reminded of French high street banks where the customer is isolated for a few moments in a glassy pod before being able to escape. Then the door in front of me slides aside and I join Seethrough in a tall and spacious inner courtyard with tropical-looking plants overhanging a cream-coloured marble floor. There are broad corridors radiating from a pair of central lift shafts. Kew Gardens, I'm thinking, meets Terence Conran. The plants are plastic.

Seethrough watches my reaction. 'Welcome to Babylon-on-Thames.' He grins. He's visibly proud of his workplace. We take the lift to an upper floor, where the pale marble turns to grey floor tiles. Halfway along an anonymous-looking corridor we come to an empty briefing room identified by a letter and a number. Seethrough offers me a chair at a large oval table with expensive veneer, from which the cables of two slim computer monitors and a pair of complicated-looking telephones run into plugs recessed into the floor. He picks up a handset and says, 'Ready now,' and a few minutes later we're joined by a woman carrying a handful of variously coloured files.

We sit down and Seethrough ignores me for a few minutes as he types at a keyboard.

'What's the reg on your car?' he asks and types it in. 'Look at that.' He grins again. 'We've got you on camera 150 times since you left home.' His eyes are glued to the screen. 'You're actually speeding in this one. Eighty-two miles an hour. I didn't know your Unimog could go that fast. What were you doing in Amesbury?'

'Petrol,' I say. 'And it's not a Unimog.'

He peers more closely at the screen, and his fingers tap and scroll at the keyboard.

'You bought thirty-five pounds of four-star. And a Mars bar. Bloody clever, this point of sale stuff,' he mutters, then looks up. His assistant is standing beside him.

'Sorry. This is Stella,' he says. 'Inside joke.' She's about fifty, slim and slightly built, and has a gaunt sad-looking face with large dark eyes. She puts the files on the table, glances at me and utters a timid hello. Then she leaves the room.

'Right, let's take care of the paperwork,' he says, opening a Manilla file and pushing it towards me. A document marked TOP SECRET in big red letters glares back. It's a copy of the best bits of the Official Secrets Act.

'Haven't I already signed this?' I ask.

'Yes, but it's got a bit more draconian since then, I'm afraid,' he says. 'Now it authorises us to kill you and sell your children.'

I let him know with a look that this isn't a good joke.

'I'm sorry, I forgot. In Washington, aren't they? Mother was American, wasn't she?'

'Yes.' As if he didn't know.

'Rotten luck. Well, just sign the bloody thing so we can get on. I can't brief you until you sign.'

As soon as I've signed, Seethrough begins a short lecture about the Service, sparing me what he calls the grisly details but wanting, he says, to give me an outline of where the operation he's planning fits within the intelligence jigsaw. Seethrough's fellow Intelligence Branch staff, of whom there are fewer than I imagined, divide their efforts between a number of regional controllerates and another called Global Issues. The combined work of the controllerates is carried out by P and R officers, standing for production and requirements, a division of labour, roughly speaking, between the first half and second half of what is called the intelligence cycle. I've already been introduced to the idea in the army during my stint with the Green Slime, as members of the Intelligence Corps are affectionately known on account of their spinach-coloured berets.

Intelligence is broadly described as having four main phases: raw intelligence is first gathered or collected by a variety of means and technologies, then converted or collated into a form useable by analysts. It is then disseminated to the right people at the right time, and finally put to use – or, as we used to joke, misuse – by decision makers. In the army intelligence is used to enhance what military analysts, with their characteristic love of terminology incomprehensible to ordinary people, call battlespace visualisation.

The vocabulary of the Firm is different. I never once hear the words secret or agent. Raw intelligence is used to produce varying grades of CX – finely sifted intelligence reports – for the top feeders in the intelligence food chain. I never find out why it's called CX, or why intelligence from the Security Service, better known as MI5 and whose members Seethrough calls the River Rats, is called FX. They sound like types of nerve gas to me.

Since its area of specialisation is the use of human assets, the Firm's officers engage in four parallel tasks: targeting, cultivating, recruiting and then running their assets. Those in the know are said to be indoctrinated; Seethrough's philosophy is to keep the number of people indoctrinated into an operation to a minimum, and is emphatic that I discuss the material he's about to show me with no one but himself unless specifically instructed otherwise. My questions, he said, will go to him. My ideas will go to him, and my contact reports will go to him. I'm to write nothing down.

'This one's at the request of the Americans,' he says, opening the uppermost file. 'Provisional code name is Elixir.' He pushes the opened file towards me with a laminated companion list of commonly used acronyms and code words with their explanations – from Actor, meaning the Service's headquarters at Vauxhall Cross, to Zulu, meaning Greenwich Mean Time. The contents of the file are divided into several sections, which we examine in turn.

The first is a description of three civilian airline crashes. Each plane has dropped out of the sky shortly after take-off, killing all on board. The three incidents have been briefly reported in the press, but none of the photographs I'm looking at has ever made it into the papers. They're too gruesome. The debris from the first aircraft is strewn over a mile, along with the bodies of 200 passengers, many of whose charred and mutilated remains are still strapped into their seats. The second and third aircraft have crashed into water, and their wreckage has been gathered and secretly reassembled in long and dangerous recovery operations. Here too the passengers have been photographed as they were found, their bloated and limbless corpses still attached to their seats. In each case the accidents have been publicly blamed on engine failure, which official investigations have later confirmed. The most recent of them occurred only a few months ago.

'Even the airlines don't know this,' says Seethrough, 'but the culprit in all three is the same.' He turns to another section in the file, and shows me a US Defense Department image of an FIM-92.

Better known by its common name: the Stinger missile.

'Not a shred of doubt,' he went on. 'The Americans have verified it and we've double-checked at Fort Halstead. There's a machine there that can identify the exact stock of explosive from a tiny fragment of wreckage. Stingers in every case.'

At the mention of Fort Halstead I think involuntarily of my strolls with the Baroness through the gardens of Chevening House, and I picture the incongruous-looking palm trees swaying above the rear porch. Fort Halstead, the secret research establishment labelled only as 'works' on ordinary maps, is over a mile away at the top of the hill that overlooks the village, but on a still day we could often hear the faint cry of the warning alarm, at the sound of which the Baroness's finger would rise like a conductor's in anticipation of the muffled thump of a subterranean explosion. Somewhere in the complex, more recently, white-coated technicians had identified residues of TNT from Stinger warheads, matching its chemical profile against a database of known explosive stocks.

'Probably by spectrometric analysis of the isotopic ratios,' I say because I know a thing or two about explosives.

'Yes, quite,' agrees Seethrough, looking up for a moment. 'PTCP reckons they came through Iran but we don't know for sure. And if you can't stop the flow, you go back to the source.'

'Afghanistan. Where we handed them out in the first place.'

'To your old friends,' he adds with a dark look.

'Only some of them.'

'Now they're easy pickings for al-Qaeda, and you know what that means.'

'Yes, I do. In Arabic it means base or capital or seat of operations. But the way you pronounce it, it sounds like *al-qa'da*, which means buttocks.'

'I refer,' says Seethrough, clearing his throat and choosing to overlook this impudence, 'to the threat, not the etymology.'

The threat is an obvious one. If sufficient of the missiles are acquired by terrorists from Afghans willing to sell them, the potential for chaos and slaughter is impossible to contemplate. Governments will be held to ransom, says Seethrough. Anti-missile technologies are too costly to install on civilian airliners. The only solution is to recover the missiles themselves from the same people they were delivered to fifteen years earlier, when the Afghans were fighting the Soviets.

'This is the update on the American buyback programmes,' he says, turning the pages of the final section of the file. 'There've been several initiatives, mostly relying on middlemen in Pakistan, and too many of the deals have come to nothing. Over the past couple of years they've had a final push and thrown a lot of cash around inside the country. Going rate is $100,000 apiece, sometimes more. In the north it's been working quite well, where Massoud's chaps have proved very willing. They get them across the border here.' He points on a map of Afghanistan to the northern border with Uzbekistan. 'But now that the Taliban control the rest of the country the Yanks haven't got anyone they really trust who can move them. There's a bloody great stash of Stingers but they can't get them out. Somewhere down here.' He points again to the map, north of Kandahar this time. 'Too complicated. They need to be destroyed.'

'Why can't the Americans drop a bomb on them from a great height? They're good at that,' I say.

'Too sensitive. The Paks won't let them use their airspace for an offensive operation and the politics are too difficult. Imagine they hit the wrong target or the missiles are moved at the last minute. We need trusted eyes on the ground. There's also a time factor. You've heard of bin Laden?'

'Isn't he wanted by the Americans for his role in financing the bombing of their embassies in Kenya and Tanzania?'

'Yes. But now we're hearing he's looking for surface-to-air missiles. If he or his people get hold of the Stingers, God knows what he'll try next. We're asking you to go to Afghanistan and do the job yourself. Find a reason to be there, get a team together, verify the Stingers are where they say they are and blow the bloody things up so we can all go home.'

I don't have to think too long. I feel a great sense of relief, in fact. The mission is a straightforward one. I have both the contacts and the know-how. I know how to move in and out of the country, and I know how to blow things up.

'I think I can do that,' I say.

'Good,' says Seethrough.

He leans back in his chair and runs his hands through his hair.

'There's a bit more,' he says, then reaches for a different file, labelled TRODPINT. 'Last month one of the Americans' tribal int teams was approached by one of bin Laden's chaps. Says he's got top-grade time-sensitive CX on bin Laden's plans and needs to get it to us. But he doesn't identify himself and doesn't show up for their next meet.' He hands me a surveillance photograph taken in Afghanistan. It shows two dark-skinned heavily bearded men in conversation beside the roof of a car with a yellow plastic housing marked TAXI in Persian letters. One wears a loose-fitting Afghan shalwar kameez, and the other an old army jacket.

'Taken in Jalalabad last month. Chap on the left is one of bin Laden's best mates. The other one's our potential source, but we can't identify him. We've run his face through every database we've got, but there's no match.'

That's because he's supposed to have died nearly ten years ago, I'm thinking as I look at the photograph. He's almost unrecognisable. His face is half hidden by his beard, his skin is dark, his face is older and leaner. But it's Orpheus, I'm certain of it. He's finally surfaced and needs to come in. I pull my eyes away from the photograph. Seethrough is still talking.

'We've asked around. The Europeans don't have anyone of their own in bin Laden's circuit. Mossad swear they don't have an illegal out there, but you never know with Mossad. This one's too good to get away. We need to make an approach, God knows how.'

He doesn't need to explain where the plan's leading.

'We can put you onto the source while you're out there and you can do some fishing to see who bites. Could be a bit risky, but if you run a tight ship we should be alright. You feeling OK? It's a lot for one session, I know. I thought I'd give you a little tour to cheer you up. There's just one more thing. It's alright, this is the fun part. Gadgets. Back in a minute.'

He gathers up the files and leaves the room while the image of Orpheus floats stubbornly in my vision. Then he returns with two small white cardboard boxes, which he opens on the table.

'Let's have a look at what the tossers have got for you. Sorry – another in-joke, I'm afraid. Technical and Operations Support. They decide on the kit for an op.'

From the first box he takes out a Motorola mobile telephone with a stubby antenna. 'Identical to the real thing but there's a chip inside that screens the call with white noise,' he says. 'Even the NSA can't get their grubby hands on the signal. It's GPS-enabled so you we can keep track of it even if it's switched off. It'll also record a conversation up to sixteen hours.' He shows me the keypad configurations for each instruction. 'Now this is good. Have you ever used a firefly?'

I've heard of the small infrared strobes called fireflies being used by special forces, but never actually seen one.

'It's the next best thing to the military version. There's no visible output, but to anyone with night vision gear it'll look like a searchlight. Land a heli with it if you need to.' I don't know if he's serious. 'There's an ultraviolet function too. Use it with this.' Opening the second box, he takes out an ordinary-looking gel-ink pen with a retractable tip. A single click causes it to produce visible black ink. A second activates a flow of ink that's only visible under a narrow frequency of ultraviolet light. To demonstrate, he draws an invisible line from the back of his hand to the surface of the table, then keys a sequence on the keypad of the phone. As he holds the phone over the table, a bright white streak appears on the table, merging with the streak on his hand as he draws it closer. The slightest movement of an object marked with the ink, when viewed under the light from the phone, will be immediately obvious.

'Use it for security when you're out and about, and you'll always know if anyone's been in your stuff,' he says. 'You need to sign for these, by the way.' He leaves the room again and returns with a final folder containing the release forms, carrying a long dark-blue overcoat and elegantly battered leather briefcase. He drapes the coat over the back of a chair, then notices a bulge in the fabric and removes from the inner pocket some envelopes and a chequebook. I just make out the Coutts emblem embossed on the black outer cover before it disappears into his briefcase.

Our briefing is over. I stand up and wander over to the windows. The river looks grey and sullen. Closer to, I can see the chequerboard pattern in dark and light tiles of the veranda below us.

'Don't do that, please,' says Seethrough.

'Don't do what?'

'Stand by the windows. We don't do that.'

I return to the table and ask him why the windows are so thick. They're not as green as they look from the outside, but they're visibly thicker than normal windows.

'Something called TEMPEST. Can't remember what it stands for. It's to stop people listening to our computers. If you're very clever you can actually detect the little bits of radiation coming out of the screens and piece them all together somehow. That's it,' he remembers. 'Tiny Electro-Magnetic Particles Emitting Secret Things.'

I'm never entirely sure when he's joking. He gathers up his coat and case and we walk back along the corridor to the lifts. As we're waiting he turns to me with a smile and says: 'Welcome to the wonderful world of deniable operations.'

'I've always wondered what exactly that means.'

'It means,' he explains thoughtfully, 'that if the whole thing goes pear-shaped and you get yourself killed in Afghanistan, then the nice people in I/OPS upstairs will make sure there's a story in the papers about a careless British tourist beheaded by a loony Afghan mullah.'

'They don't actually behead people in Afghanistan,' I correct him. 'But I agree it's certainly evocative.'

'Yes,' he muses, 'I/OPS are very good at that.'

The lift falls gently but swiftly; I imagine it will stop at the ground floor, but there are several subterranean levels and we descend to the final one. Leaving the lift, we pass through another set of double glass doors like the airlock of a high-security laboratory. On the far side we emerge in a stony-grey corridor resembling one of the passageways of the Heathrow Express. Everything is grey; it's an appropriate colour for all the grey people who move along its secret grey spaces.

'Nobody uses the main entrance,' says Seethrough. 'If we did, we'd all be famous within twenty-four hours.'

From this side tunnel we come into a broader older-looking tunnel equipped at intervals with red fire hoses and alarms. High-pressure sprinkler pipes run overhead, and the walls are criss-crossed with metal cable conduits, junction boxes and switches. Nearby is a line of half a dozen small open carriages resembling golf caddies. They must be electrically powered. At the front sits a driver wearing the same dark uniform as the security guards above us. Behind him, each doorless carriage has a single seat, large enough for two passengers.

'All aboard,' says Seethrough, indicating one of them. After a minute's wait we begin to move forward at a speed slightly faster than walking pace. 'There's another London under here,' he says, looking lazily at the gently passing walls. Tributary tunnels and doorways, marked with acronyms above their entrances, lead away at right angles. Occasionally we pass giant blast- and flood-proof doors hanging from hinges the height of a man. At each of the main intersections the train comes to a gentle halt, and passengers get on and off; twice an identical train passes us in the opposite direction. We must be heading north because a few minutes later he points out a sign indicating the Security Services building, which lies across the river on Millbank. There are many other tributary tunnels, and I realise the hidden network beneath London is far more extensive than anything I've imagined.

'God, this is nothing,' he says. 'Half of Wiltshire's a bloody great Emmental.' He points out a cryptic sign on the wall. 'There's a C4 facility through there where we can run a whole war from. Can't take you there, I'm afraid. Or there.' He points to another sign bearing the acronym of the subterranean Cabinet Office Briefing Rooms. We're somewhere under Whitehall now. The train draws once more to a halt and Seethrough adjusts his coat. 'Come on,' he says. 'I've got an appointment topside.'

We leave the carriage, turn into a tributary tunnel and come to a lift entrance, where he swipes his card and enters a number on the keypad by the doors. The lift glides up and we emerge in the lobby of an older but grand official building with an alert-status board by the entrance. It reads YELLOW. A grey-haired guard at the security desk looks up from his newspaper, then down again. Beyond him, I can make out traffic in the street, but I'm not sure where we are.

'I won't see you out,' says Seethrough. 'Cross the river and head down Albert Embankment. The walk'll do you good.' I'm still trying to take in the substance of our meeting, and perhaps it shows. He detects my feelings and, in an unexpectedly avuncular gesture, switches his long overcoat into his left arm and puts the other over my shoulders. 'Let it settle,' he says in a near whisper. 'Get your stuff tied up so that you can do some travelling, and I'll have some briefings organised. I'll contact you in a week on the mobile. Look after the things I gave you.'

I walk outside. It's overcast and has begun to drizzle. I'm at the south-east corner of St James's Park, looking along Horseguards Road and a stone's throw from Downing Street. I don't mind the walk. I can't help thinking how confident and grown-up Seethrough seems. I picture him retiring at fifty-five to sell his expertise to big businesses from his Home Counties mansion, dividing his time between Glyndebourne, charity balls and un-official meetings with heads of UK industry.

I reach Gerhardt half an hour later, remove the parking ticket from the windscreen and, resisting a momentary urge to weep, start up and head for home.

5

For days I'm hoping to continue with life as if nothing's really happened, feeling all the while like a man condemned. My meeting with Seethrough has stirred up memories I've preferred to forget, and now they return to me like ghosts, visiting at unexpected moments. From time to time I wonder whether Seethrough's proposal is no more than an elaborate hoax, and imagine him jumping out at me one day in his long coat, waving his chequebook from Coutts and declaring the whole thing a joke.

My sleep grows disturbed, and I have strange dreams in which I'm wandering along the secret corridors of Vauxhall Cross. In one I'm walking under a giant portrait of the Duke of Edinburgh that hangs in the main atrium, but the face is Seethrough's, grinning cynically at me. Recalling our meeting gives me a jittery feeling akin to panic. It's as if the visible events of ordinary life are now no more than a stage set that ordinary people believe is real, but behind which I alone know what's going on. I tell myself I'll get used to keeping things secret, and push thoughts of the future aside. But I know too that a secret can enliven one's life or poison it, and I'm wondering which way things will eventually turn out.

Seethrough has said he'll contact me again in a week's time. But the lack of news makes me anxious, and the evenings fall heavily. My working routine has gone haywire. I drink a bottle and a half of wine every night, and I'm smoking again, a vice I've managed to evade for over a year. For most of the week I avoid contact with people, stop shopping and, worst of all, run out of decent red wine. I take to going for long walks alone and driving Gerhardt cross-country on the muddy tank routes over Salisbury Plain, thinking to test my nerve in the event of getting caught and arrested by the Military Police. I shouldn't, because it would be a bad moment to be arrested. But you do odd things when the craving for adrenalin begins to set in.

Then two things happen. The following Saturday morning, along with a reminder that I haven't paid my television licence, a postcard arrives from Afghanistan. It's strangely timely. On the front is a poorly reproduced colour photograph, probably taken in the 1970s, of a turbanned Kuchi tribesman leading a caravan of camels, silhouetted against a background of barren mountains. It's postmarked Kabul, but I can't make out the date. Nor do I recognise the hand. It reads,

Be doubly warned that the journey here takes at least thirteen hours, in temperatures of up to forty degrees. We all look forward to seeing you here. Please do keep in touch. Your old friend, Mohammed.

I've had the occasional letter and postcard from Afghanistan, but I'm embarrassed not to remember a Mohammed who considers himself to be my old friend. Certainly not one who speaks English well enough to know his prepositions and such an expression as 'be doubly warned'. I think of the English-speaking people I've met in Kabul and on de-mining missions over the years. Most of them are foreigners. I wonder if Mohammed might be a Western-educated Iranian. But my mind's a blank. I've simply forgotten. Odder still, it's winter now and nowhere in Afghanistan does the temperature reach forty degrees. Perhaps the card was posted months before, and has only just been flown out. The Taliban postal service is hardly famous for its swiftness. I walk into the living room, put the postcard on the mantelpiece and stare at it. It bothers me that I can't identify the sender. I decide I'll leave it there until I can.

The second event is a phone call from Seethrough. I've yet to get into the habit of calling him Macavity. When the mobile he's given me begins to ring, I have no idea at first what it is. The tone resembles a two-tone police siren, and makes me think some kind of alarm has gone off in the house, only there aren't any alarms in the house. After a few moments of bafflement, I find the handset with its blinking green light, disconnect it from the charger lead and press the answer button.

'This is Macavity,' says a watery-sounding voice, as the data packets are digitised and encrypted, then reassembled again in the handset. At some point the Firm's special microchip begins sending out its impenetrable white noise. 'Confirm please.'

'This is Plato,' I say, feeling silly.

'All well?'

'Can I change the ring tone on this thing?' I ask.

'No, you can't. Now just listen. I'm going to send you someone.'

'That's nice,' I say. 'Will she jump out of a cake?'

'It's a he. He's going to help you to get up to speed on a few things. If you get along, I'll send him with you. He's ex-Regiment and I want you to do whatever he asks.'

'Whose regiment?'

'The Regiment.'

That's different. The Regiment is what the SAS calls the SAS. I picture a black-booted figure in body armour and respirator, Heckler & Koch MP5 at the ready, swinging through the window of the house as I lie in bed reading the Sunday papers.

'I hope it's not Andy McNab,' I say. 'He's far too intellectual for me.'

'Don't be facetious. It's not Andy McNab; it's the fellow who trained him.'

That shuts me up.

'Roger that. When?'

'That's his business. Just be nice to him. He'll introduce himself as a friend from London. By the way, he's a Mirbat vet, so I advise you not to mess him around.'

'A what?'

'Mirbat. Look it up. I have to go. Good luck.'

There's a *bleep*, and a recording of a severe-sounding woman's voice repeats, 'Please hang up, please hang up.'

I'm impressed. Both by the mobile, which seems to do its job, and by a man who seems to do his. A man so busy he has no time for small talk. I'm about to reattach the handset to its cable when looking at it gives me an idea. Hearing Seethrough's voice has reminded me of the mobile's other functions, and I wonder now if they really work.

There's a way, I realise, to test the infrared. I can switch my video camera to 'nightshot' mode, when the camera uses its own infrared source to film in total darkness, and then see what the mobile looks like. And it's easy to test the ultraviolet function. There are dyes that show up under ultraviolet light in all sorts of things.

As soon as it's dark, I'm thus able to waste several hours. In pitch blackness, viewed through the camera in infrared mode, the little screen on the mobile is, as promised, as bright as a searchlight. It lights up the entire room and is even visible from under a blanket. Handy, as Seethrough has suggested, for landing a helicopter in the garden.

The ultraviolet is equally distracting. It makes my fingernails seem luminous. I wave it over objects that take my fancy, and discover the hidden watermarks and security devices in my chequebook and passport. There are hidden phosphor bands on stamps, and images and tiny flecks of specially dyed paper in banknotes, invisible to the eye in ordinary light. Shining as if white-hot in the darkened room, they seem strangely beautiful. I also look at the postcard with it, and am disappointed to find there's no hidden message.

It's Saturday evening. I'm alone, and feel alone. As night falls, the familiar beast of despair begins to creep up on me. I have no tobacco and am too lazy to go and buy any. Worse, there's virtually nothing to drink but a final bottle of Château Batailley, which I've promised myself I'll save for a special occasion. This calls for a difficult decision. It's either the Batailley or the sole other source of alcohol in the house: roughly half a bottle of Armenian cognac, which a so-called friend has palmed off on me as a gift. It's so bad I haven't touched it for six months, having discovered what damage it can do to the untrained nervous system. I retrieve it from the back of a kitchen cupboard, mix a slug with some mineral water and discover to my surprise that it's quite drinkable. I also find a cigar, which I've similarly promised myself to save for a special occasion. I light the cigar, dig out my topographic maps of Afghanistan, and return to the cognac.

At ten o'clock I lurch into the grey morning with a sharp pain in my head where the cognac has etched Category 2 damage in the region of my cerebellum. The house reeks of cigar smoke, so I throw open the windows and put the coffee percolator to work in the kitchen. Taking the first sip, I hear myself whisper, 'I must not do this again,' and wonder how often I've uttered the same words. My Afghan maps are scattered on the floor by the sofa where I've fallen asleep. As I'm gathering them up there's a triple knock at the door. I flee upstairs, throw on some clothes and return to the door.

The daylight is painfully bright. In front of me stands a clean-shaven middle-aged man with a sheaf of paperwork in his hand, and for a terrible moment I think of all the letters from the Television Licensing Authority which I've thrown away unopened.

'Good morning, sir. I hope I'm not disturbing you.'

I don't like the 'sir' part. It makes him sound like a policeman.

But he doesn't look like one. He's wearing a black suit like an undertaker's, for which he's grown slightly too big, and a tie with green and red diagonals that hurts to look at.

'Of course not,' I reply with an unconvincing smile.

'I wonder if I can ask whether you read the Bible?' he asks. Resting in the crook of his arm like Moses in a basket is a sheaf of denominational literature.

'I do, as a matter of fact.'

A smile of pleasant surprise spreads across his face, but it's not a morning to give the enemy too much room for manoeuvre, because I don't do religion on a hangover.

'I also read the Qur'an. I have a soft spot for Marcus Aurelius too, and he was a pagan.'

The smile fades. He's not really expecting this and a slight stutter comes into his voice. 'But ... but do you believe your actions in this life make a difference in the world to come?'

'If we're going to be judged on something in an afterlife, I think it'll probably be our *inactions*. It's not difficult to live a pious life, if you think about it, imagining you'll be saved if you stick to a few rules. But think of all the good things you could have done but didn't because you were too lazy or complacent. I think we'll be judged on our potential.'

He's frowning now.

'I forget where I first heard the idea, but it does stay with you. I think it's somewhere in the Qur'an.'

I pluck a copy of the *Watchtower* from his grasp and thank him warmly, saying I hope I'll see him again soon. The speed at which he walks away up the drive suggests I won't.

With a feeling of guilty victory I return to my coffee. Then I close the windows in the sitting room because the light is hurting my eyes, and sit down at the table, taking the postcard from the mantelpiece where I left it. I read it again several times. There's nothing out of the ordinary about the text. I wonder if the picture, depicting a nomad leading a line of camels, is intended to convey a meaning. It's the identity of 'Mohammed' that bothers me. I wonder if it might be worth looking through my diaries from the period I was last in Kabul, but if the card was sent months earlier, whoever Mohammed is will have given up hearing from me.

I take the card to the kitchen and boil the kettle, hold the card in the steam and gently work a corner of the stamp with the tip of a knife. I'm not sure what to expect – anything strange or out of the ordinary.

As the stamp begins to curl back in the steam, what I see is even stranger. Under the stamp, in the same ink as the writing on the card, is a tiny drawing of a dinosaur with a smiling face.

It's a stegosaurus.

Cryptography is the science of hiding the true meaning of a message by disguising it; encrypting it by some means known to the recipient but not to others. As long as the sender and the recipient keep their means of encryption secret, the effort needed by the codebreaker is determined by the difficulty of the code. Some codes, like alphabetical substitutions, are easy to crack because the frequencies at which letters appear in words are well known. Others, like one-time pads based on random numbers, can only be cracked by computers, if at all. The most complex codes that use block ciphers and multiple algorithms need both computers and time, and modern computing power means that few codes are truly impossible to crack, given enough of the latter. But the science of hiding a message by disguising it as something which on the surface appears innocent is called steganography.

Strictly speaking, a message written in invisible ink across an ordinary letter is an example of steganography: the visible or cover message is innocuous. It's an ancient idea. Herodotus describes a king who tattooed a secret message on the shaven head of his slave, whose hair was allowed to grow before he travelled through enemy territory to deliver it. More recent applications allow secret text to be hidden in the data of digitised photographs sent over the Internet. The advantage of a steganographic message is that, unlike a coded message, the secret part doesn't attract attention to itself. It resembles something ordinary, and hides itself thereby.

My ex-wife, come to think of it, has a steganographic personality: an innocent-looking face concealing a cruel agenda.

I decide it has to be the numbers: thirteen and forty. 'Degrees' in the cover message also seems to be an overt clue. I find an atlas and look up the latitude and longitude. Problem. Thirteen degrees north and forty degrees east puts me in the mountains of northern Ethiopia. Forty degrees west is equally challenging – somewhere in the mid-Atlantic trench. Southern readings for the latitude land me in thick rainforest in Mozambique and Brazil. The numbers are not an obvious location.

They're too short to be a phone number or a postcode. The only other reference I can imagine they might give is a book code, indicating a page and line number in a book known to both sender and recipient. But I haven't agreed on a book with anyone called Mohammed.

Then it hits me like a delayed reaction, as I hear the echo of my very own words: I also read the Qur'an. The 'old friend', Mohammed, is the clue. It's so obvious I can't believe it's taken me so long to realise. Now I regret my uncivil behaviour towards my visitor.

For centuries the *mas-haf* code, virtually unknown in the West, has been used in the Islamic world to encrypt messages using the numbers of the Qur'an's sacred verses. Being identical in every version of the text, irrespective of country or date of publication, the verses retain the same numbers and provide thereby an unchanging key.

I go to my bookshelf, pull out an English translation and race to the thirteenth chapter, called Thunder. The fortieth verse, or *sura*, is a short one: 'Whether We let you glimpse in some measure the scourge with which We threaten them, or cause you to die

77

before we smite them, your mission is only to give warning: it is for Us to do the reckoning.'

There's no need to look for any more clues. The reference to a warning is confirmation enough of the message. The question now is how to interpret it and, if necessary, respond. It's strange news to get and I'm annoyed with myself for being hungover and slow. I regret my mind isn't feeling sharper and that the whole significance of the message isn't coming to me more quickly. The only thing I know for sure about the message is that it's been sent by someone who knows enough of my background to be confident that I'll figure out how to decipher it, and then how to interpret it. Whoever sent it also knows how to find me.

There's a another sudden knock at the door, which has an effect similar to a powerful electric shock. I yank open the door with a scowl. There's a different man standing on the doorstep, this time wearing a fake Barbour, jeans and trainers.

'I've told your friend I'm a Muslim,' I say gruffly.

The man's eyebrows go up and down and he let outs a gravelly chuckle.

'Well, in that case, *As-salaamu aleikum.*' His voice is low, even and has a rasping quality as if something rough is being continually ground down in his throat. I frown at him. I've never met an Arabic-speaking Jehovah's Witness and wonder if they've sent for a specialist to check my theology. He's going to get a run for his money.

'*Wa aleikum as-salaam.*' I return the greeting out of reflex and look at him more closely. His frame is lighter than the other man's, and the lines on his cheeks suggest leanness. He has short sandy-coloured hair, a neat moustache like an ex-soldier's and looks a youthful fifty. His eyes have a watchful and mischievious sparkle. But he has no documents or bag. Before I can think of anything else to say, he speaks again.

'*Ana rafiq min landan.*' I am a friend from London. He speaks

Ministry of Defence Arabic. 'I parked down the road,' he adds, gesturing with a thumb over his shoulder. Then it sinks in.

It's Seethrough's man from the Regiment. The SAS has arrived.

'Oh, Christ. Sorry. Come in.'

He smiles and his eyes dart watchfully over the hallway as he steps inside. 'It's H—— by the way. Friends call me H.' The handshake is firm. 'Late night?' he asks with a knowing look.

'Something like that.'

'We'd better have some coffee.'

'I've just made some.'

'Good man.'

He sniffs the air as we go into the kitchen, puts his coat neatly over the back of a chair and sits at the table. The room's a mess. I'm embarrassed and surreptitiously cover the ashtray in the sink with a plate as I rinse a pair of cups. I ask where he's driven from this morning.

'Hereford.' That figures. Hereford is home to the Regimental HQ of 22 SAS.

I'm about to ask whether he lives there, but he answers first.

'Settled down after I left the Regiment ten years ago, give or take.'

'Marry a local girl?'

'The whole nine yards. Wife, kids, cats, dogs.'

'What have you been doing since?'

'The security and protection circuit – rigs and pipelines, mostly. Some BGing once in a while. Sorry – bodyguarding. And the occasional special request.'

'Isn't it all a bit dull after the SAS?'

'Better than sitting around in a damp hole all day.'

This is modest, coming from a member of the most elite special forces regiment in the world.

'There's a company that helps the blokes who want to stay active – the ones who don't become postmen, mostly.'

'Remind me not to tangle with the postman.' I sit down opposite him and pour the coffee. His eyes fall on the dark red and blue bands of my watchstrap.

'Regimental flash?'

'Scots Guards.'

'Alright for some.' He grins. 'When did you pack it in?

'After the Gulf. Granby, wasn't it? Stupid name for a war,' I say. I know that military code names are chosen by computer and run alphabetically, but still.

'Stupid war, if you think about it.' He blows thoughtfully on his coffee. I like his irreverence.

'Regiment did well out of it,' I say.

'The usual balls-up,' he says, dismissing this. 'Typical Regiment story. A lot of guys spread out all over the world in different theatres, and then up comes a deployment like the Gulf.' His fingers trace a phantom squadron gathering across the tabletop. 'All of a sudden every one of them wants a piece of the action, and a lot of jostling goes on. You get guys who've been training for something else doing the wrong job, and the right guys getting bumped down the line.'

'What did London tell you?' I ask.

'I only get a phone call from the liaison officer with the where and when. Sounds like they're going to leave the details to us. We've got a month. Should be plenty of time.'

This is a very low-key approach, and unlike anything I've encountered in the military. I also find it hard to reconcile the softly spoken almost boyish manner of the man in front of me with the more sensational tales told popularly about the Regiment.

'I don't suppose you were on the balcony at Prince's Gate, were you?' I'm joking, but every soldier knows how many thousands of men have claimed they were part of the spectacular hostage rescue at the Iranian embassy in London twenty years earlier.

'No, not on the balcony,' he says in a thoughtful tone. 'Anyway, the blokes on the balcony were only there for the TV cameras.'

Good answer. I ask how long he's been in the Regiment.

'I'm a twenty-fourer.' He chuckles. 'Boy soldier.' He's served in every major theatre where the SAS has deployed. Aden, Borneo, Oman, Northern Ireland, the Falklands, Iraq, Bosnia and, between training some other military units in far-off places and what he calls 'extra-curricular stuff', a dozen other countries.

'I'm surprised you haven't thought of a literary career,' I say. 'Wasn't it your CO who started the trend?'

He shrugs cynically. 'DLB was a good soldier. Anyway, it's his memoirs they'll be reading in ten years, not the other bloke's.'

He's loyal too, I'm thinking to myself, to his former Regimental commanding officer, Peter de la Billiere. By the sound of it he doesn't care much for the celebrity authors the Regiment has also produced over the past few years. Then I remember what Seethrough told me the day before.

'What's a Mirbat vet?' I ask.

'I am, for starters,' he says.

'Then what's a Mirbat?'

'Mirbat? That's the name of the town. On the Omani coast. Operation Storm.' His eyes light up. 'The Regiment's golden hour. Have you got an atlas?'

A vet, it now dawns on me, is obviously a veteran, but I've been thinking a Mirbat is some kind of animal, not the site of a battle. Feeling very ignorant, I fetch the atlas from the sitting room, where I've left it. We push our cups aside and a few moments later our fingers are trailing southwards across the Arabian peninsula. I've forgotten how strategically placed Oman is, with its north-eastern tip pointing into Iran across the narrowest stretch of the Persian Gulf. H's finger comes to rest on the coastline not far east of the border with Yemen.

'We were down south, here, in Salalah. And there,' he says, pointing to a long mountainous shadow running east to west, 'was where the Adoo were, up on the Jebel.'

'What were you doing there?'

'We weren't. Officially. Too secret at the time. No one back home knew we were out there. But look.' He points to the map again. 'Everything coming in and out of the Gulf has to run through the Straits of Hormuz. Imagine if we'd lost it.' He smiles and then does a comic caricature of an officer. 'We couldn't very well let them have our oil, could we?' Then as if he regrets making light of the subject, adds, 'That wasn't the point at the time. We were British. We knew we'd win.'

He flattens out the sheet gently with his hand, and we lean over it to peer at the names. From the coastal plain around Salalah, several dark lines cut into the looming escarpment that H calls the Jebel, which means mountain in Arabic. The lines split and waver like veins as they travel north. They're the giant wadis that lead into the hinterland of the enemy, he explains, verdant in the monsoon season and blisteringly barren in the summer.

'That's Wadi Arzat,' he says. He smiles. 'God, I remember hiking all the way up there with a jimpy.' Jimpy is army slang for GPMG, the unpleasantly heavy general purpose machine gun. He takes a key ring from his pocket and uses the tip of a key to follow the coastline to the east, until it comes to rest on a town at the foot of the great Jebel.

'There,' he says, 'that's Mirbat. That's where I got my first souvenir.'

There isn't much written about Mirbat or Operation Storm, so I'm pleased to be hearing about it from someone who was actually there, and I fill in the gaps later. Mirbat itself was the most dramatic engagement in a six-year-long campaign spanning the final days of British control in the Gulf. In 1970 the British protectorate of Aden had fallen to a Marxist-oriented government. On its eastern border lay Oman, governed by an ageing and autocratic sultan with the help of a small army run by British officers. When intelligence reports began to suggest that communist-trained guerrillas from Yemen, as well as others from revolutionary Iraq, were infiltrating the country, there was a reappraisal of British interests in the region. The prospect of allowing the country to fall into communist hands was unthinkable.

A coup, discreetly assisted by the British, brought the sultan's son Qabus to power. But in the meantime the communist-trained rebels, the Adoo, had seized the strategic heights of the Jebel, and the new sultan's army was losing the war for control. Well trained and supplied by their communist sponsors, the Adoo were brave and tenacious.

Enter the SAS. Unofficially, under the quiet euphemism of British Army Training Teams – BATTs. And operationally, with the threefold task of wooing the local population away from the communist-trained guerrillas and persuading them of the benefits of joining the government's side, raising local irregular units called *firqats* to fight the Adoo, and taking the war ever deeper into the Jebel.

Within a couple of years a series of daring raids had pushed the Adoo from much of the Jebel, where the SAS built up lines of control and permanent bases. But the Adoo were planning a decisive comeback, and had decided on an all-out assault supported by mortars and artillery on the small coastal town of Mirbat. Their plan was to capture the stone fort and its local defenders, kill the mayor of the town and score a huge propaganda victory for the rebel cause.

They came on 12 July 1972, at dawn.

At least 250 Adoo fighters walked down unopposed from the Jebel, infiltrating the outskirts of the town and fanning out in the gullies and beyond the perimeter wire protecting the fort. The odds in their favour could not have been much better. In the fort were only a dozen local tribesmen armed with bolt-action rifles. Several hundred yards away, in the local BATT house, were a handful of SAS men looking forward to their return to Hereford at the end of their tour in a few days' time.

When the first Adoo mortars began to fall, showering the sleeping soldiers with dust from the mud walls of their HQ, no one even thought to radio the support base at Salalah. But as the volume of fire increased, it became obvious that the Adoo had launched a major assault. For a few moments the SAS men stared in disbelief from the parapet of the BATT house at the hundreds of advancing men, then opened up with their own mortar and heavy machine gun. The mist was soon sizzling on their gun barrels, and the incoming fire growing with every minute.

One of the SAS troopers, a Fijian called Labalaba, ran to the gun pit at the base of the fort and began firing a 25-pounder into the Adoo lines as their shells exploded around his position. But things were quickly getting worse. The Adoo were soon too close for the maximum elevation of the SAS mortar in the BATT house, so a desperate pair of troopers lifted it from its mounting, and while one man held it to his chest, the other fed the ammunition into the tube. Then came news over the radio that Labalaba had been wounded. Twenty-three-year-old troop commander Mike Kealey, still wearing his flip-flops, radioed for a helicopter to evacuate him while another Fijian, called Tak by his friends, ran to his countryman's aid through clouds of dust thrown up by exploding mortar shells and automatic weapons. The helicopter attempted to land nearby, but was forced to withdraw.

For an hour the Adoo poured fire into the fort, by now wreathed in smoke and dust and impossible even to see from the BATT house except when lit up momentarily by the bursts of exploding shells. But the rate of fire of the heavy gun manned by Labalaba was faltering and, unable to reach the gun pit on the radio, Kealey decided to run for it with his medical orderly, Tobin.

They sprinted in bursts, firing in turn and hearing the deadly whisper of enemy bullets all around them. Throwing themselves into the gun pit a few minutes later, they scrambled across piles of shell casings to find Tak propped up in a pool of blood, wounded in the back and head but still firing his weapon. Labalaba, with a field dressing tied around his chin, was struggling to load shells into the 25-pounder. A badly wounded Omani gunner was sprawled among the ripped sandbags and ammunition boxes. Despite sustained fire from the BATT house, the Adoo then breached the perimeter wire, and were close enough to begin throwing grenades into the gun pit. Labalaba, after slamming a final shell into the breech of the gun, fell to an Adoo bullet. Taking his place, Tobin was shot through the jaw. He died later.

Tak and Kealey, now firing point blank into the enemy, were on the point of being overrun when two Strikemaster jets from Salalah, braving the low cloud and storms of bullets from the Adoo guns, raked the enemy positions with machine-gun fire. On a second run a perfectly placed 500-pound bomb decimated the Adoo lines. The rescue helicopter now flew in and the dead and wounded and the body of Labalaba were gathered up. Tak refused all help and walked to the helicopter unaided.

The war dragged on for several more years until the guerrillas were finally pushed back to the border of Yemen, but they were never able to mount such a large-scale operation again. Back in England nothing was heard of this astonishing victory against the odds.

I ask H what his souvenir was. His hands move to the cuff of his shirt, and for a moment it looks as though he's going to show me an Omani bracelet or a tattoo. But he pulls up the sleeve to his elbow and turns his forearm towards me. There's a pale oval scar the size of an olive, matched by a slightly larger one on the other side. The bullet, he explains, passed between the bones of his forearm and lodged in the butt of his rifle, but was prevented from entering his chest by the metal base plate.

'Bet that hurt,' I say.

'Didn't feel a thing till afterwards. Bit messy though.'

'Where were you?'

'In the BATT house. Drove up from Taqa two days before, but the jeep behind me hit a mine so we had to overnight in Mirbat. I was supposed to fly out the next day with the injured driver, but the cloud was too low. Hell of a day to get stuck.' He rolls down his sleeve and sighs. 'Regiment's gone downhill since then.'

It's midday. H throws a restless look around the kitchen and asks if there's a pub nearby. 'We can have a walk and a blather,' he suggests, 'and make bit of a plan.' I need the walk and agree. We take our coats, cut across the fields from the house, and walk the mile and a half to the Crown, soaking ourselves up to the knees in the wet grass. At the pub we sit by a smoky fireplace and talk over our beers, learning details of each other's lives with a friendly complicity to which I'm unaccustomed but which I'm enjoying more than I expect.

H asks about Afghanistan. A few of his Regiment friends paid visits to the country in the 1980s, he says, training Afghan mujaheddin to use the Stinger missile. They even brought a few Afghans to Scotland to train them in guerrilla tactics and advanced communications. From a drab building behind Victoria station one or two others helped to dream up exotic operations to hinder the Soviets. But he doesn't know much else about the place, he confesses.

I try to convey the fondness, despite all the privations and difficulties of conflict, that I feel for the place and its people. I've come to respect the Afghans for their bravery and hardiness, and I'm relieved when H says he felt the same mixture of sympathy and respect for the tribesmen he trained and fought alongside in Oman. From my wallet I pull a photograph taken on my very first trip to Afghanistan, and H points to the bearded Afghan posing next to me with an AK-47 assault rifle held proudly across his chest.

'Looks like a fellow in my troop,' he says, grinning.

He asks about politics too. I say the present conflict there can be traced back to the Soviet occupation of the country throughout the 1980s. The Soviets had hoped to establish a loyal communist regime in Afghanistan, calculating that the poorest people in all Asia would be quickly subdued. Things went badly from the start. There was widespread armed resistance to the Soviet presence, and their total failure to win popular support from the rural population was equalled by their poor strategy. Pinned down in their bases and controlling only the cities and main roads, Soviet soldiers were rarely able to move freely about the country, relying on airpower and heavily armoured operations to bludgeon their enemies into submission. There was no attempt to win the hearts and minds of a deeply traditional and religious people, who had been fighting – and beating – invaders since the beginning of time.

'Mindset,' says H quietly, nodding. 'You can't win a war without understanding the mindset.'

For ten years the Soviets fought an increasingly brutal and unsuccessful conflict, killing as many as a million Afghans in the process. They withdrew in 1989, leaving an ailing communist government in a shattered nation, which further disintegrated as rival mujaheddin factions fought each other for control. American support for the Afghans evaporated in the wake of the Soviet exodus, and in the lawless provinces of the south the Taliban were born a few years later, supported increasingly by extremists from abroad. They took Kabul in 1996 and soon imposed their cruelly medieval outlook on almost the entire country. Only a shrinking province in the north controlled by Massoud continued to resist their rule.

The counter-insurgency campaign in Oman, though on a much smaller scale, made an instructive contrast. The Regiment had made it a priority to understand the local culture, realising from the outset that without local support they could never hope to defeat the enemy. The strategic emphasis was on winning allies rather than killing the enemy, and on avoiding the death of civilians at any cost. When Adoo defectors surrendered to the government side they were neither imprisoned nor even interrogated, but gently persuaded to see the logic of fighting for a progressive sultan rather than the brutal hierarchy of their communist sponsors.

'When we found a village we wanted to keep the Adoo out of,' says H, 'we'd build a well and a clinic, and a school if they needed it. And we'd never have any trouble from it again. Simple, but it worked.'

'Imagine we'd done the same thing in Afghanistan in the 90s,' I say. 'The Taliban would never have got the platform they have now.'

'Probably some accountant in the Foreign Office said it was too expensive,' he replies.

H asks how soon I can come to Hereford. As soon as he wants, I say. He suggests we meet in two days' time, and I stay with him until the end of the week. He gives me his phone number and directions to his home, and advises me to memorise them rather than write them down. I'll need boots, he says, outdoor gear, and a Bergen. He doesn't use the word rucksack.

'We'll go for some nice tabs, and work on some security SOPs,' he says. It's strange to hear army-speak again. A tab is a tactical advance to battle. Basically a long walk. SOP means standard operating procedure.

'The SOPs are common sense mostly, but we'll need to get them in our system,' says H. 'What sort of weapons do they use out there?'

'Anyone who's anyone has an AK-47,' I say, half surprised he doesn't already know. 'Russian, Egyptian and Chinese versions mostly. There's a few AK-74s around, but you don't see many.' The AK-74 is the smaller-calibre short-barrelled version of the AK-47, a prestige weapon carried by a number of distinguished commanders. There is no point in mentioning the endless variety of heavier weapons in use in the country.

'Surprise, surprise. What about shorts?'

'Makarov, I suppose.' This is the Soviet-designed 9-millimetre pistol most often seen in Afghanistan. I'd nearly bought one for myself when I'd been there, but was dissuaded by my Afghan friend and driver, who said a pistol was ineffective. He carried a grenade with an extra-short fuse in his pocket instead.

'Alright. We'll brush up on weapons,' says H, 'and you can teach me about mines. I'll see what other kit I can get out of the Kremlin. Are you fit?'

'Been fitter.'

'Try five K a day in under half an hour and we'll take it from there.' That sounds ominous. I can't remember the last time I ran five kilometres, but all of a sudden I'm looking forward to the discipline.

'Right,' says H, glancing at his watch. 'Got to get back to the memsahib.'

We walk back to the house. It starts to rain. H won't come in again, he says. He puts up his collar, wishes me luck and walks to the end of the driveway and out towards his car. I head back inside and change into my running gear.

Then I stretch out on the sofa and fall asleep.

6

I no longer recall the exact sequence of the training that begins that week. It's dark and drizzling when I leave for Hereford on the Tuesday morning. The sky begins to lighten only as I turn west on the M50, and soon the Malverns loom up on my right. An hour later, on the outskirts of a small village to the north-west of Hereford, I turn off a narrow lane and pull up facing a wooden front gate. Across a tended gravel driveway stands a small black and white timbered house typical of the county. An ageing dark blue Range Rover is parked in front of a detached garage.

A barking terrier runs up, and H appears moments later with an eager wave, opens the gate and invites me inside for coffee, defying once again my naive impression of the SAS soldier as a hard-hearted killer. In the front hallway of his home is a large framed photograph of H, looking youthful and wearing the unmistakable sand-coloured beret with the flaming-dagger badge. I imagine it lit up in the beam of a burglar's torch, the muttered curses and the swift retreat.

'Good man,' says H, noticing that I'm already wearing my boots. 'How's the running coming along?'

'Fine,' I lie. I've started a five-K routine, but not without a few pauses on the way. Five kilometres seems like a long distance until you're used to it. Boredom and the body's resistance make it seem like about a hundred. My legs aren't the problem. The protest comes from my lungs. No matter how fit I've been in the past, I've always hated long-distance running. 'I'm a bit slow,' I concede, feeling uncomfortable with the deceit, 'but fine.'

'Well, alright. You work on it. Come and have a look at the route, then we'll walk and talk.' He's put a large-scale Ordnance Survey map of the Brecon Beacons, laminated in soft plastic film, on the kitchen sideboard. 'We'll start here,' he says, pointing to a small building at the edge of a patch of forest just off the A470 in the heart of the Beacons, 'at the Storey Arms.' To the north of the road the light-brown contour lines thicken like a fingerprint.

I know what that means: up Pen-y-Fan in the rain.

'We'll leave the car in the car park and RV there if we get separated on the south side.' He traces the route with the tip of a pencil. The plan is to head for the summit, walk down Cwm Llwch on the far side, follow a small road for a couple of miles around the base of the slope, then ascend again via a point called the Obelisk before heading down to the car. He points out an alternative rendezvous point for the north leg of the journey. RVs, backup RVs and emergency RVs are an obsession with the SAS, I'm learning.

Half an hour later we're at our starting point. The weather's not ideal. I last climbed Pen-y-Fan in shorts and a T-shirt several years ago, on a brilliant summer's day. Now it's cold and raining. Not heavily, but gusting in sheets, and there's a distinct lack of ramblers. The slope above us disappears into a barricade of cloud. H offers to carry the Bergen, which holds our water, dry clothes and a heavy-duty orange plastic sheet for use as shelter in an emergency. I'm too proud to allow him to take it. We put on our waterproofs and H sees me grimace at the cold.

'Better than being too hot,' he says.

We trudge up and establish our pace. At least we're walking. For selection to the SAS, we'd be running, says H when I ask him about his time in the Regiment. Despite being known for the gruelling tabs in the Beacons that every would-be trooper had to undergo, the Regiment's selection process was designed to uncover mental resilience as much as physical grit. 'You'd see a lot of muscle-bound guys packing it in,' says H, recalling time spent as directing staff on selection. 'Not because they weren't fit enough, but because they got fed up the quickest. Too used to being tough, I suppose. It was the squinty-eyed little fellows who'd get through.'

Those who survived the gruelling Fan dance – up Pen-y-Fan and back three times – the night-time navigation to control points at memorised grid references, the heavily laden cross-country marches and mock interrogations, would end up on a month's continuation training in the jungle. Brunei was the chosen location. H calls it 'good jungle'. I don't know what bad jungle is. He says it's the jungle that really sorts people out, and where the real selection takes place.

'Everything's wet the whole time and there's beasties all over the place. A lot of guys who did well on selection couldn't handle the jungle,' he says. I ask him how he'd fared on his own jungle training.

'Me? Loved it,' he says, beaming as the rain cascades over his eyebrows. 'Happy as a pig in shit.'

We enter the cloud and feel its coldness. A purplish scar of track leads upwards. Beyond a dozen yards, every feature of the landscape is absorbed into the whiteness. H walks behind me and gives directions where the route looks uncertain. Higher up, a slippery outcrop of stone resembling a ruined wall marks the steepest portion of the ascent. The summit of Pen-y-Fan lies several hundred yards to the north-east. We reach it at the end of a narrow ridge where the flanks descend with spectacular steepness into deep glacial valleys on either side. But we can see nothing of the views.

It's too cold to stop for more than a few moments. Using the corner of his compass, H points out our position on the map as the raindrops roll across its laminated surface, and we check our bearing for the long descent into Cwm Llwch. Beyond the valley at its base, we reach Cwm Gwdi, the remnants of the

Parachute Regiment battle camp and the deserted road beyond. It loops west towards the shorter steeper ridge leading back up to the Obelisk.

Now I understand why H has chosen the route. It embraces a series of rewards and punishments – upward and downward gradients of varying degrees, from the painfully acute to the luxuriously gentle. You reap the pleasure of the gentle slopes to fight the steep ones. On a long tab there are strong arguments for stopping and others for going forward, and both spin out silently in your head. Bad weather magnifies the pleasures and the pains. The longer the route, the less seriously you take the clamour of these voices, which settle down into a kind of background grumble, while you drag your mind repeatedly back to something more concrete: the rhythm of your pace or breath.

On the final portion of the return climb, just before we re-emerge on the ridge by the Obelisk, I can feel my thigh muscles wobble in protest. The big blisters on my heels are now at the final stage of fattening up before bursting. But we've kept up a decent pace. Six hours later we're back at the car. I'm freezing and tired. H asks how I'm feeling.

'Never better.'

'Good man.'

I throw the soaking Bergen into the back of the car, and H retrieves a Thermos of deliciously hot coffee. We drive back to his house, change into dry clothes, and H fries up a late lunch. I light a fire at his request from a neat pile of logs stacked by the fireplace. We eat as we warm our feet by the flames. As dusk falls, H pours two generous whiskies, and we talk over the scope of the operation ahead of us, wondering when we'll get the go-ahead from London.

'Ironic, isn't it?' says H. 'We get sent to Afghanistan to train them how to use our kit, and then get sent back ten years later to tell them they can't have it any more.'

'Blowback,' I say. 'That's what the CIA call it.'

'Blow job, more like. Anyway. Best not to talk about any of this from now on.' Then he leaves the room and returns a minute later with a boyish look of mischief on his face.

'When was the last time you saw one of these?'

His right arm swings up, and with it the barrel of an AK-47 assault rifle. This is an unaccustomed sight in rural England, and I splutter a reply through a mouthful of whisky.

'It's been a while.'

'Know how to use it?'

'Never really had to.'

'Well, if you do ever have to, you might as well know how. Let's sit on the floor.'

He takes two cloth bundles from the map pockets of his trousers and puts them on a small table. Then he sinks nimbly to the floor on his knees and rests the weapon like an offering across the open palms of his hands.

'AK-47. Gas-operated assault rifle with selective fire, 7.62 calibre.' He waves a hand up and down its length. The blueing on the metal glitters darkly in the light thrown from the fire. 'Most successful assault rifle in the world. Any Soviet weapon with a K in its name means a variant of the Kalashnikov. There's an AKM and an AKS, both modified versions of the AK-47, a PK light machine gun, and the smaller-calibre AK-74. The Soviets designed the rifle and its ammo so that, in theory, their invading army could use captured Western weapons, but not the other way round. Pretty simple weapon, really, and that's its virtue. It's an assault weapon, so you wouldn't want to use it much over 300 metres, though it'll send a round much further. If anyone's firing at you with an AK from further than 300 metres, you shouldn't be too bothered.' A wry smile suggests he doesn't mean this too literally.

He bounces it gently in his hands as if to weigh it. Perhaps he's reminiscing. Then he squeezes the serrated edges of the rear sight and slides the range selector back and forth on its rail.

'The sights are adjustable from 100 to 800 metres. Anything up to 300, just use the battle sights. Remember it fires high and right.' He taps the muzzle. 'Later models have a different-shaped muzzle to compensate. Looks like the tip of a Bowie knife.' I've seen these in Afghanistan. 'Some have a bayonet on a hinge under the barrel. You can stick this in the ground to stabilise the weapon if you want.'

His finger moves to the selector lever.

'All the way up – safety on.' He pulls on the silvery lug of the operating handle to show that the weapon can't be cocked. 'It inhibits the mechanism.' Then there's a loud metallic click as he slides the lever down. 'One click down for automatic fire. When you're in a hurry and you need it. Good for scaring crows.'

He wrinkles his nose as if automatic fire is only for films and books.

'Two clicks for single shot. The only problem with the safety on an AK is it's bloody noisy, so don't do it unless you mean business. There's no bolt-stop device, so the bolt moves back into the chamber after the last round's been fired. You have to re-cock when you change mags.'

Then he tucks the wooden butt under his armpit as if to fire. 'If someone has the weapon on you, try to get sight of the selector. There may be dust or dirt around it. A lot of blokes carry AKs for the prestige and they're not really ready to use them. Check the position of the lever. If it's all the way up, it might give you a bit more time. Right, let's have a look inside.'

He takes the smaller bundle from the table and unfolds a triangular piece of cloth over the carpet. Then he removes the magazine, cocks the weapon to clear the breech, and pulls the trigger.

'If you have a piece of cloth with you, you can spread the pieces over it in order, then gather them up in reverse. A *shemagh* is perfect.'

'The Afghans use something called a *pattu*,' I say, and describe a few of the near-universal applications of the Afghan woollen shawl, without which life in Afghanistan would be unmanageable.

'We'll pretend it's a *pattu* then. This is the top cover.' He taps the uppermost metal surface of the weapon, then pushes in the serrated catch at its rear and slides it off, exposing the innards. A long and snake-like recoil spring emerges. Then comes the bolt, sliding back into the receiver track with a clattering sound like a miniature train crossing a junction. At its far end is a long silver rod. 'That's the piston. It's attached to the bolt carrier.' He points out the curved surface, called the camway, on which the bolt rotates, and then the firing pin and the extractor attached to the bolt itself. Then he detaches the forward section of the wooden handguard to reveal the gas chamber. There's also an easily removable rod beneath the barrel for clearing jammed rounds. But that's it. Mr Kalashnikov's brainchild, laid bare.

'I'm amazed how simple it really is,' I say.

'That's the secret of its success. Makes it less accurate than other rifles, but the clearances give it a lot of tolerance. When it really starts to fill up with rubbish, the mechanism won't return fast enough and you get a second round coming up and jamming. That's why you keep your weapon clean. Best way is to dump the whole thing in a pan of avgas.'

'Aviation fuel?'

He nods. 'But petrol will do. It cleans the dirt out and leaves the surfaces dry. Issue cleaning fluid usually comes in a fiddly little bottle, but a switched-on soldier will usually have something like this.' He reaches over to the bundle, pulls out a green plastic insecticide bottle, and mimics spraying the rifle's insides. Then he takes the head of an inch-wide paintbrush and waves it across the metal. A pull-through, stored in the butt, is used to clean the barrel. He drops it into the breech and gives a tug on the oiled strip of cloth from the other end, then closes an eye and peers into the muzzle. 'If you put your thumb in the breech, it'll catch enough light for you to see what's going on. Want to have a go?'

He reassembles the parts, then reminds me of the golden rule. 'Before you hand a weapon to anyone, clear it.' He takes off the magazine and pulls back the bolt to make sure the chamber is clear.

I strip the weapon in the manner he's shown, lining up the different parts, then fit them back in reverse order.

'Right,' says H, 'now have another go.'

I repeat the process.

'Again,' he says.

And again, as my hands grow in confidence.

'Now do it in the dark,' he says, and instructs me to close my eyes. After several repeats, he says we've come far enough for the moment, and I put the weapon aside, resting it against the table.

'That's another thing,' says H, reaching out for it. 'Don't ever prop the weapon anywhere where it can fall over. Always lie it down within reach of you, breech side up, so you don't get dirt in it.'

Suddenly I remember a question I've been wanting to ask him.

'You know those documentaries where you see American servicemen tapping the magazines of their weapons on their helmets before locking them onto their M16s? Why do they always do that?'

'I don't know,' he says thoughtfully. 'I've never worn a helmet.'

We move on. He unwraps the remaining bundle on the table to reveal a 9-millimetre Makarov pistol with five-pointed Soviet star on the grip panels. He releases the magazine, which slips into his palm.

'You've seen one of these. It's like the AK. A bit primitive, but effective and reliable. They say it's based on the Walther PPK. Double action, so you can cock it either with the hammer or by pulling back the slide. The trigger pull's a bit heavy in double-action mode. Good stopping power though.'

We go over the details of the mechanism, how to check the chamber and make safe. The pistol can be stripped by pulling down on the trigger guard, allowing the slide to be eased off from the rear. The barrel is fixed. I practise loading and unloading, thinking all the while about the expression 'stopping power'. It's a term as removed from the reality it describes as collateral damage or intelligence interrogation – death and torture respectively. Herein, I reflect, lies the terrible contradiction between two of the most momentous experiences in the life of a man: the near-irresistible thrill of conflict and the horror it produces.

Our session has a final stage. H leaves the room again and returns with what looks like a book and yet another weapon. On the dark blue cover of the book DEFENSE INTELLIGENCE AGENCY is printed in silver letters. Several yellow Post-its protrude from between the pages. The weapon in his hand is an FN HP, better known as the Browning High Power. It was originally manufactured in Belgium by the famous Fabrique Nationale, but has been copied all over the world. I'd learned how to use it in the army, where it was also known as the L9A1. I'd also killed a man with the same weapon.

'Personal favourite,' says H, as he clears it, then clicks the magazine gently back into place. The Browning has been the army's sidearm of choice for decades, and compared to the latest automatics using plastic and ceramic parts, it's starting to look old-fashioned. The Swiss-made SIG is the most recent sidearm of choice for the Regiment, he says, but the Browning's reliability and high-capacity magazine make it popular with armed forces in so many countries, it's going to be around for a while longer.

'It'd be nice to have a couple to take with us,' says H with a grin as he weighs the pistol in his hand. This one's a recent DA model, he says, a double-action version of the original that incorporates a few modifications. The magazine can hold fourteen rounds, making fifteen with one in the chamber; the shape of the trigger guard has been changed to improve the grip when firing with two hands; and instead of a manual safety catch, there's now an ambidextrous de-cocking lever mounted on the frame. There's an internal firing pin safety mechanism and another safety to prevent firing if the slide isn't all the way back.

As he points out the weapon's features, his fingers move lightly over its surfaces with the swift dexterity of a conjuror, and the dark metal seems suddenly alive to his touch, ready to spring into action. He draws back the slide, presses the de-cocking lever, takes the magazine out and replaces it, and flips the pistol between his hands.

'I used to sit for hours playing with one of these,' he says as he slides it behind his back in a single fluid motion and presents to me his open palms. Then with the same effortless gesture the pistol reappears in his hand, supported by the other in a firing grip.

'Get the feel of it,' he says, and passes it to me.

I like the feel of the ambidextrous design, which means I can reach the de-cocking lever by lifting my thumb over the hammer without having to loosen my grip.

'Do what comes naturally,' says H. 'Remember the mechanism stays open after the final round's been fired. When you put in a fresh mag, push down the slide stop to send a new round forward, and you can keep firing without having to re-cock. You can also change the mag release button so that it goes on the other side, if you want.'

He puts his hands over mine to demonstrate the correct grip when firing over the sights, and the *en garde* position for what he calls instinctive shooting with the arms straight and both eyes open, when the target is up to fifteen feet away. It's a style of shooting that the regular army doesn't teach: two rounds in rapid succession to the head of the target. The Regiment has an expression for it: double tap.

'Take them all with you,' says H, waving a hand over the AK and the pistols, 'and practise with all three. If you can strip them in the dark, so much the better. We'll test-fire them next week after you've had a chance to play with them.' Between the running, I'm thinking. I ask where we'll do the test-firing. 'We could go down to the Fort, I suppose. Good range, but it's a bit of a hike.' He's talking about Fort Monckton in Portsmouth, where young spooks go for their early training in firearms. 'But it'll be easier to get up early and have a go in the hills somewhere. By the time anyone's got out of their pyjamas to investigate, we'll be long gone.' He picks up the sinister-looking book from the table and fans its pages. 'I've marked a few other weapons you might want to look at. You can compare with the Beretta and the SIG and the HK. Let's hope we don't have to use any of them, but you never know.'

I can't help asking if he's comfortable with me taking a bag full of weapons to my home.

'Just try not to get nicked on your way. I can't keep them here anyway. Sally would kill me if she knew I had weapons in the house.' His wife's aversion to guns seems an incongruous thing in the life of a professional soldier. Perhaps it's the secret of their apparent happiness.

By degrees my training is moving from the abstract to the very concrete. H is a gentle but thorough taskmaster, who never hurries or raises his voice, nor pushes me too fast with anything I feel unsure about. He shares his knowledge freely and without any trace of pretension. I much prefer his manner and method to the arrogant mystification of Seethrough, who seems to delight in making me feel ignorant.

We walk again the following day, pushing the pace a little harder. It's overcast but mercifully dry, saving us the discomfort of getting soaked by sweat under our waterproofs. We take the same route to Pen-y-Fan, then leave the summit on the steep eastern side in the direction of the pyramidal face of Cribyn, crossing the valley by the reservoir and climbing onto the broad plateau above. After a further two hours' walking, a long downward traverse puts us on the road a mile and a half from the car. I run this stretch in considerable pain while H mutters encouragement at my side.

In the afternoon we begin drafting notes for the tasks and routines we need to cover. Then, breaking for tea, H wanders outside and feels the grass on his lawn. It's dry enough and he has an idea. It's one thing to be on the right side of a weapon, he says, but finding oneself unexpectedly at the business end is another matter. It's time to practise disarming techniques.

At the heart of the theory of disarming – jap-slapping, as it's unofficially called by Regiment men – lies the notion that, if a weapon is pointed close enough to one's body, it's possible to knock it aside before the attacker can pull the trigger. It's difficult to believe at first, so the point of disarming routines is to demonstrate the truth of it. Unless the belief is there, says H, you're liable to hesitate.

We start with the pistol, using the Browning in the manner of a hold-up. I push the muzzle into the small of H's back. His hands go up; he shuffles forward and begins to babble as if terrified, then looks at me over his left shoulder. I've agreed to pull the trigger at the first moment I sense alarm. I feel his body turn and am about to respond, but within the space of a second I find myself on the ground, looking up at him. His left hand is clenched around the shirt on my chest, which he's pulled up at the last moment to prevent my head from hitting the ground too hard. His right hand is poised above me, ready to strike. The pistol lies on the grass. I'm shaken, and very impressed.

'Easy,' he says, pulling me gently to my feet. 'Let's break it down into stages.'

Everything depends on confidence in the key idea that the weapon can be deflected before it can be fired. The rest is more or less common sense, says H. It's an expression he's fond of, I notice. There's an element of stealth – glimpsing but not fixing on the threatening weapon – and distraction – dropping one's keys or wallet onto the ground at the moment before counter-attacking. The counter-attack comes in the form of a swift turn and, at the same moment, a downward blow to deflect the weapon and open the attacker's body to further disabling strikes.

'Better not to launch into it at the first instant,' says H. 'That's when a gunman's most tense because he's expecting you to try it on. Choose your moment. Get him talking and his mind off the weapon. Then check the hand it's in by glancing over your shoulder. Pushing against the weapon is useful too, because when you start to turn it'll slide off-target. The downward strike is hard and fast. Follow up with an open hand to the chin and a knee in the groin.'

There are more precise methods for seizing a pistol without harming an attacker, he tells me, but they take too long to learn.

'Forget about Jackie Chan. The aim here is to disarm and disable, not circus tricks. Besides,' he adds with a solemn look, 'anyone who puts a weapon on you deserves whatever they get.'

This is the first glimpse I have of the steel beneath the velvet.

We practise being held up from front and back, applying the same principles with slight variations. A pistol to the head, pointed in the manner of an over-zealous gangster, is in fact the easiest of all threats to counter. But no two attacks are exactly the same, says H, and we practise until the moves come without thought. After this, he demonstrates optional refinements such as breaking the attacker's trigger finger or nose.

Then he goes into the house and returns with the AK. We run through a similar routine, as he explains that a rifle is in fact less risky to deal with than a pistol. The defender can move past the point of danger – the muzzle – and prevent the rifle returning to its target by moving in close and blocking it. The bulky foresight on the muzzle of an AK also makes it ideal to grab, and allows the defender to control the weapon. As the attacker goes down, a few jerks on the barrel is usually enough to break his grip.

'Once it's yours, you can decide what you want to do,' he says.

We try this out from the front a few times, at increasing speeds. H recommends a succession of kicks to the attacker's knee and sharp pulls on the barrel of the rifle. We move on to the variation from behind. He jabs the muzzle into my back and shouts, 'Move it!' and I turn and strike the barrel, feeling the outer side of my palm connect with the foresight. But I hit it too hard, and the skin on the edge of my hand splits open like a banana peel. I finish the move, but there's blood streaming over our clothes. H shoulders the AK with one hand and squeezes the sides of the cut together.

'Bad luck,' he says, 'but I think you've got the hang of it.' He leads me indoors, still holding the bloody hand, which drips over the kitchen floor. He stretches a few surgical strips across the wound, then binds it up in a bandage.

'Lucky the memsahib's away for a few days. She can't stand the sight of blood.'

Life at home after our sessions together seems quiet. I study the weapons manual, practise stripping the AK, the Makarov and the Browning, and wonder how the Jehovah's Witnesses might react if I came to the door with an AK at the ready. I perfect the skill of trapping small rodents, because the organisation of night-time ambushes in secondary jungle is not really practical in my garden, with the help of another manual H has lent me called *Operational Techniques Under Special Conditions*. I also force myself to run, and begin to shave seconds off my circuit times, though the margin is proving disappointingly difficult to improve on. My thighs are in fierce protest after the slopes of the Beacons, and running makes my calf muscles hurt all day long. I'm in constant discomfort.

The following week, my training with H follows the same pattern. His wife Sally is away again, visiting family over the weekend, and we have the house to ourselves. We walk and run long circuits in the mornings and go over practical skills in the afternoons. In the evenings we add more detail to the overall plan.

H says we'll need to practise car drills too.

'If our opsec is up to scratch, no one who doesn't need to will ever know what we're doing. But we have to plan for worst-case scenarios.' He's right. It's not impossible that someone might try to rob us. In Afghanistan there are unofficial checkpoints where we might be held up, or worse. 'Best way to deal with a bogus VCP is to never get into one,' says H. 'Next best is to turn around fast. Last resort is to drive through.' We agree that driving through vehicle checkpoints isn't such a great idea because trigger-happy Afghans are inclined to shoot at the occupants, rather than the tyres, of disobedient vehicles, and Afghans tend to be good shots. The problem of banditry has been much reduced by the Taliban, but their Arab allies affiliated with al-Qaeda are known to be cruel and frequently ruthless, and make Afghan bandits seem kindly.

One morning, another week later, he reverses his Range Rover into the centre of the driveway, and we stand by it as he speaks, imagining the scenario of coming under attack on some lonely stretch of Afghan road.

The interior of a vehicle, unless it's armoured, offers no protection at all, which makes getting out fast a priority. H explains that a high-velocity round has no difficulty going through the body of a car and that the only part of a normal vehicle which can provide cover is either the engine block or the wheels. Since you can't manoeuvre from behind an engine block, that leaves the wheels.

'There's just one problem,' he says, asking me to lie down behind one of the wheels and imagine that I'm trying to return fire. Between the ground and the underside of the car is a thin strip of space, beyond which the ground obscures everything. The only thing I'll be able to shoot from this position is our attacker's toes.

'You can't see a bloody thing,' I say.

'Exactly.'

At that moment I hear a rapid panting in my ear as H's terrier runs up and begins feverishly licking my face.

'Jeffrey!' hisses H. 'Get out of it! Fuck off!' The dog persists, so he leads it back into the house and, apologising, settles down beside me again.

'If you stick your head up over the wheel, you'll have a better view.'

That makes sense. Steadying my imaginary weapon over the bonnet of the car, I line up on an enemy sheep in the field beyond.

'Get the idea?' H retrieves the AK, puts it on the rear seat, and we get into the car. 'Most important is to agree who goes where, so we don't end up on top of each other. Let's say we're coming under fire from my side. You go back, I'll go front. Shall we try it?'

I throw open the door and tumble out, slamming it behind me instinctively just as H is trying to dive out. He blocks it with his hand and peers at me over the edge of the seat with a tolerant look I haven't seen before.

'Best not to slam the door in my face. Let's try again.'

We return to the seats.

'Last one out gets the AK. Enemy left – go!'

H rolls out of the passenger side and crouches behind the front wheel as I follow, grab the AK out of the back and position myself behind the rear wheel, firing imaginary rounds at our attackers.

'Better,' he says.

'You must feel pretty vulnerable with your head sticking out like that,' I say.

'You do,' he replies. 'That's why you don't want to be there too long.'

We install ourselves back in the car.

'Now we'll withdraw under fire.' He points around the garden. 'I'll move to that tree while you give covering fire. When I say, you move along the same path until we're both behind the rhododendrons. When one of us is moving, the other is firing.'

'Got it.'

We tumble out again at his signal. *Bang bang bang bang bang!* H runs to the tree. Then I follow as he covers me from the bushes beyond. *Bang bang bang bang bang!* We end up lying beside each other thirty yards from the car.

'Fine,' he says. 'But I probably would have shot you. You ran through my line of fire. Try to keep a sense of where I am.'

Leaving me feeling like a small child, H disappears inside his garage and emerges with two black nylon waist packs.

'Here,' he says, handing me one of them, 'your go bag.' From the weight of it I know the Browning is inside. We check the weapons, which are unloaded, and put the packs on the bonnet.

'You'll usually have something like this on an op,' he says, unzipping the main pouch of his bag. 'Medical kit, E & E stuff, money, maps, heli marker for your exfil, and some other bits and pieces – it depends on what you need at the time. We'll pretend these are ours and keep them under the seats.'

We stash the bags behind our heels and pretend once again to be heading into an ambush. If we're expecting trouble, the best place for the Browning is on the seat under one's leg, which saves having to scramble about for it. I copy him as he slides the weapon under his thigh with the butt facing out.

The Brownings are in our hands as we dive out again, then bound in turn across the drive into the garden.

'Good, but you forgot the bag.'

But I'm learning. We repeat the drill several more times, upping the tempo each time until we've covered all the combinations. Speed, aggression and determination are the keys to success, he says. If there are only a few attackers, a concerted counter-attack with a high rate of fire from the AK can turn the tables, but it has to happen quickly.

We break for tea and H starts his ritual note-taking at the kitchen table. We draw up some general notes on security, with a plan to refine them as we go along. He draws a map of the ideas we need to understand. He lists the possible threats we'll face, and how to defeat or minimise our vulnerability to them. He's concerned with communications and transport, and getting safely from A to B, and not letting our plans be known to others. The level of detail borders on obsessive, but being methodical is what gives the SAS its reputation.

H talks at length about vehicle security: not choosing taxis which offer themselves, avoiding fixed routes, not getting boxed in when in heavy traffic, how to carry out a quick inspection of a vehicle to see if it's been tampered with, code words for agreed sites, identifying safe havens to divert to in an emergency, and the need for back-up plans.

I realise he's working his way through his own version of a military orders plan at combat-team level. This is generally written up under several headings. The first is 'Ground', which identifies the physical terrain, both generally and in detail. 'Situation' details friendly and enemy forces in the area of the operation, as well as the political layout. 'Mission' defines the scope of the operation, summed up in snappy language: kill X or destroy Y. 'Execution' goes into the details of routes, movement, RVs, action on target and exfil procedures – how to get home again. 'Service Support' deals with weapons, rations and equipment and how to get them to and from where they need to be. There's another standard heading, which I can't remember.

' "Command and Signals",' says H. 'Radios, mostly. Who talks to who, when and how. We won't be calling in much air support. Just checking in with London from time to time.' He waves a pen over the notes. 'And we need to think of a cover story for our time in-country. Something short term.' This is my task. He then explains how I should apply for a second passport, which can be left hidden in a safe place in case we're parted unexpectedly from our things.

His wife has prepared a dinner for us in advance. We eat and then devote the evening to familiarising ourselves with the weapon that lies behind the whole operation.

'Might want to study this,' says H, putting a bulky manual in front of me. It's the American DoD training documentation for the FIM-92. The pages are marked SECRET, and there are several hundred of them.

'The Sovs would've killed to get their hands on this a few years back,' he says, tapping the cover.

'They were the first to find out the hard way what the Stinger could do,' I say, thinking of the missile's deadly effect on Soviet airpower in Afghanistan.

'Not quite,' he corrects me. 'The Yanks gave us some of these when we were down south in the Falklands. There was only one bloke from the Regiment who knew how to use the Stinger, and he was on that Sea King that crashed in the South Atlantic. A trooper in D Squadron managed to shoot down an Argentine fighter, though he was bloody lucky. That was the first combat kill with the Stinger.'

Its portability and reliability make it one of the most desirable weapons in the world. It is strange to think of the most advanced anti-aircraft technology of the time being hauled around Afghanistan on the backs of donkeys and camels. The Stinger's role in the final humiliation of the Soviet army was never really acknowledged.

The earliest Stinger models didn't distinguish between enemy or friendly targets: anything in the Afghan skies was fair game. The long thin missile is fitted into a fibreglass launch tube, and then attached to an assembly made up of the trigger and the infrared antennae, which looks vaguely like a toaster. A small battery unit is clipped in place, and when the missile has locked onto its target, a small speaker gives out the signal to fire. In case there is too much noise for it to be heard, a vibrator buzzes in the cheekbone of the firer. There are a number of checks and sensors that indicate whether the weapon is serviceable.

We need to know these things, and we go over them in detail.

Several hours later H gathers up our paperwork and locks it in a small safe. Then, when it's time to turn in, he waves a hand over his bookshelves and invites me to have a browse.

'You might like this one.' He pulls down a book about the Regiment and fans the pages until he reaches the chapter devoted to the campaign in Oman. There's a selection of photographs taken at the height of the conflict, but the images of the soldiers don't look like conventional portraits. The men wear beards, ragged-looking uniforms and frayed caps or Arab *shemagh*s; cigarettes dangle from their lips, and many of them look too old to be soldiers in any case.

H points to a photograph of a fearsome-looking bearded man with a sunburned face under a combat cap. A bulky general purpose machine gun and dangling belt of gleaming ammunition hang from his shoulder.

'That's the Ditch,' says H, looking fondly at the photograph. 'Gentle as a kitten. And that's the Monk.' There's another photograph of a man wearing what looks like a monk's hooded cassock. From the shadows of the woollen hood, a faint and enigmatic smile on the lean face does seem to confirm a contemplative temperament. Only the M16 assault rifle cradled protectively in his arms suggests a different calling.

He turns the pages again to show me a photograph of a young man peering over the sights of an 81-millimetre mortar in a dusty-looking sandbagged gun pit. His bare upper body is deeply tanned and he looks very fit. It's H, twenty-five years earlier, up on the Jebel near Medinat al-Haqq.

'We used to play with that mortar a lot.' He smiles. 'Just to let the Adoo know we could put down a round on a sixpence if we wanted to.'

It's very strange. As a teenager I owned the same book and pored over its pages, never imagining that one day I might know the names of the anonymous soldiers who looked out from them.

'Those blokes were the real deal,' says H, nodding solemnly. 'They don't make them like that any more.'

We leave the house in the morning while it's still dark. The Brownings are hidden in the go bags at our feet, and the AK under the rear seat. We're heading for an abandoned quarry about half an hour west of Hereford, practising the anti-ambush drill on the way, throwing the car onto the verge and positioning it between us and our imaginary attackers. Then, as the sky is beginning to brighten, we turn from the main road onto an unsurfaced track. At the end of it the ground opens out into a wide flat stretch of chalky subsoil, criss-crossed by waterlogged bulldozer tracks. Beyond it rises a pale amphitheatre of stone about sixty feet high.

I cut the engine and H takes two rolled-up targets from the car. We walk across the open ground and fix the targets to the soft stone with tent pegs. We count a hundred paces and I stand on the spot we mark, while H takes the AK from the back of his car. He clears the mechanism, hands me the weapon and feeds three rounds into the magazine. From his pocket he takes a small box of yellow foam earplugs, which we squeeze into our ears.

'Let's zero the sights. Put three rounds on the black circle.'

The black circle, the size of a small plate up close, looks tiny. I line up on the speck of black and squeeze the trigger. The rifle bucks as if knocked by a hammer from below. I've forgotten how loud guns are.

'One,' says H. I fire again. 'Two.' And again. 'Three. Clear it.'

We jog to the target. One round is a foot off to the left. This is probably the first. The other two are a few inches apart, in line with the centre but six inches too high. We jog back to our firing position, where H makes an adjustment to the foresight and feeds five more rounds into the magazine.

'Centre of the target. Five rounds rapid.'

The AK rises and falls. I fire at the end of each downward lull and try to keep the rhythm even. My cheekbone, which I've been holding too close to the butt, is throbbing as if someone's punched it, and despite the earplugs my ears are ringing.

'Not bad,' says H, grinning as we pull the pegs from the target. 'Must be the quality of instruction.' There are three small holes in the centre circle and two others within the second, all vertically aligned within a few inches. He looks at his watch. 'Let's see how you do with the other fellow.'

We walk to the car, put the AK back under the rear seat and retrieve the Brownings. H has also brought a plastic bag with a dozen empty beer cans, seven of which we now set on a sloping stone shelf running across the face of the quarry. We take ten paces towards the car and turn around.

'When you're ready,' says H. 'Double tap on each. Remember not to yank the trigger.'

I cock the Browning and fire at each can in turn. Four of the seven are sent spinning. Three remain stubbornly in place as little fountains of chalk erupt behind them.

'Needs a bit of work,' says H. We gather up the empty casings, then the cans, and fix them back on the shelf.

'Show me how it's done then,' I say.

H cocks his pistol and tucks it into his belt above his left hip with the butt facing forward, and lets his coat fall in front of it. Then, in a single movement of astonishing swiftness, he draws his coat away with his left hand, pulls the weapon out with his right and begins firing with his knees slightly flexed. There's hardly a pause between targets, each of which disappears as he works from left to right. By the time I look back from the targets to see him removing the magazine from his pistol, less than five seconds has passed. H says nothing but throws me a satisfied wink. Then he pockets the Browning and scoops up the empty casings.

'We'd best be going,' he says.

'I enjoyed that,' I say.

'Me too.' He looks at his watch again and gives me a pensive look. The sky has brightened in the east, but around us the land is silent.

'I was just thinking,' he says. 'Shall we try the anti-ambush, and live-fire the Brownings? We could come from up there,' he motions to the dirt track that winds upwards beside the quarry face, 'drive in close, and retreat this way.' There are some dips and mounds in the ground behind us, and roughly fifty yards from the quarry face is a long intervening ridge of bulldozed rubble about four feet high. It's the perfect hiding place to retreat to from the car. 'Just aim for the same place where the targets were. Imagine each one's an Adoo with an AK. Let's get those cans so we can scarper afterwards.'

We gather up the mutilated cans and hide them in the car. Then we sit in the front and H puts the box of 9-millimetre cartridges between us. We fill the magazines, chamber one round into the breech and add a final top-up round to the magazine, making fifteen. Then we slip the pistols under our thighs and I start the engine. In four-wheel drive we climb the badly rutted track, circle the rim of the quarry and turn the car around just before reaching the skyline at the top, from where we might be seen. With the engine running, we have a good look on all sides for any movement. It's time to go.

'Check chamber,' says H. I ease back the top slide of the pistol and glimpse the brass casing nestling in the breech.

'All set here.'

'Right, take us down.' I put the car into first gear and without accelerating let the slope carry us forward. 'Come on, make it real,' says H, and we accelerate, pitching hard across the braided ruts of the track. H braces himself with a hand on the dashboard grip. 'I'll say when,' he growls.

As the track levels off we hit the flat ground with an almighty lurch. I floor it towards the quarry face, wondering how late H will leave the signal. As the tyres bite into the mud and gravel I can hear the debris from under us smacking violently into the wheel arches. Then, about sixty feet from the quarry face, I hear H yell.

'Ambush! Ambush! Enemy front! Take the front!'

The brakes lock as I pull the wheel hard to the left. The tail end of the car swings to the right, and the front wheels grind to a juddering halt. H throws the passenger door open and somersaults out. He's already firing as I hit the ground a couple of seconds later and take up a firing position across the bonnet.

H shouts, 'Moving now!' and I aim the Browning. It leaps five times. Beyond the foresight, puffs of chalk burst from the quarry face. Then I hear H's shout from behind me.

'Move! Move! Move!'

I sprint away from the car, cowering instinctively as I see the muzzle flash erupting from H's pistol ahead of me to the left. An uncomfortable feeling. A watery dip in the ground appears ahead of me and I fling myself into it, bring the weapon up and fire another five rounds in the direction of the car. Its blue shape seems to be floating pointlessly against the light wall of stone beyond, and I think for a moment of how much it resembles a beached whale.

Then I hear H shout again and run another fifteen yards as he covers me a second time. I dive and fire as H sprints to our final position, then hear the click of the firing pin as the weapon seems to die in my hands. I make the final sprint to the ridge of rubble. He has both hands on his weapon as I dive in beside him and slither round to face our imaginary enemies at the far end of the quarry.

H ducks below the rim of the ridge and rolls onto his back to check his pistol. The air reeks of cordite and there's a high-pitched ringing in my ears, which resounds at every heartbeat.

'Alright?' asks H.

'I'm fine.'

'Right, make safe.'

I check and pocket the pistol. Then we stand up and look towards the quarry face. The place seems strangely still after all the noise and movement. H's eyes are fixed firmly on his car.

'I'm glad I wasn't stuck in there,' he says quietly.

'We certainly got out alright,' I say, thinking he's referring to our escape from fictional bandits. I haven't felt such exhilaration for years and have a strong urge to laugh out loud. The low gruff tone of H's voice brings me back.

'It's not that,' he says, still looking intently in the direction of his beloved Range Rover. I follow his gaze. The car looks perfectly intact, only the normally transparent rectangles of window have turned a different colour, as if painted in the same chalky rainwater that's splashed all over our clothes and faces. Then I understand what he's staring at, and feel myself biting my lower lip.

'You arse,' he says grimly. 'You just shot my bloody windows out.'

It's our final week of training. It changes pace and lasts longer. At dawn every day we drive to different deserted places for further shooting practice. The time I'm allowed to aim and fire decreases at each session. Then when H is satisfied that I'm shooting accurately enough, he gets me to sprint thirty yards to the firing position, which makes steadying the pistol more difficult. He wants the weapon to become an extension of my hand, he explains. He shows me a quick-draw technique and lets me keep the Browning in the spare room to practise. I need to be able to draw and fire in my sleep, he says.

Rain or shine, we run everywhere. Sometimes H sets the pace, his rhythm as steady as a mountaineer's and indifferent to gradient or temperature, and at others he lets me lead, muttering encouragement when the going gets more challenging. He drags me up the cruel slope of Hay Bluff, and we run to the far end of the long plateau called the Cat's Back, and then along the neighbouring plateau towards Lord Hereford's Knob. We tackle the lung-searing flanks of Pen-y-Fan and Cribyn in freezing rain. He pushes me beyond my habitual reach but just short of despair.

In the afternoons we work on personal security issues relating to journeys: assessing threats and risks, keeping in touch and keeping to plans, access and escape, emergency routines, and the importance of pre-established safe havens and RV points. We talk through trusted methods of anti-surveillance when on foot: crossing open spaces, doubling back on a pretext and using a friend to observe one's movements from afar.

On self-defence, things simplify. Everything I've seen in films is bollocks, he says. The key thing is making the decision between fight or flight, and sticking to it. Flight is self-explanatory. Fighting is to decide that one will make use of anything and everything possible to defeat or disable an attacker. The hand, knee, elbow and head can all be put to lethal effect, providing they are used quickly and accurately and with complete conviction. Improvised weapons are nearly endless. A newspaper, pen or mobile phone can be used in a deadly manner, and any number of household substances can be used to inflict damage: pepper will temporarily blind when blown from the hand into an attacker's eyes; bleach will choke; hot water will scald. Queensbury Rules do not apply.

We devote a session to mine recognition, which is my territory, so for a few hours I hold forth on the perverse technology of anti-personnel mines, and the lethal design refinements of the PFM 'butterfly' mine designed by the Soviets for Afghanistan, the PMN and its successors, and the almost undetectable Chinese-made Type 72.

Much of the next day is devoted to explosives in general, the improvised versions manufactured by people who can't afford jets or tanks, and the devious and unlikely ways in which they can be set off. H mentions the high explosive that comes in the form of an adhesive roll that can be swiftly stuck to a door frame like a deadly strip of Sellotape before being detonated. The technique belongs to the Regiment's curriculum on methods of entry, though we agree that blowing a door from its housing with plastic explosive is usually a last resort.

On our final day we drive to the Black Mountains, then walk for most of the day, paying close attention to one of H's maps. In the afternoon we stop at a remote and beautiful spot by a small waterfall, sheltered by a steep crag. I wonder how we'll get back before nightfall, because it'll be dark in a couple of hours and we're miles from anywhere. Over a tin of sardines, H is telling me about a Regimental reunion in Oman years after the war, where he was invited by the sultan to a huge bash with the other members of A Squadron. The sultan chartered a giant C-130 Hercules to fly them all in to Muscat. Then the subject changes unexpectedly.

'Do you really want this op in Afghanistan?' asks H. The wind is ruffling his hair as he looks at me, and the chatty tone has gone out of his voice.

'Of course I do,' I say, but as I speak the words I realise this is not the whole truth.

'I need you to think about it,' he says. 'I need you to be 100 per cent convinced that you want it. If you have the slightest doubt, you need to face up to it and find the answer.'

I'm about to reply, but he cuts short my attempt by putting the map between us and pointing to a location several miles away.

'Here,' he says. 'I want you to spend the night here. There's an old shelter on this bluff that'll keep the wind off you. I need you to meditate on all this. Find out your doubt and work through it – before you go to sleep, if you wake up in the night, and when you get up in the morning. Take the Bergen. There's a sleeping bag in it. You can meet me back at the starting point at 0900 hours. Then you get cleaned up, we have lunch in the pub, and you can drive home.'

This is a surprise. The SAS is telling me to meditate on a mountaintop. I accept the suggestion, and we plot my return route, which is a direct bearing back to the spot where we've parked, so that if anything goes wrong he knows I'll be somewhere along the line. He folds the map and pats it against my chest, then stands up. It'll be dark before he's back at the car.

'Are you alright to get back?' I ask, regretting the question as soon as I speak.

'I was in the SAS, you know.' He sets off at a jog without looking back.

A couple of hours later the moon is just rising in the east and I'm at the shelter, a ruined shepherd's bothy half open to the sky. There's a waterproof groundsheet in the Bergen, H's own sleeping bag and a small emergency strobe. I settle in behind the stones and there's nothing else to do but follow his advice. The hills and ridges sink into darkness and there's no sound but the airy whisper of the wind against my ears.

I'm wondering who, if I had the choice, I could ask for advice on all this. I think suddenly of the story told in the Bhagavad Gita of the princely warrior Arjuna, doubting whether he should go to battle because he knows there are friends and members of his own family who he's likely to meet. He turns to Krishna for advice, who reminds him that life and death are unimportant things and that righteous action is the key to life. No one, says Krishna, can get to grips with your fate except yourself, which is why it's no good imitating the life of another. There's a harsh solace to this counsel, it occurs to me now, for anyone troubled by questions of fate, choice and action.

I turn in, but my mind is see-sawing between past and future. H is right to suspect that I have doubts, and they're coming at me like demons now. I'm not so much worried about the dangers ahead. Planning and training and common sense go a long way towards dealing with the obvious dangers. I'm actually looking forward to going back to Afghanistan. My doubt is whether I can carry my secret with me, which I can't tell Seethrough or even H, and this already feels like a betrayal. No one but the Baroness knows about Orpheus or the fact that he needs to come in, or whether, in the jargon of the Network, he's still a good householder or has become a lost sheep and will have to be eliminated.

I can't sleep, not properly, anyway. It's 3 a.m. I crawl out of the sleeping bag and pace around. There's a half-moon above me and the clouds are sweeping in luminous silence across the sky, and through the tears in their fabric I catch glimpses of the stars.

Fear is a catalyst of strange thoughts, I realise.

In daily life you are swept along by events which prevent you from going too deeply into things. But now that the ordinary momentum of the world has been stripped away, my doubt is laid bare. I want to know if I am making the right choice, but I can't be sure whether I have made a choice at all, or whether it has chosen me. When a man reaches a crossroads, it's fair to suppose that the decision he takes is a free one. It's what we'd all like to believe. But you can argue that his choice, so-called, is no more than the outcome of everything that has gone before, like a mathematical equation which, however complex, really only has one answer. All of a man's experience of life is part of that equation, embracing all his hopes, dreams and prejudices, his wishes and convictions, his most tender longings, bitterest grievances, and all the dark machinery of his fears. All invisibly influence his choice, like a secret committee voting behind its leader's back. Perhaps even the future itself exerts an influence, reaching back beneath the scheme of things. Then, when this formula of near-infinite complexity is at last resolved, and his decision, in which he has really had no say, rises like a balloon into the world of his conscious thoughts, the man will declare: I have made my choice freely and am responsible for it.

But that's not the point. Any propagandist, magician or behavioural scientist can tell you a man has much less choice than he'd like to believe. The interesting question is whether a man who knows he isn't free lives a different kind of life from the one who imagines he is. And if it is different, how is it different?

I can't hold the thought long enough to calculate the answer. I'm cold and tired and shivering now, and it's time to get some rest.

PART THREE

7

Even today I am reluctant to go into the details, and the knowledge that the players and the protocols have all changed since then does nothing to ease the task. It's true I want things to be told, but to abandon the habit of secrecy on which your life and that of others has at times depended is like pulling shrapnel from a wound. It may seem like the necessary thing to do, but the act sometimes risks killing the victim. It does feel like a kind of death, a relinquishment of something that's been part of my survival, and which year after year I've managed to conceal.

His code name is Orpheus, and his real name is Emmanuel, but I've known him personally as Manny since before the beginning of all this. Fate had thrown us together in the Pakistani town of Peshawar, not far from the Afghan border, in the late 1980s, and our lives have been linked ever since.

We meet one evening in the restaurant of the notorious Green's Hotel, a favourite haunt of the many misfits and adventurers drawn by the lure of the secret and dangerous war in Afghanistan under Soviet occupation. We're starved for company and like each other at once. Manny's been hiking in Chitral in his summer holiday from university and has made his way to Peshawar, as have I, in the hope of joining a mujaheddin group who'll take him across the border into Afghanistan itself. At twenty-three, he's only a year older than me but has a worldly confidence that I admire and enjoy. He's been awarded a short-service commission by the army, which pays his way through university, after which he's set his sights on a cavalry regiment. I'm toying with the idea of Sandhurst myself in a year's time, so I soak up everything he tells me about his plans. We share a fascination with Afghanistan, and the chance to get closer to the conflict is irresistible to both of us.

Green's is a dismal hotel. It's gloomy, run-down, inefficient and, worst of all, has no alcohol licence. The Pakistani staff all know that the majority of the guests are not there for love of the hotel, but have fallen in some way under the spell cast by Afghanistan, which beckons from beyond the tribal territories some fifty miles distant. They do not share our enthusiasm for Afghanistan or its people, and make no secret of the fact they think we're misguided. We take a morbid pleasure in their cynicism, and it's in keeping with this spirit of defiance that Manny has smuggled a bottle of duty-free whisky into his room.

That same night we stay up drinking, and by dawn we're planning our trip 'inside' together. It's reckless and dangerous, but we reason that two heads are better than one because anything might happen once we're inside a war zone and it seems wiser to combine our talents. There's no way to communicate with the outside world once we're actually in Afghanistan, and we exchange addresses at home in case one of us has to pass on bad news to the other's family.

For a week we explore together, diving into the noise and anarchy of the bazaars in the old part of the town, where we buy Afghan clothes in preparation for our first journey into war. We make friends with a Pashtun tribesman who lives in the tribal territories near the border with Afghanistan, and travel with him to a few of the wild frontier settlements where the law has scarcely ever reached and where guns and drugs can be bought like sweets at a tuck shop. At Darra we try out a selection of a gunsmith's wares, and the locals are duly impressed by Manny's marksmanship. An old man, hearing we are from England, tells us the story of the charismatic faqir of Ipi, known as Mirza Ahmed Khan to the Pashtuns, who fifty years earlier led a guerrilla-style jihad against the British presence in the region. Forty thousand troops were sent to the wilds of Waziristan to hunt him down, but failed to find him in a campaign lasting more than a decade.

Then comes the news we've both been waiting for. A mujaheddin group agrees to smuggle us into Afghanistan to its regional headquarters in Logar province, not far south of the capital Kabul, and a few days later we settle our bills at the hotel and send our final letters home. At dawn the next day we're moving towards the ragged purple profile of the mountains that mark the border, where we join a party of a dozen armed mujaheddin leading a small convoy of horses laden with arms and supplies.

We walk day and night, moving from village to village, sleeping in caves and on mountainsides, and are quickly immersed in all the hazards and romance of life with our guerrilla hosts. We share our first taste of warfare. Distantly at first, in the form of long, sonorous rumbles of artillery barrages laid down miles away, and in the fleeting sight of Soviet jet fighters glinting like silver arrows against the cobalt Afghan sky. And then more closely, when the village in which we've slept is inexplicably struck by two bombs, and in the chaos of the aftermath we catch sight of the limp and broken bodies of several villagers killed by the blasts, and the war becomes suddenly real for us.

At the time we are young enough to feel immortal. Our hosts, who are as hardy and friendly as they are ill-equipped and untrained, allow us to join them on several operations against their enemies. We accompany them on mine-laying operations to cripple military convoys, and on attacks against military posts in the region. Our happy-go-lucky party is itself frequently a target, and we experience the perverse relish of hearing the musical whine of ricocheting bullets nearby and of dusting ourselves off after diving for cover from incoming shells.

At first we carry no weapons and agree only to observe the plight of our hosts. Then one night, by moonlight, we join a team of thirty-five men who steal towards an enemy position in the hope of shooting it into submission. It's a mud-walled fortified house with two small watchtowers, manned by Afghan army conscripts under Soviet command. Ten yards short of the perimeter fence an explosion sends our commander flying into the air, his leg severed at the knee by a powerful anti-personnel mine. Manny is behind him, his face blasted by flying grit from the explosion, but he manages to drag the commander into cover. We withdraw in chaos as the incandescent threads of tracer rounds tear into the darkness around us. One of our party is shot cleanly through his hand, and another has a miraculous escape as a bullet lodges in the rifle which he's slung over his back. We walk for several hours to reach our headquarters, which comprises a network of caves carved into an escarpment beneath a village. At dawn, with the name of God on his lips, our commander dies.

It's not our war. But Manny puts forward the idea that with some explosives and a few more fighters we can take the enemy post, and he begs the deputy commander to request additional forces for a follow-up attack. Unprompted, he ignites the promise of retribution in the grief-stricken minds of our group. He has a natural authority and confidence that fascinates the Afghans, and in the days following the commander's burial on the hillside above our cave, there are long discussions.

A daylight reconnaissance of the building lends force to his argument. We study it from half a mile away through an ancient pair of binoculars and discover the shape of a bricked-up arched doorway in its rear wall. This is likely to be the weakest point and it's here that Manny suggests we attack. He makes an earth model of the fort and rings it with tiny pebbles to indicate the minefield that surrounds it. In the dust he draws the fields of fire, the points at which the men are to position themselves, and where to put the cut-off groups which will deal with any attempted counter-attack. All this he communicates in the small but forceful vocabulary of Persian he has taught himself over the course of a couple of weeks, and I'm jealous not only of his grasp of tactics but also of his precocious talent with a foreign language. It's a powerful combination. A few days later, a dozen more fighters, dark-skinned, bearded and draped with bandoliers of ammunition and automatic weapons, appear at the entrance of our cave, asking for the Christian *mujahid*.

It's a daring plan, refined over the course of several evenings. A lead man will prod his way through the mined perimeter, allowing Manny to advance to the rear of the building. An explosive charge, cast from the melted TNT of anti-tank mines, will destroy the wall, allowing entry to a storming party. The fort's towers, which contain light machine guns, will be attacked by rocket-propelled grenades. Three Soviet parachute flares will illuminate the attack. Manny drives home the importance of timing and coordination, and the disciplined use of directed fire. The men are entranced.

And incredibly, it works. There is no need for the storming party. The rear wall is thinner than we calculate, and the explosive charge tears open a hole the size of a garage door. Our light machine guns pour fire into the breached wall, and we wait for the signal to move. But within seconds the terrified occupants are already pouring out, caught in the eerie artificial sun of the hissing flare overhead. Two members of the dreaded KHAD, the Afghan secret service, are betrayed by the surrendering men, and are killed resisting capture inside the building. The attack is a textbook success, and the hated post has fallen.

When Manny starts showing signs of a violent fever a few days later I'm secretly relieved. News of the Christian commander's victory has spread with electrical speed, and we both know that before long the Afghan secret police will hear of it and report the presence of a foreign mercenary to their Soviet masters. The risks of staying are too great both for ourselves and our hosts, and the decision is made for us to return to Pakistan to recuperate. On the day of our departure I witness the incongruous sight of tears in the eyes of several of the men, warriors we imagined were impervious to pain.

I have no doubts about what would have happened to us had we stayed on. Manny possesses a combination of daring and ambition which, in a war as unpredictable and brutal as Afghanistan's, will eventually end in a tragedy I don't want to witness. Two weeks later we're in England, shocked and depressed at how unreal everything seems. We long, silently, to return at once to Afghanistan and to the danger and the beauty of the place that has made us feel so very alive. We have shared in the thrill of near-death and in the agony of a nation torn apart by conflict: we are modern-day blood brothers. The prospect of ordinary life among people who care nothing for the privileges of peacetime yet whose lives are filled with a thousand petty worries, seems like a prison sentence to us both.

Manny emerges from Sandhurst to join a cavalry regiment with a reputation for dash and courage. I visit him for the occasional party at the officers' mess, where the spirit of romance is kept alive among fit and idealistic young men in red jackets and gold piping. The dinners are pleasantly rowdy and fuelled by a generous flow of wine. At one I embarrass myself by not passing the port along. Later, I watch Manny attempt a ritual capture of the commanding officer's spurs, by crawling beneath the long tables decorated with regimental silver ornaments from Balaclava. At another, the evening culminates in a fire-extinguisher fight in the corridors of the mess.

I decide to follow suit, and join my father's regiment after being awarded a short-service commission. In the dreary lecture rooms that huddle behind the grand facades at Sandhurst I plough through Clausewitz and the grand concepts of attrition and manoeuvre. My knowledge of Middle Eastern languages has not gone unnoticed, and takes me to the army language school in Beaconsfield and to Ashford to spend time with the Green Team, better known as the Intelligence Corps. In my private life, by a cruel coincidence, Manny and I fall for the same woman, with whom we both spend, at different times, our every spare moment.

For a year we are in a bittersweet competition for her favour, and our friendship is heavily strained by rivalry. When the woman we are in love with finally abandons both of us, our friendship is restored, almost magically intact.

Meanwhile, in the affairs of the greater world, there's a kind of watershed. After a brutal ten-year occupation, the Soviets make their ignominious withdrawal from Afghanistan, and their empire unravels. The Red Army's venture in Afghanistan is over, and I can't help feeling that the world's last good war has come to an end. Manny feels the same.

I have known the Baroness, or imagine I've known her, since her appearance in my childhood home as my father's guest and old friend. Her precise connection with my father is never explained and it doesn't occur to me to ask. She's an academic of the old school, and has written a book about her adventurous travels in the Middle East. I think her husband was a diplomat. She is courteous to a fault, and a woman of poise and genuine charm. I've never seen her not wearing her most formal clothes.

Of all the adults who crossed the horizon of my youth, it's the Baroness who stands out. It is to her that I owe my stock of stories about Africa and the Middle East, as well as my decision to study Middle Eastern languages at university. I introduce Manny to her not long after our first return from Afghanistan, and she takes a kindly, godmotherish interest in our future careers, going to the trouble of sending us newspaper clippings or alerting us to films or documentaries on subjects which she thinks will interest us.

One day she calls to invite us to her London home in Little Venice. We join her for dinner, and when the subject of Afghanistan comes up, as it always does, Manny surprises us both by delivering a passionate attack on the immorality of the Western powers who have abandoned the country and are doing nothing to help rebuild a nation in whose destruction they have participated.

The Baroness listens attentively. Then, in a tone of seriousness to which we're unaccustomed, she extends the argument in a direction that leaves us dumbfounded. Until this moment she's seemed to us a refined and kindly old lady.

'Have you thought,' she asks, 'of the wider consequences of the war in Afghanistan and how much we will all be affected by it? You are both seeking something out of the ordinary. Perhaps today is the day to explore it.'

We are entering a new era, she says, in which the real threat facing the West is not a military one. The Western powers will no longer fight conventional wars because the enemy of the future will be more diffuse. It will, in part, grow out of the disaffected peoples of the Islamic world, she tells us. We have meddled in and manipulated their countries for far too long. Now Afghanistan has shown that a poor but determined people can successfully resist impossible odds, and the ten-year-long war against the Soviets has served as a rallying call throughout the Muslim world. But the Afghans' hard-fought victory is being exploited by extremists, who have begun to gather in the country with the intention of spreading their violent agendas ever further afield. It is from these loosely allied militant groups that the threat is really incubating, she says, and there is a small organisation, to which the Baroness belongs, that takes an interest in such things. If we agree to speak nothing of it, she will tell us more. Manny and I are spellbound.

She calls it only the Network, and says she was introduced through a friend and former SOE agent called Freya. The Network's original goal was to establish a structure, to be activated in times of need, to penetrate key groups relevant to British interests in the Middle East and gather information on their activities. It operated independently of the more conventional intelligence services, with which its relationship was collaborative when necessary, but for the sake of secrecy never shared operational details. Being much smaller, and not limited by the approval of ministers or the political agendas of the time, it functioned with both greater freedom and greater risk. It was successfully brought into play several times over the past few decades, but the loss of British influence in Middle Eastern affairs led to its suspension.

Now the world is again facing a crisis of new proportions, and the Network has been resurrected across several continents. The Baroness's role is to address the emerging need for intelligence from Afghanistan, and this, she confesses, is why she has chosen to speak to us on the matter.

Napoleon's dictum that a single spy in the enemy's camp is more valuable than a thousand soldiers on the battlefield is more pertinent than ever, she tells us. It is not so difficult, she goes on, for someone with the relevant talents to infiltrate a group of potential terrorists. What is difficult is to gather useful information about their activities over a long period and communicate this to one's allies. The ideal structure for such a task is a pair of individuals. One disappears from sight of the world and leads a secret life inside the target's camp. The other follows at a distance, receiving and transmitting signals like the polished mirror of a telescope.

'It is the work of years, rather than weeks or months,' she says, 'and the very practice that the ordinary intelligence services have abandoned. We like to think of it as directed towards obtaining higher intelligence. The Service addresses the changing affairs of the day. We march to a different drum. By its nature it involves a fateful commitment and the sacrifice of all lesser ambitions. Above all, this task must be secret and known only to the smallest possible number of people. As long as the Network exists, its work cannot be spoken about to outsiders.'

It is for this reason, she adds, that its members are painstakingly recruited from the families of trusted friends who have demonstrated what she calls the 'appropriate spirit'.

The Network serves an idea, not an authority. It has no overt hierarchy. Even the Baroness has her teachers, she says. The role of its members is to understand a given target, to deepen their understanding and to transmit this to those who can hear. Their ambition is not to change the world, but to influence it, for lasting change is brought about by understanding rather than the application of external force. Advancement in the Network is acquired on the basis of understanding alone.

We will never know its exact numbers, the Baroness tells us, because no such information exists and its members never gather in a single place. They collaborate when necessary, but not for gain or advancement. There are Network members in government, in the military, in commerce and academia; others serve in more dangerous roles. They are content for their work to be invisible and for the most part lead ordinary lives, incorporating, without any outward show, their hidden task into the fabric of their daily responsibilities.

Such a possibility, if we wish to reflect on it, now exists for us.

She gives us time to think, but we don't need long. We are young and keen, and we accept. Nothing changes for us on the surface of things, but in our spare time we meet the Baroness whenever our duties allow, and begin our secret course of study.

There are some things you learn which, when you first encounter them, make each day seem like a gift beyond value. Our first few sessions have this quality. The fact that what we're learning must be kept secret adds a further, intoxicating aspect to our work, which is why the protocols for secrecy are drummed into us from the start.

The success of all our future work is founded on the twin arts of observation and clandestine communication – essential practices, the Baroness tells us, which have not changed since men first learned to spy on one another, and which require nothing of technology. We learn first to see and hear through a new version of our senses, as if an extra dimension has been added to their habitual function. Our task is to act at all times on the assumption that we are being observed, and to see ourselves through the eyes of our observers. We learn to watch and follow a human target, to note and then predict his actions. Then, by inverting the same skills, to evade a follower and to conceal our own telltale gestures of impatience, anxiety or relief. We must be able, the Baroness endlessly reminds us, to transmit the signals of whatever emotion we choose to whoever is watching, as well as to draw the attention of others in whatever direction we wish.

To sharpen our skills of observation, she invites us to assign a portion of our attention to something going on around us, and then points out when our attention has faltered. Our ordinary power of attention must acquire a second track, she reminds us. At meetings in restaurants she challenges us to describe the faces we have seen at the tables on our way in and to recall the numbers of buses or taxis we've used on the way. She explains how to use mental mnemonics to remember lists of things or names. We must learn these skills, she says, practise them in small ways every day, and live them until they become instinctively natural, betraying no trace of our ulterior agendas.

A large part of our time is devoted to arranging and conducting meetings. For secret information to pass between two parties, there must be a moment of contact, and this is the most perilous moment of all. A 'chance' meeting, which has in fact been arranged in advance, may be best when the exchange must be verbal. When information can be passed on without the need for a conversation, a brush contact may be best, involving a fleeting and wordless exchange of secret material. An innocent third party, or cut-out, may be another solution. Each has its advantages and corresponding risks. Brush contacts must be arranged carefully in advance and executed with precise timing; a cut-out may be unreliable and describe both parties if interrogated; and a chance meeting must stand up to intense scrutiny if suspected. But a meeting can also be arranged remotely, by an advertisement in a paper, a phone call with a disguised message, or take the form of a 'dead letter box' at an agreed location, visited by both parties at different times, perhaps days apart. The Baroness's preferred method for transmitting short messages is an 'innocent' letter, in which an ordinary text disguises a broken-up message, previously enciphered by means of a key known only to the recipient. To this end we practise a variety of codes and ciphers that can be created in the field without potentially incriminating aids such as printed one-time pads or code books, and study the theories of fractionation and homophony, and the various ways to combine codes that will render them impenetrable in the short term.

We learn of famous historical double agents and illegals and of their successes and failures. We study the career of one of the CIA's greatest spies, the Soviet GRU officer Oleg Penkovsky, and are invited to decide whether he was a triple agent or not. We learn too of the quiet English mother of three to whose children Penkovsky passed microfilm-stuffed sweets in public parks and on trains, trained by the SIS for the purpose but never caught. We are told of the reckless extravagance of Aldrich Ames, whose tailored suits, bought with KGB dollars, went unnoticed while he betrayed hundreds of CIA assets abroad. We consider the long successes of illegals with carefully constructed legends such as Rudolph Abel and Konon Molody. Abel lived in New York as a retired photofinisher; Molody in London as a bubblegum-machine salesman. Both masterminded spy rings, both were eventually caught and given long prison sentences, and both were later exchanged for Western spies captured in the Soviet Union.

We are on one occasion delivered a fascinating lecture analysing the daring escape from Moscow, organised by his SIS handlers, of the KGB colonel Oleg Gordievsky. The lecture is given by a middle-aged man with a serious-looking face, straw-coloured hair and a distinct Slavic accent, on loan to us for the day with the approval of his agent resettlement officer from the Firm. Afterwards, I confess how impressed I've been by the speaker.

'It is the lessons of tradecraft you are being asked to consider on such occasions,' she says, 'not the personalities involved.' The Baroness lets this sink in. 'Look more closely, and you will see the cold-hearted pride and ruthless vanity from which such people suffer.'

It becomes an axiom of our training that whatever the chosen means of communication and however it is passed, there must always be a credible cover story, as well as innocuous signals, agreed in advance, to indicate danger to one's allies. The closer the cover story is to the truth, the better. But there must always, always be a cover story.

When Saddam Hussein is foolish enough to invade Kuwait, the Baroness summons us to discuss things. We are both preparing to deploy to the Gulf and awaiting our final orders. It won't be real war, the Baroness tells us. She predicts confidently that Kuwait will be quickly liberated, but that the West will be blinded by its victory to the greater consequences of the conflict. America's willingness to turn its back on the heroic and ruined nation of Afghanistan but to spend billions in defence of a corrupt oil-rich state will confirm the deepest cynicism of its opponents. The time, she says, is drawing near. She offers us a final chance to withdraw. The war in Kuwait will provide the context for our operational phase with the Network. She is fond of the term context. She advises us to await our orders and do nothing except what is expected of us. We will know the signal when it is given to us. 'Like a passing bus,' she says, 'you will know when to jump on it.' It is better, she explains, that neither of us sees it coming.

We do not, in the event. When hostilities begin, we are both assigned unusual extra-regimental roles with the same interrogation team in Kuwait. Our parent unit is the Joint Services Interrogation Wing, housed at Ashford and commanded by a I Corps lieutenant colonel, hence our '2' designations, which indicate an intelligence role. The assignment is unusual because the forward interrogation team to which we're assigned – me as operations officer and Manny as 2i/c – is formed primarily from reservists who are volunteer members of 22 Int Coy, the Naval Reserve unit HMS *Ferret*, and 7630 Flight. We have relevant backgrounds, having both been through DSL Beaconsfield, but we're not regular senior NCOs or Reserve officers, and in time-honoured fashion we blame the mistake in tasking on the army. Most of the interrogation teams deploy forward to where enemy prisoners are being held, but we're assigned to Category 1 prisoners, who are usually senior officers and intelligence personnel, and our team takes over a warehouse on the outskirts of the city and converts it into an interrogation centre. We're barely up and running when the war screeches to a halt. Saddam Hussein's great army has fled before the allied onslaught, and the Baroness's prediction has proven uncannily accurate. The active combat phase of Desert Storm has lasted one hundred hours, Kuwait is liberated, and Saddam's 'mother of battles' turns out to be a rout.

When the raid occurs, we're not expecting it. Neither Manny nor I can have any notion of how deeply, and irreversibly, that ten-minute period of our lives will change things for us both. Manny has no idea that he will be seized by an Israeli commando team, beaten senseless and confined to a Mossad safe house in Kuwait City. But when the same Mossad officer – who has been beating Manny around his face so that the bruises will look much worse than they really are – slips him a narrow hacksaw blade and pats him on the back for good luck before throwing him into a cell with a suspected Arab terrorist, Manny knows that this is the bus he's expected to jump on. When Manny cuts through both sets of handcuffs and then through the metal bar that secures their window, the Arab can't believe his luck. He has no reason to suspect that his escape has been engineered. All he knows is that an enraged English soldier, vowing jihad against the Zionists, has freed him from his enemies, and he can't believe his luck. He's only too happy to introduce him to his superiors. Manny's dangerous work has begun.

Not everything goes according to plan. I am not supposed to shoot and kill a man. But the Israelis are willing to overlook the accident, since they have been allowed to seize Gemayel in the process, and they have wanted him for years. Such is the deal that has been struck. Mossad gets its man, and Manny's cover story – bruises and all – is brilliantly established from the start.

It's nearly six months before our first contact arrives at a PO box in London. It takes the form of an 'innocent' letter sent from Jalalabad in southern Afghanistan. It's what the Baroness calls a 'sign of life'. Manny, to whom we've given the code name Orpheus, has made it to Afghanistan with a forged New Zealand passport, and requests an address in Kabul to which his reports can be sent. Thus begins the new phase of my work. The Baroness tells me a vacancy has come up with a British de-mining trust operating in Kabul which favours ex-servicemen, and it's obvious she's used her influence with the founder. The fact that the plans for me to move to Afghanistan coincide with the outbreak of civil war in the country is, in the Baroness's words, 'problematic but not insurmountable'.

There is no Internet, mobile or terrestrial phone network, nor even a reliable postal system in Afghanistan at the time, so the address to which Manny's messages must be delivered is transmitted in a pre-recorded code by radio from England. Radio enthusiasts call such transmissions number stations, and rightly suppose they are the preferred method of communicating with agents in the field, though no government has ever officially acknowledged them. Orpheus needs only an ordinary short-wave radio to receive the signal, which is transmitted every day. But he has no other special equipment of his own, so his reports must be personally delivered by couriers who know nothing of their hidden content.

They begin to arrive at the trust's office in Kabul a month later, addressed to a pseudonym. The first takes the form of a book of Afghan poetry. Into its spine he's glued a sheet of paper, dense with handwritten numbers. I copy the numbers onto a grid called a straddling chequerboard, and transpose them using a keyword into letters that reveal the message.

Slowly, as the words take shape, I'm filled with a sense of awe that that our fragile link has successfully spanned so many hazards. The numbers we've agreed to use as a security device are correct and the message opens with characteristic humour: BGNS MSG 0786 ALL WELL DESPITE URGENT NEED SAQI. I am filled with relief to learn that he's well, despite a craving for wine. He's living at the Jalalabad headquarters of an Afghan mujaheddin commander called Sayyaf, known for his extreme Islamicist outlook and strong links with fundamentalists in the Arab world. Orpheus's knowledge of Arabic is allowing him to translate for his Afghan hosts and to serve as interpreter when Arab guests visit the headquarters. It's not much news but it's the sign of life we've been waiting for. The final line of the message alludes to the need for patience by reminding me that one of the Muslim names of God is the Patient One, *al-saboor*: ALLAHU SABOOR SEND GREETINGS UK QSL MSG ENDS.

I fax news of the message to the Baroness using the satellite phone at the office, knowing that she will arrange for confirmation of its receipt to be sent by a one-way signal which Orpheus can hear on a short-wave radio. Our little portion of the Network, against the odds, is up and running.

Orpheus's messages continue in the same manner for the next six months. They are, not surprisingly, irregular. Afghanistan is spiralling downward into ever more violent civil war, and on those days when the rockets rain into the south and west of the city I spend much of the time in the basement of my rented home. Because of the ongoing fighting, most of the trust's work takes me north of Kabul to the once fertile and prosperous Shomali plain, which bears the scars of fifteen years of conflict. We survey minefields sown by the Soviets and gather unexploded ordnance from settlements where people are still living. In collaboration with the United Nations we develop a mine awareness course but the daily casualties from mines and

UXOs are a constant reminder of the hugeness of our task. It is difficult at times not to be seized by depression.

The messages from Orpheus arrive with traders, drivers and refugees, who will occasionally accept a reward for their efforts and from whom I gain a picture of events in the south. Then the first of the computer diskettes arrives, hidden this time in the thick cover of a Qur'an. Orpheus now has access to a computer, which eliminates the long task of manual encryption and decryption and enables him to send messages of infinitely greater length.

It's the beginning of a series of long disturbing reports that confirm the violent intentions of the broad spectrum of foreign militants gathering in the south of the country. They are financed from overseas and the Afghan government is too weak to touch them. The Afghans, in any case, don't have the money to finance terrorists and can't even pay the salaries of their own government ministers. The religious fervour of these new foreigners has no place in their culture.

To judge from his reports, Orpheus has also gained access to lists of names, financial details and plans for plots against targets all over the world. I can only wonder about how he's being affected by the company he's keeping. He writes at length about the ideas and aspirations of the organisations he's learning about. A new kind of international war, aimed far beyond Afghanistan, is steadily incubating. Its proponents use Islam, traditionally a religion of tolerance, as a rallying banner, but increasingly stripped of its humane principles and twisted towards violence.

Extremism is new to Afghanistan, but it's on the rise. One of Orpheus's reports accurately predicts the unprecedented massacre of Hazara families in Afshar by henchmen of the brutal warlord Sayyaf, and in another he forecasts the assassinations of rival mujaheddin leaders both in Pakistan and Afghanistan. But there are also details of larger-scale acts of terror, which are increasingly inventive and ambitious. They seem fantastic and unrealisable. There are plots to blow up hotels in the Middle

East and public buildings in New York, and to hijack airliners in Europe. There are details of a plan to kill both the Pope and the US president. Orpheus has been tasked to translate American military manuals on improvised explosives, poisons and the manufacture of biological toxins. But in the very country where these unprecedented campaigns are taking shape, the powers at which they are directed have no plans to intervene.

Then the reports stop. The newly formed Taliban is advancing through the south and west of the country, and I can only assume that the headquarters where Orpheus lives has been overrun or dispersed. Communication and transport between Kabul and the rest of the country are virtually severed. I allow myself to hope that he's safe, but that it's become impossible for him to get messages out from wherever he is.

Three months pass and there's nothing from him. The daily stress of life adds to my feelings of desperation. Twice I visit the front lines in the west of the city towards the Taliban positions in Maidan Shahr, and find myself drawn too close to the fighting for my own good. I notice that I am taking risks with my own security and losing my sensitivity to danger. I don't know it at the time, but the effects of the war are reaching into me in unexpected ways, and I am being changed by them. I am surrounded by destruction and the randomness of death, which I cannot fathom. I have felt the closeness of death as tangibly as the intimate whisper of a murderous seducer, and felt the richness, twinged by guilt, of having escaped its grasp. I have seen too often the numb lost look of men consumed by undiluted grief, and heard the howl of children as their mothers are pulled from the rubble of a rocket-blasted home, and I am coming to understand the long dark pain of those who silently endure what at first seems unendurable.

One evening, in the gloomy, oak-panelled bar of the United Nations club, an Australian journalist friend who's been covering the war gives me his characteristically frank assessment.

'You're a bloody basket case,' he says. 'Got it written all over you,' he gestures, drawing a finger across his chest. 'Burned out. You need to get yourself out of this shit hole and get some R & R before someone has to pick you up in little bits and put them in a paper bag.'

A week later he's badly wounded by a mortar explosion and is flown out of the city by the International Red Cross. He's paralysed and will live the rest of his life in a wheelchair. The news hits me hard. It's as if he's shown me my own fate.

I have no wish to abandon Orpheus, but it's time to pull out, so after nearly two years I resign from the trust. Nothing can describe my feelings of devastation as I board a United Nations flight to New Delhi and circle away from the airfield at Kabul, where the surrounding fields are still littered with the debris of destroyed Soviet aircraft. My sense of ruin is complete.

I return to England. I am racked by feelings of guilt at what I have seen of a conflict to which the world is largely indifferent, and experience shock and loathing at the comforts of ordinary life back home. In Afghanistan I have lived surrounded by random death, destruction and misery of every kind, and am mystified at why people in England, a country at peace, seem so very miserable.

The Network's operation in Afghanistan has died. There is nothing more that can be done. As time passes I make my peace with ordinary life, and my hopes of seeing Manny again harden into a knot of despair. I refuse to believe he is dead, and he haunts me like the phantom limb of an amputee. There is not a day that passes when I do not think of him. I know in the deepest part of myself that one day, somewhere, I will find him, or his corpse, and be free of this pain, which is like a barrier between me and life, and through which all my experience is unwillingly filtered. When I experience moments of joy, I wish Manny were there to share them; when I am stalked by misery, I think of the difficulties and loneliness he must be having to face. He is my closest friend. With Manny I have shared the unforgettable intimacy of being alive – not only with the personal intensity that war or a shared love can bring to a friendship, but with the greater and impersonal love born of being in the service of something wholly bigger than us both.

The Baroness offers me a new role. While I start my landscaping business, finding consolation in working with nature, I'm given the task of advising and instructing new recruits to the Network. In London I teach the rudiments of counter-surveillance and field codes to a small number of men and women who will operate in places I don't know about.

One afternoon I'm in Selfridges to demonstrate the use of switchback escalators as a surveillance trap. The idea is to carefully clock the faces of travellers on a lower escalator, 'trapping' them into becoming visible. Part of good counter-surveillance is not giving any indication that you suspect you're being followed, which means techniques like stopping to tie shoelaces or peering at reflections in shop windows are never really used, and the switchback configuration of escalators in big department stores is one of the few ordinary means to see who's behind you without having to turn around in the manner of a fugitive. But life is so strange you couldn't make it up. I'm just wondering about a good way to challenge the three pairs of young watchers trying to keep up with me when I spot a striking-looking woman on the escalator below. I follow her, deciding that I'll demonstrate to my watchers impromptu techniques for getting the telephone number of a perfect stranger. I catch up with the woman I've chosen on an upper floor. She's flicking through clothes on a rail, and already I'm thinking of a story about being a designer and how, if she loves those designs, she'll love the line I've designed, which is about to be launched. But she's unexpectedly beautiful, and has the predatory gaze of a panther, and I've already fallen under the spell of her feline power and grace. I make a joke about the colour of a dress she's considering. She's American, it turns out, and within a few seconds she asks me the question that takes

English people months to get around to, enquiring what line of business I'm in.

'I teach spies how to pick up good-looking foreign women.'

'Saw you coming,' she says.

And perhaps she did. I manage to get her phone number, but I haven't had to tell a single lie. Six months later we're married, and our first child is soon on the way. But we're not happy. I've been blinded by her beauty and energy, and have failed to notice a cruel streak that makes all the other cruel people I've met seem like Good Samaritans. My attempt at family life turns out to be a multiplying sequence of disasters, and my wife is destructively angry at the whole of life. She's angry at England, angry at the English, angry at my friends and angry at me. One day, before I've lost all hope for the relationship, I call her mother in America to ask why her daughter is so angry.

'Angry?' she laughs chillingly. 'She was born angry.'

I'm two years back into life as a bachelor when the Baroness calls an urgent meeting. I drive from London to Chevening House, where she occasionally holds quiet gatherings with members of the Foreign Office. With her are two nameless officials who are eager to know my assessment of a piece of intelligence just received by the Americans. It's single-threaded, meaning it comes from only one source, and as such would normally be unaction-able. But it's so hot the CIA is screaming for help to assess its authenticity, and has turned to its allies for advice. The source suggests that a summit meeting is about to be held in Afghanistan involving all the leading jihadist commanders currently in the country. Bin Laden, who's on the ascendant, is planning to be there himself, and the Americans need to decide how to act. Based on everything I've learned from Orpheus's reports, I confirm that the details seem credible, and that the location and the names of the parties involved are consistent with what I know. The officials thank me for my contribution.

Later, I stroll with the Baroness through the grounds, and we walk to the green boathouse on the northern edge of the lake. We sit on a small bench. 'I thought I should tell you first,' she says as we look across the water. I feel a momentary sense of dread as she speaks these words, and I remember how at that moment my eyes fall on the dark green calfskin gloves she is wearing, and how her hands are folded in her lap. 'There's a rumour,' she goes on, 'of an Englishman operating in one of bin Laden's groups. He's been in prison in Chechnya for a year, which makes him a bit of a hero. The Americans felt they should share it with us.' She pauses, then speaks again before I can ask the question. 'They don't have a name, but apparently he's called the Christian commander, based on a military operation he led in the time of the jihad against the Soviets.' Then she turns to me with a slight smile. 'They remember that sort of thing, don't they?'

I hardly dare believe it. Despite periods of numbing doubt I have never fully believed he was dead. It strikes me that the east, where fate put us together like a cosmic matchmaker, is now delivering him back to me.

The Baroness has read my mind again. 'I know,' she says with a look that suggests she understands how much the news means to me. 'We need to get you back there. I shall have to arrange a context.'

My mind's racing, then comes to a sudden halt at a dark thought. 'It's been a long time,' I say. 'We don't know what's happened to him in the meantime.'

'He should come in. You either bring him back,' says the Baroness quietly, looking across the water, 'or you deal with the situation on the ground as you see fit. You were his best friend, and it must be for you to decide.'

It's February and I realise I've forgotten that the next day is my birthday.

8

It's now Saturday, five days after my temporary incarceration with Billy, the Face and the charming colonel with the nice green beret. My rib still hurts when I take a deep breath or laugh, and my eye has a purplish corona around it which gives me a slightly menacing look that I enjoy. It's time for another briefing with Seethrough and, as promised, he's laid on transport.

At dusk I drive with H to the outskirts of Hereford, where we board a black Puma helicopter fitted with additional fuel tanks and passenger seats around the sides. It's run by the best specialist pilots from the RAF and is called the Special Duties Flight, part of the Firm's special operations capability. It's the limousine of helicopters, says H, and rattles much less than others because it's maintained more diligently and they actually take the trouble to tighten up all the nuts and bolts. Even the pilot sounds quite posh. It's the Firm's preferred means of transport between London, Hereford and Fort Monckton on the coast, where among other things, H now tells me, he occasionally teaches the finer points of MOE – covert methods of entry – to selected aspirants, based on the exceptional talents of his mentor, a Major Freddy Mace.

We belt ourselves in and H gives a thumbs up to the loadmaster, who makes sure everything is properly stowed. The aircraft winds into the air and swoops south-east. I watch the Cotswolds race past beneath us as we roar at spectacularly low altitude towards London and over a carpet of glittering lights to a heliport that I didn't know existed. It hangs over the Thames not far from Battersea and is marked LONDON in big illuminated white letters. I can't imagine why anyone who already knows how to fly a helicopter to Battersea might need to be reminded of this, and H is none the wiser.

A squat and pale-faced driver meets us and whisks us along Battersea Park Road in a powerful Vauxhall. A few minutes later the towers of Legoland, bathed in orange light, loom up ahead of us. We draw to a stop alongside the building beneath a security barrier where our IDs are checked, and descend into an underground car park.

I recognise Stella, Seethrough's secretary, who's there to meet us. I wonder whether this timid-looking Moneypenny, whose face and manner are so very forgettable and who asks us meekly whether we've had a pleasant journey, has perhaps just come up from the subterranean ops room where she's been assisting the running of some far-off minor war. I'm tempted to make a joke and ask how saving the world has been for her today, but keep silent as she leads us to a row of capsule-like doors, runs her card through the reader and admits us to the lift.

Seethrough is ready for us upstairs with a briefing list of three items. The first is the latest imagery from our Cousins, as he calls the Americans. He unrolls two poster-sized satellite photographs of astonishingly high resolution and clarity, and military topographic maps that cover the same area.

For the first time we have the thrill of studying our target: a huge, medieval-looking fort with four giant turrets, nestling in the mountains north-west of Kandahar. In its cellars are the Stinger missiles that the Cousins have paid their tribal agents so handsomely to gather together. At the going rate, a minimum of $100,000 per missile, there's over ten million dollars' worth of them stashed in the fort, according to the TRODPINT reports. Some have been bought from the same commanders to whom they were originally supplied, others from profiteering middlemen, and others from the Taliban themselves. A few have been smuggled into Pakistan and spirited away by the CIA, who maintain a light aircraft at Peshawar airport for this very purpose.

An Afghan TRODPINT member will be assigned to help us reach the target, explains Seethrough. More on that in a few minutes, he says. Our job, he reminds us, is to find a good enough pretext to be in the area, to OP the fort from a distance, get inside and verify the serial numbers of the missiles, and then destroy them. We will receive a notice to move when the weather is clear enough for post-strike analysis and BDA by satellite.

I can't remember what BDA stands for.

'Battle damage assessment,' interjects H.

The maps will travel back to Hereford with H, who will study the terrain and draw up a list of our requirements, while I'm to work on our cover plan.

Secondly, I have a forty-eight-hour visit to the US.

'Go and see your kids,' says Seethrough, 'and in your spare time you can have a chat with the ops chap from CTC, who'll brief you on the set-up from their point of view and show you how to find the serial number on a Stinger. Your flight's tonight.' He hands me my travel documents and a hotel reservation in Washington. 'They want you there at night for some reason,' he says. Then he hands the rolled-up photographs and maps to H.

'Want to look those over while I have a word?' He gestures to another table. H obliges by moving across the room and Seethrough retrieves a file with multicoloured tabs poking out of it and opens it in front of me.

'Recognise anybody?' he asks.

It's a shock because I had thought him dead. He looks much older in the photograph but I do recognise him. It's Gemayel, grey-haired now but unmistakable.

'He's become a big fish since you last saw him,' says Seethrough. 'Must have cut a deal and agreed to act as a source.' That, he explains, is how these things work. Since I last saw him, nearly ten years earlier, Gemayel has become the chief financial officer

147

of a Middle Eastern organisation with a wide popular influence. The Americans call it a terrorist organisation, but in the British government nobody can decide whether it's got anything to do with terrorists or not, so we maintain contact. Gemayel is now in charge of its global funding network, and has kept open a channel back to the Firm, making him 'onside' in Seethrough's parlance. He's evidently been living in South America, where for some reason most of the organisation's funds are funnelled and then redistributed. A few years ago he resurfaced in Beirut at the highest level of the organisation's architecture, and since then has survived two assassination attempts by the Israeli intelligence service.

'Still with me?' asks Seethrough.

I nod, though it's all getting stranger by the minute.

'Most of the chatter we're getting about Stinger purchases is coming out of the Sudan. Gemayel has an area-wide network based in the capital Khartoum. We on the other hand have precisely one operational officer, whose identity is already declared. What we need is for Gemayel to ask his people to listen out for noises about the Stingers. That way we can at least do some eliminating. He may be onside, but we can't do a face-to-face with one of our known people without Mossad breathing down our necks. So when you're back from America I thought you could talk to him and rekindle the spark. You've got the perfect excuse of wanting to catch up after all these years.'

'I can remind him of our happy days together.'

'Precisely,' says Seethrough, taking me up on the irony.

'Let's say he agrees. What does he get out of it?'

'He gets to keep his head,' says Seethrough soberly, and turns the pages in the file to an IMMEDIATE-level CX report from Lebanon station. It bears the secret router indicator ACTOR, indicating that no one outside the Firm is allowed to see it. It's addressed to the head of the Global CT controllerate, which is Seethrough, and the security caveat reads: UK TOP SECRET

/DELICATE SOURCE. But it's the subject title that shocks: PROPOSED ASSASSINATION OF ELIAS RASHID GEMAYEL BY ISRAELI SECURITY SERVICES.

I scan down the page. The Israelis, if the report is to be believed, are planning to kill Gemayel with an explosive charge in his mobile phone placed by one of his own security staff. They've managed to buy one of Gemayel's own bodyguards, and the plan is to be carried out later this month, when Gemayel returns from Rome to Beirut and will receive a new mobile phone. In exchange for this deadly snippet of information, Seethrough is hoping that Gemayel will pass on whatever his people can find out about the Stinger purchases.

'Fair trade, don't you think?' says Seethrough, pursing his lips and raising his eyebrows in his signature gesture of enquiry.

'The Israelis won't be too happy when you give away their plan,' I say.

'You win some, you lose some. Par for the course. They know that. Though I shall probably be denied that marvellous Mossad cheesecake from now on.'

There are some further details, which I struggle with because my head is spinning a bit from all this. I'm given the name of my CIA Counterterrorist Center contact and a phone number to memorise for when I'm in Washington. There's also a backup number for use with a PIN and a code name in case I can't use the mobile and need to call London. The rest is transparent, he says. I'm on a trip to see my children. The hotel is paid for, but any other expenses, he reminds me with a cynical glance of regret, are not deductible.

I dread America. More correctly, I dread the prospect of seeing my ex, who holds my children hostage there, and makes it as difficult as she possibly can for me to spend time with them by skilfully inflicting the maximum psychological damage on me when I'm at my most vulnerable. It seems unfair to indict an entire nation on the behaviour of a single woman, but the feeling of anxiety returns to me whenever I board a plane to the US, and is countered only by my excitement at the prospect of seeing my kids. It's the emotional see-saw between these two extremes that's hard to manage, like the toxins and antitoxins administered by professional torturers to their victims.

Flying west, time goes backwards, so I have the strange experience of arriving at Dulles airport an hour or so after I've left England. According to local time, on my arrival it's 1 a.m. At the immigration desk a uniformed officer glances humourlessly at the bruise above my eye.

'You should see the other guy,' I say.

He runs my green card, which isn't green, through a reader, stamps my passport, and a grin comes over his face as he hands them back.

'Welcome home, buddy. It's a lot safer here.'

Which is comforting, because I'm already nervous at the prospect of encountering my ex.

I have no checked baggage and pass into the arrivals hall, where I scan for a driver holding up a sign with the name of a forgettable business written on it. He looks like a former soldier, to judge from his haircut and the muscles squeezed into his tight black suit.

'Welcome to Washington DC, sir,' he says after we exchange innocuous-sounding pass phrases. We walk outside to a line of waiting cars and he opens the rear door of a capacious four-wheel-drive Chevrolet with darkened windows. On the far side of the back seat is the ops officer from the Counterterrorist Center. I haven't been sure what kind of person to expect, but this isn't it.

At first I see only the hat, an expensive-looking dark Stetson with a leather braid around the base of the crown. I see the dark blue blazer, the starched white shirt and the jeans and cowboy boots. Then I take in the long blonde hair falling over the shoulders. The Stetson tilts up, and I'm looking into the face of a good-looking woman of about fifty, whose features break into a gleaming smile that makes me freeze momentarily in surprise.

'Howdy, amigo,' she says with unexpected earnestness. 'You look like you never saw a cowgirl before.'

This is quite possibly true. I'm stammering for a reply.

'Just not this late in the evening.'

'Well, better late than never,' she says. 'You ready to saddle up?'

I climb aboard and we shake hands. There's a Germanic-looking strength to her face, softened by the fairness of her hair and skin. Her jaw is square and tapers towards a prominent chin, and the thinness of her lips suggests a masculine hardness. I feel the steely quality of her gaze on me, as if she's assessing the nerve of her guest. We follow the convention, adhered to in certain circles, of first names only.

'Good to meet you, Tony. Heard good things about you. I'm Grace.' She leans forward to the driver. 'Full chisel, Mike.' An opaque glass screen rises between us and the driver, muffling a hiss of static as he radios the news of our departure to wherever we're going. The car surges forward and we merge into the river of lights flowing along the Dulles Access Toll Road, heading towards Tyson's Corner.

'It's a pleasure to be here,' I say, 'but do you mind if I ask why it has to be at night?'

'God, you English are so darn polite.' She laughs. 'Course you can. I understand your time here is short. I booked you for the night so's we can keep our appointment in Afghanistan. Time zone there is nine and a half hours ahead of us.'

'We're going to talk to someone who's in Afghanistan?'

'Better than that. But I hate to spoil a surprise.' She clips an ID card to my jacket pocket. 'When were you last in-country?' I'm assuming by this she means Afghanistan, not America.

'About four years ago.'

'De-mining outfit, right?'

I nod.

'Ever meet Massoud?'

'Twice.'

'Like him?'

'I never thought he was a saint, but you can't not admire him,' I say.

'Hell of a guy,' she agrees. 'Wish I could be there now. Kind of place that gets its claws into you. Ran four missions to our friend up north. Hell, I'm an honorary male Afghan.'

It's hard to imagine. Massoud's base of operations in the Panjshir valley and the northernmost province of Afghanistan called Badakhshan aren't the easiest or safest places to travel. They're the only portions of the country yet to fall to the Taliban, and are doggedly defended by Massoud and his dedicated soldiers. I travelled along the dirt roads of the region and through its spectacular mountain passes and valleys on de-mining surveys for the trust. Now Massoud's ailing forces, squeezed between the Taliban's inexorable advance from the south and the frontier of Tajikistan to the north, are fighting for survival. I've guessed that the CIA has sent advisers to the area to liaise with Massoud, the Taliban's final opponent, but I never imagined that a woman was among them.

'Choppered out of Tajikistan last year with a few of the boys on an Mi-8 that was damn near ready to fall apart. There was a few times I thought we were all fixin' to eat dirt,' she says, grinning at some recollection of peril, 'but Massoud looked after us best he could. Didn't seem to mind my being a woman.'

I ask if she thinks Massoud will survive the Taliban's advance.

'I don't rightly want to think about it,' she says. 'He's the last chance that darn country's got. If the Taliban take the north and Massoud has to ride out on a rail, Afghanistan's going to become one giant threat matrix that's going to break everybody's balls.'

'Not yours, I take it,' I say.

She laughs. 'All depends. If the State Department keeps up its no-account fantasy of cosying up to the Taliban and we don't get a result soon on Obi-Wan, then yes, mine too.'

Obi-Wan, I'm assuming, is her pet name for Osama bin Laden, a mild-mannered Saudi playboy turned anti-American jihadist. The Western world has hardly heard of him.

'Had him in our sights a couple of times, but you have to promise me you'll keep that dry. We even figured Massoud's boys could do the job for us, but he'd take a whole heap of grief for it if anyone found out we'd sponsored it. Nobody in the Muslim world wants to be known for killing their very own Mahatma Gandhi.'

It's not a comparison I would have thought of. But it's true that bin Laden is beginning to be seen as a kind of hero in the Islamic world, and his message of defiance against American domination is catching on.

Our shared respect for Massoud has broken the ice between us, though there's not much to break because she's so refreshingly outspoken. I'm enjoying the contrast between talking to her and the tight-lipped Seethrough, who only shares information when he has to. We talk as the car heads along Dolley Madison Boulevard towards Maclean. Grace works for a secret unit within the already secret Counterterrorist Center, dedicated for the past couple of years to tracking and, if possible, capturing bin Laden and bringing him to trial for his role in the bombing of the American embassies in Kenya and Tanzania. After having been hounded out of his native Saudi Arabia and then, under American pressure, from Sudan, he's set up in Afghanistan. There he can move freely between his devotees' training camps and preach his messianic message to all who'll listen, though few of his fans are themselves Afghans.

'What are the chances of getting him?' I ask.

'Take away some of the more hare-brained schemes and we've still got a good option set,' she says. The technology to launch a cruise missile strike against bin Laden is all there. There are submarines in the Persian Gulf ready to unleash their weapons. But the White House can't afford to repeat the spectacularly inconsequential strikes that took place in response to the African bombings in 1998, when a hundred million dollars' worth of cruise missiles were fired into one of bin Laden's training camps, where he was said to be holding a jihadist summit meeting. Twenty or thirty volunteer fighters, mostly Pakistanis, were killed as the missiles blasted the Afghan dust and rock. Bin Laden, it is said, had left the meeting a few hours earlier. But the failure gave him the best publicity for his cause that he could have dreamed of. Now the political climate isn't right for another strike in any case. At the time, says Grace, the great American public was really only interested in one thing: the contents of Monica Lewinsky's cheeks.

For legal and constitutional reasons, the CIA cannot sponsor or assist the assassination of an individual. They can, however, capture him. But bin Laden is both elusive and careful. His closest guards are not Afghans but Arabs, hard-core fighters from jihadist campaigns around the world. He is frequently on the move. At his compound in Tarnak near Kandahar, every inch of which has been scrutinised by Grace's team, there are women and children, another reason to rule out further cruise missile strikes. Earlier hopes of enlisting Massoud's men to kill bin Laden are dwindling, and the director of the CIA, the DCI, won't approve American intervention on the ground. It's been tried and failed. The White House and State Department, who between themselves are too dumb, says Grace, to tell a skunk from a house cat, are so tied up in legal knots they can't formulate a coherent policy towards Afghanistan.

'But there is a plan,' she says. 'We're going to fire up the intelligence collection on bin Laden all around the country, and with the help of Massoud's informers and agents the net will surely close. Doesn't too much matter if it's Massoud's boys, SF, the Paks or the Uzbeks who bring him in,' she says. 'Doubt if it'll be special forces who'll get it done,' she adds with a scoff. 'You could put bin Laden in a room with a Seal and a Delta and they'd kill each other before they even noticed him.' But it's clear what she's hoping. The successful capture of bin Laden will convince the White House to supply Massoud with greater levels of military supplies and put political pressure on the Taliban leadership. Only then might they give up on their designs to control the entire country.

'It's a tough row to hoe,' says Grace, 'but it's the only hope there is to roll back the Taliban and all the hotheads fixing to spread jihad across the universe. Sure would make a world of difference if we had one good asset inside Obi-Wan's camp.'

At the mention of this I look away, lest anything in my expression betray my thoughts. She can have no idea that my best friend has been assigned to this very task – nor that I have no idea whether he is alive or dead.

We turn left off Dolley Madison into a quiet road lined with trees. About a hundred yards along there's a security post and a chevroned barrier. The windows come down and our IDs are entered into an electronic log by a guard, who peers inside the car and acknowledges Grace with a nod and a smile. The barrier lifts and the road curves to the left. There are trees on one side and an enormous car park on the other, beyond which the main complex of buildings rises like a giant cake with layers of cream and chocolate. Footpaths lit by miniature lamp posts snake between the buildings and lend a faint suggestion of amusement park. Grace sees me looking.

'Somebody up there loves you, Tony.' I'm not at all sure what she means.

'On the seventh floor, I mean. That's where the clearance comes from. These boys don't let too many people see the toys they're playing with.'

We loop around another vast parking lot and drive past smaller clusters of buildings until we come to a halt by a building surrounded by thick woods. As we get out of the car, Grace shifts her belt and adjusts what is probably a holster under her blazer. She's tall and lean and walks like a man.

'Come and meet the Manson family,' she says, and we enter the building, press our IDs against a reader and enter a second door marked AUTHORIZED PERSONNEL ONLY.

About a dozen men and three women are in the briefing room, clustered around tables and overlooked by a giant blank screen. Grace shepherds me around with a series of first-name introductions. The majority are guarded in their manner, a few look puzzled to see a foreigner, and one or two fail to conceal their suspicion. I have the distinct feeling they are not accustomed to outsiders.

The exception is a portly middle-aged man wearing thick glasses, who I meet more or less by accident as I help myself, at Grace's suggestion, to a cup of coffee. He's ahead of me and nearly bumps into me as he turns around, and as if by reflex introduces himself. His face seems to be frozen in a perpetual grin. He mentions only his name and the acronym of the organisation to which he's attached before launching into his job description. It pours out in a low drawl with infrequent pauses. He looks at me only occasionally, preferring to rest his eyes on a point somewhere near my left shoulder. His field is 'fixed and dynamic target source analysis', a subject on which I now feel obliged to appear knowledgeable.

His main task is prioritising and occasionally deconflicting ISR input from assets on the ground, he says, so that the sequence F2T2EA – find, fix, track, target, engage – commonly known as the kill chain, can run more smoothly. I nod sagely. He advises on kinetic collateral damage assessment and target restrictions based on operation-specific ROE, LOAC, the RTL and the NSL.

'I don't remember all those,' I say. 'Remind me.'

'Rules of Engagement, Law of Armed Conflict, Restricted Target List and No-Strike List.' He takes a sip from his coffee. He's proud, he says, to be pushing the envelope on new protocols for mensuration software algorithms and datum management. But he's lost me now. I'm relieved when Grace comes to my rescue and guides me over to some of the others. One is a tall man called Rich, who greets me briefly with formal authority before turning back to the conversation he's in.

'You just met the biggest toad in the pond,' whispers Grace approvingly.

A few minutes pass before the assembly is complete, and there's a resonant tapping on the PA system, which prompts us all to sit. The room darkens.

A young technician explains, for the benefit of those of us who aren't familiar with tonight's technology, how it is that we're able to watch a live feed of imagery from Afghanistan. The screen above him flickers into life and displays a description of a Special Access Program called Afghan Eyes and the unmanned aircraft system that makes it possible: the Predator RQ-1.

A picture appears of a military-looking trailer with a satellite dish on its roof, called a ground control station, currently at an airfield in Uzbekistan, north of the Afghan border across the Amu Darya river. It's from here, it now dawns on me, that the images we are about to watch are being beamed. Inside it are a pilot and a payload operator, who direct and control the unmanned aircraft by what is called knob control.

I can't resist a sideways glance at Grace on hearing this expression, and am glad to see she's got the joke too, and signals the fact with the faintest of smiles.

While the technician reels off the equipment's characteristics, more pictures appear on the screen. The Predator itself is a long thin aircraft with weird-looking, downward-pointing tail fins that give the impression that it's flying upside down like an injured fish. It has retractable landing gear, which enables it to take off and land like an ordinary plane. It has a camera in its nose, a sensor turret and a multi-spectral targeting system. It also has an infrared camera for use at night, synthetic aperture radar to see through smoke or cloud and listening devices for picking up radio signals in its vicinity. It's a technological marvel, invisible and inaudible from the ground, and to judge from the hypnotised expressions on the audience, it impresses them as much as it impresses me. A newer version, we're told, is under development, which will enable multi-role operations. Instead of just looking at things, in other words, it will be able to shoot at them with laser-guided missiles.

Then comes the near-miraculous moment when the small square at the bottom of the screen is suddenly expanded, and we're looking at live video from a Predator's nose. Spinning numbers at the edge of the screen give the aircraft's position, heading and the time. I imagine the images will be still ones, but the video is as good as television and the impression is almost supernatural.

We are in the south-east of the country, near the border of Pakistan's Federally Administered Tribal Areas and what the British used to call the North-West Frontier. To the Pakistanis, it's Waziristan; to the Pashtuns, for whom the border has never really existed since the British imposed it a hundred years earlier, it's still Afghanistan.

The Predator is circling silently above a potential target designated by a tracking team on the ground. It's a mud-walled compound typical of the region, and the feed shows several parked vehicles in a courtyard and a single man emerging from a doorway. The angle of view is not from directly overhead so unlike an aerial photograph we can see the place in two dimensions. The man is wearing Afghan clothes and, by the looks of it, a waistcoat, but no turban. For a few moments all our eyes are on him. Then he stoops down and reaches for something on the ground. The camera is almost still. It's surreal. From 7,000 miles away, we're watching a Pashtun housekeeper sweep the dust from the doorway of his house.

A few moments later he stands up and runs across the courtyard towards the entrance gates. Behind them, two squat Russian jeeps have pulled up, and I imagine the characteristic single-tone horn of the forward jeep that has interrupted the housekeeper's task. I imagine the metallic clang of the gate as it sweeps open and the smell of dust and diesel as the jeeps enter the courtyard and park. Several men descend from the vehicles and are joined by two others from inside the house, one of whom is steadying his turban on his head as he comes out. They greet their visitors in turn. We can even see the fluttering of the untied ends of their turbans in the wind. Even at this distance the formalised solemnity of their gestures is somehow communicated, and I can almost hear the ritual exchange of blessings as they embrace, touching chests rather than shaking hands, in the timeless Afghan fashion. They carry no weapons. Who are these men? Traders? Government members? Brothers or friends? Terrorists? I will never ever know.

We hear the distorted electronic voice of the Predator pilot over the loudspeakers as he receives instructions from two men wearing headsets sitting at the back of the room at computers. They are searching for a single man in a country the other side of the world, hoping to encounter the visual signature by which bin Laden has now become known: a convoy of Land Cruisers and armed bodyguards. I'm filled with a feeling akin to awe at the effort and technological genius that makes this spectacle possible. It is matched only by private concern at the fragility of the search, which will only ever be as reliable as the informers inside the country providing the likely targets. I imagine the temptation faced by an Afghan informer, seduced by bagfuls of hundred-dollar bills, to select targets merely to please his handlers because he knows this is what is expected of him and guarantees the next instalment. But I dare not express my cynicism.

For several hours we stare at the images as they filter from the heavens onto our screen, following suspect cars and trucks along remote mountain roads and peering from afar into the private worlds of our unsuspecting quarries with angelic, or perhaps demonic, omnipotence. It's 4 a.m. when Grace taps my arm and suggests we cut a trail back to my hotel. We shake hands in parting with a few of the remaining station members as we make for the door.

'Really appreciate your input,' says one of them, although I haven't given any.

Our driver is summoned on a walkie-talkie and we speed into the city along the Memorial Parkway with the Potomac on our left. Grace asks me for my thoughts.

'Very impressive,' I tell her, then feel I should say more. 'It's a dedicated team.'

'Sure makes you feel all-overish looking at those images, doesn't it? You don't think we're barking at a knot with all that technology?' She sighs and speaks again before I can answer. 'I can tell you do, and you're right. I'll admit there's a few hotheads in the family who want the glory of nailing bin Laden in some Tom Clancy black op. They don't give a damn what happens in Afghanistan. Way I see it, the Company's a strategic entity not a tactical one. You can't do strategy with a motorised buzzard, even if it can see in the goddamned dark.' She peers from the window. 'Same goes for the DIA's data-mining programmes. We can analyse the conversations of every member of every jihad chat room across the world. We can listen to their phones 24/7. We could hear them talking in their sleep if we really wanted to. But it'll never tell us what they're really thinking. You gotta be there to know that.'

We pull up outside the Hilton on Connecticut Avenue.

'Here,' she says, leans towards me and stretches out her arm. For just a second I'm not sure what her intentions are, until she unclips the ID from my jacket pocket. 'I'd better take that. I'll pick you up at 6 p.m. tomorrow and we'll go through some details.'

'I'm seeing my kids in the morning,' I tell her.

'How do you get along with their mother?'

'I don't. She doesn't exactly make it easy for me.'

'Give her hell,' she says with a grin.

*　　*　　*

It's a brilliantly clear and cold morning, and the sky is a luminously bright blue. I haven't had much sleep but force myself to run a few miles, dropping into Rock Creek Park to get off the streets. When I run in England, I see no one. Here there's a steady stream of joggers and bikers in the latest running gear, and I feel distinctly shabby by comparison. Everything they wear is new. In my crumpled T-shirt and three-year-old trainers with holes beginning to show at the toes, I'm definitely not up to local standards. There are men dressed head-to-toe in body-hugging Lycra, women in pink tracksuits with their dogs, and octogenarians with miniature dumb-bells, which they lift as they trot along. Husband-and-wife teams tow their babies behind their bicycles in prams with suspension systems and disc brakes. I feel as though I've strayed into the recreation area of an insane asylum.

After a shower back at the hotel I pick up the phone with a familiar sense of dread and call my ex. The phone is answered by her new husband, to whom good luck. He's civil and has the annoying habit of saying 'Stand by' when asking me to hold the line. I ask to speak to my older daughter.

'Stand by,' he says. He's too stupid to realise I've been standing by for years. But it's not my daughter who comes on the line.

'Hello, Anthony,' says my ex with scarcely disguised contempt. 'You said you would call at ten.'

'Sorry about that. I'm a bit jet-lagged, actually.'

'Well that's alright,' she says. 'We're used to your excuses. But in future lateness is unacceptable. You may think you can swan in from England and expect everyone else to change their plans, but from now on you're going to have to modify your behaviour.'

'I just want to see the girls for a few hours,' I say.

'Well if you're not here by eleven you won't find us.'

The line goes dead. As much as I try, every time, to prepare myself for this kind of treatment, it never fails to have the intended effect.

Half an hour later I'm at the front door of their house in Chevy Chase, thanking God it's Sunday and the traffic has allowed me to reach the house in time. I ask the taxi to wait because I don't want to get into an argument, which I will inevitably lose. There's a silver Mercedes SUV and a convertible BMW in the driveway beside the perfect lawn.

I kneel as the girls run out and throw themselves at me, nearly knocking me over. They've both grown since I saw them in the summer and I can hardly believe how changed they are. The sight of them brings a lump to my throat but I daren't let my feelings show. I'm being watched from the doorway by their mother, who glowers at me as if there's a tramp in the driveway.

'Jesus. You look like you've been in a bar brawl. That's not an appropriate impression to give in public.'

'Yes, it does hurt, actually. Thanks for asking.'

'Make sure you're back by three. We've given up a family afternoon for this. And no sugar. They're not allowed candy, whatever you may think is alright in England.'

There's no response I can give to any of this, so we pile into the taxi.

'Alright, girls, where to? We can go to China to see pandas, buffalo racing in India, or we can go to the North Pole and hunt reindeer. Or if you're both very good, we can go and have waffles with maple syrup and loads of whipped cream.'

There's a chorus of approving giggles at the suggestion. We head for a diner and repeat the usual ritual of waffles and hot chocolate. I watch them eat, and the sight fills me with joy. But the thought that they're growing up so far from their father is like a knife in me at the same time. We catch up on news about the pond which we built together the previous summer. There's now a family of newts, the tadpoles have turned into frogs, the goldfish are fattening up and there's a big duck with a red beak from the farm across the road who comes and has a morning wash, but the last time he came the pond was frozen over so he slipped and fell on his duck bottom and couldn't figure out what was happening. The goldfish, all of whose names they both remember, will be too fat to fit in the pond by the time I next come to America to see them, I say.

'Did you catch the mouse?' asks the younger. I'd forgotten about the mouse.

'I caught him and put him in the garden,' I say. 'But he came back. He prefers his home behind the kitchen cupboards. But maybe we can catch him again when you next come to England and train him. Think mice can learn the violin?' She giggles.

'Mummy says you only come to America on business,' says the older one.

This is crushing news because it's so untrue. I've never been to America on business, with the exception of this trip, which is hardly business. I can't bring myself to say their mother is lying to them.

'Well, perhaps Mummy doesn't know everything. I always come to America to see you both because I love you and I miss you. And, well ... because you can't get such amazing waffles in England.'

We walk south a few blocks, hand in hand, to the zoo, where we seek out the animals we know from the Just So Stories. They stand inches from an elephant, peer wide-eyed at the snakes in their glass enclosures and make faces at a white-cheeked gibbon.

The penguins steal the show.

It's cold and we make for the diner for a top-up of hot chocolate. It's only when we're on the way home again that I realise one of the girls has lost a mitten. There'll be hell to pay but there's no time to retrace our steps. A renewed feeling of dread replaces that of joy as we return to the house.

'Typical,' snarls their mother from the far side of the front door. 'I can't leave them with you for a single afternoon without something going wrong.' I do not know what drives this cruelty. I don't contest it because the girls are looking up at me, wondering whether they should say goodbye, and their faces waver between smiles and expressions of concern.

'By the way,' says their mother, 'there's riding camp for two weeks in August. You can see them for the last week of the month and we can do make-up time the following summer.'

'I only have three weeks with the girls this summer. It's my only chance to have a proper holiday with them. I can't fly them to England for just a week. I don't think it's a good idea.'

There's a tightening of her jaw and a renewed look of contempt.

'Fine. If that's how selfish you want to be. I shouldn't have expected anything different from you. We can make things difficult too.'

I have no reply to this, so I kiss the girls goodbye, and they step beyond the threshold under their mother's arm and disappear. Then, as I'm walking back to the taxi, the door opens again and the two of them race out to me for a final hug.

There is a strategy, I've discovered, to manage the feeling of devastation I experience when I leave my kids. I put my mind on something different and force it to stay there until the feeling subsides. There's a radiating sensation of grief in my chest which I know will pass if I let it run its course. I need in the meantime to get back to another world where my feelings cannot be allowed to run riot. As the taxi rolls back to the hotel past the manicured lawns of the perfect homes of Chevy Chase, I force myself to the meeting I'll be having later with Grace. I wonder what level of clearance she's been authorised to read me onto. I've had top secret clearance since Seethrough reinstated me with the Firm, but it doesn't mean I'm automatically cleared for what the Americans call an SCI or sensitive compartmented information, or for SAPs – special access programmes, like the Predator missions, the very existence of which is classified.

As a British citizen I can't get top secret clearance in the US, but can be granted a limited access authorization if it can be shown, which it obviously has been, that a clearable US citizen isn't available for the same job. This allows me to be read onto the relevant SCIs. The rest is NTK or need to know, which limits access to whatever is necessary for carrying out the task involved. Seethrough has smoothed the process through with his counterparts at Langley, and as Grace has reminded me, somebody loves me on the seventh floor. Clearance isn't in itself secret, and may even lapse after a given period. But one's accountability to it is for life. It's a disturbing thought. I'm comforted by the paradoxical knowledge that at the highest levels of all, as exemplified by the Baroness's dealings, there's no such thing as clearance at all, nor any paperwork to support it. Or to deny it. Just conversations in quiet rooms, on benches in public parks, and words exchanged in chance meetings that quite probably never happened.

I have good intentions to go for a swim in the hotel pool, but instead collapse on the bed and sleep fitfully for an hour before waking with a sense of panic at not knowing where I am. When I come down to the lobby, Grace is already there, reading a copy of the *Washington Post*. I see her in daylight now and realise how blue her eyes are. There's the same mixture of hardness in her gait, voice and manner, and softness when she smiles or laughs.

Grace lives alone in a neighbourhood called Adams Morgan, jokingly called Madam's Organ by its inhabitants. An inordinate number of different locks on her front door protect a narrow house on four floors, small by American standards but huge by all others. There are Persian and Turkish carpets on the floors and Georgia O'Keefe prints on the walls. Above an elaborately hand-tooled saddle on a wooden stand in a corner of the living room hang several rodeo trophies. Among a collection of family photographs, there's one of Grace shaking hands with the president and a second woman, another with the former president, another with the CIA's director George Tenet, his Levantine features offset by a pink tie, and another with the former DCI, John Deutch. A miniature flag of the state of Colorado pokes up between them. I ask who the other woman is in the photograph.

'Secretary of state,' she answers, coming over to peer at the picture. 'Stuck-up bitch. Know what she said to me? Said Massoud's a drug dealer and we can't deal with a drug dealer. Here.' She passes me a tumbler, which prompts me to look at my watch. 'Never too early for a sip of prairie dew.' Her prairie dew of choice is a twenty-one-year-old single malt matured in port casks. 'One of life's small pleasures,' she says.

I concur. We sit and cradle our glasses.

'Massoud was never cash-averse, but he's a man you can ride the river with. I sure hope we can shore him up before he has to give up his last patch of turf.'

'What do you think are the chances of that?' I ask.

'Slim,' she says. 'Mighty slim.' Then she recalls her last mission to Panjshir, and it's obvious she was impressed, like so many others, by Massoud's charisma, energy and humility.

'We were fixing him up with a hotline to Langley and a box of tricks from the NSA so's we could listen in on Taliban comms. All of a sudden there's artillery causing a ruckus down the valley and turning his men into buzzard food. Took us up to the head of the valley so's to keep us out of range, then heads back to the fight. Damn. Still found time to look after us later, making sure we were fed and warm. Son of a bitch slept on a bedroll just like a cowboy. Next day he's directing the war again and busier than a one-legged man in an ass-kicking contest.'

'God, don't make me laugh,' I protest, clutching at my rib.

'Been meaning to ask you if you've been in a fight recently,' she says.

'Just with my friends.'

'You're not your average gringo spook,' she says, chuckling as she refills our shot glasses. 'And I've met a few. Self-satisfied sons of bitches, most of them. You're not a man who lives a life of quiet desperation.'

'You're not your average cowgirl,' I say. 'Cowgirls don't quote Thoreau, for one thing.'

I ask her how she got into the spook side of life, and she surprises me by saying it's the family business. Her father, she says, was friends with 'Wild Bill' Donovan, founder of the Office of Strategic Services, the secret American organisation dedicated to espionage during the Second World War. I know that the OSS was a parallel entity to Britain's SOE, and its daring and innovative founder became a prodigy of behind-the-lines derring-do, rather as David Stirling became a legend as the founder of the SAS. Years later her father, a dedicated cold war warrior, had ended up as head of station in a number of Middle Eastern countries, in the golden days, as Grace calls them, when the Company actually had reliable human assets in the region.

I see no reason not to tell her that my father was involved with SOE, and that I'd joined the army with the vaguely romantic ambition of following in his footsteps. 'Wasn't quite the army I thought it would be,' I say. 'I had a shot at becoming a proper spook, but made the mistake of committing what they call an indiscretion. As I am now,' I say, 'by telling you this.'

'I appreciate your looseness,' she says, meaning frankness, but it's probably no coincidence that she's plying me with whisky, probably the oldest tongue-loosening technique in the book. I try to work the conversation back to Afghanistan.

'What will happen?' I ask. 'I mean if Massoud's forced out.'

'Like I said. Whole of Afghanistan'll turn into a training camp for Obi-Wan and his hotheads. Won't leave us with a lot of choice. There's a plan,' she begins, then catches herself. 'I can't talk about that, Tony. Hell, there's always a plan.'

'For America to intervene?' It's unimaginable.

'Listen.' She puts her glass on the edge of the table. 'We know al-Qaeda's trying to kill Massoud. Someone's been guarding his shoes, for crying out loud, in case they try to put a dose of anthrax in them. If they get lucky, we lose our one ally on the ground. I don't want to have to spell it out. We've been acquiring a target archive in Afghanistan for nigh on two years. We may have survived the millennium, but the system was blinking redder than a coyote's ass in heat with all the threats cables we had coming in. Most of it single-threaded and too damn vague to be actionable, but all we need is for one of them to happen on US soil, trace it back to Obi-Wan, and you know the Pentagon's going to go to work on the place.' She retrieves her glass. 'Strategic depth. You know where that gets us?'

'Up shit creek?' I offer.

'And some,' she says. 'If we piss off twenty million Afghans, we'll have a war, my friend.'

'That's a dark thought,' I say. 'It's too bizarre. The most powerful country in the world invading the poorest?'

'Darn right it's bizarre,' she says, emphasising the word as if to extract its full meaning and filling our glasses again. 'Want to know how bizarre? We fund a ten-year proxy war against the Soviets to bury the ghost of Vietnam, and a million Afghans die in the name of freedom. Then the Wall comes down and freedom says, "Adios, amigos, we're done here." Afghanistan drops off the agenda faster than butter off a hot knife and the Afghans are left to slaughter each other with the same weapons the US taxpayer's been kind enough to sponsor. Bizarre enough for you? Cut five years till the country gets taken over by a one-eyed mullah supported by our last remaining ally in the region, Pakistan. Said mullah gets it in his cracked head to play host to a tier-zero terrorist who's declared a global jihad against guess who? America. Secstate wants to climb into bed with the one-eyed mullah, just to see how the cat jumps. "We can deal with the Taliban," she says. "Massoud's history," she says. Meantime she's fine if the Russians and Iranians send him all the guns he wants so's to keep the Taliban tied up. Pentagon says, "Engage with Pakistan, maintain the strategic relationship; Massoud's a lost cause." Know why we missed Obi-Wan in the cruise strike? Know why we fired a hundred million dollars' worth of missiles to carve up a pile of fucking rocks in the Afghan desert? Because the Paks warned him. Our dearly beloved allies. Jesus

Christ, ours is not to reason why, but how bizarre does it get? Rest of the CIA thinks we're obsessed with a hot-headed playboy who's got a fatal kidney disease and what's our fucking problem? No wonder they call us the Manson family. We could've nailed the sucker last year, but the White House won't give the go-ahead in case we hit one of his Arab buddies who's about to buy ten billion bucks' worth of F-16s, and whose government is, you guessed it, the chief supplier of weapons to the Taliban. Massoud's strongest ally? The Russians, his sworn enemies for ten years. How's that for *bizarre*?'

There's not much to add to this, except that it's consistent with Afghanistan's mysterious power, despite being one of the poorest and least developed countries in the world, to affect the affairs of the world so disproportionately.

Grace sighs heavily, pours another pair of whiskies, and her mood recovers. A businesslike tone enters her voice. 'We need to talk about those Stingers.'

She retrieves a laptop computer and brings up a collection of photographs, with which I'm half-familiar from my earlier session with H, onto the screen. The photographs are labelled to show the pressure-release valves on the weapon-round containers, which need to be opened before the missiles are removed. They also show the panel on the weapons where the lot and serial numbers are to be found. These need to be listed, she says. If there are really as many missiles as we're all hoping, I'll need to allow sufficient time for finding and photographing the serial numbers.

Once I'm in Afghanistan, a member of the TRODPINT team will advise on the situation on the ground before I move to the target. He'll meet us before and after the operation and pass on a progress report to his American handler based in Pakistan. Another trusted source will brief me before we get inside the country.

She pulls up the documents on the screen, and I notice some of the security caveats on the Defense Messaging System headers.

NODIS means that the distribution of the information is strictly limited. FGI means the document contains sensitive information concerning a foreign government. X5 is one of many declassification exemptions, meaning it all stays secret longer than the assigned number of years.

The photographs appear in turn. The first is of a thin-faced handsome young man with dark features called Abdul Sattar.

'Speaks English, Pashto and Dari,' says Grace. 'I need you to check in with him before and after the operation. I need third-party confirmation that you came and went, that's all. I wouldn't trust him with more than that. Nothing operational. We've had him signed up for a year but you can be sure he knows some bad people.'

The second is an older man in his forties, with softer features and an oval-shaped elfin face.

'Name of Hamid Karzai. Comes from a good southern family,' she says as if she's talking about Tennessee rather than Kandahar. 'He was press officer for Mojaddedi in the jihad years and deputy foreign minister in Massoud's government till he had a bust-up with Massoud's intelligence chief and rode out of town. Seems he was pretty cut up about the way he was treated and hitched himself to the Taliban for a year or two. Plans took a bath when his father was killed by the Taliban last year and now he's trying to take the fight back to them in the south. He's switched on and some of us have got money on him. He'll talk your ear off, but you can trust him.' His brothers, she adds, have Afghan restaurants in San Francisco, if I ever get to craving a *qabli pilau* while I'm Stateside.

It's Karzai who will receive the money that we've been asked to deliver. The tactical details are our business. Once we're inside Afghanistan, Grace will liaise with London as and when.

'Wish I could be there with you,' she says. Then the steely look comes back into her eyes. 'I'm counting on you, Tony.'

It's after ten now. The effect of the whisky is pleasant and has anaesthetised the day's earlier worries. I've enjoyed our talk and wish it could last longer. We walk to her front door.

'There'll be a car for you in the morning,' she says.

'Thanks. You've been good to me. I'll miss all the cowboy talk.'

'Wait a second,' she says. Her hands move to her belt buckle, which she undoes hastily and begins to slide her belt out of its loops. A few seconds later I see in her outstretched hand a woven snakeskin pouch which contains a Leatherman multi-tool. 'Take this with you,' she says. 'Darn useful where you're going.' It's obviously precious to her and she looks at it thoughtfully for a moment before she hands it to me.

'The Company's lucky to have you,' I tell her. We embrace. 'Give them hell.'

'Adios, amigo,' she says.

The streets are quiet and I decide to walk and think things over on the way. I realise the secret world into which I've been allowed sits more comfortably with me now. For a month it's as if I've been in conflict over the need for secrecy and the urge to find expression for what I know. But now the two are less at odds. The work is bringing me confidence, and I'm feeling buoyed up by Grace's frank expression of faith in me. Her gift was not a calculated act, I decide. I take it out of its pouch and look it over. It's an expensive version, well made and virtually indestructible, although only the Americans could design a multi-purpose tool without a corkscrew. I pocket it again and turn it over in my hand as I walk.

In the lobby of the hotel I announce I'll be checking out in the early morning and have a brief conversation with the concierge, from whom I've earlier asked a favour. I'm tired and it's time to get some rest. But as I head for my room I pass the lounge and my attention is momentarily caught by the sight of two women perched on stools at the bar. They're hard to miss. The blonde is wearing a dress that's open from her shoulders to the small of her back, and the black woman sitting next to her is wearing equally black leather trousers that look as though they've been sprayed on her extravagantly long legs. As I'm looking, she catches my eye and smiles, then turns back to her friend.

I think involuntarily of Tintin's inseparable companion Captain Haddock, in one of his difficult moments, tormented by the contrary promptings of the angel above his right shoulder and the devil above his left.

'You've got a flight early in the morning,' says my angel.

'You're all alone and far from home,' counters my devil, 'and you can sleep on the plane. Life is short,' he adds with a wink.

'You should be tied to a mast until those sirens are out of earshot,' protests the angel.

The devil wins.

I cross the lounge and order a top-up of whisky at the bar. A pianist is coaxing mellow jazz from a grand piano, and a dozen guests are drinking at low tables from white leather chairs and couches. The barman pours the whisky with a dextrous flourish and twirls the bottle in his hand as he replaces it on the mirrored shelf.

I turn towards the women nearby as if I've only just noticed them. They are both strikingly beautiful and look at me in unison. The blonde has eyes the colour of fresh lime juice and a finely sculpted face, from which she brushes a tributary torrent of topaz-yellow hair. The black woman, whose hair is drawn back from her perfectly oval face, has the smouldering look of a tigress, and is wearing saffron-coloured lipstick as if she's pressed her lips against the soil of a volcano in her ancestral home.

'Hello, ladies,' I say, and a kaleidoscope of fanciful scenarios tumbles into my mind. I'm in the grip of that perverse longing for closeness devoid of intimacy, and my devil is suggesting a bold approach. 'If I'd known you were both here I'd have cancelled my plans for the evening.' There's an exchange of smiles, and the blonde speaks first.

'We don't talk to strangers,' she says in a tone of counterfeit coyness that suggests just the opposite. 'But we might change our minds if you introduce yourself.' She has a Southern accent which I inexplicably associate with sexual voracity. 'I'm Summer,' she says, looking me squarely in the eye as we shake hands. I resist the temptation of allowing my gaze to fall towards her chest, but it's not easy.

'Don't tell me,' I reply, looking towards her friend. 'You're Pudding.' But the joke misses its mark, evoking looks of confusion.

'Summer,' I point to them in turn, 'and Pudding. It's a special dessert we make in England. The secret is to make sure the fruit is really ripe. You have to squeeze it without bruising it. I miss it terribly. I have a permanent craving for ripe fruits of every kind.'

'Do you ever give in to your cravings?' Summer asks.

This is a green light if ever there was. They accept my suggestion to move from the bar to a table, around which we settle into soft armchairs. I order a bottle of champagne. We chat for half an hour. Summer takes the lead, and the Tigress is sultry and largely silent. They can't get over my accent, they tell me, so I make the most of that. They're matching my innuendos as fast as I can produce them. The guests fade away, and when the pianist plays a final version of 'Georgia on my Mind', we're the only ones clapping.

'It's getting late, ladies,' I say, because it's decision time. 'What does a man do in this town when it gets this late?'

'Depends what you enjoy doing most,' says Summer with a lascivious smile.

'Well, there is one thing I'm into,' I say, 'but it's not really what you'd call conventional.'

'Try us,' says Summer, dipping a finger into her champagne.

'Think I should trust you with such a private thing?' I ask.

'We won't tell,' says Summer, and puts her finger in her mouth.

The moment is definitely ripe to let them know.

'Pond life.'

'Pond life?' They giggle uncertainly.

'Ponds,' I say. 'Absolutely fascinating. The whole of life is represented in even the smallest pond. As small as this very table. Every kind of life is in it. Things that swim, run, crawl, fly, burrow and slither. I don't just mean toads and frogs and newts. Everybody loves them, right?

'Right,' says Summer, exchanging glances with her equally perplexed friend.

'Think of all the lesser creatures that people never bother to mention: water beetles, water scorpions, water fleas, damselflies, skaters, dragonfly nymphs, nematodes, flukes and tapeworms. They're all there.'

'I'm with you, kind of,' says Summer, but I can tell she's wondering where I'm going with this. Understandably.

'But it's right at the bottom of the pond where things get interesting,' I say. 'That's where all the debris sinks to, where you find all the life that has no place in ordinary pond society. There's a whole world down there with its own rules. That's where you get the mud dwellers and the scavengers, the parasites and the leeches.

'Don't get me wrong,' I say. 'Some of the creatures that live in the mud are actually beautiful, so beautiful you can't really imagine what they're doing down there.'

I'm watching their faces quite closely now. Summer is confused, but trying hard not to let it show. The Tigress is ahead of her and close to glowering at me.

'There's a family of parasitic worms, I think they're called planarians, which produce slime that allows them to move over any surface. There's little hydras which hunt by waving their tentacles around to entrap their prey. Then there's the medusa. Surely you've heard of them. They belong to the Coelenterata phylum. They're free-swimming. Free agents, you might say. Difficult to identify if you're not trained to spot them of course, but unmistakable if you know their distinguishing features.'

The girls exchange glances again, and their body language is betraying their restlessness. Neither of them is smiling any more. There's actually a frown on the face of the black woman.

'There's little crustacea. They're very active. Nocturnal too. They swim on their backs and capture their prey with their legs. Imagine that. I mean, what creature would fall for that?'

'We need to go,' says the black woman, quietly but abruptly.

'I do believe you're right,' says Summer, or whatever her name really is. The smile hasn't entirely left her face, but it's a different kind of smile now. Her lips are held tighter against her teeth than before, in the manner of someone swallowing a bitter medicine. The two of them reach for their handbags.

'Wait,' I say. 'I haven't told you about the best creature of all. It's a beetle which beats the surface of the water with its little feelers to attract its prey. They say it's a sexual signal, but who knows what sex with a beetle is really like. Anyway, there's another beetle that knows this trick, so you know what it does? It swims up and goes through all the motions of being attracted to the other one, and it gets really close, and just as the other one is getting ready for its snack – gotcha! It swallows it whole. Doesn't even *chew*.'

I don't get up as they stand. They leave without looking back.

I feel bad that I've deceived them. It isn't pond beetles that trick their prey at all, but a tropical species of land beetle, which flashes fake signals to fireflies. Somehow I don't think this detail will get as far as the reports they have to make. But I do wonder if Seethrough will reconsider when he's about to make another joke about ponds.

I finish the champagne and walk back to the lobby. I give a twenty-dollar bill to the concierge and thank him for his vigilance, because it's he who's told me about the two good-looking women asking after me by name earlier in the evening.

Then I'm alone in my room. My mind spins in a black whirlwind of thoughts. Soon I will meet Gemayel and confront him with the news that one of his own staff will attempt to be the instrument of his murder. I'm sickened at the deceitfulness of the people I'm mixing with. I wonder if I will be sent to the Sudan. And I wonder about a friend I haven't seen for ten years.

But it's something Grace said that worries me the most. All they need is an excuse, she says, and there'll be war in Afghanistan.

I loathe the duplicity of some of my own countrymen, but I am even more afraid of the power of America, and of what will happen if the giant is unexpectedly provoked.

9

In the few days that I've been in America Seethrough has been busy, as usual. He's liaised with the Italian intelligence service, SISMI, and managed to borrow a team of watchers to help arrange a meeting with Gemayel. The Italians have been kind enough to let us know that on Fridays Gemayel has the habit of walking from his apartment on Via Hongaria and strolling along the shady gravel paths that criss-cross the gardens of the Villa Borghese. He is accompanied by two armed Arab or Italian bodyguards, who trail discreetly behind him in expensively tailored casual jackets and Ray-Bans. So on the chosen afternoon, instead of calling up Gemayel and requesting a meeting like a normal person, I'm sitting in the back of an Italian telecom van watching him from half a mile away through a high-powered miniature telescope.

My partner for the day is a former Italian special forces soldier from Naples called Gaetano, who tells me a funny story about surrendering to a troop of British paras on a joint escape and evasion exercise in Germany. When he's caught, which is not supposed to happen on E & E training, he produces a fine bottle of Montepulciano and a large Parmesan from his Bergen, and settles down with his captors to a picnic, after which they generously decide to let him go. Mysteriously, he is the only member of the Italian team to successfully complete the exercise, and receives a commendation from his proud commanding officer.

The old rule of surveillance applies. We must assume at all times that our target is being observed, so the plan is to deliver a message directly to one of Gemayel's bodyguards under cover of an innocent encounter. The message is a piece of paper on which I've written a note requesting an urgent meeting. There's enough detail for Gemayel to know who I am, and though I don't put my name, I've given him details of my hotel. I have to trust that his memory is still intact and he isn't too upset about the past.

For the contact, two SISMI officers, a couple posing as American tourists, have rented bicycles for an afternoon ride through the Villa Borghese. Directed by Gaetano through their hidden body comms, they're able to position themselves ahead of Gemayel as he turns along one of the tree-lined pathways. They keep their backs to him and pretend to be consulting their tourist map of the park from the saddles of their bikes. The timing has to be just right. Gemayel walks past the couple, and the bodyguards are a few yards behind.

'*É proprio dietro di te*,' whispers Gaetano into his microphone. Right behind you. '*Cinque secondi – adesso, vai vai vai*.'

I watch through the scope as the female team member, pretending to lose patience with the map, turns around and catches the attention of one of the bodyguards as he passes and asks him directions to the exit of the park. They talk for a couple of seconds. Then her partner reaches out his arm in thanks to the bodyguard, and shakes his hand.

'*Fatto*,' says Gaetano. It's done. The bodyguard is well enough trained not to show any reaction to the message that's been pressed into his palm, but closes his hand and walks on. The bikes speed away, but the message has been passed.

By the time Gaetano has taken me on a tour of his several favourite bars in Rome it's not only dark but I'm pleasantly drunk. I take a taxi to my hotel, recounting to myself the list of things which Gaetano says the Italians have invented.

'Everything that matters in life,' is how he puts it. Electricity, the radio, opera, fashion, the violin, the atom bomb, the best cars in the world, and pizza. Not to mention the most beautiful women of infamy in the world, he says with a wink, calling them *donne di costume facile*, meaning easy virtue. A pair of whom, he adds, are available to us this very evening.

It's a kind offer, which I decline politely.

There's no message for me at the desk. I'm wondering how and when Gemayel will get in touch when the answer is unambiguously provided. As I open the door of my room and reach for the light switch, I feel a sudden and overwhelming force pulling me down. I'm totally off my guard and whoever's doing the pulling has done this kind of thing before. Before I hit the floor my arm's already in a half nelson, and pressing into my temple is the muzzle of a pistol, which now emits a series of clicks as the hammer is drawn back. It's a little too close to be in focus and I can't turn my head, but I can just make out the design from the configuration of the slide assembly, which I recognise from my evenings spent poring over H's weapons manuals.

'*Bella pistola*,' I say. 'Beretta 92.' Another very accomplished Italian invention, it now occurs to me.

'*Chi cazzo sei?*' says a voice at the other end of the weapon. Very colloquial Italian, somewhat lacking in humour, with what I suspect is a Lebanese accent.

'*Sono un amico del tuo capo*.' I'm hoping if I tell him I'm a friend of his boss, he'll think twice about misbehaving.

'*Cosa vuoi da lui?*'

'*É una faccenda privata*.' It's time to switch to what seems likely to be his native language. '*Haida beini w'beinu w'bein Allah*,' I say, switching to my best Lebanese. That's between him and me and God.

While his partner watches me from a standing position beside the door, he turns me over, returns the Beretta to its holster and frisks me carefully twice, emptying my pockets in the process.

'*Siediti*,' he says, more calmly now. I oblige by sitting in the chair by the window, as he tosses my phone, wallet and passport onto the bed. I massage the side of my head as he scrutinises my things. Then he takes a mobile phone from his pocket, dials a number and speaks briefly in Arabic. The phone is passed to me and, as I've hoped, I hear Gemayel's voice. He sounds older and I'm unexpectedly reminded of how much time has passed since I last saw him. But the tone is unmistakable.

'I will be happy to meet an old friend,' he says. 'You have some news?'

'I can give it only to you.'

'My men will bring you. Forgive me if I do not tell you the location on the telephone.'

Without much further ado, because Gemayel's men don't seem to be the type for small talk, I'm escorted in silence to a black Mercedes parked outside the hotel. We speed through the Roman night. To judge from the number of times we change direction, I'm guessing the driver is doing his best to disguise the location we're heading for, and he's succeeding because I don't know Rome and we might be anywhere. But I'm not too bothered. Even though it's switched off, my phone will keep track of me and, more importantly, I've got my meeting.

It's past midnight. I have no sense of where we are. The car pulls to a halt in a narrow cobbled street and I'm hastened towards a heavy wooden door in a high wall. Beyond it I find myself descending several steps from street level towards a crypt-like space which smells faintly of incense and ancient stone. A second door opens into a small windowless church, its vaulted roof supported on three pairs of polished pillars in oak-coloured Carrara marble. The walls are ochre and the lines of the vaults are decorated with elaborate floriated mouldings in white plaster. There are a dozen dark wooden pews on the chequerboard marble floor, and the whole space is poorly lit by a pair of bulbs inside frosted domes.

I'm shown forward to the apse, to one side of which is a dusty velvet curtain. Another, smaller door lies behind it, and opens onto stone steps leading down. I count twenty-four, which means we are a good way underground and the signal from my mobile won't survive. Nor will any sound carry to the outside world.

It's the perfect site for a clandestine meeting. A transmitter won't work, and there's no chance of eavesdropping through the walls. But the isolation makes me uncomfortable.

There's a crossroads of passages and we descend again as the walls roughen and take on a prehistoric look. They are cold to the touch, though the air is surprisingly warm. One of the bodyguards leads and the other follows me as we turn into a long broad tunnel with horizontal niches on either side. I realise now we are in a portion of one of the city's many catacombs, and the ghostly mounds lying in the niches are the calcified contours of human skeletons. Then the tunnel opens into a series of rooms decorated with ancient murals depicting gardens and animals. They have a primitive beauty about them but it isn't really the moment to stop and lecture my escort on the iconography of pre-Christian murals.

We pass into a larger chamber almost as big as the church above us. The floor is bare but the walls are covered with more faded but colourful murals of mythological landscapes and encounters. There are blind windows and door frames carved meticulously out of the pale stone and, running the length of the base of the walls, a low platform. On this platform, at the far side of the chamber, sits Gemayel.

The guards settle on either side of the entrance we have come through. Gemayel stands up and greets me warmly. His hair and moustache are grey now, but he looks in good health. There's a patrician look of approval on his face.

'You were a boy when I met you,' he says. 'Now I see a man.'

'I did not expect to meet you again in a church,' I say, for lack of a better reply.

'Our Prophet recommends that if you cannot find a mosque to pray in, then you should go to a church.'

'Better than a prison, I think.'

'For some, even a church can be a prison.' He smiles. 'But for me the churches of Rome are the most beautiful in the world. This is the best city in which to take the Prophet's advice.'

He knows I have an important reason for calling a secret meeting but is happy to delay the moment of asking until we have caught up. We talk a little of our lives and are led back to the fateful events of his capture by the Israelis, ten years earlier.

'I do not forget what you did,' he says. 'I am still in your debt.'

'There is no debt,' I tell him. 'What I did was my duty.'

'To protect me, you killed a man.'

'I failed to protect you.'

'There is honour even in failure,' he says, and smiles again.

It's strange, but at this simple statement I feel a burden lifted from me. It's as if he's exorcised an old and troublesome ghost that's been haunting me for years, and I feel suddenly grateful towards him.

'Ask anything of me, and it will be repaid,' he says.

'*Insha'allah*, the opportunity for that will come. Now I have other news.'

I tell the truth, as much as I'm able. He will never know the full story: that his violent release from prison was a favour to the Israelis for providing the cover for Manny's infiltration. That he was sold, in effect. But the rest is true. I explain I've come not only as a friend but as a representative of my government, and that we are seeking his people's help in Sudan for any word of the Stinger purchases. If bin Laden is involved, we need to know. He listens attentively and nods in agreement at the request. He can guarantee no result, he says, but will alert me to any news as to whether Sheikh Osama, as he calls bin Laden, is connected or not. He reminds me that his own organisation wholly rejects the killing of civilians and has no policy of contact with any of the groups calling themselves al-Qaeda. But he will ask his people to listen.

I thank him and then tell him about the plot we have discovered against him. He says nothing but shifts his position a little and grips the bridge of his nose between his thumb and first finger.

'First they want to save me, then they want to kill me.' He lets out a heavy sigh. 'But God knows best. There are details?'

I tell him what I know. Then I give him a phone number and instruct him to notify me, using a code, if our intelligence proves to be correct. He agrees again, knowing that we also need to verify the reliability of our own source.

'Remember, our friendship is outside all of this,' he says, and stands up. 'We have work to do.' His guards come to their feet as we cross the open space, and then he pauses, as if he's remembered something.

'You will go to Khartoum?' he asks. 'Perhaps there is a better way to search for such knowledge while you are there. There is a woman who has been in contact with the people in my office, to speak about our charitable work. She works with the *mellal al-mottahed* – the United Nations.'

I'm puzzled, because a woman with the UN isn't much of a lead. Then Gemayel speaks again, and it's as if he's put gold dust in my hand.

'She belongs to the family of the Sheikh, and she knows many things that will interest you. Her name is Jameela. I believe she is very beautiful, as her name suggests. If you become her friend ...' A vague wave of his hand suggests both uncertainty and promise. 'You are young and handsome. You know how these things are done.'

I don't. But it occurs to me I'll be interested to find out.

'Not exactly house style,' says Seethrough, tapping the nail of his index finger against a pink file which I'm guessing is the contact report I've written up for my meeting with Gemayel, 'but you get the message across. Have a seat.'

I've been escorted to another anonymous-looking room at Vauxhall Cross to talk things over with Seethrough, who's there to meet me with another man who epitomises the description grey man. He's about sixty, wears glasses and a shabby grey suit, mumbles a greeting, avoids eye contact and says nothing else while Seethrough turns the pages in the file.

'This isn't bad for your first approach,' he says. 'Now we have to make it fly. At least she exists.'

'Who exists?'

'Your Sudanese floozy exists,' he says, opening the file towards me. I haven't forgotten about the woman Gemayel mentioned, but haven't expected a file to be put together on her so quickly. She's even been assigned a code name: Hibiscus.

'She wasn't in the CCI,' he says, referring to the giant database that the Firm maintains on every operational contact. 'So we asked Santa's little helpers for some details. Titbits from CX KHARTOUM and our friends at the Mokhabarat. Good-looking girl.'

He's used this phrase before, and he's right. There's a photograph of her, taken only two days earlier by the Sudanese security service, whose members Seethrough is pleased to call the elves. She's standing outside a shop talking to a passer-by or friend. One arm is half-raised as if in the process of giving directions. I can't tell if she's tall or not, but her face is slender and intelligent-looking, and her features suggest seriousness. Her eyes are large and expressive. Over her head she wears a long and loose white scarf, which accentuates the smooth dark brow it encloses, and the impression of youthfulness is at odds with the intensity of the gaze that the photograph has captured.

'Clever too,' he says. 'Parents moved to Paris when she was a teenager and she ended up with a doctorate from the Sorbonne. Married into the bin Laden family six years ago after she moved back to Sudan, but we don't have any details. She's worked for UNICEF for the past two years. We think she's worth cultivating.'

'Cultivating?' Spy-speak, I now remember, for winning a target's trust.

'All you have to do,' says Seethrough, 'is be there when she drops her shopping. Play the game. Get to know her. And find

184

out everything she knows about bin Laden and his best friends in the Sudan.'

'What if she doesn't know anything?'

'If she doesn't know anything, you can take lots of pictures of Khartoum for us instead. Enjoy the local food. Spread goodwill, that sort of thing.' Then the other side of him surfaces. 'But she does know. And as long as she knows more than we do, she's an asset and a potential source.'

'How close,' I ask, 'are you expecting me to get to her?'

'As close as the situation on the ground permits,' he says with a leer. 'If you think she'll have you, I don't care if you sleep with her and all her sisters. But do be careful about her brothers.' He gives a signature bounce of his eyebrows. 'We don't want to unleash the Mahdi's revenge. Just judge the situation as it develops. I need gradable CX that we can't get anywhere else.'

'When?'

'Saturday alright for you? We'll put you in a nice guest house in a quiet part of town. Shouldn't be too many cruise missiles this time of year.'

It's over two years since the retaliatory American strike reduced Sudan's showcase pharmaceutical factory in north Khartoum to a pile of rubble, and it seems unlikely there'll be any more. The US needs all the help it can get from the Sudanese intelligence services, and cruise missiles have proven a poor way to win friends.

There's a satellite picture of the city on which a number of key points are marked, to which now Seethrough points.

'On Mondays our target drives on her own to a refugee camp called El Salam in Jabal Awliya, about forty klicks south of the city. Your best place for a first meet will be on the road, out of the city and where nobody'll be watching.'

'So what do we do, give her a puncture?' I'm half-joking, but he's already considered the scenario and his seriousness comes to the surface again.

'No. She parks in a gated compound at home and at work. A puncture's too unpredictable in any case. If she's clever she'll suspect something. Better to be in charge of the moment ourselves, and make it quick and unexpected.' He doesn't elaborate. 'You'll get help with it when you're there.'

His eye falls back to the photograph of Hibiscus, and lingers there.

'Ant,' he says. 'CX is like an investment account. You have to have some capital to put in to start with. That's you. It has to outperform anything else in the same field. If the CX reaches the threshold, you put some more money in. But if you're putting in money and nothing's happening, you close the account. I'm giving this a couple of weeks. Three at the outside. That's what you've got to work with. George here will run you through the SOPs and help you sort out your legend.'

Then he leaves.

I spend an hour with 'George', a retired Security Branch officer who's previously served in Khartoum and now offers his services to the Firm in the manner of a consultant. It's a challenging hour, which begins with a geography lesson.

'The Sudan is the largest country in Africa,' he begins in a dreary monotone, 'and the tenth-largest country in the world, with a population of approximately thirty million.'

I haven't been this bored since Sandhurst.

'The capital Khartoum is centred around the confluence of the two major tributaries of the Nile, the White Nile and Blue Nile, the latter being the source of most of the Nile's water and fertile soil, but the former being the longer of the two.'

George uses a pencil to point to the features on the map, but is careful not to let its tip make contact with the paper. 'The White Nile rises in the Great Lakes region of central Africa, and flows north from there through Tanzania, Lake Victoria, Uganda and southern Sudan, while the Blue Nile starts at Lake Tana in Ethiopia, flowing into Sudan from the south-east. The two rivers meet at Khartoum.'

He moves on to history, racing me through the Mahdist revolt against the British that leads to General Gordon's untimely demise at the siege of Khartoum in 1885, the British withdrawal and subsequent reoccupation after Kitchener's victory at Omdurman, where Churchill rode with the 21st Lancers. He mentions the long British efforts to resist the unification of Egypt and Sudan until the country's independence in 1956, when a seventeen-year-long civil war began. He points out that the ongoing civil war has been rekindled after a hiatus of ten years, and is now being fought between the government of the north based in Khartoum and the Sudan People's Liberation Army based in the south. The SPLA, he points out, is a non-Arab secular movement with an interesting history, having been supported in turn by the Soviets and the Americans.

Consulting nothing but his own memory, he moves on to average temperatures and rainfall. Land use and natural resources. Different types of law enforcement. Different types of electrical outlets, traffic hazards and places to visit. He points out that the city is divided into three parts: Khartoum, Omdurman and Khartoum North or Bahri. Alcohol can be legally served only in the small Pickwick Club, which forms part of the British embassy.

My initial bemusement has turned into a kind of awe. He identifies the location of the UNICEF headquarters in Street 47, the whereabouts of the British embassy, the embassies of several other countries that can serve as a refuge in an emergency, and the location of other emergency RVs, as well as the main routes in and out of the capital. The CIA station, he tells me, closed down five years earlier, although the American and Sudanese spooks have been talking again since the bombings in Kenya and Tanzania.

He shows me the target's home address and her route to work. He shares with me a frighteningly long list of organisations considered to be terrorist outfits, all headquartered in the city. And he ignores my joke that, with so many terrorist organisations, it's probably the safest city in the world to be.

My legend should remain as close to the truth in every detail. He asks if there's a particular one that I'll feel comfortable with. I suggest that I be working on a mine awareness project, since mine awareness is all the rage nowadays. He likes that, and notes it down in spidery handwriting. It will give me a reliable pretext to be in the UN building and to mix with its staff, because the UN has its own mine programme in the country, he says. We invent a mine awareness organisation based in London that sounds like the real thing but doesn't really exist. He'll have Central Facilities, whoever they are, check the name and print business cards with phone numbers that work in the UK. Then other details. The car reserved in my name at the airport is a four-wheel-drive Isuzu. My visa, he tells me, has already been applied for.

George gathers up the maps and papers and returns them to their files. I realise it's the only trip I've ever planned where all the relevant documents are deliberately left behind in the office.

'Khartoum?' says H, when I call to tell him the op is on. 'Well, say hello from me.'

'Have you been there?'

'Can't remember now.' I picture a wry smile spreading across his face, the way it does when he's not telling the whole story.

10

No one who's been to Khartoum can forget the place. You fly for hours over weird and lifeless corrugations of rock and desert until the land turns to the colour of mud. Then, descending towards the city, the sun flashes from a broad snake of water, and in the centre of a sprawling grid of roads and houses streaked with green lines of trees you see what looks like a crescent-shaped samosa, wrapped in the dirty braid of the Nile. This is Tuti island, where the Niles converge.

On the ground, the heat hits you like a wall, and suddenly your white face feels like a lonely beacon as you move among crowds of ebony-coloured faces. You feel the vastness of Africa, like a vibration that stretches back to the beginning of time. A reddish dust moves in snakish wisps above the surface of the tarmac and quickly settles into everything.

The entry stamp in my passport is a swirl of Arabic script, delivered with a flourish by an immigration officer who welcomes me to Sudan with a gleaming smile. I return the smile, and when his pen runs out of ink, I offer him mine.

'Thank you, my *friend*.' He beams and looks like he means it.

Changing money and collecting the car that's waiting for me involves an hour of form-filling and official stamps. Then I pay a taxi driver to drive ahead of me to the district called Riyadh, and I follow him along a broad highway with chequered kerbstones, overlooked by giant advertisements which I try to decipher from the Arabic as I drive past. The taxi pulls over as we reach a grid of sand-covered streets lined with charmless modern villas, and the driver waves goodbye to me from his window.

I'm greeted by a housekeeper called Kamal, who guides my car into a small compound, carries my things indoors and prepares hot sweet tea, over which he alerts me gently to the danger of scorpions in my shoes in the mornings.

I shower and lie under the ceiling fan for a solid hour. Then out of curiosity I go by taxi to the centre of the city, a term the driver doesn't understand, but suggests instead the presidential palace, which I remember lies near the water. He drops me near the palace, around which the city's more interesting buildings lie, and for a couple of hours I walk along roads parallel to the banks of the Nile lined with fat palm trees. I'm adjusting to the heat, and savouring the scent of datura and frangipani blossom and others I can't identify. And I'm taking pleasure in the innocent charm of strangers who say hello as they pass, then look back and ask my name and wave. Their friendliness reminds me of Kabul, where the visitor quickly gets used to the spontaneous smiles of passers-by, whose sincerity renders irrelevant all the bad things you hear about the place back home.

There are no mountains around Khartoum, but the city is blessed by the presence of the two Niles that converge there. The water is nearly half a mile wide and more powerful and serene than I imagined. I walk much further than planned. As evening falls I'm sapped by the heat and retreat to my room. I shower again and position myself back under the ceiling fan, wondering how long it will take me to get used to the heat, trying in vain not to think about the future and whether it is really written or not.

My meeting is at midday. I take a taxi halfway to the embassy and walk the rest, stopping to sample fruit juices at cupboard-sized shops along the sand-covered streets until I'm satisfied that no one is following me. I turn left from Sharia al-Baladiya between the Turkish and German embassies into a smaller

street, and a little further on catch sight of the Union Jack fluttering on a rooftop. At the reception desk I introduce myself to
an English-speaking Sudanese member of staff, asking as agreed
for a Mr Halliday. He asks me to repeat the name, then speaks
for a few moments on the phone while I sit wiping the sweat
from my eyebrows.

There's a door a few yards away to my left, which opens
suddenly and takes me by surprise. I turn and see the head and
shoulders of a man wearing a white shirt and tie studying me with
a severe look of enquiry like a professor who's been disturbed at
his papers. The impression is strengthened by the thin circular
gold frames of his glasses, behind which he blinks a few times
before speaking.

'Ah,' he says, as if he's making a mental calculation that seeing
me has interfered with. 'You'd better come with me.'

I follow him through the door, which he closes behind us, then
shakes my hand.

'Welcome to the Dark Continent. I'm afraid it is a bit hot,'
he says. He has an unctuous voice which sounds faintly comic
to me, as if he's trying out an impression of Noël Coward. He
doesn't introduce himself. I guess he's no more than thirty, but he
has the boffin-like mannerisms of a much older man, and looks
as though he belongs on a university campus in the vicinity of
some high, perhaps ivory, Gothic towers and carefully tended
lawns. He's tall and unnaturally thin and I can see the bones of
his shoulders outlined under his shirt. We cross what looks like
an interview room, where a photographic portrait of the Queen
hangs above a wall of filing cabinets, and on the far side enter a
smaller windowless room secured by an electronic lock. There's
the hum of an air-conditioning unit, and it's mercifully cooler. We
sit at a large wooden table.

'Oh dear,' says Halliday, or whatever his name really is, 'I seem
to have forgotten the map.'

'I've got one, if it helps.'

I take the tourist map of the city from my small backpack and hand it to him.

'Bravo. That's actually the same one we use,' he says with a comic expression of mischief. 'Shall we have a look at where you're going to walk the dog?'

'I'm sorry?'

'Walk the dog. The term applied to the chance meeting of an acquaintance, most often achieved while innocently exercising one's pooch.'

'Right,' I say.

We open the map and he points to Jabal Awliya and the road that links it to the city. Halliday steadies his glasses and blinks as he sweeps back a mop of dark hair from his forehead.

'The target vehicle will be returning on this road at four o'clock tomorrow afternoon. It's a white Daihatsu. Your helpers will be looking out for it at the halfway point and you'll be waiting a little further along. In the event of a successful interception I won't expect to hear from you, but if anything goes wrong I must ask you to return here and let me know.'

'There isn't much that can go wrong, is there?' I ask.

A schoolteacherish look of disapproval comes over his face.

'Oh but I think there is. Target vehicle changes route unexpectedly. Target vehicle has mechanical difficulty. Target vehicle fails to yield to persuasion. Target vehicle crashes. Pursuit vehicle fails to execute manoeuvre. Pursuit vehicle crashes. Target is seriously injured, summons civilian assistance, summons law enforcement; law enforcement vehicle stops at interception site before you do—'

'I get it,' I say. He's from the health-and-safety generation.

'I think you'll find you can't be too careful. Any of the above, and you drive on. We can't have you getting into a local imbroglio.'

We talk over a few more details, and on the way out he collects a small bag of tokens, redeemable against drinks at the Pickwick Club in the embassy grounds.

'Very exclusive,' adds Halliday with a buffoonish wrinkle of his nose. 'When you feel the need for a G & T. Just next door. Do be aware there are two listening devices pointing at the club enclosure from the eighteen-storey building opposite.'

'I'm sure you've told the Hanslope Park people about them,' I say. He hands me a small packet with the Firm's specially designed tamper-proof seal on it, and I recognise the code card for my satphone.

'There is one other thing,' he says, by way of a reply. 'The pool isn't in use on Thursday nights and if you fall in you receive a lifetime ban.'

Seethrough called the local Sudanese helpers elves, but they don't look like elves. The pair I meet the next morning are tall, lean and fit-looking men with serious faces. Their blue-black skin does not seem to sweat. They are in a pickup truck, which the locals call boxes, laden with what looks like the contents of somebody's house, half-covered in canvas and lashed with an old nylon rope. Their vehicle pulls out ahead of me as I leave my compound, and then stops as the driver gets out, opens and closes the tailgate as if to check it's properly closed and gets back in. It's the agreed signal.

I follow them out of the city to the south, and we drive past the dilapidated suburbs for about half an hour before stopping in a sandy enclave of small warehouses, where we park in the shade. One of the men is in contact by two-way radio with the watcher vehicle a further quarter of a mile south, who confirms his position every fifteen minutes.

After an hour's waiting there's a sudden burst from the radio confirming the target is heading our way. The elves' pickup moves to the edge of the road and gets ready to turn into the traffic, and I start the engine of my jeep but keep out of sight of the road for the moment. There's only a small chance of it happening, but I don't want the target to see our two vehicles together – mainly because the one ahead of me is going to deliberately run her off the road.

I can't see her clearly as she passes. The pickup pulls out and settles two cars behind her. I follow after they're several hundred yards ahead. We've gone about a mile when I make out the elves' pickup veering out of the flow of traffic to overtake the target. They're dangerously close to an oncoming car, but that's the idea. They pull in suddenly and disappear from view again, but the move has worked, because to my right I see the target vehicle lurch onto the unsurfaced shoulder, sending up a cloud of dust before plunging into the sand beyond.

But it doesn't stop. I'm reminded suddenly of H's maxim *no plan survives first contact with the enemy*, and I feel a mixture of frustration and admiration for the driver, who's kept control of the Daihatsu and is now circling away from the road at high speed. It looks as if she's going to try and drive back onto the road. If she succeeds, we'll have to come up with a new plan, and I hear myself cursing out loud as she manages the turn and begins to head back towards the road. But the offside wheels of her car are fighting the sand now, and throwing it up in little waves as she slows just before the circle is completed and ploughs to a stop before she reaches the road again. From a hundred yards away I see the driver get out and wave her arms angrily in the direction of the pickup, which has now disappeared. As I pull over she's kicking at the front tyre in frustration, and it sounds like she's swearing.

I get out and wave, and in reflex she pulls a white scarf, which has fallen onto her shoulders, back onto her head.

'*As-salaamu aleikum.*' It's time to play the role of the helpful passer-by.

She returns the greeting peremptorily and looks up at me full of suspicion. She says something angrily in Arabic which I don't catch, then rolls her eyes as if help from a white tourist is the last thing she wants.

194

I walk down from the shoulder of the road to where she stands beside her car, the wheels of which have sunk into the sand up to the axles.

'I saw what happened. Can I help?'

'No, thank you,' she says, putting up her hands in a gesture of refusal. 'Everything is OK. I don't need help.' She has a clear soft voice with a distinct French accent.

'Are you sure?'

'Yes,' she says testily, 'I'm sure. I'm a woman, but I'm sure. Thank you.'

She looks even more annoyed now. Her reaction has caught me by surprise. I had the impression from her photograph that she'd be meek and reserved, a timid Muslim woman who only speaks when she's spoken to. I couldn't be more wrong. She's all fire and pride, conspicuously strong-willed and too stubborn to admit how angry she is. She's also more beautiful than in the photograph, which is perhaps why I'm staring. Even without having seen her picture, I'm certain I would have this feeling that I already know her, as if we've met before. But we haven't. I catch myself and look away, as if breaking free from the spell of a hypnotist.

'I can help to pull you out,' I say. It worked with the Uzbek girl.

'Thank you,' she says. 'I don't need your help. I can take care of this.' Then, half to herself but distinctly enough for me to hear, she mutters '*Imbecile*' under her breath.

I say nothing. It's a stand-off. She won't accept help, and I'm too proud to be rebuffed. We look at each other for a few seconds. It's the first time our eyes really meet. Her face is still but her scarf is moving slightly in the breeze. My mind's racing with unexpected thoughts and I'm reluctant to take my eyes off her. I walk back to my car and fetch the tow rope. She's still glowering at me as I return, but there's a hint of curiosity in her eyes now.

'*En cas d'urgence*.' I put the tow rope on the bonnet of her car.

'I don't need that,' she says.

'I'd say you need it more than I do,' I say. 'In case you have trouble parking again. Nice to meet you.'

She opens her mouth to speak but then decides not to. I turn and walk back to my car. I have my pride too.

On the roof of the guest house I can sit unobserved and power up the satphone. It's been modified by the operational support geeks back home to accept a memory card with randomised codes on it, which makes it the modern equivalent of a code book and one-time pad combined. Each word of my contact report for Seethrough has a corresponding code number which is then encrypted and sent in a burst that lowers the probability of recognition or intercept to virtually nil. The most challenging part of the operation is shielding the screen from sunlight so as to see the words as I select them: FIRST CONTACT HIBISCUS SUCCESSFUL ARRANGED NEW RV NEXT WEEK. It's not perfectly accurate, but he's not to know. I'm just hoping I can think of a way to meet Jameela again before the week is out.

The solution comes after I pay a visit to the UNICEF office in Street 47 and am given an armful of documents about the organisation's activities in the Sudan. Among them is a list of upcoming events in Khartoum, which I scan down until Jameela's name leaps out at me beneath the title Global Programme for Polio Eradication. In three days' time she's giving a briefing on the progress of an immunisation campaign in the Nuba mountains in the south of the country. Staff and NGO partners, it reads further down, are welcome.

When the time comes, I find a seat among an audience of about thirty people and remind myself that I'm supposed to have found my way there by accident because the woman I've come to see hasn't even told me her name yet. Listening to her speak about the inter-agency appeal targeted at multi-sectoral activities, I'm reminded that the world of humanitarian aid is almost as afflicted by jargon as the army. But when it's time for questions, I make sure I'm the first to raise my hand, introducing myself and my company in the process, to ask about the risk of anti-personnel mines to children in the region.

There's a flicker of puzzlement on her features as she wonders where she's seen me before then delivers a textbook answer. At the end of the session I linger by the door as the others file out, and am glad to see that while she's talking to another of the participants her eyes turn in my direction several times. I don't make any effort to hide my pleasure at seeing her again. She walks up to me, clutching her papers across her chest.

'So, Mr Tavernier.' She's Frenchified my name. 'Is it a coincidence that you are here, or are you spying on me?' The charm in her restrained smile robs the suggestion of seriousness, but her manner is bold all the same.

'It's a coincidence.' I return the smile. 'Although I'm sure I would enjoy spying on you too. Unfortunately I'm in Khartoum only for a short time.'

She puts out her hand and introduces herself. She uses her maiden name. The surname bin Laden is not mentioned. 'It's nice to meet you again,' she says. 'I gave your rope to a village chief. He liked it very much. I have a few minutes before my next meeting. Would you like some tea?'

We walk to a small cafe in the gardens behind the building and sit in the shade under a canopy. She asks me about mine awareness in the Sudan and I tell her what I know: that the problem of mines and unexploded ordnance affects not only the central and southern areas where there's been recent fighting, but also the Eritrean border east of Kassala, and places on the country's other borders with Chad, Congo, Libya and Uganda.

She nods approvingly as if satisfied that I really do know about mines. I go on to explain my hopes for designing a mine awareness programme in collaboration with the UN. As I talk, I realise I'm having trouble taking my eyes off her and am hardly listening to my own words. She's exceptionally beautiful. Her eyes are dark and calm. At moments they express a faintly imploring quality, magnified by her habit of tilting her head almost imperceptibly downwards as she looks at me, as if she's hiding something she wants to tell me. Her face is narrower and her skin lighter than the Sudanese women I've seen, and her smooth rounded forehead and high hairline are unmistakably Ethiopian.

'You have Tigray blood in you,' I say impulsively, then regret it. It's too personal a detail for our first meeting and she's visibly taken aback, as if I've reached too suddenly into her world. I apologise, explaining that she reminds me of a friend's wife, who was from Ethiopia. She was very beautiful, I add.

'From my mother,' she says, and her tone is both curious and guarded.

Yet the conversation survives, and remains unexpectedly personal as we speak of our parents and families. Her mother was born in Ethiopia to a Christian family and her father in Khartoum to a Muslim one. Their marriage was a rare combination but the difference in religion had not interfered with their happiness.

'The Islam of the Sudan is not like anywhere else,' she says. 'Have you seen the stars in the desert yet?'

'Not yet.'

'You must, before you go. The stars are great teachers.'

I'm watching her closely as she speaks, observing her face as it traces over each different emotion that rises in her, and catching what I can of its beauty like the glimpse of a butterfly that settles and opens its wings in the sunlight before dancing away. Then suddenly I remember that my purpose in meeting this beautiful woman is to deceive her, and this hits me like the guilt of a murderer. For a moment my head sinks into my hands. I look up again and she's staring at me with a look of concern.

'Something is wrong?'

'I have to go. I have to get in touch with my office.'

'And I must go too,' she says, looking at her watch.

The unexpected intimacy has robbed of us our sense of time. Now we both want to make light of it, as if it hasn't happened, and neither of us really knows what to do next.

'I hope we'll meet again,' I say.

She nods casually. '*Insha'allah.*'

But I just can't leave it at that. 'Perhaps … perhaps one day you'd be kind enough to be my guide. Or you could advise me where to go. It would be a pity to waste time. Life is so short.'

'You're right,' she says. 'We should not spend time on things which have no purpose.' She says this in a way that charges the words with meaning, but I don't know if it's a warning or something else. Perhaps she doesn't know herself.

'I'd like to see the Souq Arabi. The wrestling in Omdurman. And there used to be a statue of General Gordon on his camel somewhere, but I think it went back to England.'

'It is better that the English keep it.'

'Yes, I know, but there's a funny story about it. One day a little English boy goes with his grandmother to see it, and they stand under it and look up and the grandmother, whose father fought in the Sudan, says, "My boy, that is the great hero General Gordon, who fought the Mahdi in the Sudan." So the little boy says, "Gosh, Grandma, that's amazing. But why is there an old man sitting on his back?" '

'I would be happy to be your guide,' she says. The full intensity of her dark gaze is on me, but she's smiling now.

Two days later I hear the honk of Jameela's Daihatsu outside the gate, and leap aboard with my little backpack feeling like a schoolboy on his first day of school. She drives us across the river to Omdurman, where the life of the city, although poorer than the centre of Khartoum to the south, becomes infinitely more colourful and intense.

We leave her car and wander through the spectacle of the open-air markets. The dust-laden streets are lined with mud-walled homes, and shared with camels and donkeys, and the air is heavy with the scent of spices and smoke. There are piles of fruits and vegetables I've never seen before, and everywhere there are tall and sometimes strikingly handsome men in long white *jellabiyas*. Their teeth flash in gleaming smiles. The women wear the brightly coloured *tobe*, a long swathe of loose fabric worn like an Indian sari, and there are just as many who are as tall and handsome as the men. We are offered food by a hundred strangers in turn, and after numerous refusals of raw diced camel's liver with onion and hot *shatta* spice I succumb at last to a plate of *foul* and gallons of sweet tea. In a jewellery market I bargain hard for a tiny silver casket and joke with the owner of the stall about being British, to which he responds by pulling out a large dagger from behind the counter and brandishing it theatrically above my head.

We take an old ferry to Tuti island, an undeveloped enclave of peace in the chaos and bustle of the city, and we stroll by the Nile, where women are washing vegetables for market in the muddy water, and we sit in the shade of a lemon grove to share a watermelon and take turns brushing the flies off each other's piece. A few laid-back locals try out their English on me, and chuckle at my half-remembered Arabic. Jameela is looking at me with a faint and affectionate smile.

'You seem at home in such a poor country. It is rare. You are not a typical Englishman.'

'I don't know what a typical Englishman is.'

'An Englishman does not show his feelings.'

'Perhaps there are feelings I am not showing you.'

Then she says thoughtfully, as if she's been wondering about it, 'We should visit the tomb of the Mahdi.'

It's the most revered site in the city and probably the whole of the Sudan. At the end of the nineteenth century the Mahdi, hated by the British but much loved in the Sudan as a saintly warrior, led his tribesmen to repeated victories against their imperial overlords in battles of stupendous bloodshed. The charismatic champion of Sudanese independence became the most celebrated Muslim leader in the world, and formulated a unique version of Islam which was distinctly upsetting to other Muslim powers of the day. He considered the Turkish rulers of neighbouring Egypt infidels, and claimed to be preparing the world for the second coming of Christ.

His most famous victory resulted in the slaughter and humiliation of the British and their Egyptian allies after the ten-month-long siege of Khartoum, where General Gordon waited hopefully and in vain for reinforcements from Egypt. Gordon's command and life ended on the point of a Mahdist spear. The Mahdi himself is said to have respected Gordon greatly, but was mystified by his refusal to accept Islam, choosing instead a humiliating death. The Mahdi died of typhoid a year later, and a shrine was built over his body in Omdurman.

The Sudanese paid a heavy price for their defiance. Thirteen years later, under no-nonsense imperialist General Kitchener, an Anglo-Egyptian force returned to avenge Gordon's death and reclaim the Sudan. They were heavily armed with the latest weapons. On the outskirts of Omdurman 50,000 tribesmen threw themselves at the British Maxim guns and were decimated by waves of dumdum bullets. The white *jellabiyas* of the slaughtered warriors were said to resemble a thick carpet of snow across the battlefield. Twenty thousand wounded were executed where they lay, and their bodies thrown into the Nile. Moored in the water beyond the town, British gunboats took range on the Mahdi's shrine and reduced it to rubble with volleys of fifty-pound explosive shells, the cruise missiles of the era. Kitchener had the Mahdi's body burned, but was discouraged by fellow officers from presenting the skull as an inkwell to Queen Victoria.

The silver dome of the tomb rises from a palm-filled enclosure like the nose of a rocket. Jameela greets the old guardian with affectionate respect, and calls him uncle. We walk barefoot around the custard-coloured walls of the octagonal shrine while the old man rubs the steel-grey stubble on his chin and recounts the more famous exploits of the Mahdi and his ill-fated warriors.

'I said you were a Muslim brother from *Britaniyyah*,' whispers Jameela mischieviously as we enter the shrine, savouring its cool stillness for a few minutes before emerging blinking into the sunlight.

The old man asks if we will be his guests, and insists on tea. He leads us past the accommodation for pilgrims and dervishes adjacent to the shrine, and we settle at a table under a tall acacia tree. By both tradition and law, he tells us, the grounds of the shrine are a place of sanctuary, an ancient version of diplomatic immunity. When it's time to leave, he heaps blessings on our families, and we promise to return.

We drive back to the city as the sun is setting. The temperature has dropped to a comfortable thirty-five degrees celsius. It's also Thursday evening, so I suggest we go to the Pickwick Club, where Halliday has put me on the guest list. We are shown straight in and head for the bar, close to the swimming pool. On the far wall Pickwick is written in lights. There's a plastic parrot at the bar, and I'm reminded Halliday has told me that the club takes its name from the late embassy parrot, which is buried inside the wall.

After the intensity of life on the streets of Omdurman, we feel out of place among the clientele of mostly lonely and bored-looking foreigners, and I suggest we go somewhere more real. Jameela agrees gratefully. We walk to an Ethiopian restaurant. There are no knives and forks, so she takes my hand gently in hers and shows me how to fold the food into the traditional pancake-like bread called *injera*. It's the first time we've touched since we shook hands, and this tiny act of closeness feels like a landmark to me, as if I've discovered the source of the Nile.

The pyramids are her suggestion. I've heard of the enigmatic site at Meroë, two hours north of Khartoum, but never imagined I might actually go there, much less in the company of a woman I'm struggling not to fall in love with. She lets me pick her up the next morning, and I'm shown into her home by her Sudanese housekeeper, who, judging from the twinkle in her eye when I appear, knows what's afoot.

We drive north for about two hours on the road to Atbara. Seeing how quickly the complexity and prosperity of the city fall away, as if from the edge of a flat earth, I'm reminded of Kabul, where the surroundings beyond the capital return to almost prehistoric simplicity after only a few miles.

At a small settlement called Bagrawiya on the east bank of the Nile we turn off the main road and bounce along an unsurfaced track. It's oppressively hot. Then the pyramids loom up, some pointed and others broken, reaching like ragged sets of teeth out of the orange sand. There's about a hundred of them, much smaller than their Egyptian relatives and much less well known, fashioned from black stone nearly two and a half thousand years ago as tombs for the kings and queens of ancient Nubia. There is no one else there except a solitary local who wants us to ride his camel for an outrageous sum, and we send him guiltily away.

'Quite a place,' I say to Jameela, 'for your ancestors to be buried.'

'Do you know anything of the history?' she asks.

'Only that Meroë was the southern capital of the kingdom of the Kushites, who ruled Nubia for a thousand years, invaded Egypt and ruled as the pharaohs of the twenty-fifth dynasty. They traded with India and China, and their warrior queen Candace, riding a war elephant, confronted Alexander the Great himself, who withdrew rather than fight her magnificent warriors.'

'You're funny,' she says.

'I read it in the guidebook last night. I wanted to impress you. Did you know the gods were so jealous of the beauty of the queens of Nubia that they struck the tops of the pyramids with lightning to humble them?'

'Good try.' She smiles. 'The tops were destroyed with dynamite by an Italian explorer in 1820. He was looking for gold. There wasn't any.'

We walk among the ruins in wonder at the lost civilisation that created them, ducking into the coolness of the few tombs that are open. As we enter one of them, Jameela reaches behind her for my hand and guides me gently inside. On the walls we can make out carved stone panels with Egyptian-looking winged gods. I run my hands over them and turn my head towards Jameela to see an expression of worry on her face, which I haven't seen before but which disappears as my eyes meet hers. Outside again, under the stone gateway to the entrance we lean against the walls, facing each other in the silence. I'm just looking at her, and she's returning the look, because we have somehow reached the end of the words we want to say to each other. The sun is low and the golden light catches the perspiration on her upper chest, and for a moment it's as if her dark skin is glowing.

I'm not sure what would have happened had the elderly guardian of the place not emerged from his nearby hut, and waved to us with a shout to let us know it was his time to clock off.

'We should go,' she says.

It's hot in the car. We drive for a long while in silence, as if the spell of the place is still on us. We pass trucks piled precariously high with cargoes, as well as passengers clinging to sacks of food and supplies, who wave and smile at us above the billowing fumes and dust.

'Sometimes,' says Jameela suddenly, 'I miss the sea. I want to swim in the sea. I want to go to a desert island and feel the sand instead of this dust, and feel the water instead of this heat.'

'Then let's go to the sea,' I say.

'It would take too long.' She sighs. 'Several days just to get there and back. It's impossible to get to the islands in any case.' She changes the subject. 'Do you know anyone in Khartoum?'

'Not yet,' I tell her. 'I haven't done much socialising.'

'Listen,' she says. 'I'm having dinner with a cousin and his family tomorrow. They're nice people. You could come and impress them. With your knowledge of history, perhaps.' She throws me an ironic smile.

'I don't want to impose,' I say.

'It's fine,' she says. 'My cousin can be a real pain sometimes but his wife is a good friend of mine. They're quite traditional. Religious. Can you handle that, Englishman? I'll call them to say you're coming.'

I am suspicious of him from the start. Jameela's cousin is an Arab and his features are Mediterranean. His skin is fair. He is tall and lean and has an angular face with a sharp nose and chin. The most disturbing thing about him is his eyes, which are grey and lizard-like, and settle with a faint look of disdain wherever his head is turned, as if they are fixed in their sockets. His gestures are slowed by an affected piety.

It's an untypical configuration. I know that in Sudan only family or the closest of friends are invited to the traditional family home. Something is different here. An accommodation has obviously been made for their foreign guest, and a table and chairs have been put together in the room, which is the equivalent of an English family deciding to eat on a carpet on the floor. They have also invited a Sudanese man and his wife who have lived abroad for a few years and whose family connection I never catch. I suspect that their presence is intended to be a bridge between the traditional environment and the strange ways of a foreigner, which is me. Jameela is family but thoroughly westernised in her ways, and is accepted like a foreign film on television.

Her cousin sits opposite me at the table with Jameela to one side. His wife, a young Sudanese woman with big soulful brown eyes, ferries the dishes to and from the kitchen, settling from time to time at the end of the table like a young deer drinking warily from a stream. Her eyes never meet those of her guests. They all speak in Arabic for most of the meal, until our host fixes on me and reveals that he does in fact speak nearly perfect English.

'It is to be commended that you speak Arabic,' he says to me with a sinister smile. '*Insha'allah* you will one day read the Holy Qu'ran.' His teeth are perfect white.

Jameela rolls her eyes.

'My cousin has said you were in Afghanistan.'

'My work took me there for a while,' I say.

'You were not there at the time of the jihad?'

'For a short visit. It's a long time ago now.'

'You are not a Muslim,' he says, as if this disqualifies me from travel. 'What did you do there?'

'I did what my friends did. Just lived.'

'Did you fight?' he persists.

'There was fighting. It was wartime.'

'It is an honourable thing to participate in jihad. Did you participate?'

I don't like where he's trying to lead me. I don't like his curiosity. I think of the grace and dignity of the old man at the shrine, who wouldn't have dreamed of prying into the private life of a visitor. My host, it seems, links the idea of going to Afghanistan with fighting the jihad and nothing else. It's impossible to explain to him that my sympathy for the Afghans at the time wasn't anything to do with religion or its decrees, but simply because I liked the people I met.

'I believe the Prophet – *sala Allah alaeihu wa aleihu as-salaam* – said that the greatest jihad is the struggle with one's own personal weaknesses, and that the jihad against the worldly enemy is the lesser struggle – the jihad *as-saghir*.'

I glance at Jameela while my host's head is turned, and she shoots me a look of fond disapproval. But her cousin isn't impressed.

'How do you know such a thing?' He ignores the implication of the question. 'Did you fight or not?'

'I lived as my friends lived. So I lived with them, ate with them, fought with them, prayed with them.'

'You *prayed* with them?' His hands settle deliberately on the edge of the table, as if he's about to get up.

'Omar,' says Jameela, 'let him eat.' The conversation is making us both feel uncomfortable.

'Yes,' I say, recalling those serene moments at dusk when the men would lay their weapons quietly aside and turn their minds to God before resuming their worldly preoccupations. 'Sometimes. Not always. It would have been strange not to.'

'But you are not a Muslim?'

'Omar,' says Jameela, with a note of protest.

He looks at her then back at me as if to say, I'm talking; don't interrupt me.

'In wartime everyone prays in their own way. There it was a part of life.'

'You did not feel …' he looks up, searching for the word. Then he finds it, and his eyes fix on mine again with new intensity. 'You did not feel like a *hypocrite*?'

'Oh *merde*! That's it, I'm leaving,' says Jameela. She pushes her chair back abruptly and stands up. Her cousin looks up at her like a lizard, imperturbable, and then directs a strangled smile at her as if he's found a hair in his food but is too polite to say.

'It's fine, Jameela,' I tell her. 'Your cousin is asking a legitimate question. He has his interpretation and others have theirs. That's the basis of *ijtehad*. It's what makes Islam interesting.'

'How do you know such a thing?' he asks again, almost angrily, as if his religion is a secret that no one else has the right to take an interest in.

'He can't talk to you like that. You're his guest. This is not Islam.' She utters the word with a sneer.

Omar ignores Jameela's outburst as if it's beneath him to respond to it.

'The answer to your question is no, I did not feel like a hypocrite. God speaks many languages, not just Arabic.'

He sighs tolerantly, like a teacher who's been let down by a promising pupil but sees that this isn't the moment to pursue the issue.

'I would be most interested to speak to you more about this subject. Perhaps you can come back and I will introduce you to some friends who would also be interested. We can make a small interview and you can also read some verses of the Holy Qur'an for the radio. There are many other things we can discuss.'

'I would be happy to do that,' I say. It's a lie because I have no intention of allowing him to exploit me for his own style of propaganda. His version of religion is too political for me.

Later, after the conversation has changed direction, I wonder whether I've judged him too harshly. Perhaps he is just genuinely curious and has never been exposed to the notion that you can be interested in a different culture and religion without becoming a fanatic. But the atmosphere never quite recovers.

'I'm so sorry,' says Jameela when we're back in the car. She's more distressed than I am. 'He can be such an idiot. Only religion matters to him and his friends. They're so medieval, and they're all like that.' She calms down a little. 'I was mixed up with them for a while.' She starts the car and we pull away.

'How mixed up? You're scaring me.'

'Family stuff,' she says, as if it's a chapter in her life she prefers to forget. '*Ils sont tous des fanatiques*.' She looks at me. The smile has gone from her face. 'I married one of them. Have you heard of Osama bin Laden?'

'I think so,' I say. 'He's becoming quite well known.'

'I married one of his brothers. He was a good man.' She pauses. 'But he changed. Osama's people changed him. Osama was a good man. He did good things for Sudan. But they changed him too. I used to see him and his people, and every time he was becoming more extreme.'

'I don't think I want to know about them,' I say. 'Watch the road.'

'You have to understand,' she says as a look of sadness crosses her features, 'there's a beautiful side to Islam and an ugly side. You're a Christian. Christians have done cruel things. Evil things, I mean. But cruel people will always find cruel things to do. You don't judge a whole civilisation on them. At the heart of Islam there's a ... a *peace*, an unimaginable peace and beauty. You find it in the simple people here, in their lives. Their gods are the sky, water and trees. Real Islam accepts all that. The Prophet was from the desert. He was a simple man who understood hardship.'

We drive in silence for a while. There's something raw about this issue for Jameela, and it's exactly the kind of discontent that a proper spy would try to exploit, deepening the grievance to obtain information. But there's no need to try to bring it out. It bubbles up again a few minutes later.

'You don't deny your religion and civilisation because there are some fanatics who call themselves Christian? You don't deny all the goodness and beauty because there is some ugliness. You don't have to feel guilty because the Church ordered the crusades, or a massacre, or – I don't know – a Hiroshima or a Srebrenica, or because your Christian leaders built concentration camps or enslaved millions of innocent people? But if a Muslim is involved in something unspeakable, in the West they always point out his religion. They talk about Muslims as if a single word could describe a billion people, as if the word was really useful.'

We pull up outside her home. The engine is still running, so I reach towards the ignition and turn off the engine. Jameela turns to me. She's still upset. The issue has caused a division between us like an argument, and cast a shadow over the closeness I feel for her.

'Do you know who the most extreme ones are?' she's asking. 'They're from Saudi, Egypt, Palestine. The ones who have the closest contact with the West. That's where they learned their politics and their violence. And they're always the ones you hear about. You never hear about the millions and millions of people who live quietly and tolerantly and peacefully and with the happiness that Islam brings to the heart of their lives.'

But I'm not really listening. I lean across, reach behind her head with my hand, and draw it gently towards my own. Then I kiss her on her lips.

'I am in love with you,' I say quietly. 'And each time I say goodbye to you, it hurts.'

She looks at me in stunned silence. Her breath is uneven.

'Go,' she says. 'Just go, please. *Va t'en, je t'en prie.*'

11

Her letter arrives the next day. Kamal brings it to me while I'm drinking tea on the balcony.

> *À mon très cher Antoine,*
> *I cannot describe my feelings at this moment so I will not try. I*
> *am happy that we have met and I will always treasure the time*
> *we have spent together. But soon you will leave Khartoum and*
> *we will both be alone. When that happens, I know only that for*
> *one of us, or both of us, there will already be too much pain.*
> *Let us not make that pain greater than it needs to be. Please*
> *respect my wish that we not meet again.*
> *Je t'embrasse,*
> *J.*

Her housekeeper is outside, watering the bougainvillea, and greets me with a smile. Jameela is not at home, she says. I know, I tell her. I just want to leave her a present, I explain, and take the bags upstairs to her bedroom. The rose petals are fresh and fragrant. They are mixed with hibiscus and jasmine. I plunge my hands into them and scatter them over every surface, across the bed and dresser and bookshelves, until there is a thick layer of them from one side of the room to the other. The note which I leave on her table, by way of an answer, reads: *'Please come to a picnic on Friday morning, to discuss your important letter (bathing suit optional).'*

On the Friday, when I drive to her house Jameela is still in bed. She descends a few minutes later in a pair of white silk pyjamas, brandishing the note I've left.

'Why are you doing this?' she asks. She's trying to look angry.

'Trust me,' I say. 'We'll be back by this evening. Just one picnic and then I'll leave you alone.' Which I have no intention of doing.

At the airport an official leads us to the plane. It's a Cessna 172R with just enough range to get us to our destination and back. I've already filed a flight plan and the plane is chartered for twenty-four hours. I haul my bags into the hold.

'Are you at least going to tell me where we're going?' asks Jameela.

I pull open one of the bags and show her a pair of diving fins.

'You wanted the sea. I'm taking you to the sea.'

She shakes her head very slowly, but she can't conceal the faintest of smiles.

'You're crazy,' she says.

I press a hundred-dollar bill into the hand of the official, who mimics a machine gun as he warns me thoughtfully not to stray into Eritrean airspace. After a few minutes of pre-flight checks we're airborne, heading north-east from the city and watching the Nile snake away under our port wing.

Jameela's head is pressed against the passenger window in silent fascination. Over the intercom I hear her voice from time to time, pointing out the features of the landscape beneath us. Later I hear a strange sad music in my headset and realise she's singing to herself.

Two thirds of the way, a range of black and waterless mountains looms out of the wilderness below. Beyond, we can make out a thin blue band on the horizon which I point out to Jameela, who bites her lip in anticipation. I make the aircraft swing from side to side in celebration and Jameela's face bursts into a dazzling smile of delight. Then, just shy of three hours' flight time, I talk to air traffic control at Port Sudan and begin our descent.

Above the coast I turn south and the lonely Red Sea port of Suakin passes under us. It's an ancient place, abandoned by the Ottomans in the 1920s, now inhabited by a dwindling local population and crumbling steadily into the sea. A few minutes later I spot the airstrip and make a single low pass. There's a solitary white jeep parked by a tin shed at the end of the runway, and beside it stands the driver, waving his arms slowly above his head. I think almost warmly of Halliday, who hasn't had long to make the arrangements I've requested.

It's a dusty landing. I taxi down to the shed, turn and cut the engine. There's a blissful silence. The driver runs forward to help us with our bags, and we bundle into the jeep and head for Suakin. At the ramshackle port we transfer to the boat he's found for us. It's an ageing Zodiac with powerful twin outboards, and I don't ask where it comes from. Nor does our driver ask where we're going. Some black identification numbers on the prow suggest a military provenance, so perhaps he's got a cousin in the army. He runs over the controls with me and points out the several large jerrycans of water aboard, as well as a box of fruit which he indicates was his personal idea. I reward him appropriately and arrange when we'll meet. In the meantime he'll return to the aircraft and guard it in our absence.

Not far away we see several fishermen selling fresh catches from their boats. One of them is hacking steaks off what looks like a small version of a tuna fish. He cuts two wedges of the dark flesh for us using a blackened machete, which he has to knock through the fish with a mallet. We stow it in the Zodiac with our things, I set the GPS to start acquiring, and the engines splutter into life.

We motor out of the channel and into the open sea, bouncing across the water under the sun. It's burningly hot, and I'm grateful when Jameela, who's been eyeing me throughout all this with a mixture of suspicion and admiration, takes off her scarf and ties it over my head. It's the first time I've seen her without it. She runs her fingers through her long dark hair as if a portion of her spirit has been released with it, leaning into the wind like a dog from the window of a car, and she's loving it as I hoped she would.

Fifteen minutes later the coastline behind us is a thin black line. But ahead, just where the GPS predicts, a dozen deserted islands have sprung out of the sea. Some are tiny and barren, others larger with thick bands of vegetation stretching along the bleach-white sand of their coastlines.

'Choose your island,' I say.

She points her slender arm to a small sandy cove a few hundred yards distant, flanked by rocky entrance spurs, between which stretches a dark green canopy of trees. We haul the Zodiac onto the beach and take the extra water and bags to the treeline, where I fuss over an improvised camp. There's no sound but the ticking of the cooling engines. I look up to see Jameela running to the water and plunging in, fully clothed.

Then she races back to me and flings her arms around me.

'Thank you,' she says, 'thank you.' I hold her wet body against mine, savouring the scent of her skin for a few moments until she releases herself and rummages in her things to find her swimsuit.

She changes under a towel and I struggle not to show any reaction as she throws it aside. She wears a cream two-piece swimsuit which I'm guessing she bought in Paris and which makes her skin seem all the darker. I keep forgetting she grew up in Paris. The headscarf she wears in the city sends out a protective signal that cools the physicality of encounters between the sexes. Out here she's not wearing it and the signal has evaporated, and the shock of closeness makes me faintly nervous. I see her body silhouetted as she turns towards the water and adjusts the strap of her top. Her legs are long and graceful and my eye rests guiltily on the flare of her hips beneath her slender waist, and I am filled with longing.

We walk to the beach with the fins and snorkels. For the next couple of hours, hardly aware of the time that is passing, we float on the water's surface, gazing into the silent world in front of our masks. The water is spectacularly clear, and every fish we see is a strange and unexpected shape, and each one seems as bright and delicately coloured as a living rainbow. Then we walk along the sand together, picking at shells until she notices the redness of my shoulders and suggests we return to the shade above the shoreline.

I collect some wood from under the canopy of trees, and when I'm out of sight of Jameela take the satphone from its waterproof case and send our exact location to Seethrough via the GPS function on the keypad. He'll relay it to the buffoonish Halliday at the embassy in Khartoum so at least he'll know where to find us if, as I fantasise, I get stuck on the island with Jameela. Then I make a small fire, wait for it to burn down, wrap the fish we've bought in thick green leaves and put it into the embers. The white wine I've procured from the regional security officer who doubles as barman at the Pickwick Club is slightly warm but hits the spot, and in the heat it makes us pleasantly drunk. It's the first time I've seen Jameela drink wine. She allows me to feed her slices of mango, and we let our faces get very messy.

She sees me look at my watch and asks when we have to leave. We need to fly before dark, I tell her. I can fly at night but I'd rather not.

She looks pensive. 'Let's stay,' she says. 'Here on the beach. Under the stars.'

I have, as it happens, considered this possibility, and brought two nylon hammocks with us for the purpose. She's impressed, as I hoped she would be.

I tie them between the trees, side by side a few yards apart.

'Separate beds. I must be old-fashioned,' I say.

There's a force of attraction between us that's no longer a secret. It's invaded my body and thoughts. I wonder how long we can preserve its innocence, which is a fragile thing that won't survive if we both cross the line that we're now drawing towards and from which it will be impossible to turn back. But we both know what intimacy is and the pain that comes with its dissolution, and perhaps it's this that gives us the strength to approach the line more cautiously.

'Thank you,' she says, but then she doesn't make things easier by drawing her body against mine and resting her head on my shoulder, so that I can look down the muscles of her long back towards the swell of her hips.

I build up the fire and we sit by it as the sun falls into the sea and the world turns to shadows. Jameela's face gleams in the light of the flames and seems more beautiful to me than ever. When I add wood to the fire a shower of sparks rises and imprints itself among the stars overhead. They're so bright, and there are so many more stars than are visible in England I can't even make out the constellations I can see at home.

We clamber into our hammocks. She's close enough for me to hear the sound of her hand against her skin as she rubs mosquito repellent over her arms. We're tired and happy.

'I enjoy our friendship, Jameela,' I say, half to myself.

'*Moi aussi*,' she answers from the edge of sleep.

When I wake, Jameela's not in her hammock and I have a sudden sense of panic until I catch sight of the splash of her fins. She's already in the sea, snorkelling. We breakfast on mangoes, wash in the water, and then it's time to pack. As I'm doing up the bags I imagine once or twice that I hear the sound of an engine, dismissing the thought each time because the islands are uninhabited and the water is too shallow for fishing. Then as we're getting ready to put the bags in the Zodiac, we hear the distinct whine of an outboard motor, which gets suddenly louder as a boat rounds the mouth of the cove and heads for the very spot where we've dragged the Zodiac onto the beach.

'Fishermen,' says Jameela.

They don't look like fishermen to me. We watch them together in silence, and Jameela's look of unease mirrors my own as they come to a stop a few yards away from the Zodiac and cut their engine.

Without acknowledging us, they point out the Zodiac's features to each other as they drift nearby. I wave, but the wave isn't returned, which is unusual. I wave again, thinking that perhaps they haven't seen us. But we're less than a hundred yards away and they must have. They lift their propeller from the water and one of them jumps overboard to pull the boat to the shore. The other, who is bare-chested, picks up what looks at first like a harpoon, but it isn't.

'Oh my God,' whispers Jameela, 'he's got a gun. They must be pirates.'

'Keep very calm please,' I tell her. My mind is going through a list of options which is not as long as I'd like it to be. I have no weapon. We are barefoot. There is no shelter and nowhere to run.

They look the part. The one who pulls the boat ashore is a bulky man with cropped hair and deep black skin. His chin protrudes like the kind of fish that patrols the floor of the sea. The bare-chested one has wild-looking hair and seems to be giving the orders. The weapon is an AK-47 with a folding metal stock, a variant known in Russian as the *Partisan*. He barks something at us as he approaches but I can't tell what language he's speaking. Whatever he's saying it's not particularly friendly, and as he nears us he shifts his grip on the weapon so that his left hand moves under the stock as if he's planning to use it. He's lean, strong and young, which is not good from my point of view.

'Speak English?' I call out, to try and slow down the whole process.

He's asking a question which I can't understand a word of, but it doesn't sound like he's inviting us back to his place.

'He's speaking Amharic with a weird accent. He wants the key to the boat,' says Jameela in a shaky voice. 'Give him the key.'

She's standing next to me and has wrapped a towel protectively around her waist, but she's still a sight to behold and the effect is not missed on our visitors. The one with the weapon looks at her and says something to his partner, who advances towards Jameela. He tries to grab her wrist, which is still wet and allows her to break free, so he has another go and the same thing happens. On a third try he pins her arms against her body from behind and lifts her from the ground as she kicks frantically and uselessly against him.

It's obvious they want to take Jameela, and once they've got her, getting the key to the Zodiac isn't going to be too difficult to achieve after a 7.62-millimetre round has passed through my head. But there's something so improbable about the timing of their arrival and the fact that only Seethrough knows our exact location that I'm not too bothered. I'm impressed, in fact, with the thinking that's gone into it, but I mustn't let it show because I've got a part to play.

'Tell your friend not to do that, please,' I say to the one with the weapon. 'It's rude.'

I take a step towards him because I need to see the position of the selector lever on the right side of the AK. And to put a little more space between him and his friend. The safety's on, which gives me a slight but meaningful advantage. I raise my hands a little further, take another step towards him and now start babbling in English, which I'm hoping will make him think I'm telling him something important.

He bares his teeth in a snarl as I near him and raises the line of the weapon so that it's centred on me. The muzzle resembles a giant cannon, which gives me an unpleasant feeling, but his finger hasn't moved to the safety yet. I hope Seethrough has built in some form of compensation for the men he's sent, because they're not only doing a very good job of pretending to be pirates, but what's about to happen is going to hurt one of them a lot more than it's going to hurt me.

He raises the barrel of the AK to my chest and pokes it into me, barking another incomprehensible instruction. I raise my hands a little higher. It's a textbook replay of the very same defensive drills I did with H all that way away in Herefordshire, which does indeed seem a very long way away.

He pokes it into me again, stepping towards me now, and since all good and probably bad things come in threes, I wait for the third time. At the instant he gives another push with the weapon, I bring my left hand down hard and fast onto the barrel and turn my body to the left. He lurches forward and my right hand connects with his chin and drives it up and back, forcing him to try and regain his balance by stepping away from me. But my foot is there to meet his, and as he begins to tumble his left arm leaves the weapon by reflex in the attempt to break his fall. I yank it by the barrel and it passes almost miraculously into my hands. His efforts to scramble to his feet again are put to an abrupt end by the single round I fire into the sand just near his ear.

There's a scream of fright from Jameela, and then an immense shrieking fills the air as a cloud of birds erupts in a single swarm from the trees behind us. Jameela and her attacker are momentarily frozen in surprise. She breaks free from him, and in an impressive move whacks him squarely on the jaw. He's about to retaliate, but seeing his friend cringing on the sand has a different idea and sprints for the trees. I fire two rounds by his feet and he gets the message.

We need to leave. Jameela gathers up the bags as I cover the two men, make them take off their shoes just in case anyone feels like running anywhere, and direct them on their knees back to their own boat. I'd rather they didn't go and fetch any of their friends, so I break off the top of the spark plug of their outboard with the butt of the AK. Having to paddle with their hands will slow them down and have the added advantage of keeping their minds off robbery and kidnap.

Jameela finishes loading the boat and throws a look of contempt at the men.

'They would have killed us,' she says in a frightened voice. Then she shouts something at them in what I suppose is Amharic and probably a curse.

'Want to shoot them? The sharks will be happy if you do.' I offer Jameela the AK, guide her hand to the grip and the trigger, and point out the foresight for her to line up on her cowering targets.

'They would have killed us,' she repeats.

'Women with guns.' I shrug my shoulders at them as if the decision is out of my hands. 'Scary, isn't it?'

They're not laughing.

We move out of the shallows and throttle up the engines. The two stranded men are stooping over their boat as we gain distance. Jameela sits next to me, gripping me in silence and looking back from time to time as we race across the water. At the halfway point I pass the AK to Jameela. I'd love to keep the weapon, but it would be hard to explain. She flings it into our foaming wake and returns to my side.

The first moments of intimacy are never really equalled. She hasn't tidied up the rose petals, and their perfume wraps itself over us as we fall onto the bed and submit to the momentum that feels as though it was set in motion the instant we first saw each other. A frontier rushes beneath us as if we are entering territory new to us both, and where before there has always been restraint, there is now abandon.

Her skin is still salty and smells of the sea, like a mermaid who has miraculously survived the journey ashore. She laughs, weeps and laughs again, grips me repeatedly with unexpected force, then gives way again as if her body has returned to liquid and been reclaimed by the sea. I have never given myself so fully before, nor received so generously.

I wake in the night with a shock, as if roused by a gunshot. The shots I fired on the beach have been carried into my dream. Somewhere a dog is barking. Jameela is asleep next to me like a baby, half-wrapped in a sheet. I go to the bathroom to drink from the tap and notice the pattern made by all the sand washed off our bodies in the shower. Then I retrieve the satellite phone and step onto the balcony, where the air smells of dust and jasmine. I prepare a coded sitrep for Seethrough and thank him for his part in the arrangements of the previous day. I'm not really expecting an immediate reply and I'm just sitting in the silence thinking of Jameela when I see the blinking light in the phone display that signals his reply: YOUR REFERENCE 'PIRATES' NOT UNDERSTOOD PLEASE CONFIRM.

And it's only after about a minute of thinking this over that it really hits me.

I see Jameela every day, and return to her home with her after she's finished work. The hours of daylight are spent in anticipation of the hours of darkness, when we can travel ever deeper into the territory of intimacy that has opened itself to us. I planned nothing of this when we first met. But now it has us in its grasp and we are powerless against it, and care nothing about where it will take us.

The elements themselves seem to be conspiring in our favour. One afternoon Jameela calls to say she's returning home early. I drive to her apartment to meet her, and we sit on her balcony, where the air smells so strongly of jasmine, and drink cold white wine. I notice that the sky seems darker than it usually is and wonder if a storm is coming in.

'Not a storm,' says Jameela, as if she knows something I don't. 'Come.'

We climb to the roof by some narrow brick stairs and she points over the rooftops. Beyond the river to the west, rising out of the desert beyond Omdurman, is a sight I've never even imagined. A billowing wall of sand, a thousand feet high I'm guessing, is rolling towards the city. It stretches for what must be miles, an opaque, boiling, blood-orange wave, creeping visibly towards us. The scale of it is stupendous, like a biblical plague. The outline of the city seems puny against the advancing bulk of sand, and the sky grows darker as it nears as if under the command of an irritated god. I have no idea what will happen when it reaches us.

'Have you seen this before?'

'It's a *haboob*.' She smiles. 'The desert's way to clean itself. It's beautiful.'

It's a magnificent reminder of the scale on which nature prefers to do things. We watch its course for a few minutes. Its beauty is inescapable. But as I look at it I feel more than anything a sense of foreboding, as if a kind of reckoning is about to unfold. It signifies only danger to me. Then I turn to Jameela and see her beauty and am reminded how often beauty and danger can be found close together, and the symmetry of the moment seems complete.

'It will pass,' she says. 'We should go inside.'

We leave the roof and return inside, and close the doors and windows of the apartment in turn. The sky darkens even more. We can smell the sand as the *haboob* advances into everything, suffocating even the daylight and robbing the world outside the windows of colour like an eclipse of the sun. We retreat to the bedroom and make love once more as if to take shelter in one another, celebrating our intimacy in defiance of the affliction visited on the city beyond us.

Later, lying against each other in the muted light, feeling as though we've survived a natural disaster, Jameela speaks, prompting me to wonder whether she can read my thoughts. She faces away from me and asks quietly if I am awake.

'I know you are a spy,' she says. 'I don't care.'

'I'm not a spy,' I tell her.

There's a long silence. She's not happy with my answer.

'But I do know people who are.'

'They sent you here?'

'Yes.'

'To spy on me?'

'No.' Lie. 'My meeting you has nothing to do with that.'

'What do they want?'

'To find out about bin Laden and his people.'

'From me?'

'No. From anybody.' Lie.

Another long silence.

'I knew sooner or later somebody would come,' she says.

She rolls over, looks into my face without speaking and runs her finger across my eyebrows, my nose, my lips.

'I didn't want this to happen,' she says.

I omit no detail of what she tells me, writing for reasons of security at a glass table from which the imprint of my pen can't be lifted, and with a single sheet of paper at a time. She begins with the story of her husband, one of bin Laden's many half-brothers, and describes her marriage in Khartoum six years before and her early meetings with his family members at parties and gatherings. She names the dozen other bin Laden brothers she has met, and describes their prosperous lifestyles, their homes in California and London, their love of business, racehorses, boats and cars. These are not the profiles I'm really expecting. Bin Laden himself, she says, is one of the few brothers who lacked the family's love of wealth, perhaps because he's the only child of his father's tenth wife and lost his father when he was a teenager. Much of this, she says, she knows from her husband, who worked on the periphery of bin Laden's circle, helping to raise money for his projects in Sudan. Her husband is a good man, she says, but fell under the spell of the extremists who formed bin Laden's closest associates. I'm guessing that this is one of the reasons for their separation but I don't ask.

Bin Laden has been in Sudan for several years when she meets him, not long after what is said to have been an attempt on his life by the Sudanese authorities, acting on instructions from powerful Saudis who are hoping to silence bin Laden's criticisms of the Kingdom. It's in Sudan, says Jameela, that he acquires a penchant for black women, and has a string of Sudanese girlfriends. Can't really blame him for that, I'm thinking. His other great fondnesses are for earth-moving machinery and hunting with falcons. He also has an incongruous love of growing sunflowers.

The bin Laden I know from the cables and reports I've read over the previous year bears no resemblance to the man Jameela describes. The impression of a bloodthirsty mastermind simply doesn't tally with the diffident, almost shy man she knows from family meetings and parties. He's known to his admirers as a quiet philanthropist, sponsoring construction projects in Sudan and encouraging wealthy Saudi friends to invest in farming and real estate there. But those who knew him better, says Jameela, observed a man going through changes.

The unworldly teenager she's described is marked by a single overwhelming experience: his involvement with Afghanistan. It's there, after living and fighting among Afghan mujaheddin during the Soviet occupation, that his life is given a different direction. He becomes passionate about supporting the Afghans in their struggle against their invaders, and puts his personal fortune to work sponsoring camps, hospitals and a support network for Afghan fighters and their relatives. Like so many others, he simply falls in love with the place.

The simplicity and austerity of life in Afghanistan leaves a deep mark on him. When he returns to Saudi, he sees his own country through different eyes: a place run by corrupt and worldly men who care little for the true face of Islam. It is this true face that he has encountered in Afghanistan. He works against the Saudi regime, and when American troops arrive on Saudi soil for the Gulf War he calls for the overthrow of the royal family. He wins friends in low places and is forced to leave his homeland.

He's hounded from country to country, and settles in Khartoum. A puritanical hardness has entered him. He bans music in his household and puts his teenage sons through hard physical tests. Two years after his arrival in Sudan the Saudis strip him of his citizenship and freeze his assets. Around him circulates a loyal entourage of 'Arab Afghans' from the days of the jihad in Afghanistan, and their agenda becomes increasingly political. A few of them take an interest in steering bin Laden in a new and more violent direction, simultaneously nurturing his grievances and idealism in accordance with their own more cynical agendas. By the time bin Laden is expelled from Sudan and returns to Afghanistan in 1996, he has fallen entirely under their spell, espousing a new kind of global jihad which makes no distinction between its targets and their civilian subjects. Jameela lists the names of his radical associates with contempt, calling them cold-hearted hypocrites who have brought shame on Islam, men who exploit the legitimate grievances of ordinary people for their own violent ends. She tells me the names of the organisations they use and of the places in Khartoum where she thinks they sometimes meet. With other men, she says, suffering leads to goodness. But not with these ones.

By the time she's finished I've filled a dozen pages. When she leaves in the morning I rewrite them using the pen supplied to me by Seethrough and the pad of water-soluble paper that he's shown me how to use with it. Double spaced and in capital letters. Then I press the blank sides of a twenty-page United Nations de-mining report against each page in turn, and press them together for several minutes as the invisible dye contained in the ink of my report transfers to the blank sheets. Even under a microscope, there is no physical disturbance to the fibres of the paper, and the ink is virtually undetectable using chemicals. Then I re-staple the pages, and the result is what looks like an ordinary printed document, together with a scribbled covering note, sealed into an envelope addressed to a Mr Halliday of the British embassy. I burn my original notes in the kitchen sink, then run the tap over the sheets of my finished report. They dissolve within seconds into a translucent sludge. Then I throw a single unused sheet which I didn't need into Jameela's waste-paper bin. It misses by a tiny fraction, and bounces from the rim onto the floor.

I wonder, now, about such things.

A piece of paper, crumpled into a ball and propelled by the force transferred by the muscles of my hand and arm, tumbles through the air. Its direction and speed is in turn influenced by the immeasurably smaller forces that act on it from the air through which it passes. The resulting momentum, partially dissipated by the metal lip of the waste-paper bin, determines its final position, a few inches from the edge of the wall under Jameela's dresser. And this tiny deviation from its intended goal, of which the paper itself cannot possibly be conscious, prompts me to stand up and retrieve it from the floor with the intention of putting it into the bin where I had hoped it would land. But as I lean down to pick it up, something catches my eye.

On the floor tile at the base of the wall under the dresser where the paper has ended its flight is a tiny mound of white powder. It must be recent, otherwise it would have blown away or been swept away by now, and I can't help but wonder where it comes from. It's the kind of mound generated by making a small hole in a wall with an electric drill. I smell it. It's plaster dust. I look up to see where such a hole has been made, bemused at the same time by the habit of my own curiosity. An oil painting hangs directly above the dresser. It's a sample of raw but striking art from a local painter, depicting half a dozen women in brightly coloured *tobes* carrying pots of water on their heads. The dust, I reason, must come from the hole made to hang the painting. But this would have been made months or even years before, and no trace would be left today.

The dust, I decide, comes from a hole in the wall which is actually above the frame of the painting. I haven't noticed it before because it's just a few millimetres across and just above the frame. But this is the puzzling thing: the dust made by the drilling of the hole hasn't fallen onto the frame of the painting but onto the floor instead, which suggests that the painting was removed when the hole was made. None of which would have the slightest significance, had I not, out of curiosity, run my finger over the hole, which turns out not to be a hole at all but a slightly convex bump. It's the wide-angle lens of a covert fibre-optic surveillance camera.

It's not exactly a three-pipe problem, but it does raise questions. If the hole was made from the side I'm on, there's the question of who made it. I can't really picture Jameela with a covert entry and surveillance kit, so it's probably been made by someone who's got access to the other side of the wall. Whoever it is has a strong reason for wanting a camera that looks into Jameela's bedroom, and provides a panoramic view of the bed on which I've spent a good part of the preceding week with her.

It strikes me, the following morning at 5 a.m. as I'm about to break into the neighbouring apartment, that I'm here because of the irregularity in the flight of a ball of paper. Which suggests to me that large events are determined, at least in part, by smaller events, and those in turn by even smaller ones. Following this idea to its extreme is problematic, because you end up with the vibration of atoms determining every measurable event; and if everything really is determined, no action has any significance other than its own unfolding, and one may as well stay in bed. Thinking of the flare of Jameela's hips beneath the slimness of her waist, staying in bed does indeed seem like the most sensible thing. But I know intuitively that the apparently random position where my sheet of paper came to rest and the sense of foreboding I felt on seeing the giant *haboob* are somehow connected. Not by scale, but by their significance.

My lock picks live in a panel of my wallet that only the most diligent search would uncover. They are made from a high-tensile ceramic coated with tungsten carbide and are much stronger than steel but have no detectable metal content. The six picks are black, and moulded, like the pieces of an Airfix model, into a panel the size of a credit card with a thin plastic cover, which

I now slide off and twist out the tension wrench. I put the short end into the keyway, using my third finger to apply pressure and resting the other two gently on its length. With the other hand I use the snake pick to lift all the pins in one go, listening as they snap down when the pressure from the tensioner is released. Five tiny clicks tell me it's a five-pin right-handed lock.

To judge from the slightly gritty feedback I'm getting from the pins, it's either a fairly new lock or there's dust on them. Probably both. It doesn't matter which. I push the diamond rake to the back of the lock and work it a few times to get the feel of things, then work the pins one by one, feeling the tiny variations of pressure in the tensioner as the cylinder struggles to turn. There are few tasks more satisfying that can be accomplished with the fingers of the human hand than picking a lock. One minute you're locked out, blocked from your goal by a device that seems so inflexible and defiant. Then comes the magical moment as the tensioner gives way, the cylinder turns, and the door swings magically open.

I clear the lock and close the door gently behind me. Jameela has told me that the apartment is empty and that nobody lives there, and she's right, almost. Nobody lives there, but the place isn't entirely empty. There's just enough light to make out the shapes of things, and I feel my way from room to room and then up the stairs. The layout of the rooms is the mirror of Jameela's apartment. In the bedroom that lies next to Jameela's there are two folding tables against the wall and two empty chairs. A black fibre-optic video cable comes out of the wall above them, more or less where I expected it. What I didn't expect is the sophistication of the equipment. The cable feeds to a digital video recorder, next to which there's a control console, flat-screen monitor and a keyboard. It's all switched off, which suggests that the watching is done selectively. I squat by the edge of the table and study the equipment without touching anything, and I can hear my heartbeat pulsing in my ears. A strong smell of stale cigarettes comes from an unemptied ashtray, and there's a crumpled empty packet of Marlboros on the floor. Then a muffled thump sends a shock wave through me and I leap to the door.

Someone has come in downstairs. I can just make out an exchange of male voices. There's no time to leave by the window. A light goes on at the foot of the stairs. I close the door silently and go to the adjoining bathroom and feel my way into the shower, leaving the curtain open and pressing myself against the tiled wall. A yellow band of light spreads under the bathroom door as the light goes on in the room, and I hear voices and footsteps.

My heart's thumping now and feels like it'll jump out of my throat. I close my eyes and try to regulate my breathing. The bathroom door opens and the light, which seems blindingly bright, comes on for a few seconds and then, to my inexpressible relief, goes off again. They are checking the place but not searching it, and not really expecting to find anyone. They have perhaps seen me follow the path to the entrance of the building, and wonder why I haven't reappeared. Perhaps I should, to appease their curiosity. Perhaps they have decided I have gone into another apartment. Perhaps they have seen nothing at all, and one of the men who works the equipment has simply come back for something he's forgotten. But I doubt it.

I leave the apartment via the roof, cross it noiselessly, and climb down by the steps that lead to Jameela's balcony. A few moments later I am lying at her side. For another hour I can't sleep.

I half-expected them to come for me, though I'm not sure why, and I'm not anticipating being detained for long. I wonder if Jameela is still officially married, and whether the technicality of adultery will see me expelled from the country. We are lying naked next to each other when the buzzer sounds. I have never heard it before and wonder what it is at first, but the loud simultaneous pounding on the door confirms the unfriendly nature of the visit.

Jameela and I dress hastily and are buttoning our clothes when two black men wearing suits and open shirts enter the room and announce abruptly in Arabic that they are members of the Mokhabarat, the intelligence and security service.

'I am a British citizen,' I say in English, holding my passport in front of me. 'I have the right to contact my embassy.'

The man nearest to me looks me up and down with a scowl, takes my passport and flicks through it. Then he hands it back, and his reply stuns me.

'You are British. *She* is not.' He points to Jameela on the far side of the room and snaps his finger. The other man grabs her arm and leads her to the door.

'I'm sorry, Antoine,' she says. She looks utterly demoralised and bites her lips as her eyes fill with tears.

'Jameela, what is happening? Tell me what is happening.'

'I'm sorry,' she says again.

The man pushes her though the bedroom door and guides her down the stairs without looking back. The sight of her disappearing has a strange effect on me. I cannot bear the thought of her being harmed. I see the sudden image of the *haboob* and the boiling wall of sand drawing towards me, and feel myself being swallowed in its immensity. I try to follow her down the stairs, but the other man blocks my way by putting his arm across the doorway.

His eyes have a fierce coldness to them. He looks straight at me and says something slowly in Arabic which I don't understand, but the language of threat is universal and the cruelty in his eyes tells me the warning is a serious one. Something in me is snapping. It's as if I can hear it, taking up the final moments of strain before it reaches its limit and shatters into fragments. I don't want it to, because there'll be no return when it does. I meet his gaze.

'Let me go, now,' I say very slowly.

'Mister,' he says, 'you should not fuck Sudan woman. She make too much noise.'

People will always tell you about the horrors of conflict, but seldom about the exhilaration that so often accompanies it. War is one of the rare performances on the human stage where every taboo is lifted, every restraint lifted, and the limits removed from behaviour that's unthinkable in peacetime. The result is that people do extraordinary things, sometimes performing acts of selfless courage that defy belief, and at others carrying out acts of depravity that make the world shudder. The lack of limits brings out strange things in people. It's as if, when war is declared, something else takes over where reason leaves off, a promise of freedom that will always be denied in ordinary life, the taste of which is incomparably sweet. Perhaps that's why war is likened to a fog, a mist, a *haboob* even. I know there is no return from this. I have declared war.

I push his arm sharply in the crook of his elbow, and as it gives way I walk out of the room. He doesn't like that idea. Almost instantly I feel his arms on me, grabbing me from behind and pulling me violently back inside. But I'm not in the mood to be thwarted now. I draw my mind and breath towards my centre of gravity and keep my balance, turning as he pulls me so that I move around him, then drop suddenly to one knee as I sense his momentum beginning to follow mine. As his body begins to fall onto me, I reach back with both hands to get a grip on his wrist and upper arm, and pull as hard as I can.

He's not prepared for the move. As his centre of gravity shifts over mine, I heave on the arm and straighten my legs, pushing my hips into his and propelling his body over my shoulder. I release the air from my lungs and a yell explodes from my abdomen. His body flies over me. He's heavy and smashes a chair as he falls, then tries to roll and get onto his knees, so I kick him in the face as his head is rising. He lurches to one side like a torpedoed boat, his right hand moving to the holster on his left, but I'm above him before he can unclip the pistol, and swing the edge of my hand onto his nose. There's a crunching sound and he's unconscious before his head hits the floor.

I want his pistol, but the time it takes me to release it is too great, and his partner seems to be flying through the door, weapon ready. But not quite ready enough. If he'd come into the room in a firing stance he might have found the time to shoot me, but his right arm is flailing and I throw myself at him before he can take aim. We end up half in the doorway, and his right arm flies back and the pistol clatters down the tiles of the stairs. I feel his nails dig into my neck. I can smell his breath and the oily scent of his skin. I drive my forearm into his throat without giving him a chance to draw breath from the fall that's winded him, and hear a gasp as he begins to choke. If I can keep up the pressure it shouldn't take too long.

I don't want to kill him. My right foot finds the door frame and I use it as a brace to put all the force I can summon onto his windpipe and my weight onto his chest until he runs out of air and passes out, but I'm not expecting what happens next. His left hand is free and has found, perhaps from his belt, a short-bladed knife, the tip of which he manages desperately to sink into the calf muscle of my left leg. It's strange. I don't feel much, except the warmth of the blood as it spreads across the fabric of my trousers. But his next attempt will probably end up in my ribs. I don't want to, but I release the hold from his throat and grab his wrist with both hands to twist the knife out of his hand, but he's too strong and I can't do it. He's sucking the air back into his lungs like a diver who's just surfaced. It's time to bail out.

I roll back into the room and tear his partner's pistol from its holster, cock it on the move and turn. The doorway's empty. He's pulled himself down the stairs to try and get his weapon back, but I'm there, thank God, before he reaches it, and fire five rounds into the stairwell above the outline of his body until he's screaming at me to stop.

The contest is over, but whoever has driven Jameela away will sound the alarm. I need information. I don't know these men who have burst into my life, and I don't know why they have. I don't know why they've taken Jameela, and I don't have much time to find out. If I get away within a few minutes, a dim reasoning tells me I can make it to the embassy and take refuge there. But I need this man to talk first. With the muzzle of the pistol jammed into the back of his neck, I don't give him time to think between questions.

'*Amur amniyati*,' a security matter, he says. That the reason they're here.

'What security matter? What matter?'

'*Al jasoos. Britaniyyah*. Spy ... spy,' he splutters. 'British spy.'

I realise I've broken the rules somewhere, but how I've been classed as a spy is a mystery. I need to know what, or who, has betrayed me.

'Why?' I yell. 'Why do you want me?'

He shakes his head furiously, or as much as the space between his head and the ground allows.

'*La, la*. Not you,' he says. 'The woman.'

The world's gone mad. I suddenly hear my own breathing, but I'm not saying anything because I don't know what to say. I can make no sense of this. Jameela isn't a British spy. Jameela is the woman I love. Jameela has nothing to do with all this.

'Explain.' I dig the pistol deeper, which has the desired effect.

'She is agent. She meet with your MI6 from embassy. Every day.'

The answer comes in a rasping whisper, half in English, half in Arabic, but I still can't believe what I'm hearing. Jameela, he's telling me, meets a contact from the British embassy every day in a hotel for a few minutes of conversation. He doesn't know why they meet, he says. That's why they've been watching her. It's one of their SOPs to take an interest in anyone who meets the intelligence officials of another country.

I can understand that much. But when I ask him to describe the agent she meets with, he gives me a perfect description of Halliday.

'Thin, like skeleton,' he says, and mentions his glasses and his stupid mop of hair. The same Halliday who so enjoys playing the buffoon, and who's pretended from the start never to have met Jameela.

It's only when I discover the camera in Jameela's apartment, he says, that they decide to bring her in to question her. It's not me they wanted.

But they'll want me now.

It's time to disappear. I lock the two Mokhabarat men in the bathroom leaving the key in the door so at least their rescuers won't have to smash it open, and though I doubt it'll win me too many favours, leave the unloaded pistols outside the door on the floor. In my go bag there's a first aid kit from which I take a bandage to bind my leg. Then I limp to the main road and take a taxi to my guest house.

There's no time to do much packing. The taxi waits outside for me. I change out of my blood-soaked trousers and re-bandage my leg. I head for the north of the city, making sure on the way to casually ask the driver where I can find trucks heading for the Eritrean border. When he comes forward to help the police with their enquiries, perhaps he'll throw them off my trail. Then I take a bus west across the river and head for Omdurman, towards the last place they'll look for a foreign fugitive.

Beneath the silver dome of the Mahdi's shrine, the elderly guardian remembers me, and greets me with a warm but grave look of concern as he notices my limp. He escorts me to the buildings behind the shrine. I don't make any attempt to conceal the trouble I'm in. I tell him I'll understand if he is unable to give me refuge and offer to make a contribution to the upkeep of the shrine. He eyes the bundle of hundred-dollar bills I put before him. There is a grave and untainted steadiness to his eyes, which perhaps a lifetime of prayer and piety has forged into his soul. Meeting his gaze, I have a momentary sense that my own life seems a frivolous thing. I am saved from the inexplicable impulse to admit to this when he chuckles loudly.

'We will show you more mercy than the General Kitchener showed to our warriors, but not for money. Your protection is my duty, as a Muslim.'

He hands me back the bundle and leads me to a small room where there's a simple bed. I sit. He points silently to my leg as if he wants to see the wound. I pull the fabric of my trousers to the knee, and as I take the bandage off, it starts pouring blood again, and I realise it won't close on its own unless it's immobile and bandaged for several days, which I don't have. When I make a sewing gesture with my hands he understands immediately and fetches a towel. From my go bag I take the first aid pouch, and retrieve a small bottle of Betadine and a suture kit. I give the old man one surgical glove and put the other one on my left hand.

The pain makes me tremble. The suture needle is crescent-shaped and glides through my skin while the old man holds the two sides of the wound together. He's unflappable and would have made a good surgeon's assistant. He even mops the sweat from my head as I do the sewing, and cuts the black thread where I point, just above the final knot. Then I drench the wound in the Betadine again and cover it tightly with the bandage.

'*Khelaas*. I will pray at the shrine for your health,' says the old man. '*Insha'allah* you will recover quickly.'

'*Insha'allah*,' I hear myself whisper.

The pain invades my whole leg now. I feel the double toxins of adrenalin and exhaustion, and though my mind is still racing I long for sleep. But there's one more thing. When the old man leaves, I take the satphone and thank God and the Mahdi that I can receive a signal near the window.

There's a watery-sounding ringtone and a succession of clicks.

'Hope you I didn't wake you up,' I say when it answers, 'but they say cowgirls don't sleep much.'

'Goddamn it, Tony, you sound like you're at the bottom of a creek. You on a satphone?'

'I need to find a good travel agent,' I tell her. 'Someone to get me home quickly without showing up on anybody's grid.'

'Hell,' she says, 'so long as it's illegal, I'll help any way I can.'

This distant promise of help fills me with the strange urge to cry. I tell her where I am, that I need a new passport, ticket and some supporting identity. She doesn't waste time on trying to find out how I came to be on the run from the Sudanese secret service. She just wants to know my exact location, preferred time frame and route for the exfil, whether the immigration system at the airport is computerised, and whether local law enforcement has a photograph of me. She asks what languages I speak. I tell her I'll buy her dinner at Nora's in DC when this is all over.

I feel burningly hot and then cold. I can't sleep. My mind's a whirlpool of black thoughts and things I don't understand and my feelings are too strong for me to think properly. I feel brutalised by the thought that Jameela was expecting my arrival in Khartoum and played along with every part of it. I wonder, since everyone else I've trusted seems to be lying to me, whether Grace will betray me too.

Halfway through the night, sleep closes in on me.

So it's with nothing short of a feeling of the miraculous that I open the package that arrives at dawn the next day. The old man delivers it when he comes to wake me, saying that a child came to the shrine and asked that it be given to the foreign guest. There's a printed reservation number for my ticket, a Canadian passport in the name of Cousteau and a worn leather wallet complete with credit cards. There are even some Canadian dollars in it. I see from the passport that I entered Sudan three weeks earlier. I was told the CIA station in Khartoum had been shut down but they've obviously kept some talented employees on the payroll, and I've never been quite so grateful for the no-nonsense American attitude towards getting things done.

The rest is a gamble. If the police are stopping cars on the way to the airport I'll call it off and try my chances to the south. But if they're only checking passports, I have a good chance of slipping through. They won't have my photograph, and only the two Mokhabarat officials can personally identify me.

I take a taxi to the airport and sit in the car with the driver until I see a party of foreigners disembarking from a hotel minibus. I pay the driver extra and ask him to wait, though I'm not planning to come back, and amble to the group of tourists, who are gathering up their bags. Scanning the building for signs of extra security, I break away from the tourists, head for the airline counter, and give the reservation reference to an attractive Sudanese girl wearing a purple veil. She thanks me and hands me a ticket in my new name. She bears a cruel resemblance to Jameela, whose face haunts me now. Then I head for the immigration desk, where the group I joined earlier are fussing over their departure forms, and fill out my own, remembering only at the last minute to check my signature against the one in my passport, which I copy as well as I can.

I will myself to be invisible, merging into the flow of the others in the hope that I'll look like a member of the group. We go through security and form a line ahead of the final passport check. I'm nearly there. I shuffle forward, looking at the ground, not daring to look up and draw attention to my face. But I can't resist a glance around to see what's happening, and it's at this precise moment, as if the very atoms in my surroundings have conspired to make it happen, that the uniformed immigration officer looks straight at me.

I turn my eyes away, but he calls out to me, and suddenly the world begins to slow down as if I'm in a dream, and I feel my heartbeat pushing up into my throat as he calls out again, tapping his pen on the kiosk to get my attention.

I pretend not to notice and turn towards the doors, wondering if there are any police between me and the exit, and whether I can make it to the taxi before things turn noisy. But the woman ahead of me in the queue, an earnest American in a safari hat, is tapping on my shoulder to get me to turn around, and now it seems the whole line is staring at me.

I'm trying hard to disguise my own dread. I wonder if I can manage the sprint to the doors, but my leg won't take it. I force a bewildered smile to my face. The official is waving me impatiently towards him. I feel as if I'm standing above an open trapdoor and about to be forced to take a step forward. I walk to the booth, where he's pointing his finger energetically at me. It's only then I realise dimly that I've seen him before, and that it's the same officer who stamped my passport when I first entered the country.

He takes my passport, opens it at a random page without even looking for my entry visa, and brings down the exit stamp with a thump. He doesn't notice that I have a different name and nationality now. He points to himself and then to me, and with the same gleaming smile that flashed at me on the day of my arrival, says, 'My *friend*.'

Then he returns my passport to me, and the pen I have earlier lent him, and waves me on.

12

The Firm likes its staff to live nearby. It makes them less depend-
ent on public transport in case of 'incidents' that mean they have
to get to work in a hurry. North or south of the river doesn't
make much difference these days, and the stigma attached to
living near the Firm's former headquarters at Century House
in dreary north Lambeth has been thoroughly exorcised. So
Kennington is fine; anywhere near the Oval but south of the
gasworks is desirable; Fentiman Road is very nice if you can
get it; and the quiet streets off St George's Drive in Pimlico are
rather perfect.

Seethrough, I now discover, lives a little further away, but at
under three miles it's not so far as to refute his claim that he
sometimes jogs to work. According to the BT engineer I rely on
for the occasional discreet enquiry, he lives a stone's throw from
St Luke's Church in Chelsea, and it's here that I wait for him in
Gerhardt with some food and a Thermos and enough paraceta-
mol to keep the pain in my leg under control.

His house doesn't have a garage so he has to walk from his
car to the front door, and it's 9 p.m. when I finally catch sight of
him. He's moving at a pace that makes it painful for me to catch
up, and his hand is just moving to the keys in his pocket when he
senses the presence of someone behind him. As I reach him, he
turns his head slightly but not enough to see my face.

'Keep your hands by your sides,' I tell him, 'and keep walking.'
I'm pointing the antenna of the mobile at him through the pocket
of my jacket.

'Alright,' he says quietly and very slowly, in the manner of a surgeon on the point of extracting a bullet. Then he realises that it's me.

'Oh, for fuck's sake. You're supposed to be in Khartoum.'

'Keep walking, please.'

'Fuck is going on, Ant?'

'Did you hear what I said?'

'Just don't do anything bloody stupid.' After a few yards he regains his habitual composure. 'You've got a bit of a suntan, Ant. And you're limping. Are you sure you're alright?'

I know he'll try to work the conversation around so that he's in charge of it. I'm almost curious to see how he does it. He's throwing out lines now, to see which one I'll bite at. We turn into Sydney Street and move south.

'Who helped you out, Ant? Cheltenham says you made a call to an unlisted number in America.'

'You were running Hibiscus without telling me,' I say.

There's a pause before he replies.

'Yes.' He purses his lips like someone who's deciding from the look of the sky whether it's going to rain. 'Course we were.'

'I need to know why.'

'Perfectly normal precaution, and none of your business. How'd you find out anyway?'

'I found out,' I tell him, 'because two armed Mokhabarat officers came to take my source away, and that wasn't in the plan.'

'Well.' He muses again. 'They are very much more efficient than they used to be. Get picked up at her place, did you?'

He's already figured out the scenario.

'It wasn't very nice. One of them tried to stab me too.'

'Is that why you're limping? Have you had it looked at? Christ, we would have brought you home.'

'You were running Hibiscus before I ever got to Khartoum. You set me up.'

240

'Rubbish,' he says dismissively. 'Don't be so melodramatic. Keeping an eye on her was just a safety net. Imagine it hadn't been us. Imagine someone else had got her on their payroll. Ever occur to you? Rate you were going, you might have compromised the entire op. Anyway it's not unusual. Makes the source feel special, like they're doing something important. Secondly we get to compare what she says with what you tell us. Like matching up a couple of fingerprints. If there are any discrepancies we know something funny's going on.'

'Were there any discrepancies?'

'As yet, no. I wasn't expecting any, but that's how we do things.' His tone softens, and I recognise the gentle introduction of charm. 'We also get to see how you handle your first cultivation. I, personally, was impressed with the way you handled Rome. Your meeting there is already bringing us some half-decent CX. I thought you should be given a chance with Hibiscus, but not everybody agreed with me. You haven't exactly come through the right channels, but you could have a future with the Service, Ant.'

'I don't believe a word of what you're saying.'

'Excellent.' He stops and turns to me. There's a disarming grin on his face. 'You're showing the first signs of a competent Intelligence Branch officer. Wouldn't it be better if I put that on your appraisal form rather than mention that you assaulted me with a weapon while I was on my way home?'

'It's not a weapon.' I pull out the mobile from my pocket. 'And I didn't assault you.'

He sighs.

'Come on,' he says. 'You're upset. Let's go to the Phat Phuk. Good Vietnamese scoff. It's just up here.' He searches my face for a signal of assent and, as he knows he eventually will, finds it.

True to his apparent concern, Seethrough does have my leg looked at. He arranges for a car to take me the next day to a surgeon in Wimpole Street, who's unimpressed by my do-it-yourself repairs.

A sour look comes over his face as he peers at my attempt at stitches through an illuminated magnifying glass. Then he deadens the leg with an injection and a stout serious-looking Polish girl fastens a surgical mask to his face. My ragged black stitches are pulled gently free from the enclosing skin and replaced with neat loops of biodegradable suture that doesn't need removing. I lie on my stomach and feel nothing, thinking of the steady eyes of the guardian of the Mahdi's shrine.

'It feels much better when it's done with anaesthetic,' I tell the surgeon.

An hour later I'm limping to Regent's Park and marvelling at its greenness. After the dust and desiccation of Khartoum, it's so much easier to understand why the Islamic vision of paradise is a verdant place with running streams and fountains. I sit for a while on a bench beside the main avenue and watch people passing. They seem extraordinarily preoccupied and utterly unaware of the luxury of their surroundings.

Later I walk along the shady paths by the ponds and through the rose garden and back to the Outer Circle, where I've parked Gerhardt. I have not paid attention to the time and there's a ticket on the windscreen. England is unreal to me again.

At home, nothing seems to have changed, although my private world has gone through indescribable tumult over the past few weeks. I mow the lawn and clear the pond of leaves, and count my fish to see if they're all there. I write up a long report for Seethrough on everything that's happened in Khartoum, and send it as an encrypted email via the Firm's server.

I call Jameela at her home for three days in a row but there's no answer. Then, on the fourth, she picks up. Her faint voice carries on it a flood of memories. She was released without harm after twelve hours. But I have a burning question.

'Yes,' she says, in answer to it, 'it was real. All of it.'

'What do we do now?' I ask.

'I don't know.' She weeps.

I don't know either. I want to ask when we'll see each other again, but the question sticks in my throat and the result is a long and agonising silence in which each impulse to speak is superseded by its opposite. Neither of us knows what to say. There is only a silent knowing which we both instinctively feel is undermined by words; it's the very thing we detected in each other when we first met and which took us both by surprise with its intensity. Even at this distance from each other we are in its grasp again.

I call H too, and he invites me to his home to catch up. I drive there the following day. It's sunny and H is in his garden on a ladder, picking caterpillars from the leaves on his rear porch.

'They're eating my wisteria,' he says, 'but I don't like to kill the little buggers.' I help him gather them up and put them in a box which he's planning to empty in a neighbouring field.

He doesn't like the look of my limp, so a long walk isn't part of our plans.

'Thought we could put in an hour's target practice,' he says. 'Good for morale. We've got permission to use the drive-in range, so we don't have to creep around any quarries.'

It's not far. Eight miles from the bridge at Hereford we reach a village where there's an ancient church with an illustrious history. I half expect to see a WORKS ACCESS ONLY sign of the kind that usually indicates a secret government facility, but there's nothing of the kind. We turn off the main road opposite the church, and drive almost a mile along a country lane barely wide enough for two cars. At an unremarkable crossroads H turns along the way he knows. We pass a derelict-looking farm and suddenly there are high chain-link fences on both sides of the road, beyond which any view is obscured by thick twenty-foot-high deciduous hedges. Poking above them are some high-frequency antenna arrays resembling rotary washing lines, the kind used for long-range agent communication, but there's not much else to betray a special forces training camp.

We turn in opposite a cluster of low buildings. H slows the car, puts his window down and waves to the man emerging from the security post, who smiles as he recognises him.

'Alright, H——?' calls a thick Scottish voice. 'Nae seen you fra while.'

'You know how it is,' says H, and tells him we'll be about an hour.

'Nae grief, mate,' comes the reply.

We pass a small car park with a fleet of scruffy identical vehicles which look as though they're used for training. A helicopter with no registration markings sits in a neighbouring field. To our left, a quarter of a mile away, rises a wooded slope which H calls Gibbie's Hill, where he fondly recalls catching wild eels to eat on an E & E exercise. We drive towards it across some innocent-looking open land, past some equally innocent-looking buildings, and then some slightly less innocent-looking ones. These, H says, are former ammunition storage facilities, protected by mounded blast-protecting revetment walls and once linked by rail when the site was used as a hideaway for government munitions. The Regiment calls them bunkers. H points out the bunker with the mocked-up interior of a house where he used to practise hostage rescue scenarios. One of the rooms contains a comfy sofa where, despite the bullet holes, H says he used to sleep when it got too late to go home.

At the foot of the hill the road loops around and we pull up at the entrance to what at first looks like a small open-air stadium.

It's a hundred and fifty feet square, with steep grassy banks on three sides, which rise to about thirty feet. The whole area is fenced off and guarded with a barrier on its open side, which faces south so that no one has to shoot into the sun. Vehicle drills of the kind we've earlier practised are carried out within the central enclosure, but H doesn't want me to risk aggravating my leg, so we work on grouping and then snap shooting with the Brownings. Then, because H can't resist the opportunity, we practise shooting from a moving vehicle, which is as noisy as it is exhilarating. And as he rightly suggests, good for morale.

We drive back in the afternoon. As we reach the village near his home I offer him a drink at his local. But he seldom goes there any more, he says. He used to when he first moved to the area years ago, he says, but that was before the SAS became such a big deal. He stopped going to the pub not long after the Prince's Gate hostage rescue, when people who heard he was in the Regiment would treat him disturbingly, like a kind of god.

The thing I like about H is that he prefers to be invisible. I can't really picture him, after all this is over, going public and giving lectures to the local British Legion in pubs around Hereford and Leominster. Nothing makes him stand out in either habit or appearance, unless you count the small knife that always hangs from the back of his belt or the length of opaque plastic that he carries in his wallet, which can be put to so many different uses.

The few Regiment men I've met all share this quality. They are the last ones you would identify as members of the most feared military unit in the world. They are all exceptionally fit, and exertion comes easily to them. They enjoy order and precision in physical tasks, and prefer action to theory, which makes them wary of pretence or self-importance and suspicious of men who wear moleskin trousers. They take solace in beauty of the kind not found in art galleries but in the mist that hovers over a bend in a river at dawn. They rarely smoke, but tend to drink more than most. Much more, in fact. They love the quiet life of the English country village until the next operation in a country that most of us have never heard of. It's true they keep strange things in their garages, but they get points on their driving licences like anyone else.

So H cooks us an early dinner instead, and afterwards produces a bottle of whisky, which we broach in front of the fire that he lights in his living room. We get on to stories about people H has met who claim to be members of the Regiment. His favourite is the time he gets into conversation with a former soldier who's just delivered a lecture to a gathering of security experts and claims to have been in the SAS for years. H invites him for a friendly drink, over which the man reveals, confidentially of course, that he's a former member of the Regiment's F Squadron. There's no need, on this occasion, to make a call to the security cell at the Regimental HQ to check on him, because the SAS has never had an F Squadron.

Stories about the more stubborn Walter Mitty types sometimes reach *Mars and Minerva*, the Regiment's newsletter. H finds me a copy. It's mostly titbits of news and reunions. There's a mention of the sophistication and expense of the security features incorporated in the double fence around the new camp at Credenhill. There are letters from former members and their wives, details of the Regimental Association's benevolent fund, and obituaries. Members can even buy wine with the Regiment's insignia on the label. It's as interesting as a village parish magazine. Nothing could be further from the sensationalism of all the books with flaming daggers on their fronts, which now seem so absurd to me.

'It's weird,' I say.

'What's weird?'

'It's just that in films when they have to train someone for a special op, they take him off to a huge underground secret base.'

'You mean one with those doors that swish open like they do in *Star Trek*?'

'Exactly. And a thing that X-rays you and scans your eyeball. You don't see them saving caterpillars or sitting on the floor in somebody's living room with a dog asleep on a chair.'

H looks affectionately at his terrier Jeffrey, who occupies the largest chair in the room, and tugs on his sleeping chin.

'Welcome to the real world,' he says.

On the way home, Gerhardt has difficulty pulling away from a crossroads, and I realise I've forgotten to top up the transmission fluid. I stop at a garage and it occurs to me, as I burn my hand on the cylinder head in the attempt to remove the transmission fluid dipstick, that it's time to call in the favour from Gemayel before I leave.

It's also time to see the Baroness. I arrange it in the usual way, but she's not at the club and a note is waiting for me instead, indicating that I come to her home. I'm not expecting to be followed but take time for a careful dry-cleaning before reaching her front door. She buzzes me in. I feel my calf aching where the stitches have yet to heal as I walk up the stairs to the second floor.

The curtains are half-drawn as if she hasn't had the strength to open them fully. She's visibly more frail and I can't help thinking that the end of an era is near. She uses a hand to steady herself against the furniture as she walks across the room, but stubbornly insists on preparing a pot of tea on her own and not letting me help.

I tell her about Khartoum, my illegal escape, and about my feelings for Jameela.

'It does happen sometimes.' She smiles. Her teacup tilts imperfectly on the saucer as she returns it. Then her expression grows more grave and I can tell she has something on her mind.

'I have some news,' she says. 'It's not what you would call good.'

I'm imagining it's something personal, so it's a shock when she refers to the operation we're planning in Afghanistan.

'It is only a whisper, but it's been suggested that some parties would prefer the operation to fail.'

'To fail? Who could want it to fail? Is this Macavity's idea?'

She shakes her head and frowns.

'Elsewhere. There's no reason Macavity should know. The contrary.' She lets out a wistful sigh. 'Have you considered the possibility of the missiles being allowed to fall into the wrong hands in order to be turned against us? To permit such a catastrophe may even be desirable to some. Imagine,' she smiles darkly, 'a new crusade. It would reach across the world and drag on for a generation.'

'That sounds dangerously like a conspiracy,' I tell her.

'What is coherent at a more organised level may be incomprehensible at a lesser one. If it is true, as I fear it may be, we must hope that the plan is uncovered along the way. The Network has always been a counterweight to the abuse of power, but it cannot change the weaknesses of human nature.' She sighs again, then looks up at me. 'You must be especially vigilant. When will you leave?'

'Soon. In a week or so.'

'Well,' she sighs, 'I have passed on what I could.'

I'm not certain what she's referring to, but I sense that it's more than simply the news she's given me. It's her habit to assign more than one meaning to the things she says, but now it's as if a mask is dropping from her, and she's preparing to relinquish the role she's steadfastly played all these years. I have the feeling she knows that, before long, loneliness and infirmity will rob her of all the worldly authority and guile her character has accumulated over a lifetime, and that now she must relinquish it voluntarily, shedding herself of its burden to allow her life to at last become simple and unencumbered.

'You will remember,' she says quietly, 'that the great art is always to find an activity which serves a practical visible purpose but which serves your hidden purpose as well.'

'You have taught me that and much more,' I say.

'Context ...' she begins, but then coughs harshly. 'Context is everything. I'm a little under par,' she says. 'Will you forgive me if I don't see you out?'

'I'll see you as soon as I'm back from Afghanistan.'

'When you're *both* back.' She means Manny, which I'm glad for.

'Yes, both of us will come and see you.'

'Of course.'

As I cross the road from her front door I look up to see her standing at a window. She's waving. But it's not a modern wave, where the hand flaps from side to side like a metronome. Her arm is upheld but remains still, and her hand rotates with only a slight and stately motion about her wrist. Then her gaze rises towards the sky, and it looks as though she's holding up an antique ornament towards the light, tilting it back and forth experimentally, as if to glimpse across its surface some tarnished hieroglyph which she alone can decipher.

It's a Sunday when the call comes.

'Why not come round for tea?' asks H in his characteristically gritty voice. It sounds an odd request until I remember it's the expression we've agreed on for our order to move. I make sure the letters I've prepared are left neatly on my desk, together with instructions for my sister in case she's the one who ends up having to deliver them.

Then I go for a short walk, because it's the last I'll see of this damp and peaceful world which my countrymen take so blissfully for granted. As I walk, I hear three sounds. One is the whispering of a light wind in the nearby trees, which at moments seems like a conversation between the leaves. The second is a succession of calls between a pair of wood pigeons. The last is a distant cyclical pealing from a church somewhere. The notes descend in an eight-bell octave, but grow confused as the notes begin to sound out of sequence. Soon they become a sonorous tangle, the last note sounding after the first and the others steadily more disordered, until gradually they begin to rearrange themselves. Then, in the manner of a knot that magically unravels itself, the octave regains its proper sequence and the scale is finally resolved and returns to its original harmony. After which there is only silence.

At dawn H and I fly to London in the Puma and are escorted to our final briefing at Vauxhall Cross. We surrender our mobile phones to security and are met once again by Stella, who leads us wordlessly to an upper floor.

Seethrough is waiting for us with what looks like a pair of shopping bags, which contain our personal hiking boots. We scrutinise them in turn but can't see where the heels have been opened and resealed to accommodate the tiny satellite transmitters that will keep track of our precise locations. The transmitters are almost identical to the kind covertly installed on ships and aircraft sold to allied forces around the world. Seethrough reminds us that they can also be used to designate a target or any other site that requires attention.

Then we move line by line through our operational plans, basically an actions-on list, or what we'll do in the event of various mishaps. Seethrough plays the role of ops officer, questioning us like a quizmaster and making sure in the process that we all agree, to the extent that things allow, on what happens and when.

He confirms that H's kit list, which consists of things that we can't easily explain to curious immigration officials, has been approved. Some items will be picked up at the British consulate in Peshawar, and the rest in Afghanistan through one of the few remaining foreign embassies that still function in Kabul, the identity of which we undertake never to reveal. The only exotic item we actually carry ourselves is our new codes, which are a more personal matter. They're stored on stamp-sized memory cards and easily concealed.

Then there's what Seethrough calls last orders, and we hand over the sealed copies of our wills. Nothing in his manner suggests to me he's aware that the operation will be deliberately threatened. It's obvious he doesn't know of any means by which our plans might be compromised, but is conforming faithfully to a well-established chain of command, the tainted origins of which lie far beyond our mutual reach.

No other place I know smells like Peshawar. The city is wrapped in smells like an Oriental tramp in an old coat from which he can't be parted. There are three main layers to these smells, and infinite lesser ones, the proportions of which depend on your luck, or lack of it.

The first is the smell of the land itself, an ancient alliance of fragrances that probably hasn't altered since the Buddha, Alexander, Chengiz Khan, Mahmoud the Great and Marco Polo passed through the city in turn. It's the one that reaches around you as you step from the featureless atmosphere of the plane. It's a warm smell, humid, sensual and faintly exotic. It comes from the mixture of dust, eternally recycled by wind and rain, and tropical vegetation, the fragrance of which suggests deep green canopies of untamed foliage on an immense scale.

The second layer rises unstoppably from the narrow open channels that run alongside every city street, carrying the full spectrum of human waste like a peeled-open intestine of infinite length, which you spend a good portion of the day anxiously hopping over or crossing on imperfectly balanced paving stones. The opaque slime contained in these primitive sewers cooks slowly in the heat, generously giving up its perfume of decomposition to the surroundings in a constant reminder of earthly dissolution and decay. It is strangely muted and inoffensive, and after a few days ceases to register.

The third layer is the toxic twentieth-century addition of vehicle fumes, which billow into the air from what seems like every passing vehicle. The main culprits are overworked buses and trucks, all obscenely laden and straining under their loads like ageing weightlifters. Clouds of eye-watering black exhaust follow them. On lesser streets and side roads their junior partners in olfactory crime are everywhere: plagues of three-wheeled rickshaws, trailing spumes of unburned oil from their soot-caked two-stroke engines.

Then, depending on where you find yourself, this basic range of smells is refined by the presence of countless others: the bluish smoke of low-grade wood charcoal burning on a million improvised stoves, betel nut, turmeric, cardamom, mildew, wool, concrete dust, whitewash, freshly skinned animal hides, baking bread, dung and the acrid fumes of burning rubbish.

Mercifully, our accommodation lies in the least polluted part of the city called University Town where, since we're officially working for them as consultants, we'll be staying at the official guesthouse of the de-mining trust. It's the western and most prosperous suburb, where the streets are overhung with dusty eucalyptus trees and sprawling vines, and where the UN and foreign NGOs have made their headquarters in spacious houses with gated compounds and gardens behind high walls. Beyond them, from the car that takes us to the trust's Peshawar headquarters, we catch glimpses of the villas built for the city's politicians, high-ranking military and all the dealers and players who've made their fortunes from the endless war in Afghanistan, and whose white marble towers and balconies gleam like poisonous wedding cakes.

Our first meeting in Peshawar is at the British consulate. It's there we've arranged to collect a large quantity of cash, to be delivered on behalf of the Cousins. It arrived from Islamabad a few days earlier, the consul tells us. He's a likeable, gangly and urbane figure in his sixties and probably on his last posting. He doesn't ask what's in the padlocked bag, though he probably knows.

'No end-user certificate required, I presume,' he mutters charmingly as he hands it over, then asks if we'll stay for lunch. Over the meal he briefs us informally on the situation in Afghanistan: the Taliban's steady advance into Massoud's shrinking stronghold in the north of the country and the stalemate in negotiations between the Americans and the Taliban on the ongoing issue of bin Laden.

'Poor old Massoud,' he murmurs, working his fork into a Yorkshire pudding. 'Never met him, but one feels terribly for him all the same.'

On our way back I ask the driver on impulse to take us to the Qissa Khane bazaar, which I want H to see. For an hour we wander through the clamour and chaos of the narrowing streets of the Old City, where the memories of my first visit with Manny return to me in unexpected flashes. I seem to remember the very places where we drank glasses of greenish iced sugar crushed from the raw cane in front of us, and shared kebabs with wild-looking mujaheddin who told us our first real tales of war, and I remember too how we sensed the magnetic pull of the war just across the border, and both felt immortal.

Time still holds this place less tightly in its grasp than most. On the way back we see a little crowd that has gathered around an elderly Punjabi snake charmer. He wears an orange turban and plays a strange sonorous melody on a reed flute to a jaded cobra, which he taps on the back of its neck when it's too tired to dance. It's how the two of them make a living. The sight reminds me how quickly we've been transported into a different world with different rules and ways which most Westerners don't even know exist, let alone really understand. I know, at least, that I don't.

We call our contact the following day. He agrees to visit us for lunch. I'm not sure what kind of person I expect, but he isn't it. At midday there's a banging on the gate and the chowkidar admits a lightly built man pushing a bicycle with dusty woven saddlebags. He wears a flowing white shalwar kameez, waistcoat and a black karakul lambskin hat, beneath which his ears project prominently. It must be Hamid Karzai. I recognise him from the photograph that Grace has shown me in Washington.

'Ah, Grace.' He chuckles, propping his bike against the wall. He takes off his hat and sweeps a hand over the perspiring and almost smooth crown of his head. 'She's a real cowboy. When she came to Afghanistan they treated her like a man.'

He has a quick mind and a keen sense of humour, and H and I both like him from the start. He talks freely in almost perfect English, and our conversation moves rapidly over the burning issues. The situation, he says, has never been more dangerous.

Massoud's forces are hanging by a thread, and unless more help comes he'll be unable to withstand the Taliban. With help, he'll be able to survive until rebellions can be spread among Pashtun groups within the Taliban's own heartland. It's an ambitious plan, which prompts H to ask if the Taliban can really be defeated. The answer surprises us.

'Nobody can defeat the Taliban militarily,' says Karzai, shaking his head. 'As long as Afghanistan exists, the Taliban will exist. They are the sons of Afghanistan and they will always have their place. But the Taliban are not one entity. They are like – what is the name of that Greek monster with all those heads? If you cut off one, another will take its place.'

'A hydra.'

'A hydra. But the Taliban can't unify my country. They cannot repeat their earlier success.'

'Success?' asks H. 'Do you call their kind of government a success?'

'My friend,' he says, 'for a scorpion, even hot sand is a relief. We have to start where we are. The Taliban have their place in that. You cannot deny them their achievements. People who have not seen the conditions in the country cannot understand their popularity. But by bringing foreign fighters onto the Afghan earth they have done a thing which Afghans cannot forgive. People can see where they are taking our country. That is why we need friends, real friends, who can help to defeat them politically.'

'Does that include America?' I ask.

'Of course,' he says. 'Why shouldn't it? I don't dislike America. But America is like the Taliban. It doesn't have one head. Listen, my friends. I have talked to American diplomats here and in Islamabad. I have talked to the State Department in Washington. I have talked to the CIA and the military. Every one of them has a different idea about Afghanistan, but only America is powerful enough to help us.' He sweeps his hand again over his head. 'Their great weakness is to see the world in black and white.

It's always good guys and bad guys with them.' He chuckles. 'In meetings they always ask, "Is he a good guy or a bad guy?" They want it to be black and white. But nothing is black and white in Afghanistan. There are a thousand shades between black and white.'

I ask if he thinks that bin Laden will be handed over.

He sighs deeply. 'Before, it was possible. Now, I doubt. After they tried to catch him, he is too cautious.' I didn't know anyone had tried to catch him, but thinking back to some of the things Grace alluded to back in Washington, it makes sense. Karzai raises an emphatic finger in the air. 'Osama will bring big trouble to Afghanistan, I guarantee. Even though he himself is not the most powerful one. Make no mistake. This is an international war with international players.'

We move on from this dark thought to more immediate things. Karzai doesn't know, or want to know, the operational details of our onward journey. But he sits with us over our maps and tells us in detail about the Taliban's deployments and what we can expect in different places. He agrees that to drive to the south via Kandahar will invite too much attention and that our planned approach from the north will be safer.

'Whatever you think of them,' he says, 'the Taliban are Afghans, and unless you do something very foolish they will treat you as their guests. But al-Qaeda is a different matter. They are trained to think that Westerners are the cause of all evil. If they suspect something, you will have difficulties.'

'When you say difficulties,' asks H, 'what do you mean?'

'I mean they will shoot you and your bodies will never be found. Fortunately for you the majority are in the south of the country and you are unlikely to meet them. God forbid it should be so.'

He agrees to send a message to our contact in Kabul to alert him to our arrival and advises caution in the matter of who we trust. When it's time to give him the money that we have promised to deliver on Grace's behalf, we hand over the shrink-wrapped bundles of cash, each one of which contains a hundred thousand dollars. He picks them up, stuffs them cheerfully into the saddle-bags of his bicycle, wishes us good luck and pedals away.

'He's pretty switched on for a bike messenger,' says H as we go back indoors.

Not many foreigners take the overland route into Afghanistan. We haven't actually got permission to enter the tribal territories between Peshawar and the border, but it can take weeks to arrange and H wants to see the Khyber Pass, which is actually a dramatic series of switchbacks on the Pakistani side of the frontier. It's an unforgettable way to get to Afghanistan and there isn't anywhere quite like it. So at dawn two days later, after our visas come through with the help of the trust, we change into local clothes and head for the border with our driver.

From the tribal point of view, we're already in Afghanistan. The British drew the frontier a hundred years ago, but it was never recognised by the Pashtuns who live along both sides of its thousand-mile length, and Afghans still like to joke that they in fact own much of Pakistan. It's wild territory. There are Pakistani police checkpoints along the way, but you get the sense their power doesn't reach much further than the distance they can swing their long bamboo truncheons. As we leave Peshawar behind, the mountains swell and the road begins to sway between their steepening flanks as we approach the pass that officially connects the two countries. Everything looks more dilapidated except the mountains, which rise steadily higher and magnify the feeling that you're entering a different world, with different and harsher but simpler rules. Even the sky begins to clear as the dust of the plains falls away, and the air cools as it thins.

The border post at Torkham is a chaotic place. There's a scruffy collection of buildings and a pair of wide gates flanked by fence posts that are no longer vertical, beyond which an Afghan flag flutters in the wind. Hovering near the gates are about a dozen Pakistani policemen in khaki uniforms, picking at random on individuals from the flow of men and women approaching the crossing point.

As long as we are not recognised as foreigners, there is nothing to stop us from entering Afghanistan here, and I sense that H is enjoying the idea of reliving the Great Game for a day and slipping unnoticed into the country. So a hundred yards from the gates we get out of the car and our driver agrees to wait until he sees us cross before he leaves. I catch the attention of an Afghan boy pushing a dusty cart laden with sacks and boxes, to which I add our bags and pay him a small sum to meet us on the far side of the gates. Then we say goodbye to our driver and merge into the flow.

'You look good in an Afghan hat,' I say to H.

'See you in Afghanistan,' he says.

We walk past the police as nonchalantly as possible and meet gratefully on the other side of the gates. It's an anticlimax. There doesn't seem to be any passport control. We wander into the courtyard of what looks like a customs post, where an armed Talib is dozing under a tree with an AK-47 across his lap. We rouse an official and are invited to sit, and a few minutes later a boy brings us tea. Then from the building someone waves us inside to a run-down office with a dusty desk beneath a bare bulb and a ceiling fan that doesn't work. He smiles and stamps our passports without much interest, then points us in the direction of some decrepit cars waiting to ferry passengers to Kabul. We're officially in Afghanistan.

Nothing has escaped the years of war here. For almost the entire route, the surface of the road has long since disappeared. For lengthy stretches even the road itself has simply been torn away by flooding or collapsed. Even on the best sections we weave between craters and gullies gouged out by years of neglect. The telephone poles and pylons beside the road have been stripped of their wires. There is no building, wall or human structure that is intact. Everything seems on the verge of collapse or to have been reduced to its most elemental parts. All along the way we see the vestiges of conflict: destroyed and rusting armoured vehicles, stripped of every salvageable part, crouching silently beyond the shoulders of the road or in the surrounding fields.

'That's not a tank,' says H, when I point out the first of them 'It's a BTR-70. Armoured personnel carrier. That one over there's a BMP combat vehicle.' He knows his Soviet armour from the days when the West feared the might of the Red Army, which fought its last engagement not in Europe but in the valleys and passes of Afghanistan.

The landscape is beautiful none the less. Perhaps it's even more beautiful because the evidence of destruction is never far away and makes us think of the fragility of life. It's also as if we've gone back in time. The surrounding villages, clinging to hillsides as if they've grown out of the ground itself, are made from timber and adobe and have a biblical look. White-bearded men in turbans and flowing gowns lead camels by the roadside or guide wooden ploughs behind oxen. We return briefly to the twentieth century as we enter Jalalabad, where the streets are paved again, and we stop to eat kebabs and freshly baked bread at a tiny stall. The owner jokes with us and asks if we are looking for Osama.

The capital bears all the scars of war. We drive in from the east, about six hours after leaving the border, and pass the shattered suburb of Microrayon, where every building is half-ruined by gunfire and rocket blasts.

'Bloody hell,' says H gloomily as he looks over the destruction. 'They really went to work here.'

Even on the outskirts of Kabul there are hollowed-out carcasses of Soviet-made tanks, whose turrets have been blown from their housings by anti-tank mines and lie upside down a few yards away. I wonder how many wars some of them saw before they ended up here. Some date from the era of the Soviet occupation that ended twelve years earlier, others from the long civil war that saw the city torn apart by rival factions. Some may have even seen action in the Gulf War, after which the CIA had the bright idea of gathering them up from Iraqi battlefields and bases and sending them on to Afghanistan.

Kabul seems half-deserted since I was last here, probably because the Tajik population championed by Massoud, the Taliban's arch-rival, has largely fled. Nor is there any sign of the *pakoul*, the flat woollen hat worn all over the north of the country. On the advice of our taxi driver, we've already hidden ours. There are few cars other than taxis and the occasional pickup truck with tinted windows, the preferred means of travel for Taliban commanders and their bodyguards. It's as if the place is on holiday and every normal activity has shut down. There are no kites in the sky. The Taliban have seized a ghost town.

Our guest house is in the least-destroyed residential part of the city called Wazir Akbar Khan, where a grid of homes for Kabul's most prosperous families was built in the 1970s. The trust provides a housekeeper and a chowkidar, who welcome us warmly and fuss over our every request. The windows on the ground floor are heavily sandbagged, and upstairs the panes have anti-shatter tape across them in case of nearby explosions. We install ourselves gratefully in big rooms with marble-floored bathrooms where the taps don't work because there's no electricity to pump the water. But we've made it to Kabul and we're happy to be here.

From the upstairs room we can just see a snow-covered ridge, miles away in the high mountains to the north. The final moments of sunlight are just settling along it with a bright pink glow, and it looks almost as if a luminous flamingo feather has gently fallen to rest there from the beyond.

13

The mine clearers are brave men whom I respect. Their work is dangerous and by normal standards they are paid a pittance for it. Though they save countless lives, they don't get the recognition they deserve and are frequently treated with suspicion or ridicule, especially in rural areas, by people who are too stupid to understand the importance of what they do.

They have never been introduced to the notion of life insurance. When one of their team is wounded or dies, the others contribute to a sum which is then delivered to the man's wife, who may be able to live from it for a few months. But this is Afghanistan, and they are among the most privileged of the city's employees.

We walk to their headquarters in Wazir the following morning, and are greeted with spine-crushing hugs from the manager, a burly and jovial Pashtun in his fifties who I've known for years. I call him Mr Raouf because he used to call me Mr Anthony, and the habit of using our first names stuck. Even as a junior member of the de-mining team his natural confidence and authority told me he'd do well, and I did everything to see he was promoted as swiftly as was fair. Now he's the local director and has thirty men working under him.

'Thanks be to God,' he smiles, 'life is good. You see how religious we have all become?' he asks with an ironic chuckle, and tugs at his thick beard. It's a decree of the Taliban that men let their beards grow. Being clean-shaven is associated with the irreligious devilry of the communists, who brought ruin to Afghanistan, though not everybody agrees. Like many Afghans, Raouf doesn't see why not having a beard should make him less religious, and like any Afghan, he dislikes being told what to do.

Mr Raouf gives H and me a tour of the trust's new facility in Wazir, then drives us to a training area on a hillside in the east of the city, where his men are learning to detect mines. We have lunch in his office, where the shelves are lined with a slightly macabre collection of deactivated anti-personnel mines.

'In a few days,' I tell him, 'I need to drive to a place in the south-west of the country. I need a few reliable men who can help me and who will not talk about what they have done.'

'*Dorost*. Right. They will be at your service,' he says without hesitating. 'What will you do in this place?'

'I will make a big explosion.'

A smile spreads slowly over his face, and he strokes his beard as he nods admiringly at us both.

'I am proud to help you,' he says. 'Especially for an explosion.'

To confirm that I will make it worth his while would be to offend him, so I don't.

'Your men will be generously rewarded,' I say.

There's a knock at the door and one of his staff announces that the men are ready for their afternoon game of soccer, but that they're short of two men. Mr Raouf looks at us with a questioning twinkle in his eye, and we're too surprised to refuse. I am lent a pair of boots several sizes too small, and hobble to the pitch outside. It's a grassless stretch of land that's as rough and hard as bulldozed rubble. The air is so thin I can't seem to suck enough of it into my lungs. And since the Afghan body is made out of a substance harder and more durable than ordinary flesh and bone, when our shins and arms make contact with our opponents, H and I agree that it's as if we've been hit with wooden bats.

We haven't had so much fun for ages.

The mornings are quiet and cool, and on the balcony we soak up the rays of the sun like lizards. There's little to suggest that the country is a place torn apart by conflict. The occasional rumble of artillery far to the north can be easily mistaken for distant thunder, and the sound of AK-47 fire on the outskirts of the city is indistinguishable from that of a horse trotting on tarmac, carried from afar on an uneven wind.

H busies himself with the equipment we'll need for the overland journey, with which Mr Raouf has agreed to help us. We also receive a message from London to tell us that the special items we've requested are ready to be picked up. The friendly embassy is one of the few that has not been abandoned, and lies in the centre of town. We are given two large black nylon bags, which we take back home and unpack on the floor of a locked bedroom. It feels like Christmas, and we lift out the layers of supplies with the thrill of children who've never had presents before.

Uppermost are several maps of Afghanistan printed on silk, of the kind usually issued to special forces. They can be easily concealed without being damaged by crumpling up into a ball, and it doesn't matter if they get wet because they can still be read and will dry in the open air within a few minutes. There's a pair of two-way radios with chargers and adaptors for use in vehicles. There's a modified weapons sight called a Kite which looks like a stubby telescope and will allow us to see in near-total darkness, and a second telephone which like my own switches to satellite frequencies when there's no cellular signal. There's a fifty-metre length of black nylon climbing rope, which I idly presume is for H in case he needs to abseil through any embassy windows. There are also two quick-draw plastic holsters and the pair of Brownings that H has been secretly dreaming of, together with several hundred rounds of 9-millimetre ammunition.

'It's like an Andy McFuck novel,' says H with a grin, removing the magazine from one of the pistols and peering along the sights. 'Not very deniable, though.'

I reach into the bag to see what's left. In another moulded plastic carrying case there's a Trimpack military GPS receiver and a metal mounting bracket for use in a vehicle. It's not new and has seen a few years' service, though God knows where. Then I find what looks like a man's black leather belt, which is so unexpectedly heavy I need two hands to pull it free.

'Feels like it's full of gold,' I joke.

'It is full of gold,' says H. He takes the belt and pulls open a long zip on the inside face, revealing a line of twenty solid gold sovereigns nestling in a waterproof sleeve. I don't know the exact value of a sovereign, but each one must be worth several hundred dollars, so there's roughly ten thousand dollars' worth of gold in a belt. There are two. 'Should get us a few kebabs,' he says.

We hide the equipment in the roof space of the house and I mark it with the ultraviolet pen. Reminded of its usefulness, and as a further precaution, I also mark the handles on our bedroom doors. Even the tiniest variation in their position will be detectable, and tell us if our rooms have been visited in our absence.

The biggest present is yet to come. When we get the message from Mr Raouf's office that there's been a delivery H is mystified, but I already know what's waiting for us. We drive with Mr Raouf in the trust's pickup to an immense car and truck park in the north-west of the city. In so far as the Taliban have a customs clearance centre, this is it. It's here that the goods that have survived the long drive from the Pakistani port of Karachi are finally unloaded and spread over an area the size of several football fields.

It's guarded by two armoured personnel carriers at the gates. We drive past several thousand truck containers and vehicles and are escorted by an armed Talib to a succession of run-down offices. Endless paperwork is endlessly inspected and approved over equally endless pots of tea. But it's worth the wait. Several hours later, we're led to a long line of dusty pickup trucks with registration plates from Dubai where an unmistakable shape leaps out at me. The design hasn't really changed for twenty-five years.

'Meet son of Gerhardt,' I say. My hand comes to rest on the bonnet of a Mercedes G400 CDI. It's the more serious version. It has a four-litre turbocharged diesel V8 engine that generates 250 brake horsepower, which makes it rather more powerful and sophisticated than Gerhardt. It also costs about fifty times more.

'How the bloody hell did you manage that?' asks H.

'Called in a favour.'

'That's quite a favour.'

It is. I don't know how Gemayel has done it. I'm guessing that his friends in the Arab world have friends in the Taliban world, and things have been smoothed over at a high level.

Mr Raouf looks a bit disappointed.

'Is this it?' he asks, stroking his beard thoughtfully. I suspect he's a Land Cruiser sort of man. The G-Wagen is unheard of in Afghanistan, where its talents are unknown, and its boxy profile has yet to become an object of desire. From carjackers and bandits whose idea of heaven is the cab of a Toyota Hilux, at least we'll be less of a target. They'll also be unlikely to know about its built-in satellite tracker.

I offer Mr Raouf the key but he defers with a grimace. He'll drive back in the trust's pickup, which is more to his taste.

H circles the vehicle and taps the greenish glass of one of the windows.

'Bloody thing's armoured.'

He's right. I didn't ask Gemayel for the armour, but he's had it added anyway, which is a thoughtful gesture. All the windows look about half an inch thick, which will be useful if anyone is in the mood to have a snipe at us, because they'll need a 50-calibre to get past these windows. We climb in. The armour makes the doors feel as though they weigh half a ton each, and the windows don't come down. The interior smells of leather and dust, but has a luxurious feel, as if we've entered the private quarters of a billionaire's yacht. I recognise and am at home with the basic layout, but there's more buttons on the steering wheel alone than all the cars I've ever owned. For those with sensitive fingers, I notice, the steering wheel itself can be heated. The rear-view mirror darkens automatically in response to glare, and there are sensors to monitor the tyre pressures. My eye is caught by the satellite television and the triple electronic differential locks, which means I can drive it almost anywhere except a vertical rock face and watch a badly dubbed Arab soap opera beamed out of Dubai at the same time.

'Shall we see how it goes?' I ask H.

In Afghanistan cars sound as if they're about to fall apart when you slam their doors. This one sounds as if we've just closed the hatch of a nuclear shelter. The engine starts first time and purrs. It's done less than a thousand kilometres and is good for about another half-million. Mr Raouf drives ahead of us and heads back to the office, but I take the road to Kart-e Parwan and turn west around Aliabad hill. I have my reasons. As we reach the Deh Mazang crossroads by the zoo I turn onto the broad avenue that leads in a straight line to the presidential palace, nearly a mile away. The surface is scarred by shell and rocket blasts and the G weaves between the craters, handling magnificently.

It's a surreal drive. We see the world through a greenish haze, silenced and deceptively harmless-looking, as if we've descended like aliens and are observing the life around us from a protective bubble. Some men on bicycles and the occasional taxi pass us in the opposite direction, but there's no other traffic. Men haul at overloaded carts of timber and sacks, and ghost-like women in pale-blue burqas float past us as if carried on air.

I've never dared to visit this part of the city before because it was so vulnerable to attack and came under rocket fire almost daily when I was last in Kabul. The buildings on either side of the road are in a state of utter ruin. Floors, columns and lintels all sag and droop, held together only by the metal reinforcement inside them. Lesser structures are shattered and split and crumbling into the earth. There's isn't a square foot that hasn't been riddled with gunfire. Sometimes we see the dark scar of a rocket blast that looks as if someone has thrown a bucket of paint against a wall, only it's been caused by an explosion of white-hot metal.

We are in the centre of a capital city, but it looks more like one of the battlefields of the First World War. In the early 1990s the area was first devastated by Hekmatyar's rockets, vast stockpiles of which were generously financed by American taxpayers and supplied by the CIA. Later it became the southern front of prolonged battles as the government's rivals converged on the city from every direction except the north. They were fought off in a series of desperate counter-attacks organised by Massoud, whose exhausted forces were unable to counter the swift advance of the Taliban a year later.

Ahead, the palace looms. It's a shell of a building now. The roof has been torn open in several places by rocket blasts, and resembles a botched attempt to open a tin can. The walls are saturated with bullet holes. I park nearby, and for a few minutes H and I wander around the deserted arcades of the lower floor, where kings and heads of state were once received and where our feet now crunch the fragments of its shattered walls.

Then we return to the G, circle the palace on a dusty track and drive north again along the equally devastated Jade-ye Maiwand, named after the battle in which the British 66th Foot were decisively defeated by Afghan forces in 1880. The Afghans were rallied, so the story goes, by a Pashtun woman called Malalai.

As we near the house, we round a final bend and nearly collide with an ageing Land Rover, whose occupants gawp at us with a look of horror. It's the BBC's official car, and I recognise the pale and scarved face of the Kabul correspondent. I've had a bit of a crush on her ever since she interviewed me years ago in Islamabad, when I was on my way home and Kabul was going to hell. I feel guilty at not stopping to say hello, but it's better that H and I remain as invisible as possible. I don't want a journalist to be able to position us in Kabul just before a rather large act of sabotage is committed.

Back at the guest house I park the G in the garage and put a new lock on the door.

'Looks a bit like a hearse,' says H, 'but very impressive. Let's look at the manual and check the consumption. We need to sort out how much fuel we need.'

You never quite know what a person has gone through in life to make him what he is. This is especially true in Afghanistan, where no one has escaped the effects of more than twenty years of war without some sort of scar. I don't want to pry too much into this young man's life, but he's a sullen character and I wonder what's made him that way.

He comes to the house after dusk but before curfew begins. I'd prefer him not to know where we're staying, but H and I agree it's a necessary risk, and it would somehow be a breach of Afghan proto-col to show mistrust. He's supposed to be our ally, after all. Sattar is a member of the tribal intelligence unit raised by the CIA. He's the only one who can provide a link to Orpheus because he's the one who made contact with him in Jalalabad and knows what he looks like, though he knows nothing of my connection with him.

'You remember this man?' I ask, showing him the photograph taken of Manny earlier in the year.

'The foreigner,' he says.

'You can deliver him a message?'

'Sure.'

'How will you do it?'

'I will just do it,' he says. 'It will take a few days.'

'You speak good English, Sattar.'

'I learned at University of Kabul.'

'I thought the university was closed.'

'It was open when I was there.' He smiles but only with the lower part of his face.

I'm not entirely sure I believe him. I don't know when the university was last teaching English, but I've never met an Afghan who made the same claim and was under fifty years old. I wonder whether his English wasn't acquired from a spell with the Afghan secret police or the Pakistani ISI, the intelligence service on which the Americans rely too much. And I know it's wrong to expect him to be cheerful so that he better fits my idea of how Afghans should be, but he noticeably lacks the friendliness and spontaneity of nearly every Afghan I've known, and the combination of these things amounts to a kind of private suspicion. It's not such an odd feeling to have towards someone who you know is a spy.

We talk over the situation around the country and discuss the best route to take for the operation, though I don't reveal the exact location of where we're going. He suggests as a precaution that we travel via Bamiyan, where the Taliban have a regional headquarters and can give us a letter of safe passage through the area under their control. I can't help suspecting that this might be the trap that is waiting to be set for us, but I thank him for the suggestion.

'What is the message?' he asks.

I take out a fifty-afghani banknote, almost worthless in itself.

'Give him this note,' I say, 'and this one only. Tell him it comes from England.'

He looks at it with an expression of disappointment. He doesn't know that I've made several tiny holes in the note with the point of a needle. There's one in the centre of the note, over the engraving of the Darul Aman Palace, and several more over the serial numbers in the corners. It's taken me a while to find a note which contains the right numbers, but I've got about a thousand of them.

If Manny gets the note and knows it's from me, he'll know that there's a message contained in it somehow, and will examine it minutely for clues. He'll find the pinprick that shows him I want to meet at the ruined Darul Aman Palace. Then he'll look at the numbers and realise they represent the time, 1800, and the days of the week, indicated by the Persian initials for Monday and Tuesday. I space the holes so that even under inspection they'll look as though they were made by a staple, and add Manny's initials to garble the signal. Only he will recognise them and know to eliminate them from the message.

'How will I know if you've delivered it?'

'You just wait,' he says.

So I wait. The weekend passes. H and I visit the famous walled gardens of the sixteenth-century ruler Babur, who despite conquering much of Afghanistan and India expressed the wish to be buried in his beloved Kabul. Once the most popular venue in the city, the park is deserted but for an elderly guardian, and his shrine is peppered with bullet marks. We also pay a visit to the former British embassy, once the grandest foreign residence in Kabul. It's a burned-out shell now, and the emerald lawns have turned to dust.

On the Monday I take a taxi to a suburb in the south of the city called Deh Qalandar and walk the final stretch alone to the ruined palace. The giant rooms have long ago been stripped of their furniture and fittings and are strewn with smashed masonry, plaster and glass. I wait an hour, but no one comes. I return again at the same time the following day. There are a few children playing in the rubble, but there is no one to meet me. Realising how slim the chances are of re-establishing contact with Manny in this way, and dwelling on the many factors that make it unlikely, my sense of expectation begins to waver.

'Don't let it get to you,' says H, who spent a good deal of his time in Northern Ireland waiting in unmarked cars for informers who never showed up. He knows I'm hoping to meet a source useful to London, but he knows nothing of my history with Manny and can't know how disappointed I am.

On the Thursday a message comes from Mr Raouf. Our supplies are ready, which means it's time to get the operation underway. We drive to the trust's headquarters, where Mr Raouf is waiting for us, beaming mischieviously. He leads us to a store-room and throws aside a dusty tarpaulin to reveal several metal trunks.

'*Befarmaid.*' He grins, stretching out his hand. 'Be my guest.'

We unpack the trunks with a feeling of awe. There are several wooden boxes of plastic explosive, each containing half a dozen blocks the size of small bricks wrapped in brown waterproof paper to keep out moisture. I recognise the type. It's Iranian Composition 4, C4 for short, made from the high explosive RDX with a small percentage of non-explosive plasticiser which allows it to be cut or shaped. It has a detonation velocity of nearly 30,000 feet per second, which makes it more powerful than dynamite and an ideal demolition charge.

There's a long roll of waterproof blasting fuse resembling thin black rope, which H calls time fuse. The design hasn't changed much since Guy Fawkes' time. It's a modified form of gunpow-der, wrapped in a waterproof fabric sheath to enable it to burn underwater if necessary. It's this that will give us our time delay, though we'll have to test its burning rate to see what length we'll eventually need.

H lifts out what look like two rolls of bright orange electrical extension lead. It's detonating cord, filled with the high explo-sive PETN and sealed in plastic. There are different strengths of detcord but a six-inch length has about the same power as a military blasting cap and a few turns will sever a telephone pole when detonated. We'll use it to link the charges so that they detonate simultaneously. Then there's a further box of lesser but essential accessories: masking tape for securing detonators to the detcord, a pair of crimping tools, some old-fashioned time-delay explosive pencils and non-electric ignitors. H takes out a block of the plastic, sniffs and squeezes it, and fits it back into its box.

'Let's see the dets,' he says to Mr Raouf.

For safety, detonators are always stored separately from the charges they will eventually initiate. Mr Raouf has put them in a safe in his office, from which he returns bearing a small red metal case with a black and yellow sticker on the front depicting a skull and crossbones. There are twelve cigarette-sized detonators inside, six in each half of the case, separated by individual clips. H nods approvingly.

'We can blow up a small town with this lot,' he says. 'You need to thank your mate. What about the other stuff?'

Mr Raouf leads us across the storeroom to another pile of equipment. There are some camping supplies and tarpaulins, several military-looking sleeping bags, a length of steel towing cable and half a dozen jerrycans for our extra fuel.

'*Khub ast?*' Asks Mr Raouf. 'Alright?'

He's supplied everything we need for a minor expedition.

Very *khub* indeed, I'm thinking. From my map pocket I take out a fat packet of hundred-dollar bills and press it into Mr Raouf's hand. He makes a brief effort to refuse it, saying the whole thing is a gift to me as a friend, but we both know this is a ritual. Then he tucks it away into his jacket because he's too polite to count it in front of me, but I know what he'll be doing a few minutes after we've left.

He sends three men to the house that afternoon so that we can meet and talk over the general plan. H and I like them all at once. The oldest is called Sher Del, and has worked as a mine clearer for several years. His name means Lion Heart. He's in his forties but looks at least a decade older and served as a soldier in the Afghan army before defecting to the mujaheddin during the Soviet occupation. He has dark hair but his beard is nearly white, and he has the indestructible look of a seasoned warrior. His swift physical reactions are allied to a habit of directness which, tempered by long experience, lends him a quality of charm and worldly reassurance.

His colleagues are younger men, in their late twenties or early thirties, though they have the old-fashioned civility of an earlier generation. Aref is one of the trust's managers and speaks passable English. He's tall and thin, has a hawkish nose and a thick black beard, but his voice is soft and almost feminine. His mind enjoys details and concepts, and he translates for me, with both care and precision, into Pashtu for the others. Momen is another mine clearer, and reminds me of an Afghan version of Friar Tuck. He is stocky and always seems to be smiling, and his beard is dyed orange with henna. 'I could have been a doctor,' he complains with a rueful grin, 'or an engineer. But in Afghanistan there is nothing but war. Afghans are all donkeys,' he jokes, and the others laugh. 'They are too stupid to stop fighting each other.'

We look at maps. Our destination is in the south-west of the country and most easily reached from the southern city of Kandahar. But there will be checkpoints along the way, around the city and beyond it, and our convoy will not escape attention. Sooner or later we'll be searched and the purpose of our mission will fall under scrutiny. It's a risk we can't take. We'll travel through the remote centre of the country, and although it will take much longer, we'll be much lower on anyone's radar.

All the men agree that, given the military situation, it's probably a good idea to travel via Bamiyan and get onward permission from the local Taliban commander there. We'll take the southern route from Kabul through Wardak province, because to the north there's fighting and the environment is more dangerous. There's some discussion about the famous Buddhas, which were destroyed earlier in the year.

'It was wrong to destroy them,' says Sher Del. I ask him why. 'Because no other Afghan rulers destroyed them before, and before our time the people were better Muslims than now. So what right did the Taliban have to destroy them?'

'All the rich countries were unhappy that the idols were destroyed,' says Momen. 'But they didn't care about all the Afghans who were being killed.'

He has a point. Before their destruction, most outsiders didn't even know the Buddhas existed, much less that their faces had been removed hundreds of years ago. Now nearly everyone has heard of the Buddhas of Bamiyan, but few know of the Taliban's massacre of thousands of Hazaras at roughly the same time, of the levelling of southern Kabul by Hekmatyar a few years earlier along with the loss of perhaps 20,000 human lives, or the carnage unleashed on the Afghans by the Soviet army and its communist underlings.

'The Buddhas were destroyed on the orders of al-Qaeda,' says Aref, 'to make the world angry. Afghanistan will be much better when the Arabs have gone.'

After everything I've heard of the Taliban it seems like a kind of madness to introduce ourselves to their commander in Bamiyan, but the men are all for it. I feel a twinge of guilt at having suspected Sattar of leading us into a trap because it sounds like his advice was sensible after all. It involves a longer route, but I agree to it.

From Bamiyan, we'll head west to Yakawlang and then across the mountains to Panjab. This much everybody agrees on. But the route after that is a little confused, which is not surprising because there aren't actually any roads, but dusty and unmaintained tracks instead. The men's fingers trace over the approximate route, but only Aref is really interested in the details.

I'm not too worried because the Afghan way of moving cross-country is simply to ask the route from whoever's coming in the opposite direction. The maps of the country are in people's minds, not on paper, and trying to follow a map too closely in Afghanistan is an almost sure way to get lost.

The following day Mr Raouf approves our request to test the explosives. His team is clearing a minefield an hour's drive east of Kabul, in the vicinity of an old Soviet military position. We drive there together two days later. Mr Raouf proudly introduces us to the men at the site, who are mapping the cleared areas and marking the perimeter of the danger zone with stones daubed in red paint. An unexploded mortar round has been found and Mr Raouf allows us to place a charge next to it. Explosives are generally arranged in the form of a chain, each successive part creating a larger explosion, so we want to use as many of the components as possible to see if they all function as they're supposed to. So we take a slice of the plastic from one of the blocks, wrap it in a length of detcord, tape a detonator to the free end of the detcord, and finally attach a short length of blasting fuse to the detonator.

The area is cleared and from somewhere comes the wail of a siren. Our little team, along with a dozen other men from the local group, stare fixedly at the point where I lit the fuse several hundred yards away. Thirty seconds later a brown cloud of dust leaps from the ground and a moment later there's a spectacular bang as the sound wave reaches us. There are grins all round. All the components of the chain have performed as they should. It's as if our faith has been restored in the purpose of the op, and now at last it's within our reach. Back at the trust's HQ we load the explosives into the G and return it to the safety of the garage at the house.

We send a report to London and receive a signal from Macavity approving our forward passage. We're nearly ready to move now, but I must try to make contact with Manny one last time before we go. On the Monday, once again, I change into my shalwar kameez so as to be relatively invisible, adjust my nylon belt and holster and slide home the loaded Browning. I put my phone in one pocket, one of the silk E & E maps in the other, and walk ten minutes from the house before hailing a taxi.

There is no one waiting for me at the palace, and once again I have to struggle with my disappointment. I have one more day to try, and then we'll have to move because we can't wait another week. Apart from anything else, I'm not happy about the risk of our meeting place having been compromised, which increases as more time passes.

For the final time I repeat the process the following day. The taxi driver asks if I'm Iranian, and I tell him I've grown up in Iran but come back recently. He gets talking about his life.

'I fought with Massoud in Panjshir at the time of the jihad,' he says, referring to the period of the Soviet occupation. 'I was wounded and went to live with my cousin in Mazar. After he was killed I had to fight with Dostam. When we came to fight in Kabul I was captured by the government and my brother paid for my release with his house. Then the Taliban accused me of being a spy and tortured me. They put me in a freezing basement and beat me with cables. My uncle gave them his house, so they let me go. I was lucky. What is there to come back to?' he asks cynically, waving a hand towards the destruction on either side of the road.

I reach the palace at exactly six o' clock. There's no one around. I walk across the central courtyard and marvel as I always do at the volume of gunfire that must have once filled the air. But it's silent now, and nothing stirs but the light breeze that so often rises in the moments just before dusk. I observe my feelings of disappointment as if from afar. The first few times I came I was full of expectation, but the emotion's gone now and I'm forced to admit that I'm merely a solitary spectator at a forgotten battlefield of which the world knows nothing.

I'm full of morbid thoughts about the uselessness of the destruction around me and the folly of the people who inflicted such misery on themselves, albeit with considerable help from abroad. I walk on impulse along the arcade of the eastern wing and enter one of the ruined rooms. The empty windows stare back at me, but then something catches my eye. It's a tiny fire, burning at the far end of the building. It's in the north-east corner of the building and corresponds exactly, I now realise, to the position of the pinprick I made in the note.

I hear the crunch of my footsteps amplified by the bare walls as I approach the flickering light, beside which a human shape is crouching. For a moment I allow myself to believe that at last

Manny has made an appearance, then curse myself again because I know it can't be him. The figure is wrapped in a dark *pattu* and doesn't move as I approach. But the coincidence won't let my mind rest, and I have to make sure.

'Peace be to you, *watandar*. May this traveller warm his hands on your fire?'

In a slow gesture, as slow as a man on the point of death, a lean and dark-skinned arm emerges from the shadowy bundle as if to offer me the place opposite. A ripple of shock passes through me as I register how thin the arm is, like that of a starving man. There's not enough light to make out the face, and a nightmarish train of thoughts suddenly spins across my mind. Perhaps it really is Manny, but he's been disfigured or suffered some cruel affliction that's left him withered and prematurely aged.

'Manny?' I say his name experimentally, because I'm not sure. I can just make out the grey bundle of beard that hangs from a chin and the vague contours of a face within the shadows. The outstretched hand looks horribly old, and repeats the beckoning motion for me to sit. I'm only a few feet from him, and the fire is between us. The stone floor is cold.

'Manny? Say something, Manny. You're scaring the shit out of me.'

Then with unexpected suddenness the face looks up at me. It's not Manny. It's a half-toothless old man, whose gaunt and almost fleshless face looks into mine as the flames bring to life a mad glint in his eyes, and from his ruined gums comes a wheezing cackle.

'Oh Christ.' I leap up in fright. 'Oh *Christ*.' My heart's pounding and the spell is broken. I take several steps backwards, slipping on the rubble as the old man's dreadful laughter subsides.

And then I hear the voice.

'As you were, Captain.'

I whirl around in reflex, and my right hand flies by instinct to the grip of the Browning. Behind me, ten feet away and emerging from behind one of the plaster pillars, I see Manny, dressed in a black shalwar with a *pattu* thrown over one shoulder. He's tanned and lean and has a full beard, but it's him, unmistakably, and he's smiling now and throws his arms open towards me.

'You bastard. You absolute bastard,' I say. 'Didn't anyone ever teach you how to stay in touch?'

'Sent you a postcard,' he says as we walk towards each other. We embrace, and I feel his chest trembling, as he does mine, with the breathless rush of feeling somewhere beyond laughter and tears that expresses all the long-awaited relief of deliverance.

Sometimes, just sometimes, your hopes are exceeded beyond all measure. What you dared to hope for is not only granted but heaped up with unexpected dividends you haven't been able to imagine. It's akin to falling in love with someone whom it seems likely will never glance at you, and then finding that your feelings are reciprocated with even greater intensity.

I had thought Manny dead, or at best imprisoned or gone mad. But I've seen him in the flesh now, and I still can't really believe that he's alive. It's not only that. He's sane. His sense of humour is intact. My greatest fear, worse than the fear that he'd been killed, was that he might have become like the men he'd been living among.

'We have our way and they have theirs,' he says when I share this fear with him. 'They are human too,' he adds. And though he has the odd habit of speaking in Pashtu when he gets excited and cursing in his prison Chechen, his mind seems whole and healthy.

'It's time to come home,' I tell him.

'Home,' he repeats, as if dimly recalling an old friend. 'Yes. I need to come home.'

'When we're back from the op I'll get you out.'

He looks at me and shakes his head as if I haven't understood. 'I can't just disappear.'

'Why not?'

'I need to die,' he says, and for a moment I'm full of dread.

'You don't need to die,' I tell him.

'Why are you so stupid? I need to be seen to die. If I just disappear I'll be considered compromised. All the plans I know will be changed. All this will be useless.'

From his pocket he produces a memory disk the size of a cigarette lighter. I've never seen one like this before.

'What is it?' I ask.

He holds it up solemnly between us with the fingers of both hands, in the manner of a priest about to administer the sacrament.

'Unless we stop it,' he says, 'it's the future.' The light is fading now. 'Can you get the contents to London, FLASH priority?'

'What's on it?'

'It's better I don't tell you. There's no time to explain now. It's everything I know. They've got plans you can't imagine. Huge attacks. New York, London.' He shakes his head. 'The Sheikh wants a war, a global war. This is how he's going to get it.'

I can't help thinking as he speaks that perhaps he's grown too enthused by the ambitions of the men whose world he's managed to infiltrate. I doubt whether Islamic militants, especially those living in a remote corner of Afghanistan, have either the means or know-how to provoke what he calls a global war.

'I can't stay here much longer,' he says.

I tell him about the operation, unfolding the silk map and pointing out the location of the fort and the route we're planning to take there.

'Are you sure it's there?' he asks emphatically. 'My *firqat* was in Sangin until a month ago. I know the men in that area.' He strokes his beard thoughtfully. 'The Stingers,' he says quietly. 'I've been wondering where they were being kept. They've got plans for those.'

'So have I,' I say.

His finger swerves over the map as he studies it closely. Then he looks up at me, his finger still tapping the map where it's come to rest.

'We need to make a plan,' he says.

It's dusk when I leave. I walk for a long way before finding a taxi, which drops me at the Shirpur crossroads. No one pays any attention to me as I walk the quarter-mile to Wazir. The entire city seems to be hurrying home to safety as darkness falls. I experience a sense of bemusement that no one can detect the torrent that's racing through my head as I endlessly repeat to myself the details of my recent encounter. As I walk I'm making a list of the things I've talked about with Manny, linking them against mental images that rhyme with the numbers one to ten, which I'll write up more fully when I'm back at the house.

With one hand I'm turning over the flash disk in my pocket, hardly daring to believe the significance of its contents. I don't have the software to examine it myself but I can email it from the trust's office and wait for a reply. I run my hand absent-mindedly against the stone wall beside me and feel its warmth, even though the sun has set. Then I reach the roundabout in Wazir and cross into the grid of streets beyond.

Up ahead I see the fruit stall that I pass in the daytime. There's a tall Talib who looks like he's buying fruit, and parked on the opposite side of the street is a signature Toyota pickup. For a moment I think of turning around and taking a different street because I don't want to tangle with anyone. But the moment the thought takes shape I dismiss it because I'm just an invisible Afghan peasant and I must act as if I'm just that and not a fugitive.

As I draw nearer I realise there's something going on between the Talib and the boy who runs the stall. The Talib has said something to him in Pashtu and now repeats it, but the boy doesn't respond, so he asks again but this time he yells it. I'm close enough now to see the boy's expression. He's just looking down at his feet, scared as hell and not daring to answer.

So the Talib hits him. His right hand flies up and slaps the boy violently on the side of his head. The boy winces and holds his hand to his ear and mumbles what I take to be an apology. That's probably the end of it, but the scene has caught my eye, and without realising it I've stopped.

Mistake.

In the greater context of things a man slapping a boy is not much to be concerned about. Especially in Afghanistan. It's a tough country and the boy has probably been dealt worse punishments. And it's none of my business. But it's an unprovoked act and I feel a disproportionate sense of outrage at the sight of someone being bullied, and I'm allowing it to show.

In another place at another time it wouldn't matter. I'd say, 'Pick on someone your own size,' and the other man would say, 'Get lost,' and that would be the end of it. But this is Afghanistan and its people are at war and the Taliban have come to Kabul to show who's in charge.

The Talib notices me a few yards away and his head turns. He has a huge black turban and a thick black beard, and the strange thing is he's strikingly handsome. But his expression tells me he's an arrogant belligerent bastard, and for the second or two that our eyes meet I want him to know that's exactly what I think of him. I realise that I've let my gaze linger an instant too long, issuing thereby a silent challenge. I've unwittingly threatened his pride, and the pride of an Afghan is not a thing to underestimate. I look away but it's too late.

'What are you looking at?' He's speaking Pashtu, which I don't understand, but the question is obvious.

I walk past him, and his body turns to face mine.

'I'm talking to you,' he says.

I raise a hand in a gesture of dismissal, to indicate that I meant nothing and that I'm leaving him in peace. My back is turned to him now. He calls after me but I keep walking because it's not a moment for confrontation. With a military map in my underwear, encrypted computer files and a weapon on my waist, it'll be a challenge to pass myself off as a passer-by. But he's not letting it go.

Behind me I hear his boots on the ground. He's running towards me. I turn around and raise my hands to my throat and make a strangling noise to let him know I can't talk properly. He stops just short of me and he's staring at me with a look of both anger and curiosity. I pull desperately at my throat to convince him I can't talk and turn away again, and it's just as I turn that I feel the first blow.

The strange thing is that the pain erupts not from my back but my stomach, and I look down in astonishment as my hands clutch the front of my body in reflex. It feels like a powerful electric shock and as I begin to double over in agony I'm just able to turn enough to see what's caused the blow. The Talib is standing behind me with a length of thick black electrical cable in his right hand, which I now realise has whipped over my arm and across my abdomen.

I can't speak. Nothing comes out of my mouth. I stare at him in astonishment, and his hand comes up in a lightning motion. The wire hits my other arm, curls over it and sends another electrifying jolt of pain across my back. Where the cable has struck it feels as if a red-hot piece of metal has been pressed against me, and I'm gripping my sides trying not to speak, because I mustn't.

I'm amazed at how quickly pain affects the consciousness. There's a few gawping bystanders now, gathering at the periphery of the street, but as I take in the sight of them they already seem unreal, like characters in a dream the significance of which I don't really understand. The Talib is yelling at me, but I don't understand and I can't respond. I hear only a weird, animal-like moan of anguish escape me, but my attacker wants more, and the cable leaps out at me once again, delivering another burning jolt to my wrist, arm and back, and making me stumble down into the dirt.

I can't take much more of this. If he hits me again I know I'll be in too much pain to function. I can run, but another Talib who's been sitting in the cab of the Toyota has got out now, and has an AK in his hands, half-raised into a firing position just to let everybody know this is their business and nobody else's. I'll have to shoot him first, while my vision is still good and my hand steady. But if I do, my options are not too good. I can run through this maze of streets, but I won't escape for long. If I'm not killed, I'll be found soon enough and the entire op will be ruined. I may or may not have time to conceal the flash disk somewhere, but I'll then have to find a way to transmit its location to H or someone I can trust.

I can't bear the prospect of all this. If I own up to being a foreigner he'll stop hitting me, but I'll be taken prisoner and searched and my map and weapon will incriminate me. God knows what will happen to me if I end up in a Taliban prison. Every scenario spells disaster.

I'm lying in the road now, propping myself up with one arm, looking him in the face, deciding that if his hand goes up again, I'll roll to my left and shoot the one with the AK who's leaning against the door of the pickup. He won't be expecting it. For the moment he's just enjoying the sight of his friend beating the hell out of an unlucky passer-by. Then, unless he acquiesces very quickly and very politely, I'll shoot the one with the cable.

He walks towards me with a menacing swagger. Slowly, as if nursing my ribs, I move my hand under my shalwar to the holster, and find the grip of the Browning. Safety off, finger to the trigger.

'What have you got to say for yourself now, you Panjshiri son of a whore?' he says, or something very like it.

In a movement calculated to cause further terror, he winds an extra turn of cable over the hand that holds it, and runs his other hand along its length, as if preparing it for its next journey. But it never comes. At the moment he's about to hit me again and, though he doesn't know it, to be shot twice through the chest, there's a high-pitched squeal of brakes from a few feet behind him, where a car has pulled up alongside the Toyota. At the sight of it I experience a strange sense of recognition. It takes me a few seconds before I realise why, but I get there in the end. It's the BBC Land Rover on its way home, and behind the windscreen I can clearly see the female passenger, leaning across from her seat and honking the horn to get everybody's attention.

She gets out, strides up to the Talib with the cable and with a minimum of ceremony introduces herself as the BBC correspondent and asks what the hell is going on. She has no idea it's me, but sees only an apparently defenceless man lying in the street and a big Talib looming over him with an electric cable in his hand. She's blathering fearlessly at him and the effect is so dramatic I'm transfixed by the spectacle. At the sight of this obviously mad, shrill foreign woman, the murderous warrior turns into a sullen schoolboy who looks as if he's just been caught by the headmistress behind the bike sheds. He skulks with his partner back to the cab of the pickup without even looking at me, and as I stagger to the pavement the pickup roars angrily away.

Then, summoning her interpreter, she marches over to me. I avoid meeting her eye.

'Bastards,' she mutters in English. 'What have they done to you?'

I'm still gripping my sides in pain.

'*Khub ast*,' I growl. 'It's alright.'

I try to keep my face turned from her towards the shadow. But as she looks at me, her expression turns from one of concern to curiosity.

'I know you,' she says quizzically. She's squatting beside me. 'Don't I know you?'

I want to shake my head, but I mustn't show that I've understood.

'Zekriya,' she calls to her driver, who's been sensible enough to stay clear of the fray, 'ask him if he's alright, can you?'

'*Khub ast*,' I repeat, disguising my voice with a wince of pain.

'That is *so* weird,' I hear her say with a sigh as she stands up and walks back towards the Land Rover. 'He looks just like someone I know. Zek?' she calls with her hands on her hips. 'Ask him if he'll agree to an interview. Honestly, these poor bloody people.'

14

I'm not good for much the following day. But while my body's been immobile, my mind's been careering back and forth over the events of the previous twenty-four hours. The mind hungers naturally for certainty, but I can't be as sure as I want to be about any of the things that are troubling me. All that is possible is an interpretation, and the one I've come up with has a dark side and a light side.

The dark side is that, as the Baroness indicated, someone is attempting to sabotage the operation and wants us to fail. I have accepted the cynical possibility that, somewhere along the line, there's an agenda in favour of the survival of the Stingers. I must accept, possibly, that the Talib who accosted me yesterday was perhaps expecting me, and had been paid or persuaded to disable or kill me. Perhaps he wasn't really a Talib at all. Perhaps Sattar, on whom my suspicion has largely fallen, has been watching the house, seen me leaving on Mondays and Tuesdays, and arranged for the Talib to intercept me on my return. The planning and effort involved in this, as well as the fact that a much simpler method could have been found to make me disappear, render it unlikely. But not impossible.

The trouble with small conspiracies is that they lead contagiously to larger ones. When I dwell on the notion that there really is a plan for the Stingers to fall into the wrong hands, I can't help remembering Grace's solemn prediction that there are people in America just waiting for the excuse to invade Afghanistan. All they need, she said, is to trace an act of terrorism on US soil back to Afghanistan.

The Stingers could certainly provide the means. Yet the chances of planned American military involvement in Afghanistan seem so utterly remote, I have to mentally dismiss this possibility.

The light side is that if my encounter with the turbanned cable-wielder really was a devious attempt to stop us, it has failed. And if someone is still going to try to stop us, he'll have to come up with another plan. If we leave quickly, the chances of another attempt will be much reduced. I share this idea with H when he looks in on me the next morning, because it feels right that we should move without delay.

'Let's leave now,' I say.

'What, today? What's the hurry? You need to rest.'

'No. We pick up the men and leave without warning them. That way no one has time to talk.'

'Are you serious? Let's have a look at you.'

I sit on the edge of the bed and H inspects the deep-red welts that run across my back and stomach. Dark bruises are beginning to extend along them. The skin isn't broken, but it looks as though I've had an unusual accident with a very large barbecue. I wonder if they'll leave scars.

'Give it another day,' he suggests.

Then we make a new discovery. I ask H to retrieve the first aid kit for me, which is with our stash of equipment in the roof space. I remember at the last minute to give him my phone so that he can check the markings I've left on the bags and cases with the ultraviolet light. He returns with the first aid kit, but there's a new expression on his face.

'How did you mark the stuff?' he asks.

'Vertical lines across the front that join up with the floor.'

'Well,' he says, 'either there's a bloody great Afghan rat in that attic or someone's been poking around in there. None of the lines match up.'

We've both been out of the house over the past few days. It's possible that a determined visitor could have taken an interest in our stuff. We call downstairs to the chowkidar, who says there have been no visitors but that he's had to leave the house at times.

'I didn't check the doors when I got back yesterday. I was too distracted.'

'Yes,' he agrees, 'you were a bit out of it.'

It's an unpleasant feeling. There's nothing for it but to recheck every piece of our equipment and all the supplies in the G. We start with the kit in the attic, hauling it down into the room and scrutinising every item minutely for any signs of tampering. H even inspects each individual round of ammunition for the Brownings. It's all there, along with everything else, and none of it seems to have been interfered with.

Then we descend to the garage and unload everything from the G, paying particular attention to the explosives in case they've been altered in any way. H takes out every block of the plastic and smells it. We unwind the blasting fuse and I coil it over my arm as I inspect its length, and then rewind it onto its original spool. We do the same with the detcord. The detonators are intact.

If nothing is missing, then perhaps something has been added. Most likely is a bomb. Less probable is a transmitter to track our movements. Either one will take up a certain amount of space. We run our hands over every seam of the G's interior, probing the seats, panels and carpets for any sign that they've been disturbed or modified. We check with minute care to see if there's any indication of modified or extra wiring in the vicinity of the ignition or the panels around the dashboard. We lie on the ground with our torches and search the wheel arches and bumpers and chassis. Then we roll the G forward into the daylight to check under the bonnet, using a strip of paper to detect any tripwires before opening it fully. We peer into the fuel tank, radiator, reservoirs and lamp housings. Anything that can be readily removed and replaced, we remove and replace.

There is no bomb. There is no transmitter. No one seems to have installed a tilt switch that will go off when the car meets its first slope after leaving the house. Nothing is missing. I wonder, but not out loud, whether I could have accidentally moved the kit in the attic myself. I do not know.

It's late afternoon. We spend the rest of the day packing, and agree to leave in the morning without telling the chowkidar or giving any advance warning to the other men. An envelope with a letter of thanks and a generous tip will express our appreciation.

Not long after sunrise, we drive to Mr Raouf, who's not expecting us.

'We have to leave immediately,' I tell him. 'I'm sorry.'

'*Moshkel nist*,' he says, no problem. He summons the other men on a two-way radio. While we wait for them to arrive, I ask if I can use his computer to check my email. He lifts a scarf from the keyboard, dusts off the screen with it and pulls back the chair for me, observing me wince as I sit. It's an unpredictable process, and takes a dozen attempts before the modem finally connects. I log into the secure server maintained by the Firm, encrypt and send the contents of the flash drive using my own public encryption key, and ask Mr Raouf if he'll keep the original for me in his safe, along with our second passports. What happens next is a surprise.

'I have something for you,' he says. From under his desk he pulls out an AK-74SU Kalashnikov with a folding stock, and presents it proudly to me.

'For your journey,' he says.

H's eyebrows rise as Mr Raouf hands it over. It's a compact automatic weapon which fires the 5.45-millimetre low-recoil round, and the barrel is much shorter than the AK-47. It can be easily hidden under a jacket and will fit snugly under a car seat, which makes it popular in Russia with special forces, drivers and bodyguards. It's a generous gift because I suspect he's deeply attached to such a rare and highly prized weapon, and I promise to return it to him on our return. He nods gravely as if to say 'when you return'. At least I hope that's what he means, and not 'if you return'.

On journeys at home the road is a means to an end. It's a featureless thing which doesn't attract the greater part of your attention, and you take for granted that it won't crumble to dust under your wheels as you while away the time with distracted thoughts, thinking of your final destination. You take for granted that your journey implies arrival.

In Afghanistan all this is reversed. The road demands your attention from the start. Every aspect of it requires effort and stamina and determination. It does, literally, crumble to dust under your wheels, and offers you no time for distracted thoughts. In the meantime your destination becomes an ever more abstract idea, a thing you doubt and question and wonder if you'll ever reach, and as your journey lengthens you feel like a fool for blindly assuming that your eventual arrival is guaranteed. The road, in short, becomes the goal, and arrival a luxury.

Our caravan is made up of two vehicles. The trust's white Toyota pickup leads the way, carrying Sher Del, Aref and Momen. H and I ride second in the G. Our doors and bonnets bear the vinyl stickers that Mr Raouf has supplied us with, so that our true purpose, like that of many a charitable institution operating in this part of the world, is amply disguised.

We drive through the devastated western suburbs under a brilliantly blue, clear sky. On the outskirts of the city the surfaced road ends. There was one, years before, but it's simply been worn away. Now it's a pale scar on which every vehicle lurches and weaves in a perpetual cloud of white dust. Which side to drive on is only an approximate convention.

Beyond the dust we can see the long chains of peaks to the north and south of the city. It's late spring now and the mountains are draped in ice on their upper ridges, and lower down their snow-filled gulleys resemble the camouflage of a killer whale. It's hard to believe that a country so beautiful is in the midst of a brutal conflict, and has been for years. But there's always the ruined armoured vehicles, tilted at the verges of the road like ships that have run aground in the shallows and been abandoned, to remind us otherwise.

An hour west of the city centre the road divides. The route to the north-west leads up to Paghman and the southern towards Ghazni. We take the lower branch and move beyond Maidan Shahr, the natural pass that protects the city's western flank. Then an hour later, at the next main junction, we turn into the mountainous folds of Wardak province, where the road deteriorates a stage further.

It's the Afghan version of a B road, virtually impassable by Western standards but not at all bad by Afghan ones, and it's more like being in a boat than a car because of the constant pitching and rolling. Sometimes the rocky surface of the road changes to packed earth and suddenly the crunch of stone under us is silenced as if by a ceasefire. But it's only ever for a few miles before we are fighting the dust and stone again.

In the early afternoon we stop to buy some apples from a farmer who's put up a stall by the side of the road. As I'm talking to the farmer, our men take their *pattus*, lay them over the ground near the road, and perform their afternoon prayers.

We move west through a landscape of great beauty, winding through a succession of long broad valleys where the surrounding slopes glide gently down towards the emerald-coloured patchwork of the valley floors. Beyond Jalrez, the slopes begin to steepen and grow less gentle, and the grassy bloom turns to darker stone, which rises steadily on both sides of the road.

Several hours later I hear Aref's voice on the two-way.

'We're coming to Gardandiwal,' he says. 'I think we should stay here tonight. We won't reach Bamiyan today.'

Gardandiwal sits at the crossroads of four mountain ranges and has the feeling of a primitive gold miners' outpost from the nineteenth century. We install ourselves at a tiny *mehman-khana* beneath the clusters of mud-walled homes that sprawl up the hillside. At sunset we sit on the wooden veranda and the owner brings us kebabs and rice. The river that runs through the place is called the Helmand, says the owner of the place. It rises in the mountains to the north-east and flows all the way through the centre of the country, surrendering itself eventually to the deserts beyond Kandahar.

We move on shortly after dawn. The road begins to rise and the mountains to tighten around us. There's no ongoing fighting in the area but the next day several pickup trucks with heavily armed men pass us in the opposite direction. They look battle-weary and well travelled, and their clothes and turbans and weapons are thick with dust. I wonder where they've come from and where they'll end up. It seems likely they're moving back to Kabul from the recent fighting in and around Yakawlang, avoiding the northern route via the Shomali plain, where Massoud's forces are harassing their fellow fighters.

We are less than a hundred miles from the capital but we seem already to have moved back centuries. As we near the Hajigak Pass there's a construction team hewing a new section of road from the mountainside, and there's a long wait as we allow trucks coming the other away to squeeze past. There is no machinery. Just 500 men with pickaxes and spades, working at a furious pace, carving out and levelling the black rock. Watching them work, I have the feeling once again that we're going back in time.

You can't get this feeling from a map. The speed at which the influence of Kabul drops away is like a stone falling into a well.

'Look,' I say to H, pointing to the men hacking at the rock. 'Afghan infrastructure.'

'I can see why the Soviets failed here,' he says. 'If you invade a country you have to control the infrastructure. There isn't one.'

H is right. Afghans depend on so little for their survival that there isn't much for an invading army to control. The mechanisms by which a modern government influences its people simply don't exist. Power, and its pursuit, is a fragmented and intensely local affair, and central government has never meant much to Afghans. The capital has never had significant influence in the countryside, except to take taxes or conscripts. Rural Afghanistan is made up of communities that depend on a close-knit structure of local rights designed to protect fragile resources. And since Afghans live from their land, their lives are bound up with the practical realities of survival, not abstract political or social goals. Fifty miles from the capital might as well be a different country. Five, even.

We pause at the top of the Hajigak Pass to admire the spectacular view. The men pray beside the cars. The engines smell hot. The peaks to the east and west of us soar to 15,000 feet, and the road behind and beyond us swoops down to loop between the intersecting spurs of the valleys. Then, from just below our line of sight, a man wearing a giant brown turban appears as if from out of the ground, flanked by a pair of grinning friends. The fact that he's lost his right leg to a mine and must have ascended the pass on his crutches gives the sight a surreal quality. He stares at us with a mute grin, which reveals a wide gap where a tooth has been knocked out, and I marvel at his physical hardiness before giving him a few afghanis for his troubles, wondering how far he'll have to go before he reaches home.

A long and winding descent leads us towards the Bamiyan valley. The surrounding geology seems to pass through every colour of the spectrum as we creep down, deepening to a purplish shade of red as we near the valley floor and turn west towards the site of the famous Buddhas. I catch glimpses of stairways and walls and ruined galleries in the cliffs above us and am reminded that Bamiyan was once a Buddhist state that resisted its Muslim overlords until well after their arrival in the seventh century. Its natural setting has always enchanted visitors. I don't know if it's because of the time of day, but the light seems particularly magical, and now that we've been released from the grasp of the mountains the valley seems a place of delicacy and charm, where slender poplars line the riverbanks and their pale leaves shimmer in the soft flame of the afternoon sun.

'This place is stunning,' says H. 'I thought Afghanistan was all rocks and desert, but this is something else.'

Closer to the town, in the folds of reddish stone above us, we can make out the crumbling towers and ramparts of another long-abandoned fortified settlement. It's Shahr-e Gholghola, the City of Lamentation, laid to waste, so the story goes, by Chengiz Khan himself in 1222.

But the town itself brings a different feeling. It's strange to look at, because the last time I was here there was a thriving bazaar where there are now ruins. A whole section of the town has simply been annihilated. Its obvious there's been heavy fighting and the majority of the local Hazara families have fled. They are still the underdogs of Afghan society. Their virtually autonomous kingdom was smashed by the nineteenth-century king Abdur Rahman, and the Pashtun tribes have treated them like slaves ever since. Their recent battles with the Taliban have been particularly fierce.

The radio crackles into life, and I hear Aref's voice.

'Taliban checkpoint ahead,' he says. Then Momen grabs the radio from him.

'Make sure your beard is long enough.' He chuckles.

'So long as it's only my beard they want to measure,' I say, because there are lots of jokes like this about the Taliban. Cackles of laughter erupt from both men.

'Drive up slowly and stop,' I say.

It's time to introduce ourselves to the local Taliban commander. A black flag flutters from a small command post on a bluff above us, towards which Aref and Sher Del walk. They are met by two armed Talibs. They are not unfriendly, but have the tense look of people who know they don't belong. A few others descend from the post and circle the cars but don't quite dare to search them.

H and I get out, distribute some cigarettes to break the ice and ask if we can walk up to the Buddhas. The fighter standing next to me shrugs as if to ask why we'd want to bother but walks up with us. He leads us through a warren of steps and tunnels until we emerge above the hollow niches from which the giant statues have gazed for 1,500 years. From the top we can see a fantastic range of snow-covered peaks to the south. Closer to we can make out a red jeep racing towards our position, trailing a plume of dust.

'That'll be their commander,' says H.

We meet him as we emerge from the dusty doorway at the foot of the niche. He's unexpectedly friendly, intrigued to meet foreigners, and suggests we be his guests for the night, even though it's obvious we have no choice in the matter. We follow him in the vehicles to a fortified compound, where we park inside the gates and unpack our things.

Whether as a courtesy or precaution, an armed Talib follows us everywhere. I suspect it's a bit of both. We are all shown into a long room strewn with carpets, and the first of many glasses of tea is poured. As dusk falls, the room fills gradually with about thirty armed men.

'It's like a dinner party in Notting Hill,' says H, as the men lay their AKs by their sides like napkins. The magazines of their weapons are doubled and taped together to give them twice the amount of ammunition without having to grope around for a fresh magazine.

The commander is a man of about thirty. We sit next to him as the meal is served. His manners are peculiarly modern, and I wonder whether he grew up in Pakistan. He has none of the formality or reserve of most Afghans I've met, and asks me directly about the work we've come to carry out. I tell him that even in England we're concerned about helping Afghanistan with its mine problem. And because everything in Afghanistan is about establishing allegiances and invoking the names of powerful strangers,

I make up a speech about the Queen, whose authority they can't quite assess from this distance, and how keen she is to see peace and prosperity in Afghanistan, and emphasise how grateful she'll be for the assistance we're receiving here in Bamiyan.

'We beat the British,' he says cheerfully, 'last time they came to Afghanistan.'

'War was different then,' I say, 'and battles were fought man to man.'

'Perhaps they will come back,' he says with a smile, 'and we can fight them again the same way.'

As darkness falls a fighter shows us to our room. We've been on the road only a couple of days but for some reason it feels like weeks. For a moment we wonder whether to position ourselves near the door or the window.

'If they're planning to kill you,' I tell H, 'the preferred method is to drop a rock on your head.'

'With all those weapons they hardly need a rock.'

'You forget how thrifty Afghans are. A rock will save them the expense of a bullet.'

'Well,' he says, 'I hope it's big enough. I've got quite a hard head.'

We leave the next morning, our heads intact. The commander has given us a handwritten letter of permission to travel as far as Yakawlang, but can't guarantee much after that. I'm glad we've got the letter. There are several checkpoints as we head west, and at each we're waved to a halt by a pair of fighters whose surly manner improves once our letter has been inspected and passed around. We've chosen the right combination of personalities for the lead vehicle. Sher Del is not only a Pashtun, but his white beard and confident manner give him an authority that no one will easily challenge. Aref plays the role of boffinish administrator to perfection, and between the two of them all suspicions are put to rest.

Beyond Bamiyan the high mountains draw apart, the cultivated plain broadens to a width of several miles, and the glittering braid of the river and its tall green poplars runs beside us. The lesser hills are bare and reddish, and against their starkness the valley and its carefully tended fields and borders once again seem all the more delicate.

We reach Yakawlang in the afternoon, refuel the vehicles and eat a meal of kebabs. The town has an unhappy air and looks as though it's suffered from recent fighting, which a number of abandoned armoured vehicles confirm. We don't want to linger, and drive south into the mountains towards Panjab. There's almost no wheeled traffic, but we pass several families struggling on foot with their possessions piled onto donkeys, and a woman clutching a child begs us for money. The desperation in her expression is obvious and she claims the Taliban have forced her from her home. Her face and gestures haunt me like a presence as we drive further south along a deteriorating route, and our pace slows to a crawl. Several times we catch sight of trucks which have fallen from the road and tumbled into the ravines below.

As we near the Isharat Pass, the lead vehicle has its first puncture, and while Aref and Sher Del are changing the wheel, H and I get out to admire the spectacular scenery.

'It's not like anywhere I've ever seen,' he says. 'Every part of it's different, like a different country. You could never win a war here.'

I ask him why not.

'It's the people. They belong too much. They'd never give it up.'

We're looking over to the east where about thirty miles away the highest peaks of the Koh-e Baba range rear up from among the lesser summits in a magnificent glistening knot of ice. A purplish haze is settling over the landscape and after the relentless lurching of the route the silence is almost overwhelming. Quietly, H recites the lines of a poem.

'We are the pilgrims, master; we shall go
Always a little further: it may be
Beyond the last blue mountain barred with snow
Across that angry or that glimmering sea

'Regimental poem,' he says as if emerging from a private trance. 'Don't know the rest.' He looks back over the darkening mountains. 'I'm glad I came. This is a special place.'

'There's some things I haven't told you,' I say.

'That's normal,' he says. 'There's stuff I haven't told you either.'

'Like what?'

'You killed a mate of mine, for one thing,' he says after a pause.

The fact that this doesn't make any sense to me does nothing to lessen the shock.

'How? When?'

'In Kuwait. The team that busted your Lebanese mate out. They were all Regiment blokes. You took out the team leader.'

For years I've never really understood why the man I killed hesitated when he was about to shoot me.

'I didn't know,' I say.

'You weren't supposed to. It was a Special Projects op. We had the order to go in as an Israeli team. Weirdest thing is that it was going to be me leading it.' He smiles. 'You would have slotted me instead.'

'I'm sorry about your friend.'

'Kenny was his name. He was from up north, Glasgow, I think. Couldn't understand a word he said half the time. I nearly killed him myself once on a hostage rescue practice. That's the way it is.' He brushes some dust from his arm. 'Anyway, what aren't you telling me?'

I wonder how much I should say, but the power of the land has stripped us of our secrets now, and there seems no purpose in hiding anything from him any longer. So I tell him what I can, because I cannot tell him everything, right up to my meeting with

Manny in Kabul, and about the plan that we made together in the ruins of the Darul Aman Palace.

At dusk we stop in a tiny settlement and the five of us sleep on the floor of a small room in our sleeping bags. In the morning the old man who provided our accommodation brings a bundle wrapped in newspaper and says he wants to show us something very old. He unwraps a dozen small yellowish figurines that do indeed look very old, and tells us they come from somewhere nearby and that they date from the time of the *Younan*, the Greeks. The faces are carved from some sort of bone or tusk and portray a series of men with staring eyes and long moustaches wearing crowns or ornate headbands. They look more like the faces of the Lewis chessmen than anything from this part of the world, and it's impossible not to wonder what uncharted portion of the region's history they really belong to. Then he shows us an enigmatic oval-shaped stone medallion depicting a soldier with a lance, wearing a kilt-like skirt and sandals with long leather straps like a centurion's. The script resembles nothing I've even seen.

We skirt north of Panjab the next morning and begin the slow and winding route towards the south-west that will take us out of Bamiyan province and into Oruzgan. It takes us five days. The landscape seems ever more wild and beautiful and untouched by the world beyond. An entire day is spent losing and refinding the correct route, driving into valleys where the track ends at the foot of a mountain or dissolves into a rock-strewn wilderness. Aref surprises me by remembering that he has some old maps in the pickup, and produces them the next morning. They're 1:200K Soviet military maps from the 1980s, and they're far better than the ones we've got. It takes a little longer to transliterate the place names, which are printed in Cyrillic script, into English and then into Persian, but they're extraordinarily detailed.

The problem is that the locals we ask have no idea of the names of villages only a few miles distant and give us contradictory directions because they've never driven there and travel on paths where we can't. To the villagers we are like aliens from a distant planet, and whenever we stop we are endlessly questioned as to where we come from by men who are barely aware that there's even a war going on.

In one village we are sung to by a melancholy blind man who predicts that our journey will end in fire. In another we meet a man with a dancing bear, and are shown the grave of a teenage boy whose body is said to have remained intact and undecayed more than three years after his death. At another we give a lift to an old man with a club foot and a fat-tailed sheep from one end of the valley to another. By the time we are a day's drive away from the fort, it's our own mission that seems unreal, and the strangeness of our surroundings that has become real.

When we reach Sarnay, beyond a spectacular final pass that crests between two 13,000-foot peaks, it's as if we've broken free of the grasp of the mountains. There are still some high peaks beyond us, but nothing over 10,000 feet, and the route we're planning to follow stays on the valley floor from now on. But in the *mehman-khana* where we settle for the evening there's news from an unexpected quarter.

There's a wiry jovial old man staying in the place, who's walked with his donkey from a village about ten miles away called Daymalek. He sits among us as the owner of the place lights several oil lanterns and puts them on the floor near us, and tells the story of how he used to smuggle weapons on his donkey past a Soviet checkpoint in the days of the jihad.

'He's a big smuggler,' Aref jokes with him, 'famous across Afghanistan.'

The old man wheezes with delight.

'What are you smuggling these days, *Hajji*?' asks Sher Del teasingly. 'Come on, we won't tell.'

'Donkeys!' exclaims the old man, and a ripple of laughter spreads through the room. 'Right under the noses of those cursed Arabs!' He chuckles.

But at this we all fall silent, and the old man looks at our faces wondering what it is he's said.

'*Hajji*,' says Aref, 'there are no Arabs around here.'

'*Wallah*,' he says. 'By God there are. Where the roads meet between Sharow and Dasht, not half a day's walk from here. A cultureless people,' he adds dismissively. 'I've heard Arabic, and I know what it sounds like. They're Arabs alright. They dress wrong too.'

And suddenly we all know it's time to revise our plan because this means there's an al-Qaeda checkpoint further down the valley.

In the morning when we're alone, we gather over the maps. There's no other way out of the valley except through the checkpoint, but we're all agreed that if there really are al-Qaeda there, they won't take kindly to the presence of foreigners.

We all move cautiously down the valley later in the morning, but when we're beyond the village called Dasht, H and I climb a ridge that will give us enough height to OP the checkpoint. We keep our ascent hidden and stay below the skyline, settling after a half-hour climb between some boulders from which there's a clear view of the valley floor.

H takes out the Kite sight and positions it carefully so that it's shielded from the sun. He puts it to his eye and adjusts the focusing ring on the eyepiece.

'Definitely a checkpoint,' says H. 'PK on the roof. Generator out the back. And it looks like they've got comms. Have a look at that antenna. We don't want to get involved with them.' He hands me the Kite. 'What do you make of those blokes outside the building where the jeep's parked?'

I put the sight to my eye and the world shoots forward, shimmering in the heat haze. They're half a mile away but I can clearly make out a man leaning against the wall with one foot propped behind him. His hand rises and falls as he puts a cigarette to his mouth. Another man is talking to him, then turns and enters the building. As he turns I can see he's wearing bulky webbing across his chest. They both have AKs over their shoulders. What distinguishes them from the others around them is that instead of the traditional shalwar kameez, they're wearing desert combat trousers and nothing on their heads, which is almost unthinkable for an Afghan. And though it's harder to define, they don't move like Afghans either. I share these observations with H.

'Time for a meeting,' he says. He covers the end of the Kite before packing it away, then sinks down and away from the skyline.

The others are waiting for us below, where we agree on a plan. H and I, accompanied by Momen, will move on foot to the neighbouring valley to the north, cross the Kadj river, and rejoin the others at a village called Garendj. We'll take the Kite and one of the radios, and wear the Brownings against our bodies. I'll carry Mr Raouf's AK-SU so that in the event of a search the others won't be incriminated. And before we move we'll watch the others from the ridge above as they negotiate the checkpoint, and wait until they've passed safely through.

'Your equipment will be ruined if you have to cross the river,' protests Sher Del.

'Tell him not to worry about that,' says H. 'And don't use the radio,' he says to Aref. 'Keep it switched on in your pocket and press transmit three times if there's an emergency.'

Aref nods.

'What will we do if there is an emergency?' I ask H.

'We'll *emerge*,' he says, throwing me one of his dark looks, so I leave it at that. Then we gather the things we need from the G and pack them into his Bergen.

Like everything else, it takes longer than anticipated. From the ridge we watch as the vehicles reach the checkpoint and are waved to a halt by one of the Taliban guards. Another Talib comes out of the nearby building, and reads what we assume is the permission given to us back in Bamiyan. Aref gets out of the pickup, and is joined by Sher Del, who's driving the G. The Talibs circle the vehicles like hyenas around their prey.

It's an exasperating sight. Another Talib is observing the proceedings from the roof of the building. Then they all disappear inside for fifteen minutes, until Aref returns to the pickup to retrieve some documents. One of the foreign fighters we've seen earlier is with him, and seems to be asking a lot of questions.

Momen, who is so surprised by the power of the Kite sight he can't take his eyes off it, agrees that the men we've seen aren't Afghans. We take turns watching the checkpoint for about half an hour, sharing our observations. Occasionally one of our team comes out, smokes a cigarette conspicuously as a signal to us that things haven't got too bad, then heads back inside to join what is obviously a protracted discussion.

'Maybe,' says Momen, with characteristic mischief, 'those Taliban are lonely, and they want to make new friends.'

More than an hour passes, but eventually the men leave the building and return to the vehicles. H is watching as one of the Talibs gets into the passenger seat of the pickup.

'Bollocks,' he hisses. 'Things have just got more complicated. They've given us an escort. Time to move.'

We leave the ridge, ascend the slope on the far side of the valley and make our way down again along a wide ravine towards the floor of the neighbouring valley, keeping enough height to be able to scan the villages on the far side of the river. There are clusters of low adobe buildings at intervals along the length of the far bank, but we've no way of knowing the exact position of the village where we've agreed to meet the others. All we can do is get as close to it as we can determine from the map and wait for nightfall.

It's a huge relief when, on the far side of the river about a third of a mile away, we spot the signal we've been hoping for. It's the satphone, blinking in infrared mode, which I've fixed to the roof pouch inside the G-Wagen. Through the Kite sight it's as distinct as a parachute flare but invisible to the naked eye.

At our chosen point by the water's edge H lays all our kit carefully in the centre of the tarpaulin we've brought, to which we add our folded clothes after stripping to our underwear. Around everything he lays brushwood for flotation and then rolls the tarpaulin over the contents and ties the ends of the bundle tightly with two lengths of paracord. Then he folds the ends over the centre and ties them again. Finally he cuts two short lengths from the black climbing rope, ties a triple bowline at the end of each, and steps into the loops he's tied.

'Second man ties on with the kit using this,' he says, clipping a small karabiner onto the improvised slings he's made for me and Momen. 'Last man ties on to the far end.' He loosens the remaining coils and passes me the rope. 'Pay out and try not to let go. I'll signal you from the far side.' He screws a red filter over the head of a small torch. 'Give me time to get opposite you.' He waves the torch. 'Side to side for OK and up and down if there's a problem and you need to wait.'

Momen and I watch as he steps into the whispering black water and looks back at us.

'I bloody hate cold water,' he says, and there's just enough light for me to make out the grimace on his face. Then he pushes off and quickly disappears from sight. There's a steady tug on the rope from the current as he swims across, tracing a diagonal twice the width of the river as he's carried downstream. I'm peering along the length of the rope, trying to picture how far he's gone, but the pull on the rope is steady and I can't tell where he's ended up.

It's Momen who sees the signal first on the far side opposite us. It looks like a cigarette glowing in the distance, and it's waving side to side. Momen ties on, and we loop the bundle that H has made onto the rope.

'*Boro bekheir*,' I say. Go well. And then he too disappears into the blackness.

When I see the red glow of the torch for the second time, I detach the rope from the boulder we've secured it to and step into the flow. It's unpleasantly cold and I hear myself swearing inventively. Then all thoughts fade as I swim as hard as I can, feeling glad of the tension on the rope as the others pull me across from the far side. I'm trembling violently when in the darkness I'm suddenly aware of hands pulling me onto the bank. We hurriedly unpack our kit and retrieve our clothes. Everything is perfectly dry.

It sounds straightforward. You need to leave a vehicle, let it go through a checkpoint and rejoin it the other side. But several factors make this apparently simple scenario more problematic than it sounds. It's dark and you're cold. You've got cuts and bruises on your body which demand attention you can't give them. You don't know the terrain. Your vehicle now has an armed and potentially hostile escort, and your sole human link with safety can only communicate with you in secret, via a two-way radio that he can't use. Your friends also appear to be lying up in a small settlement nearby, where there are other civilians, so you can't simply charge in because word of your presence will reach the wrong people far too soon for your purposes. So you will have to somehow deal with the armed escort, and do so in such a way as to not be observed. But you don't know which building to enter, because you don't know where anyone is. You are not in a film, where such things are achieved without hesitation or doubt, and unfold with magical ease. You are instead cold, frustrated, tired, hungry and you have no choice but to wait and watch, and perhaps pray, hoping it doesn't get any colder.

By late morning the following day, I have my first insight into what it must feel like to belong to a criminal gang or team of kidnappers. There is something powerfully attractive to it. In the back of the G, somewhat resembling a nodding dog on the back shelf of a car only with an Afghan scarf tied over his head, the Talib escort has become our reluctant passenger.

We owe our success in part to Aref, who as night falls leaves the room where they're all gathered on the pretext of paying a visit to the outdoor privy, from where he contacts us in a whisper on the two-way radio. They're staying at a primitive *mehman-khana* with several others travellers, and there's nothing to be done until the morning when they all leave.

So we wait for the dawn, taking two-hour stretches on watch in a dried-up irrigation ditch which, if cold, is surprisingly comfortable. It's the nearest we can get to the vehicles, which are several hundred yards away, without breaking cover. In the early morning we all hear the triple burst of static on the radio as Aref attempts to alert us. A few moments later we hear the urgency in the near-whisper of his voice.

'Come now,' he says.

We're about thirty yards from the vehicles when the others emerge from a nearby building. Momen waves to them. Aref and Sher Del wave back as if they've seen an old friend. The Talib escort turns in our direction as we walk up, and we see the look of uncertainty come across his face as we approach, but he makes no move for his weapon. He's in his early twenties. The tail of his black turban hangs over his left shoulder. The look of uncertainty turns to confusion as H cocks his Browning and lines it up on the Talib in a swift and unambiguous motion. I follow up with Mr Raouf's AK-74, and all that remains is for Sher Del to lift the victim's weapon from his shoulder and put it on his own, and then for H to tie a scarf around his bewildered features.

'We don't want him doing much sightseeing,' he says as he tightens the knot. 'He can come in the G with us. That way he doesn't get to overhear anything except my bad English.'

We have a certain sympathy for our extra passenger, at whose expense we're unable to resist a few jokes.

'Do you think he's got a mobile? Ask him to call his girlfriend so she can come and pick him up later,' says H.

'He says he hasn't got a girlfriend. But he's got a nice-looking donkey who he misses a lot.' And so on, because for the time being we have the advantage.

A single range of mountains separates us from our objective. In a straight line we are a little more than fifteen miles from the fort, but there's no way to cross the range with vehicles, so we're forced to take a route that is three times the distance and loops north and then south again around the mountains. It takes all day and half the following day. A few miles from the target we pass through a small settlement called Kadjran, where we stop to buy a few supplies. We don't stay long, because we don't want to be noticed, and camp out in a high deserted fold of the hills, where the GPS tells us we're only half a mile away from the fort.

As darkness falls we take the scarf from the Talib's head and, this being Afghanistan, allow him to eat with us because there are courtesies to be observed. Then we tie his hands again, and return him to the metal bed of the pickup with a blanket.

The colour of the sky turns imperceptibly from turquoise to an ever-deeper purple, and we see the first stars appear. Above us, silhouetted against the sky like a primeval saw blade, lies the ridge to which we'll walk in the morning, and from which we'll have a view, at long last, of the place we've come so far to see.

15

The fort stands on a high narrow spur with a commanding view of the valley below. It is perhaps a hundred years old, and built in the form of a perfect square, the walls linking four circular bastions with defensive slits in their upper sections. A driveable track, cut into the steep approach from the front, links it to the valley floor in a coil of tight switchbacks. Behind the fort and on its flanks the barren slopes of the mountains rise another thousand feet or more. The closest of these rising slopes is at least 300 yards distant. Nearer to, a footpath leads from the side of the fort over the shoulder of the spur and into the next ravine, and a bigger track gives access to the ravine on the other side. They are too steep to be negotiated by vehicle. On the neck of the spur overlooking the fort sits a Soviet BMP like a stranded turtle, abandoned at least a decade ago and stripped even of its wheels. There's no sign of life from within the fort other than a tiny plume of grey smoke, which drifts silently skyward from the central courtyard. It's a picture of rural peace.

From a nest of boulders on a ridge above our final lying-up point, H and I have been watching through the Kite sight since dawn. Sher Del is with us, taking turns to peer at the target, and agrees that there's nothing to indicate we shouldn't drive there and back again without any surprises.

At 10 a.m., as the sun begins to lose the innocence of early morning and climbs with growing strength into the clear sky above, H looks at his watch and then at me.

'We shouldn't wait much longer,' I say.

'Then let's go to work.'

We scramble down into our little camp, where Momen and Aref are nursing a kettle over a small fire. Our captive sits cross-legged on the ground with a scarf still tied over his head and his hands fastened behind his back.

'Time he went back to find his donkey,' says H after we have packed up the vehicles and are ready to leave. He cuts the cord on the Talib's wrists and unties the scarf. We give him a glass of tea and he drinks it in silence with a strangely matter-of-fact expression. Then H gives him enough money for a few days' food.

'Now fuck off and get a proper job,' says H, the gist of which Aref kindly translates. He'll walk down into the village, get his bearings and begin the long walk back to his headquarters, by which time we'll be long gone.

We drive to the valley floor and then ascend again, winding up through the dust until, beyond the final bend, the fort looms suddenly above us. The walls are about fifty feet high and broken only by a giant pair of wooden doors, within which a smaller door the size of a man is framed. Aref and Sher Del walk to it, rattle the heavy iron loops and exchange some words with a voice on the far side. The small door opens and a turbanned armed man emerges. After a few minutes he goes back inside and the two main doors swing open. We drive in.

A double storey of dilapidated rooms runs around the wide central courtyard. Above them the turrets are linked by a narrow earthen parapet. It's strange to think that in London we've seen a satellite photograph of this very place. The two guards are local men, who tell us they've kept watch over the place for the past month. They both have AKs, and when H asks what other weapons they have they point to a PK light machine gun in one of the turrets and an RPG-7 grenade launcher in a corner of the courtyard, beside which lie several bulbous rounds.

The two guards ask whether, now that we're here, they can leave. For a small sum we persuade them to stay a little longer.

'Get one of them on stag up there,' says H, pointing to one of the turrets. 'We don't want to be interrupted. Then get the others to turn the vehicles around and tell them to come and help.'

One of the guards leads us to a door and unlocks the padlock that secures it. Inside it's about the size of a double garage, and is half-filled with a brooding mound covered in dusty tarpaulins. We pull them off, throwing up a bright slanting wall of dust made suddenly luminous by the sunlight. There's an assortment of crates and black boxes, which we stand before in silence. I can't really believe it's them. Ten million dollars' worth of missiles, give or take.

'We could go into business with this lot,' says H. 'Come on.'

With the second guard we work in pairs, hauling everything from the room and laying it out in the courtyard like bodies in a morgue. Some of the missiles are in their original plastic weather-proof cases; others are in wooden crates; and some are wrapped up in sacking which we have to cut through. There are a few surprises. Three of the missiles are British-made Blowpipes, and there are half a dozen Soviet surface-to-air missiles. There's also a Soviet 82-millimetre mortar with several boxes of ammunition.

'Good piece of kit, that,' says H, rubbing the stubble on his chin. 'Seems a shame to blow it up.'

H and I work from opposite ends, photographing the serial numbers and logging the condition of the battery units in our notebooks. One by one our men return them to the room and pile them around a central open space. It takes us more than two hours. Then, as they look on, brushing the dust from their clothes, we unload the explosives from the G.

The layout of the explosives takes the form of a chain of two circuits, linked together. In the unlikely event that the primary circuit fails to detonate, the secondary will fire, detonating the first in the process by the power of the blast. Detcord firing systems with detcord priming are the safest, so we lay a long circular length of the bright orange cable over the pile for a ring main, and tie on six shorter lengths as branch lines leading to the individual charges. The plastic explosive is toxic so we leave the blocks in their paper covering, wrap each one with several turns of detcord and place them among the missiles. One of them will go into the central space that we've left open for the purpose. It's probably not necessary but reassures us. The process reminds me faintly of arranging Christmas lights on a tree.

Then we repeat the same system, using the detonators, which we tape to the six ends of each branch line. Then we make a cut into each block of plastic so as to enclose the detonators in cosy beds of high explosive.

'They call this the direct insertion method,' says H.

'Please don't make me laugh,' I say.

'Case of beer would go down well after this.'

'I'll take the juice of a Kandahari pomegranate,' I say, savouring the thought.

Then, as final back-up, we attach time pencils to the detcord. If the blasting fuse fails, the pencils will fire after thirty minutes. All that remains is to attach the two final detonators, one for each circuit, and the time fuse.

'Time to get the vehicles out,' says H, and begins unwinding the reel of fuse.

I start up the G and drive it out of the gates, and the others follow with the pickup. Our engines are running. The two guards clamber into the bed of the pickup and cling a little anxiously to the sides. Then I walk back to H as he lays out the fuse in a long trail around the deserted courtyard.

We calculate the length required by multiplying by sixty and dividing by the burning rate per foot. Twenty minutes of burning time will need forty feet of fuse. We check and double-check its length, make sure it doesn't overlap, verify the position of the circuits and the plastic, and agree that everything looks ready.

'Pencils,' he says. 'Pull them.'

I remove the safety clips and pull the rings in turn. We look at our watches. Then H holds up the end of the time fuse.

'Got a light?' he asks, running his hands absent-mindedly over his pockets. I know he doesn't need one, because there's already an igniter attached to the end of the fuse. We look at each other for a moment.

'I insist,' I say.

'*Allahu akbar*,' he replies, and pulls the ring. There's a spluttering sound and the fuse bursts into flame. We resist the urge to run, heave on the gates, run the chain through the iron loops and fasten the padlock.

I'm wondering what to do with the key.

'Keep it,' says H. 'Souvenir.'

I wave to Aref, who gives a thumbs up from the cab of the pickup. We climb into the G and lead the way at a good but restrained pace. Then we follow the track to the valley floor, and turn against the slope along the way we came. H is looking ahead and behind us.

'Let's get up to that ridge and stop,' he says, pointing to the spot from which we made our final recce of the fort. We get there ten minutes later. Keeping the engines running we stop and wait for the explosion.

'Thirteen minutes,' I say. The other men get out and, taking their cue from us, look back in the direction of the fort.

'Fifteen minutes.'

'Wait for it,' says H, quietly now.

It's agony. I want to keep my eyes fixed on the fort, but they stray to the surrounding slopes and the valley beyond and then back again, but the explosion doesn't come. I look at my watch and back to the fort again.

'That's twenty minutes,' I tell H.

He's running his tongue around the inside of his mouth. Another minute passes.

'Might be a kink in the fuse cable. Give it a while. The time pencils will kick in in a few minutes.'

We wait. Half an hour passes. The other men begin to talk in whispers. We take the Kite sight and look over the fort in turn. There's no sign of life. No one can have tampered with the charges. I ask the guards whether there could have been anyone else hiding inside the fort. They shake their heads.

Forty-five minutes has passed. Then an hour.

'Misfire,' says H quietly. 'Fuck it. Let's go back.'

It's a depressing feeling to be returning. None of us is very happy about it. The unexpected delay is acting like a silent poison on our nerves. We know we can't give up on the task, but it's as if fate itself has suddenly and personally turned against us. I know I mustn't give in to this feeling, but as we drive up once again under the looming walls of the fort it seems a wounded place, resentful at our having abandoned it to destruction and planning sullenly to punish us in turn.

I retrieve the key to the padlock, pull out the chain, and we heave the gates open. There's a long scorch mark on the ground where the time fuse has burned. Gently we pull open the second door onto the missiles. Everything is intact.

Carefully, H unties the primary detonator from the detcord and examines it. He hands it to me. It hasn't fired. The open rim is scorched where the fuse has burned it. It also has a faint but distinct smell, which it shouldn't have.

'Wax,' I say. 'Smells like some kind of sealing wax.'

We disconnect the time pencils. They've fired as they're supposed to, but the detonators attached to them are intact, as are all the others. H takes a short length of fuse and fits it into the open end of one of them, lights it and stands back. The fuse burns perfectly, but the detonator remains stubbornly inert.

'These dets are all fucked,' says H.

The news is particularly bad because the detonator is arguably the most crucial component of an explosive chain, and our plastic explosive cannot be initiated without one.

'Sattar,' I say. 'In Kabul.'

H nods. 'Crafty fucker. Must have switched them before we left. We've been stitched up.'

For a few moments there is only silence. We look at each other. It's a long way to have come to be thwarted at the final moment.

'Right, let's deal with it. Options.'

The other men are lingering on the far side of the courtyard, looking a bit let down but too polite to ask what the problem is. I wave them over, and we explain the challenge and listen to their suggestions in turn.

'Fire an RPG into the room,' suggests one of the men.

'Bollocks,' says H. 'That's suicide. Who's going to do that?'

Someone else asks whether a piece of detcord, pushed into an emptied 7.62-millimetre round, could be made to detonate when the round fires.

'Doubt it,' I say. 'But you still have the problem of how to fire the round from a safe distance and make it reliable. There are dets in the Stingers, but we'd have to take them apart first. There are dets in the mortar rounds too, but even if we got them out we'd still have the problem of how to prime them.'

'What about the 82?' asks H, meaning the Russian mortar. 'If we can get it up on a ridge we can drop a round right through the roof of the room. We could drive it up, past where that APC is.'

I translate the idea to the others. Firing an ageing Soviet mortar into the fort from a distance isn't the most reliable solution. H is silent for a few minutes, and the men break into a heated discussion. Turning away from them, one of the guards puts his hand gently on my forearm to get my attention.

'*Ba motor bala rafte nemishe,*' he says, shaking his head. 'You can't drive up there.'

'We have a *motor* that can get there,' I reassure him.

'No,' he says, 'it's not that. You can't go up there because of the mines. *Mayeen hast.*'

'What kind of mines?'

'Big Russian ones,' he says, his hands describing a plate-sized circle. 'They're for tanks. From the time of the jihad. I can show you where they are if you want.'

It's a long shot, but we're getting accustomed to long shots. Any Soviet anti-tank mine will contain a powerful detonator. If it's a TM-type mine, which is the most common, it won't be difficult to remove and attach to our own explosive chain. We agree that we have to try. If the effort fails, we'll bombard the fort from a distance with the 82, and keep firing until something happens.

Hunting for the mine itself isn't dangerous. At least at first it isn't. Anti-tank mines have an actuation pressure of a hundred kilograms or more, so a single man's weight can't set one off. The danger comes when you try to move one from its original position. There's no way of telling whether the mine has been booby-trapped by another, smaller mine laid beneath it, which actuates when the main mine is lifted, setting both off. In some mines there's even an extra fuse well underneath or on the side, made for an anti-lift device, which will detonate if it's moved. There's a charge of several kilograms of TNT in most anti-tank mines, so the prospect of failure is at least unambiguous. The blast will kill us all.

The guards stay in the fort. We work four abreast on our knees, probing the ground at intervals of a few inches while Sher Del acts as a kind of marshaller a few yards ahead of us, keeping us in line. A thin metal rod with a pointed tip is best, but we're using what we've got: one knife, a long bayonet from the guards' machine gun and the oil dipsticks from the G and the pickup, which are improbably ideal. Glancing across at the others I can't help feeling it's a strange symmetry of fate that they are professional mine clearers, and that's exactly what we've ended up doing to save the operation. I'm glad it's them.

There are several false alarms as the others strike stones, and we stop to probe the ground more closely. Then after about half an hour, which feels like a year, Momen announces quietly that he thinks he's got something. I kneel beside him and take his bayonet and push it gently forward until it stops. The tip feels as if it's moving against something smooth. I try from different angles and feel the same response at the correct distances. We've found one.

H comes up beside me. He's sweating.

'I'll clear this one,' I tell him. 'Get everyone back inside the fort. Is the 82 ready?' I don't add the obvious 'in case this doesn't go quite the way we're hoping'.

He looks down at the bayonet in the ground, then at me, and then nods as if he's forgotten the question. He draws his forearm across his forehead.

'Leave you to it,' he says. 'Try not to drop it on the way back.'

I hate to see him go. I find the perimeter of the mine and discover it's circular and about a foot across. There don't seem to be any others next to it or beneath it. It feels like it's metal. I'm guessing it's a Soviet TM-type because most of the other kinds have plastic outer housings, which feel different when you scrape against them with a probe. I calculate the centre and carefully begin to remove the earth until a portion of the dusty pressure plate appears.

There are six evenly spaced depressions on the plate. It occurs to me, at this unlikely moment, that they resemble the finger-marks that Italian bakers press into their dough when they're making focaccia. Then I think how odd it would be to be blown up by this mine in particular after having come all the way to Afghanistan, because it's not a Soviet mine. It's a British-made Second World War-era Mark 7.

The body is made of sheet steel with a domed upper surface, and it uses a Number 5 single- or double-impulse fuse. It can be fitted with an anti-lift device, but they're rare, which is good. The mine's weight makes it easy to booby-trap, which is bad. It contains twenty pounds of high-explosive TNT, or roughly the equivalent of sixty hand grenades.

I scrape away the soil from the upper part, working slowly down, watching the drops of sweat from my forehead fall onto the plate to create dark stains in the dust. The drops fall as if in slow motion and seem unnaturally large, though I know they're not. I reveal the circular upper edge of the mine. I want only to know what's underneath it, as a man wants to know the future, which, although closer to him at every moment than he ever suspects, is impenetrable.

I have a strange feeling as if I'm passing through a door, beyond which time no longer behaves in the usual way. I see the point of the bayonet pushing into the dirt around the mine and my hands tugging at the loosened debris. I see the tiny particles of dust swirl across my skin and tumble down in microscopic spirals of air onto the hairs on the backs of my hands like drowning sailors clinging gratefully to wreckage. I see blood appear under my fingertips, creeping along the curve of my nails as I claw into the rocky soil, only it seems that the blood is a flash flood in high summer driving across a boulder-filled canyon. There is more life compressed into these microscopic worlds than I have ever suspected, and for a few moments I've been carried into the full drama of their existence.

I reach under the mine to feel whether there's anything sinister there and sense the weight of the metallic structure resting patiently on the earth waiting to corrode into its component elements, and all the passions and mysteries that can ever be known seem to have let me into their invisible secrets. They are all there, like a silent film we can't see or hear, but they're there all the same.

There's no second mine or anti-lift device. As I lift the mine and it comes free I hear the sound of my own breath, and the world is back to its ordinary self. I have no idea how much time has passed and look back to the fort, where H is standing on the nearest turret, giving me an on-the-double hand signal like a steam-train driver pulling frantically on his whistle.

316

I run back and the men greet me like a long-lost friend with pats on my back.

'It's like working for the United Nations,' I say. 'We drive a German car to an Afghan fort to blow up American missiles with a British mine.'

'And decide on it by a Chinese parliament,' says H, using the SAS term for a meeting that involves all ranks. 'Can you get the det out?'

'One does rather hope so,' I say in my best officer's accent.

There's a depression on the cover plate like the head of a screw, which I now attempt to loosen with the screwdriver on the Leatherman which Grace gave me. The plate doesn't budge, so I add a little pressure, and the body of the mine slips along the ground. H sinks to his knees and holds it firm while I try again.

I'm fairly sure that I can't exert enough force on the plate to set off the mine, but it's not a pleasant feeling. It would be a shame to have come this far only to blow ourselves up by pushing too hard. I lean over the mine and grip the Leatherman with both hands and turn as hard as I can, while H uses his forearms to push in the opposite direction. I hear a strange growl of exasperation escape my mouth, and I'm almost oblivious now to the consequence of pushing against the plate with all my strength.

Then there's a sudden metallic cracking noise as the screwdriver snaps. Our heads knock together with such force that my vision darkens for a second, and little sparks seem to be spilling in front of my eyes, prompting me to wonder whether we've been killed. Then the light pours in again, and we're both staring at the top of the mine. The pressure plate is free.

I've never known such a roller coaster of emotions. We're alive, but as I lift the mine fuse free I realise it's integral to the plate and can't be separated.

'I don't think this is going to work,' I say.

'Tell me you're joking,' says H quietly.

We can't spend more time hoping to improvise a solution. It's six hours since we released the Talib guard, and we must assume that before long he'll make it back to the post where he originally joined us and report to his commander. We make a brutal calculation. We have already passed our cut-off time.

I feel sick.

'Then let's get the mortar on the truck,' says H grimly.

And just as our hopes fall to their lowest ebb, with a precision that renews and affirms a private notion that all things are inevitably connected a shout goes up from the guard who's keeping watch in the southern turret. We turn and see him waving frantically, so H and I run up and join him in the curve of the wall, which resembles the conning tower of a submarine, and follow the line of his outstretched arm to the floor of the valley.

'We've got company,' says H, reaching for the Kite sight in his map pocket. He flips open the covers, rests it on the dusty lip of the wall and brings his eye forward. 'Jesus Christ,' he says. 'I thought you said he was only going to bring his bodyguards.'

'That's what he told me.'

'That's a lot of bodyguards.' He hands me the Kite.

'We might need to revise the plan,' I agree because not even in the emergency plan that I made with Manny is there a scenario like this one. For a moment I can't prevent the thought that perhaps Manny has betrayed us, and involuntarily picture myself having to shoot him. Then I hear the voice of the Baronness and the story of Ali and the knight, and the feeling of dread is lifted.

Below us, at the mouth of the valley about a mile away, there are six pickup trucks travelling at speed, throwing up pale clouds of dust in their wakes. There are at least half a dozen armed men in the back of each one. It won't take them more than fifteen minutes to reach us. I pass the Kite to the guard, who peers intently into the viewfinder then turns back to us.

'By God,' he says, 'those men are no Afghans.' And a look of relish spreads slowly across his face.

H calls down to the others, who are looking up at us expectantly. 'I need an ammo count. Everything we've got.' He pats the metal ammunition box that's fixed to the PK belt-fed machine gun at our feet.

'*Chand hast?*' I ask.

'*Devist*,' answers the guard. There's two hundred rounds of link in the box. H slaps the guard firmly on the back, points to his own eyes with two fingers and then to the horizon. Then we run to the rear turrets and look over the terrain.

'No way out there,' says H. 'Right track's mined and the left one's too steep.'

The track that leads to the neighbouring ravine is far too steep for an ordinary vehicle, but looking at it gives me an idea.

'We can do it,' I say. 'In the G. It's steep but we can do it. With all the diffs on and in low-range gear. All we have to do is get out of the front and along the side of the fort. They won't be able to follow us.'

'Then we need a diversion,' says H. 'Let's get the others set up.'

We speed down the earthen steps that lead to the courtyard, where the men have gathered the weapons and ammunition. Everyone has heard by now of the approaching trucks, and their faces have the solemn look of men who feel the closeness of the unknown.

Our weapons are spread on the ground. There are four high-explosive rounds for the RPG launcher, three AKs, including the one we borrowed from the Talib, and Mr Raouf's AK-SU, which means each of us has a weapon of some kind, except for H. In the guards' webbing there are six full magazines, which H divides between the AKs. We also have the Brownings and several magazines' worth of 9-millimetre rounds.

Spontaneously the men have drawn themselves up in a rough line, which H now travels, assigning each of them a weapon after examining it and telling him where to position himself. Then he asks Aref to translate for him, and steps away from the line.

'It was not our intention to bring you into a battle,' he says, looking into the faces in turn. 'But if the men who are on their way here have evil intentions against us, we must be ready to defeat them. They are not our friends. They are not your countrymen. I hope to avoid fighting them, but if they choose to fight us, they will pay the price.'

'*Allahu akbar*,' says one of the men, quietly but distinctly.

'There are many of them and few of us. But remember they will not be expecting us to resist them, and the surprise will cost them dearly. We have a strong position of defence. And they know nothing of how many we are, or how determined we are.

'Be aware of these things. If our enemy reaches the slopes around us they will be able to destroy us. Allow nothing to move above us, and nothing to come through the doors.

'If we fight hard, we will succeed. Everybody clear?'

There's a moment's silence, then one of the guards speaks. 'We're Afghans,' he says evenly. 'We already know how to fight.'

'Then be ready to fight,' says H, 'and God help you.'

All the men deploy to the turrets except Sher Del, whose experience and help we need. The three of us move to the room where the missiles are piled and haul out the wooden case which contains the 82-millimetre mortar. While H manoeuvres it onto its baseplate in a corner of the courtyard, I drag the ammunition boxes with Sher Del out from the room and open them alongside. There are twelve rounds, which Sher Del shows us how to prime and charge. H adjusts the mortar bipod to its maximum elevation.

'I'll need you to spot for me,' he says. 'Watch for the fall of shot and call out the range.' He pats the mortar tube. 'This ought to keep their heads down.' He smiles at me and wipes the sweat from his face with his forearm. 'Don't fret,' he says. 'There's only fifty blokes out there. There were two hundred of them at Mirbat.'

I feel strangely at peace. The pure and uncomplicated purpose of battle, which tranquillises all thoughts of past or future, settles on me now. It displaces the habitual tyranny of the mind and opens onto a luxurious quietness, which one longs for but never quite attains in ordinary life. Life seems miraculously beautiful and fragile.

The three of us walk to the forward turret and watch the convoy of pickups as it ascends the track. I take the magazine from the Browning and slide two rounds into my hand. Then with the pliers on the Leatherman I pull free the lead slugs in turn and remove half the cordite charge from the casings. I replace the slugs, then return the two rounds to the magazine.

The pickups swing onto the flat ground beneath us. The guard in the opposite turret, tightening his grip on the stock of the PK, looks across to H, who returns a gesture of restraint. The men below us are not expecting a fight, which means they've been put at ease by their commander. I'm hoping it's because they've been told we're unarmed and not in a position to resist. They dismount casually from the trucks, shaking the dust from their clothes and looking up at the walls of the fort like tourists beneath a cathedral. Three or four men with scarves tied Middle-Eastern-style around their faces dismount more cautiously and position themselves defensively behind the cabs of the trucks. There are perhaps some Afghans among them but it is impossible to know. They have all become our enemy now. H is lying on his stomach, watching them through the Kite.

One of the pickups is black. Clusters of RPG rounds are fastened behind the cab like satanic bouquets of flowers. Six or seven men sit in the back, but two have jumped out and are conferring with whoever's inside. Then the nearside door opens, and a man in a black shalwar emerges with the confident manner of someone in authority. It's Manny. I feel the pounding of my heart.

'Is that your friend?' asks H in a whisper.

'Yes.'

'Doesn't look much like he's come to save us.'

I don't reply. To judge from appearances, H is right. It's hard not to suppose that Manny has brought this overwhelming force to attack us. The next few minutes seem to confirm this worst of scenarios.

Manny takes a loudhailer from the pickup and blows into the mouthpiece. Two men behind him unsling weapons from their shoulders but their posture is still relaxed.

'You in there, Ant? Hello?'

He walks brazenly to the centre ground in front of the fort, looks up and brings the loudhailer to his mouth again.

'Open up, Ant,' he calls. 'You've got something in there that we want. If you don't come out, we'll have to come in and get it ourselves. Think we can arrange something that suits everyone? *We've all come a long way.*'

It's the pass phrase I've been waiting for. H nods at me then whispers an instruction to Sher Del.

'Why don't you come in so we can talk about it?' I shout.

Manny confers with the man who comes to his side. He's a bulky-looking fighter with a black scarf tied around his head revealing only his eyes. Ammunition pouches stretch across his chest.

'Mind if I bring a friend?' calls Manny.

'Just the one,' I reply.

H and I descend to the courtyard, where H positions himself against the wall next to the entrance. I pull on the bolts of the smaller door, open it fully and walk back towards the centre of the courtyard. There's a clear but narrow view to the flat ground outside, which is momentarily obscured as Manny's bodyguard steps inside, followed by Manny. The bodyguard looks under-standably puzzled and anxious. He sees H, unarmed, behind him, but no one else, because they're hidden by the walls. The two of them walk towards me. The bodyguard is standing to my left and a couple of paces behind Manny, who gives a nod of reassurance to him, then steps forward.

We embrace in the Afghan manner. As our bodies touch, Manny's hand brushes my jacket, out of sight of his bodyguard. I feel a slight but distinct pull against the fabric as something small and heavy drops into my pocket.

'Present for you,' he says quietly, taking a step back. 'Ten-second fuse.'

'Who told you we needed that?'

'Our little bird in Kabul, who switched your detonators. You were right about him.'

'You said you'd bring a couple of guards, not six truckfuls.'

'Couldn't help that, I'm afraid. They all wanted to join the party. I seem to have scooped up all the bad ones.' He's silent for a moment. 'They're not planning to let you go, if you surrender.'

'Somehow I didn't think so.'

'You ready for this or do you need me to buy some time?'

'Ready as we'll ever be.'

'Well then. Let's get it over with. I suppose it's time to die.'

He calls to his bodyguard in a language I don't recognise. It must be Chechen. Then he turns around and, walking slowly towards the door, raises his arms out in what looks like a gesture of resignation, so that the others beyond the door can see. It's safe to say that none of them is expecting what happens next.

I wait until Manny has taken about ten paces and is nearly at the door. Then I pull the Browning from the holster on my hip, aim squarely for the centre of his back and fire twice.

His body tumbles forward and falls face down. Without pausing, I roll to my right, bring up the Browning in a firing stance on Manny's bodyguard, who's dropped instinctively into a squat and is raising his weapon to his shoulder. It's the last thing he ever does. Before I can fire another shot rings out, as H sends a single round into his head. His body slumps like a collapsed puppet. H runs forward like lightning, picks up the bodyguard's weapon, drags his body away from the doors and calls out to Sher Del as he leaps up the stairway to the tower.

'*RPG! RPG!*'

He's predicted, accurately, that for a few seconds after the first shots are fired the men outside will scramble for cover before returning reactive fire. It's these same seconds I use to slam the door closed, throw the bolts and haul Manny away into cover.

The shock of the rounds has sent his body into a kind of paralysis. I prop him against a wall and tear at the straps of his body armour as he coughs and gasps for air.

'Feels like you broke all my fucking ribs.'

'Breathe. I took out all the powder I could.'

He's about to say something else but at that moment there's a high-pitched bang which makes us flinch as the shock wave goes through us like a physical blow. Sher Del has fired the first RPG round into a truck below and is taking aim at a second. H is by his side as I run up, and Manny follows behind me, his lungs heaving in pain.

'*Down!*' yells H a second before the backblast from the RPG roars over us, and the turret fills with hot smoke. There's another incredible bang from below. We grab our weapons.

'Support him,' shouts H, pointing to the other turret. We can hear the first smack of rounds against the wall as we run across to reach the PK, which is chattering deafeningly.

From the slit we look down to the open space in front of the fort, which a minute ago was so peaceful. It's a chaos of debris, flames and scattered bodies. The PK is firing bursts into the trucks, from which men are tumbling onto the ground and staggering across the dust.

We know our task, and shoot into the nameless shapes until they are still. Cordite-laden smoke surrounds us. Sher Del fires a third RPG, and a thin grey plume streaks down towards a truck attempting to withdraw, exploding with a bright orange burst against the tailgate. The engines of the other three are screaming and their wheels throwing up dust as they lurch frantically towards the track. Bodies are spilling from the flat ground and finding cover among the crags beyond, from which their return fire now begins, struggling to find its mark.

There's a loud crack as a burst from below hits the turret and a cloud of disintegrating mud erupts behind the Afghan who's firing the PK. He leaps sideways and I grab him to stop him falling into the courtyard. He rubs grit and blood from the side of his face and returns to the weapon, muttering thanks to *Mushgil Gusha*, one of the Afghan names for God, before lowering his eye to the sights again and hunting for movement below.

I hear H call to us and run over to him. He points out the pockets of men making their way from our front towards the sides of the fort.

'Concentrate on them, then spot for me. Vehicles first.' He pushes the Kite into my chest and runs at a crouch towards the rear turrets, where Aref and Momen have begun firing. Our work becomes more precise as our targets dart between the rocks at a growing distance. Sweat interferes with my aim. From somewhere a round finds the slit and slaps into the wall behind my head.

Now in the courtyard, H is crouching behind the mortar. Manny stands beside him with a mortar round in his hands, waiting for my signal. The three vehicles have emerged from the dead ground about 300 yards away, turning along a track towards the higher ground.

I watch for the fall of shot and see the impact before I hear it. A ragged brown column of dirt flies into the air a hundred yards beyond the vehicles. I see their brake lights flash. I signal to H and see him furiously adjusting the trajectory. Manny drops another round into the tube and the two of them crouch with their ears covered as a burst of flame leaps out. Another geyser of earth flies up ahead of the vehicles, this time on the opposite side. A third round lands directly ahead of them. H can fire for effect now. A fourth lands almost between them, and a fifth forces the lead vehicle from the track. A sixth destroys it. A seventh falls into a cluster of fleeing men. The driver of the final vehicle has figured out the deadly game and veers off at right angles to our fire. We cannot track it, so I signal for H to cease fire. There is so much smoke in the courtyard I can hardly see him.

A yell goes up from Momen, who's gesturing frantically to the area behind the fort. I run to him. A group of men equipped with RPGs is ascending the slope above him. Manny and H struggle to turn the mortar around and line it up on them, and fire a ranging shot which explodes far above. They're too close to us for the minimum range of the mortar, so Manny struggles under the tripod to superelevate it until it's nearly vertical. There's another deafening explosion as they fire again, and a fountain of rocks bursts from the slope nearby. Another falls beside the attackers, spreading its lethal shrapnel in their midst. I point to another flicker of movement in the rocks, yell out the range and watch another two explosions erupt from the slope. Then the mortar falls silent as the final round is fired, and H and Manny run up to the rear turrets, emerging like wild apparitions from the smoke, filthy and glistening with sweat.

Manny stays behind while H and I run to the front. The PK has stopped firing. The Afghan guard lies beside it with his arm pinned under him. His neck, where a round has passed through it, resembles a bloody rag.

'Check on him,' shouts H, pointing to Sher Del in the opposite tower. Sher Del, warrior that he is, looks almost at ease. He looks at me and grins wildly. The left side of his face is drenched in blood but he doesn't seem to notice. But the lapse in fire from the other turret has allowed a pocket of men beneath the lip of the open ground to reorganise themselves, and I don't know who hears it first, but I see the telltale plume of smoke simultaneously with H's cry.

'*Incoming!*'

The whole fort seems to shudder with the impact as if it's about to collapse. We hear a clamour of shouts from below and see shapes running towards the doors, which the RPG has blasted from their hinges. H fires quick bursts into the running men, who are making a suicidal bid for the entrance, and together with Sher Del we cut them down in their tracks. Then along the perimeter of the open ground I see bursts of dust blossoming out of the ground where H is firing to discourage a repeat effort. Then he runs up to us.

'PK's out of ammo. We can't let that happen too often. Fuckers aren't giving up.' He looks at us and slaps Sher Del heartily on the back. 'Reckon it's time to go before they rush us. Warn the others and get them down.'

The idea that we're about to leave fills me with an unlikely sense of calm. It's as if he's suggested that it's time for us all to go home, and I can't wait to share the news with the others that it's time to move. But as I'm running to the far turret, where Manny and Aref are crouching, a puff of smoke catches my eye from high up on the slope beyond the rear of the fort. It shouldn't be there.

I know I'm yelling for them to take cover, but I can't seem to hear my own voice, and the whole of time seems to be stretching out again as if I can't get things to happen fast enough. I dive to the ground along the parapet and cover my ears and head with my forearms and distinctly see Manny turn towards me. The whole turret seems to disappear in a burst of smoke and I feel a shower of debris as if I'm suddenly being pecked to death by a flock of crazed birds. When I look up, there's a gaping space where the turret used to be.

I throw myself off the parapet onto the stairs and run down to the room into which Manny has fallen. The roof has absorbed the force of his fall and he's struggling to his feet, dazed and gripping his head. Aref has been blown into the courtyard, and either the blast or the fall has killed him outright. His clothes have been partially stripped from his body by the blast, and I involuntarily register how white the skin of his chest seems in comparison to that of his face.

We have to leave. We are being killed and will soon be overrun. I help Manny to the car, then run to the missiles. It seems a lifetime since we were calmly examining them in the sunshine a few hours ago. I'm aware, as if a quiet matter-of-fact voice is telling me so, that it's cooler and darker in the room. I take the grenade from my pocket. It's a dark-green egg-shaped Soviet-made RGD-5. I unscrew the fuze, see that's it's a UZRGM and wonder if it really is the ten-second version, though it hardly matters now. There's a strip of black tape still hanging from the detcord, so I use it to bind the detonator end to the cord, then look back into the courtyard to see where everybody is.

The doors to the G are all open. Manny's already inside. Momen and the other Afghan guard are lifting Aref's body into the back. Sher Del runs up, hauls the others in and pulls the door closed. A round from beyond the gates somehow finds the windscreen of the G and richochets from the armoured glass with a whizzing sound like a party firework.

I call to H to start the engine and briefly contemplate the stretch of open ground I have to cover in order to reach the G. Then I pull the safety ring on the grenade and release my grip on the fuse handle. It springs onto the ground. I run.

I can't hear the engine because my ears are ringing so loudly, though it's the first time I'm aware of it. I slam the door closed and see the rev counter leap as I test the accelerator. Sher Del grabs my shoulder from behind and I turn to him and it's then I see that his earlobe has been shot away.

'*Besyaar khub jang mikonid!*' he says. A huge grin reaches across his face. 'You fight really well!'

The empty pickup is in front of us with the brakes off, so that as it emerges it will roll to the edge of the flat ground and draw the enemy's fire. They won't know we aren't in it, at first. And we're glad we're not, because as the G surges forward and pushes the pickup onto the open ground we see the rear window of the cab grow cloudy with bullet holes as the rounds tear into it, scattering fragments of its interior into the air.

Then as we gather speed I throw the G to the right, feeling the power of the engine surge as the pickup rolls away from us, and we circle under the foot of the turret, and suddenly it's as if a team of people are hammering at the doors and windows with all their might. The windows emit a high-pitched crack but the rounds that hit the doors make a deep thud like stone into mud. The spare wheel on the rear door bursts with a violent hiss of air. Then as we climb the slope that leads to the track beyond the rear of the fort, the back window finally shatters and collapses inwards, torn from the frame of the car by repeated impacts. An AK-round thumps into the seat behind me like the blow of a sledgehammer but is stopped by the layers of Kevlar stitched inside.

My hand scrambles for the diff-lock switches as we reach the crest of the shoulder, and as I make the turn the wheels judder against the loose surface of the ground. There's a succession of loud thuds against the roof, and the skyline lurches up like the view from a fighter plane going into a dive, and our weapons clatter forward onto the dashboard. It's steeper than I thought, and the G pitches down as if it's not going to stop, and H braces his hand against the windscreen and curses.

'*La illaha ill'allah,*' cries Sher Del. There is no God but God.

And then it happens. The first thing we feel is the compression, as if our ears are being sucked into our heads. Then we hear the blast, which shakes the ground so strongly the force is transmitted to the steering wheel like a blow against the wheels. A deep rolling booming sound, followed almost instantaneously by several more, sweeps over and through us. The gunfire is silenced.

'Hope someone's taking pictures up there,' says H, bracing himself against the roof and grimacing as the G yaws dangerously to one side. My thoughts seem to be taking shape in slow motion, and his comment makes no sense to me until I realise he's talking about satellites. Then it occurs to me that we are actually still alive. Against the odds, we have completed the mission, and the missiles will never be used. I recall the Baroness's words, *I want you to succeed*, and suddenly I want to laugh because we really have succeeded. Whoever was planning a catastrophe using the Stingers will now have to come up with a very different plan, and whoever was planning to let it happen will have to wait for a very different catastrophe.

The wheels are holding like glue onto the rocky slope, but our pace is agonisingly slow. Then there's a bright flash a few yards ahead and an explosion that scatters a violent cloud of rock and shrapnel against us. Bits fly up from the front of the car, but we're still moving.

H clambers with astonishing agility into the back, rests his AK on the rim of the rear door and fires towards the ridgeline above us where the RPG has come from. The sound of the shots is deafening and the interior is thick with cordite smoke. But the ravine is beginning to open up now and the slope is reducing so I take the gearbox out of low range and accelerate.

As we crash forward, I'm aware of a kind of moaning sound behind me. It's Momen, chanting prayers. There are warning lights blinking on the dashboard but I can't look at them. The ground begins to flatten out and with a final bounce we hit the dirt road. I turn towards the head of the valley. H scrambles into the seat behind me.

'Let's get some distance behind us,' he says.

We race up the valley, savouring the sweetness of our escape. After half a mile the slopes steepen on both sides as we draw closer to its head. Then, just as we're beginning to feel like we're finally beyond the reach of our enemies, a black shape plunges across the track a hundred yards ahead of us, blocking the way. I recognise the pickup from earlier outside the fort and wonder for a moment whether it's just an unpleasant coincidence that we've now run into each other. Perhaps they're lost. But the truck's bonnet pitches sharply downwards. The driver is braking hard, because that's exactly where he wants to be: directly in front of us.

'Jesus Christ,' yells H. '*Ambush front!*'

'I can't turn.' The slopes are too steep. 'Can't stop either.'

We see two men jump from the cab of the pickup and run into cover. Two others position themselves behind the bonnet. One has an AK and the other readies an RPG. The AK doesn't worry me too much. We hear the crack and thump of rounds smashing into the G head on, but it'll put up with a few more. What worries me is the RPG. If I stop or reverse, we'll be sitting ducks.

H realises this too, and turns to me. 'Give it all you've got.'

I don't know what the minimum arming distance for an RPG round is. When a round is fired from the launcher, it won't explode if it hits a target that's too close because it doesn't have time to arm itself. It will simply bounce off, leaving a trail of smoke from the propellant. But I don't know what that distance is. I think it's thirty feet, but it might be five. It seems a pity to be killed having come so close to escaping, but there's nothing more to do. I can only hope that seeing us hurtling towards him will make our enemy think twice about lingering in our path.

I push my foot to the floor and hear the transmission kick into lower gear. There's a roar from the engine as the full power of the cylinders burns its way to the wheels, and we feel the front of the G lift as if it's struggling to take off. We must be doing sixty miles an hour but it feels like we're driving through treacle. Five or six seconds pass. It feels like a year.

I don't know if the RPG is ever fired. I aim the G for the rear of the pickup, where it's lightest and will do the least damage to us, and the impact, when it comes, is surprisingly mild. As we spin to a halt beyond it, everything is still happening in slow motion. H dives and rolls from the passenger door and I follow him automatically, just as we've trained for. We fire over the bonnet of the G, and I distinctly feel a round pass by my ear with a watery thud. Our enemies, now that we have passed behind them, are unprotected. An injured man staggers into view and falls backwards as I fire. Another shape falls, as if in a clownish dance. H darts from the cover of the car and signals me to do the same to the left, and we advance in turn towards our enemies' final hiding places. In the folds of rock about twenty yards away I see a flicker of motion, and fire at it. The hammer of the AK falls on an empty chamber, so I throw it aside and pull the Browning from my hip. Sweat blurs my vision and I cannot be sure where the movement has come from. I fire three rounds from the Browning until it too falls silent as the magazine empties. There is nothing but rock. I turn my head momentarily as I hear a double tap from H's weapon, and then a strange stillness descends.

On H's hand signal we withdraw back to the G.

A plume of steam is rising from somewhere under the bonnet. The windscreen is opaque and the bodywork is perforated with bullet holes. The engine's still running but it's faltering now and making a high-pitched wheezing sound like a man with a bullet in his lungs. H's shirt is stained with blood where a round has nicked the muscles between his neck and shoulder, but he hasn't noticed it.

We cover about two miles driving on the rims of the wheels, and then the engine finally dies. H and I remove the weapons and the gold, and from the back the others pull Aref's body and lay it on the ground. Then we soak the hand-stitched leather seats with diesel as if in a demonic funeral rite, and push the G from the track, pointing it down a slope, where it tumbles and eventually cartwheels onto a boulder-filled arena far below us.

'It was a bit ugly, anyway,' says H.

'Would have cost a fortune to service.'

'Especially the way you drive.'

The sun spreads its liquid gold over the landscape. We carry Aref's body in a *pattu* up a nearby hillside to where a cluster of poplars is swaying, and bury it in a shallow grave, over which the other men kneel and pray.

Afterwards, the Afghan guard from the fort comes up to me.

'I'm going,' he says. 'Back to my village.'

I take several of the gold sovereigns from the belt and give them to him. He looks at them, pockets them and says nothing. Then he embraces us in turn and walks away.

Manny is in poor shape. The blast at the fort has blinded and deafened him, though I can't tell for how long. We agree to walk to where the map indicates a tiny village, and follow an animal track that leads up towards the neighbouring valley. For nearly two hours we trudge in silence. H and I take turns to support Manny, who walks with difficulty.

Then we descend towards the village beyond, as if into a tranquil and unconnected world where violence is unknown. The silent houses are surrounded by a patchwork of green fields in gently differing shades. An old man, working in the irrigation ditches that run between them, leaves his work and walks up to us as we approach, guiding us without asking for any explanation to the tiny settlement, beside which a glittering stream is flowing.

I press a gold sovereign into the hand of the old man.

'For your help,' I say. Then I give him another. 'For your silence.'

'*Aqelmand ra eshara kafee ast,*' he croaks. A sign is sufficient to a wise man.

'Give it to the poor, then.'

He lights a fire in the courtyard of his simple home and brings us tea as we wash the dust and grime from our bodies beside the stream. He gathers our clothes to wash them, and brings us his own spare garments. I tie a strip of fabric around Manny's eyes so that they can rest and hope that the damage is not too great.

We move inside, and the old man brings us a platter of rice. I eat a few mouthfuls. Then I feel the onset of fatigue like an advancing unstoppable tide and, leaning back against the wall, close my eyes for a few seconds.

I wonder, when the morning light wakes me, where I am. I sit up in a panic and feel pains flare up all over my body. Someone has thrown a blanket over me, and the others are sleeping in a row next to me. Only H is absent.

I walk outside, shielding my eyes from the sun, which is already high. I realise that my ears are still ringing, but that there's no other sound. It's ten o'clock and already warm, and our clothes are dry and swaying gently from a rope stretched across the yard. I open a rickety outer door and walk a little way towards the river, where I catch sight of H. He's already dressed, but his chest is bare, and he's splashing water over the wound on his shoulder and pressing on the muscle experimentally. I call to him, quietly.

He turns and looks at me. He says nothing but smiles. Everything in our friendship seems contained in it. An Afghan proverb springs suddenly into my memory, and I hear myself repeating it quietly to myself.

Yak roz didi dost, roze dega didi bradar. One day there is friendship, the next there is brotherhood.

The silence is broken by a single shot. I don't see where it comes from because I am watching H, whose body suddenly jerks, then wavers at the water's edge. He looks down slowly at his chest, where a dark stain has suddenly appeared, and looks up again in bewilderment. There's another shot a few seconds later, and H's body topples backwards into the water. I open my mouth but no sound comes out.

A momentary paralysis lifts, and I turn in the direction of the shot. A man is standing thirty yards away. His clothes are filthy and torn, and I realise it can only be the fourth man from the black pickup. I can see his face and the look of coldness on it as he swings his weapon towards me and takes aim. There's a faint click. A scowl crosses his face as he throws the empty magazine to the ground and reaches for another in his webbing.

Then a raging energy enters me and I run across the open ground towards him. I'm already halfway to him as he sends the magazine home and draws back the bolt. I see the muzzle swing up and see his head tilt as he takes aim at me, and I realise I will die, but I'll die trying.

I hear the shot but feel nothing. Something is happening I

don't understand. Another shot rings out, and then another and another, and the man's weapon falls from his hands as he tumbles back under the rounds from H's Browning. The man is dead by the time I reach him.

I look back towards H, who's standing in the water with his pistol at his side, and for a second I wonder if it's all been an illusion and he's fine after all. But as I run back to him he sinks to his knees, and the water flowing behind him is red, as if someone has been pouring wine into it.

I catch him as his body falls sideways and yell to the others, and I carry him to the wall of the house. Sher Del and Momen have run out and tear strips of cloth to press against H's chest where the blood is gushing as if from a broken tap. I prop him against the wall.

'Did I get him?' he asks. He's trying to smile.

'Yes,' I say.

'Good. I thought there might be one more. Everyone else alright?'

'They're fine,' I say.

His eyes roll up then back again, like the bubbles in a spirit level. He's dying.

'Do me a favour? Help me up the hill, can you? I want to look at the view.'

I pick him up. The others stay behind because they know what's going to happen. I carry him across the stream and through the line of poplars beyond, where the dappled light falls across his face as he tries to keep his head up. He's struggling to hum a tune, but the sound only comes out as my feet fall against the ground, pushing the air from his lungs in tiny bursts. Then he coughs convulsively, and a trail of blood descends from his lips, and there is nothing I can do now but watch the life flow from him.

'Here's a good spot,' I say. I lower him to the ground and lean him against a slope that allows him to look across the valley, and sit next to him, wiping the tears that are streaming from my eyes. I can't stop them.

'It's nice here,' he says. His head lolls forward, then corrects itself. 'I think I might stay a while.'

We sit for a few minutes in silence as the mystery of death draws in. Then, as gently as if he has fallen asleep, his head comes to rest on my shoulder, and I have the distinct sense that something has been released, like a river that has finally reached the sea.

We wash his body in the stream and carry it into the old man's courtyard. Two women from the village come to wrap him in white cloth. I dig the grave myself, concealing in it the boot which contains the tracker, though I have no idea how long it will give out a signal. The four of us carry him to the grave, Manny walking with one hand on my shoulder as a guide, and we're watched from below by the old man, a few villagers who have emerged from their houses and some brightly dressed, curious children.

Sher Del and Momen offer prayers over the grave in turn, and as the first handful of dark soil falls onto the whiteness of the fabric, the grief is just too strong and I have to turn my eyes away.

I look up through a blur of tears, and my gaze falls on an eagle soaring high overhead in the centre of the lapis-blue sky. It seems to be circling us, and I watch its silhouette turning effortlessly through the pure clear air until the sound of the men's prayers brings me back. When I look up again, the eagle is gone.

We agree to stay together, though I give Sher Del and Momen the choice.

'Together,' Sher Del says, 'we will be stronger.'

We've still got the silk maps, the pistols, enough gold to sponsor a minor coup, and between us a healthy stock of stories to keep us entertained along the way. If we steer clear of the main tracks and roads we're unlikely to be seen, and should be able to make our way to Kandahar within a few days and blend into the life of the city. From there we can split up and travel invisibly on public transport back to Kabul.

The old man gives me his own shalwar kameez to wear, and we roll our things into a *pattu*, which Sher Del throws over his shoulder as we prepare to set off, resembling nothing more than an impoverished team of weary native travellers.

I look up once more and search the air to see if the eagle has returned, but it's gone now, and the sky is magnificently empty.

In memory of

H

1949–2001
A Sqn 22 SAS

BEYOND THE LAST BLUE MOUNTAIN BARRED WITH SNOW

Acknowledgements

With special thanks to:

His Master's Voice
Lola Beaumont
RayF, J & B
Mephisto
DE &
'C'

Jason Elliot is a prize-winning British travel writer, whose works include *An Unexpected Light: Travels in Afghanistan*, a *New York Times* bestseller and winner of the Thomas Cook/*Daily Telegraph* Travel Book Award, and *Mirrors of the Unseen: Journeys in Iran*. *The Network* is his first novel.

A NOTE ON THE TYPE

The text of this book is set in Linotype Sabon, named after
the type founder, Jacques Sabon. It was designed by Jan
Tschichold and jointly developed by Linotype, Monotype
and Stempel, in response to a need for a typeface to be
available in identical form for mechanical hot metal
composition and hand composition using foundry type.

Tschichold based his design for Sabon roman on a font
engraved by Garamond, and Sabon italic on a font by
Granjon. It was first used in 1966 and has proved an
enduring modern classic.